D0046552

THE
MAN WITH
NO FACE

Also by Peter May

PETER MAY

THE
MAN WITH
NO FACE

Quercus

New York • London

Quercus

New York • London

© 1981 by Peter May
First published in the United States by Quercus in 2019

ISBN 978-1-63506-122-2
Library of Congress Cataloging-in-Publication Data

Names: May, Peter, 1951– author.
Title: The man with no face / Peter May.
Description: New York ; London : Quercus, 2019. | Identifiers: LCCN 2018044839 (print) | LCCN 2018046234 (ebook) | ISBN 9781635061246 (ebook) | ISBN 9781635061253 (library ebook) | ISBN 9781787472570 (HB) | ISBN 9781787472587 (TPB) | ISBN 9781635061222 (hardcover) | ISBN 9781635061239 (paperback)
Classification: LCC PR6063.A884 (ebook) | LCC PR6063.A884 M3 2019 (print) | DDC 823/.914–dc23
LC record available at https://lccn.loc.gov/2018044839

Distributed in the United States and Canada by
Hachette Book Group
1290 Avenue of the Americas
New York, NY 10104

Manufactured in the United States

10 9 8 7 6 5 4 3 2 1

www.quercus.com

For Bryan

The wolf also shall dwell with the lamb, and the leopard shall lie down with the kid; and the calf and the young lion and the fatling together; and a little child shall lead them.

Isaiah 11:6

INTRODUCTION

First published in 1981, *The Man With No Face* was only my third book to go into print. I wrote it almost forty years ago during my last couple of years working as a journalist in Glasgow.

When my editor at Quercus suggested we republish, I read it again for the first time in decades and was struck by just how topical the subject matter and setting were in the context of today's world.

The story takes place in the winter of 1979. The setting is Brussels. The backdrop is a British general election, and a political debate about Britain's membership of the European Union.

I was struck, too, by its sense of noir (not dissimilar to the Scandi Noir of today), of murders in the bleak midwinter of a snowbound city, as well as cultural observations that belonged to their time and have long since passed into history. I am speaking of milk bottles on doorsteps. Of typewriters rather than computers. Of a pre-internet, pre-mobile-phone age when the flow of information was infinitely slower.

The political landscape has changed, too. In 1979 the apartheid government in South African was regarded as an international pariah, with sanctions imposed upon it by the United Nations. So, too, the illegal régime of Ian Smith in neighbouring Rhodesia, which was soon to become the independent state of Zimbabwe.

One of the characters in the book is an autistic child. In the forty years since it was written there have been many advances in the understanding and treatment of this condition. What appears in the book is a reflection of prevailing opinion at the time.

I undertook what I would describe as a light revision of the text ahead of publication, and found myself having a dialogue with my 27-year-old self. I am sure that the younger me might have taken issue with some of the (very minor) changes I made, but in the end forty years of life and writing experience took precedence.

Finally, I have to say that I am delighted with *The Man With No Face*, and I very much hope that you will enjoy it, too.

Peter May
France, 2018

CHAPTER ONE

Kale watched the train through the rain-spattered glass and thought, this time will be the last. But even as the thought formed in his mind it clotted and he knew he would kill again.

He twirled his cigarette nervously between nicotine-stained fingers and sipped the sour dregs of his coffee. The coffee machine on the counter hissed and issued steam, and with the rain beginning to fall outside the window was misting over. The first drops of condensation formed and ran clear lines through it.

An old man sat in the corner making his coffee last so he could remain in the warmth, and a hard-faced woman behind the counter sat smoking a cigarette and watching Kale. She had seen the likes of him before. A place like this was a constant stream of men and women who had seen better days. There was the familiar suit, perhaps expensive once, but now fraying at the cuffs, crumpled, baggy, shiny at the elbows and the seat of the pants. The old blue overcoat, rubbed and coffee-stained down the front, dandruff on the collar. The clothes hung loosely on his lean frame. She had seen worse, but maybe this one was just starting out.

He would be around thirty-nine or forty, hair thinning, greased back. A hollow face with high cheekbones; clear, pale, slightly yellow skin, remarkably unlined. It was his eyes that interested her, if it was possible to say that she was interested in anything. They were dark, deep-sunk eyes, set too close, and they burned with a bleak intensity that she had not seen before. There was something sullen in his face, but it was not the face of defeat as was the face of the old man in the corner – as were most of the faces that came in here to stare morosely into endless cups of coffee.

Kale caught her watching him and she looked quickly away, becoming aware for the first time that she was actually afraid of those eyes . . . almost intimidated by them. *You're letting your imagination run away with itself, Nance*, she told herself without conviction.

'Oi, you!' she shouted with a voice as hard as her face at the old man in the corner. A Cockney voice, a long way from home. 'You've 'ad yer coffee. Now clear aht!'

The old man looked up with resignation. He had learned to accept such things. You grew used to them, as you grew used to the constant gnawing pain of an ulcer. He pushed back his chair, rising slowly with what might have been an attempt at dignity, and shuffled past the counter and out into the wet. Nance had only done it to take her mind off Kale, but now she realized her folly. She had left herself alone with him. She stubbed out her half-smoked cigarette and lit another between thin, painted lips, crossed to the jukebox and punched two plays. The noise would make her feel more secure, and still she wished she could have called the old man back.

But she need not have worried, for Kale had barely noticed his going, and was only mildly irritated when the jukebox began belting out a scratchy hit record. And Nance was of no interest to him. He was thinking about his meeting with Swinton in a dingy London tearoom three days earlier.

Swinton was a small, fat, busy man. He had sat across a wooden table from Kale. One of those people who perspire constantly.

'It's a big one, Kale,' he had said with an air of confidentiality, leaning across the table and breathing garlic at the other man. 'Big money this time. You could retire. Where you been anyway? The boys was thinking you was maybe dead or something. The word's been out for over a week.'

Kale had felt uncomfortable there, surrounded by elderly ladies drinking tea from china cups. But Swinton had insisted they should not meet at the usual pub. 'How much and who's paying?'

Swinton's smile widened. 'Oh, come on, Willy boy. You know me. Even if I knew I wouldn't tell you who. But truth is, this time I don't even know myself.' He paused and sat back as a waitress scurried by with a pile of empty cups and saucers clinking on a tray, and then leaned forward again. 'It's not the usual form. You'll deal direct. I'll get my commission for finding you, but honest to God I don't know who's paying.'

'How much?'

'A hundred thousand smackers, Kale. A hundred thousand! Jesus, I'd do it myself for a quarter of that, but I'm not in your class. No one's in your class, mate.'

Kale toyed with his cup, the undrunk tea cold now, milk solids forming a scum on the surface. He was not happy. If he had not needed the money . . .

'Tell me.'

Nance was relieved when Kale pulled up his collar and pushed back his chair. She watched him out the door then crossed to his table to collect the empty cup and found twenty pence under the saucer. Funny, she thought, how some of them never lose the habit. Maybe he wasn't as bad as he seemed.

Kale crossed the railway yard, asphalt crunching under his feet, the January rain stinging his face. The locomotive had shunted three coal trucks into a siding and was chugging back towards the depot. Ahead of him this small industrial township rose up the hillside, a jumble of blackened brick terraces. The tall chimneys of the mills belched smoke into a heavily laden sky away to his right, and he could hear children playing somewhere behind a wall that ran alongside the road down to the station. The cobbled street shone in the wet, reflecting the grim poverty of the place. On the station wall a fly-blown poster urged a vote for Labour, its red vivid against the grey, a smile on the candidate's face above the slogan – *FOR A BETTER BRITAIN*.

He crossed Church Street to the newsagent's on the corner

and stood looking out across the town square with its black memorial statue, hands sunk deep in the pockets of his coat. For three days he had come to this spot every morning and every afternoon, checking all the routes that led to and from the square. He knew this town now as well as anyone could who had walked every street. Each road leading out of it was marked in red on the map in his pocket, each identifiable by some feature that could not be seen, but might be felt or heard. He had been relentless and thorough, and yet he was still far from satisfied. He shuffled uneasily and watched the traffic carefully. Three days, he told himself, was not enough. The clock on the church tower showed three but did not chime. The minutes ticked past slowly and the rain stopped, leaving only the chill wind to sweep across the square.

He saw the van come in from the north side and watched it as it drove past him, along the top end and back round again. This time it stopped, a white Ford Transit. Kale saw the fresh mud splashed along the side from the front wheels, and took a mental note of the registration, though he doubted if that would prove useful. Still, every scrap of information might help. A slight smile curled his lip. Others would not have gone to such lengths.

A short, thickset man stepped from the van, his crop of white, wiry hair catching in the wind above a brown leathery face. He wore a heavy tweed coat and was not what Kale had been expecting. His blue eyes incongruously honest.

'Kale?' he said. Kale nodded. 'Into the back of the van then, lad.' He rounded the van and opened the doors for Kale to climb in. 'Here, stick this over your head. And don't think you can whip it off when we get moving. I'll be watching you in the mirror.'

Kale pulled the black cotton hood over his head and squatted down on a rug on the floor as the driver shut the doors. There were dog hairs on the rug and there had been fresh mud on the man's brogues. Despite the good coat and shoes, his hands were those of a working man. Heavy, hard-skinned, calloused hands. His accent was northern, and he had a weathered out-door air about him, uncomfortable in his expensive city gear. Kale adjusted his senses to the darkness, pressing his back up against the side of the van. He smelled dog and stale cigarette smoke.

They seemed to have been driving around the town for an eternity. Several times Kale had lost his bearings, but always he picked up their position again. The hoot of a train as it approached the station, the steep cobbled climb up Cotton Street, the quarter-hour chime of the church clock on the edge of the new housing estate – the only chiming clock in the town. They were leaving the town now, he was certain. The roundabout on the north side with roads leading north and west. The sound of a pneumatic drill, and a slight delay at temporary traffic lights erected for roadworks. They had taken the A road west. It was a road Kale had checked on his first day.

The driver stuck to the A road for what must have been

nearly twenty minutes. That would take the time to around three forty. Kale would check the time when they stopped. Another seven or eight minutes perhaps, and then the van turned off the main road. Kale heard the click, click of the indicator before they slowed to take the corner, tight, the driver forced to crunch into first gear. It would be a narrow road, maybe a farm track. The van bounced and clattered over the uneven surface. Kale heard the splash of mud along the side. Then they stopped, and above the idling engine Kale could hear a man's voice and the sound of hooves, the lowing of cattle. He strained to catch more. The scraping of a wooden gate, again a man's voice calling, cattle retreating, and they were moving again, very slowly. Up a sharp incline and then suddenly down. A bridge? Over water? Yes, he could hear the water. The driver had rolled down the window. And now they were picking up speed, the surface a little better, the swish, swish, swish of fence posts or perhaps trees along the route. Slowing again, the clatter of a cattle grid, and then the crunch of gravel beneath the tyres. They stopped. The driver cut the ignition and climbed out.

'Just keep yer hood on, lad.' The back doors opened and Kale felt the working man's hands help him out. Even in his enclosed darkness he could sense the presence of trees and a building. Stone. Something big, impressive. Up steps and into a hall, a great sense of space around them. A flagstone floor, or tiles maybe. The man with the white hair and the big rough hands felt the tension in Kale's arm. 'Okay, lad. Take it easy.' Kale was surprised by the odd friendliness of the voice, its inappropriate innocence. This man could know nothing of what Kale was about. It's strange, he thought, how much a voice can tell you about a man when you cannot see his face. 'In 'ere.' The big hands guided him across the hall and through a doorway. 'You can take yer hood off when I've shut the door. There's a bell press below the light switch when you're ready to go.' The door closed, the key turned in the lock, and the sound of the man's heavy tread receded across the hall.

Kale removed the hood and screwed up his eyes against the sudden glare of electric light. It took nearly half a minute for his eyes to adjust fully. He checked his watch. It was just after four. Then he looked around. This was a small room. No windows, no fireplace, cream-painted walls, bare floor-boards. A smell of dust and age. Perhaps a storeroom. But there were no clues, the room completely bare save for a wooden bench against the far wall. Kale's eyes fixed on the bench. Towards one end of it lay a briefcase, a heavy black phone placed beside it. He was startled by the sudden loud ring of the phone – a short, single ring. He crossed the room and lifted the receiver, checking the dial as he sat. It was not an outside line, but an internal phone with only an extension number. Four.

'Kale?' a voice rasped in his ear.

'Yes.'

'Good. Now understand this . . .' The voice seemed without

particular accent, but it was an educated voice, mature. Even from the five words Kale had heard he detected a quality of confidence. A man used to speaking, a man used to having others listen. 'You and I are the only ones who will ever know the purpose of this meeting. You do not know who I am and so it shall remain. I know very little about you except for your reputation.' The voice paused. Kale let the silence drag out and became aware for the first time that he was cold in this empty room. Then the voice was there again, insistent, demanding his attention.

'In the briefcase you will find fifty thousand pounds in cash, the first half of your fee. On top of it you will find a folder containing two photographs marked A and B.'

Kale switched the phone to his other ear and opened the briefcase. The money was there beneath the folder in bundles of £100 notes, but he did not count them. He lifted the folder and opened it to take out the photographs and lay them side by side on the bench.

'Listen carefully to what I tell you because you will receive nothing in writing and you may not take the photographs with you. If you wish me to repeat anything, ask.'

'Hold on.' Kale took out a small, dog-eared notebook and a biro pen. 'Okay.'

'Photograph A is Robert Gryffe. He is a Minister of State at the Foreign Office.' Kale had recognized the face but been unable to place it. So, political assassination. It meant nothing to him. 'Gryffe has special responsibilities in acting for the

Foreign Minister at the European Commission of the EEC in Brussels. He is there at least one week a month, during which he stays at a terraced house he owns in the Rue de Pavie, number twenty-four. Today is Thursday. On Sunday morning Gryffe has an appointment there to meet the man pictured in photograph B. That man's identity is of no importance to you, just so long as you remember the face. I want both men dead . . . without suspicion of murder. How you do that is your business.' The voice paused and Kale waited.

'You will then proceed to the Rue de Commerce, the top-floor flat in the apartment block at number thirty-three. It will be empty. There is always a key below the mat. Let yourself in and go straight to the main living room. On the fireplace wall hangs a painting by Brueghel, behind it a safe set in the wall. The combination is three, zero, five, nine, six, two. Inside you will find a black briefcase . . .'

'Burglary ain't my thing,' Kale interrupted, his voice flat and cold.

The other hesitated. 'The apartment has already been checked out by a professional. You will simply be required to collect the case and leave.' Again the hesitation, the reluctance to answer Kale's unasked question. Kale was only too aware of the power of his silence. 'The case cannot not be taken before the . . . before you have fulfilled your task at the Rue de Pavie.'

'Go on.'

'You will take it straight to the Gare du Midi and deposit it in box thirty-nine at the left-luggage lockers. The key is taped to the inside of the lid of the briefcase beside you. If you return to the station at midday on Monday you will find a further fifty thousand pounds in cash in the same locker – assuming, of course, that you have successfully fulfilled the contract. Do you have any questions?'

'No.'

'Good. Then I shall allow you five minutes to study the photographs. Should anything occur to you in that time, dial six. Ring the bell by the door when you are ready to leave and remember to replace your hood.'

A click and the line went dead. Kale replaced the receiver. He lit a cigarette and looked at the two photographs. Gryffe would be around forty. A smooth, prosperous face. The other man was, perhaps, a few years younger. A lean, bearded face below a crop of fair, or perhaps red, hair. Two anonymous faces. Two men whom Kale would kill. There would, he knew, be no satisfaction in it, but neither would there be conscience or remorse. For Kale was the complete killer: cold, efficient, deadly. A man who showed no mercy, a quality he reserved for no one, including himself.

He sat for a while drawing slowly on his cigarette, a small shabby figure in the nakedness of the room. He would find this place again. On the map, or physically if need be. It was invariably important to know who it was that employed you to kill. And this one had taken such elaborate precautions to conceal his identity. *You all think you are so clever*, Kale thought.

But in the end I have always got you, one way or the other. He stood on the last inch of his cigarette and closed the briefcase, leaving the photographs on the bench. He lifted the cotton hood, and his money. Then crossed to the door and rang the bell.

CHAPTER TWO

It was raining. Not a particularly auspicious day. It had rained yesterday and it would probably rain tomorrow.

Bannerman remembered a cartoon he had seen once in an old *Punch* magazine. Two crocodiles basking in a jungle swamp, heads facing each other above the muddy waters. One of them was saying, 'You know, I keep thinking today is Thursday.' Bannerman smiled. It had amused him then, as it amused him now. What bloody difference did it make . . . today, tomorrow, yesterday, Thursday? It was ironic that later he would look back on this day as the day it all began. The day after which nothing would ever be quite the same again.

But at the moment, so far as Bannerman knew, it was just a day like any other. He gazed reflectively from the window a while longer, out across Princes Street, the gardens beyond, and the Castle brooding darkly atop the rain-blackened cliffs. Even when it rained Edinburgh was a beautiful city. Against all odds it had retained its essential character in the face of centuries of change. There was something almost medieval about it; in the crooked hidden alleyways, the cobbled closes, the tall leaning tenements. And, of course, the formidable shape of the Castle itself, stark and powerful against the skyline.

In the office the day had barely begun. Reporters sat around reading the morning papers, sipping black coffees and nursing hangovers.

'Morning, Neil.'

Bannerman turned from the window in time to see George Gorman drifting past. 'Morning,' he called after him, and watched the retreating figure as he headed for the news desk. Bannerman felt some sympathy for his news editor. Gorman was a dapper little man, good at his job without being inspired, nervous under pressure. A nice man, just waiting for the axe to fall.

It had already fallen on a number of his colleagues: John Thompson in features, Alex McGregor in sport. And there had been casualties in the reshuffle on the subs desk. It had been inevitable really, ever since it was announced that Wilson Tait was being brought up from London to fill the recently vacated editor's chair.

The *Edinburgh Post* had never been able to boast a particularly high circulation. For years it had lived off its reputation as a serious newspaper of quality and reliability. It was read by politicians, members of the legal and medical professions, teachers, academics. But their patronage alone was no longer enough to balance the books. Profit was more important than prestige. Hence the appointment of Tait, a hard newspaperman of the old school; a Fleet Street-toughened Scot returning to his old hunting grounds and bringing with him his personal hard core of hatchet men whom he was moving into key editorial positions. Blood was being spilled. And only the approaching general election – just three weeks away – had provided a stay of execution for Gorman. When it was over, he would receive a quick sideways promotion to make way for one of Tait's rising stars. And while Gorman was allowed to vegetate quietly in some out-of-the-way office with an ambiguous brief from the editor, the paper would move slowly but surely downmarket, where it would endeavour to pick up new readers, almost certainly alienating its existing readership in the process.

It was then, Bannerman thought, that he would have to consider his own future with the paper. Though that was already in doubt. He and Tait had clashed almost immediately over Bannerman's role with the *Post*. And there was no love lost between them.

The phone rang on Bannerman's desk. 'Bannerman.'

'Good morning, Neil. You're in early.'

Bannerman smiled. 'What is it, Alison?'

'The editor wants you.'

'You mean he's in early, too?'

'Ha, ha.'

'I'll be right there.'

Alison smiled up at him when he came into her office. 'Set your alarm an hour early by mistake?'

Bannerman grinned. She was a good-looking girl, easygoing

but very efficient. 'Actually I came in early to ask you if you might be free tonight.'

'Oh, that's nice. I am actually. But you're not.'

Bannerman frowned. 'Oh? You know something I don't?'

'Only that you'll be too busy packing. I've just booked you on the first flight to Brussels in the morning.' She nodded towards the editor's door. 'Orders from His Imperial Highness.'

She watched him go through into Tait's office and wondered what it was that was so attractive about him.

Tait was hunched over his desk in shirtsleeves. He glanced up momentarily from his paperwork as Bannerman knocked and came in. 'Take a seat. I'll be with you in a moment.'

Bannerman sat down and watched the other man patiently. Tait liked to make you feel that he was seeing you on sufferance, that you were interrupting much more important matters. Bannerman was not impressed.

The editor was a small man and had the arrogance and puffed-up sense of self-importance of many small men. A compensation for lack of height. He was of indeterminate age and could have been anything between forty and sixty. His hair was steely grey, cut short above a squat, ugly face.

He gathered together several printed sheets and slipped them into a folder before looking up again. He surveyed his investigative reporter with caution. He disliked him, but was also intimidated by him. By his calm, powerful presence, his obvious self-confidence. Bannerman didn't jump, as the others did, on Tait's command. And that annoyed him.

'I'm sending you to Brussels for a few weeks,' he said.

'Oh?' Bannerman endeavoured to show no surprise.

'We need some good stuff on the EEC in the couple of weeks after the election. Corruption, fraud, political back-stabbing, that kind of thing. Particularly when Common Market issues have been given such high priority in the election speeches of the major parties.'

Bannerman gazed at him thoughtfully. 'Why so keen to get me out of the way?'

Tait leaned back in his seat and eyed Bannerman coldly. 'Because I need time to consider what I'm going to do with you. You're a troublesome bastard, Bannerman. A one-man band. I want to build a team here and there's no room for buskers.'

Bannerman pursed his lips thoughtfully and Tait watched him with apprehension. Bannerman wasn't tall, perhaps five feet nine or ten, but he was stocky, broad, and gave the impression of a bigger man. Tait knew from personnel records that he was thirty-five, but it would have been difficult to judge had he not known. He could have been younger, or older. Dark, wiry hair without a trace of grey fell carelessly across his forehead. He was not what Tait would have thought of as good-looking, but he had a certain presence, and there was something compelling in the gaze of his hard blue eyes.

Bannerman said, 'Maybe you would rather I got a job somewhere else, Mr Tait.' His voice was flat, toneless.

Tait grinned maliciously. 'Trouble is, Bannerman, you're too good just to ditch. Probably the best investigative journalist in Scotland right now, and very highly regarded south of the border. I'd like to keep you. But on my terms.'

'I'm flattered. Maybe I should be asking for a rise.'

Tait laughed. 'Cheeky bastard!'

Bannerman tilted his head. 'So long as we both know where we stand.' And he knew that he was going to have to think about his future sooner than expected.

CHAPTER THREE

A blinding whiteness lay below like an Arctic landscape. The sky above it a clear, deep blue, sunlight flashing on the windows of the jet as it swung east. Bannerman sipped his coffee and felt the plane begin its long descent. Somewhere below would be the Belgian coastline. They would be in Brussels in under twenty minutes. He checked the time. Almost ten-thirty, Friday morning. They would lose an hour flying into Central European time. He turned his watch on sixty minutes.

The two seats beside him were occupied by an elderly American couple, he a minor cog in the wheels of NATO, and she a vigorous, unselfconscious woman who seemed well used to speaking for them both.

'Henry Schumacher.' The American had reached across his wife to shake Bannerman's hand when they first sat down, his fat amiable face broadening into a grin. 'And my wife Laura-Lee.'

Bannerman had taken the proffered hand reluctantly. 'Neil Bannerman.'

Laura-Lee had then begun a monologue, peppered with

frequent questions which she never allowed Bannerman the time to answer. The Schumachers' dreary, early married life in Chicago, the unconvincing and undistinguished rise of Henry Schumacher in American politics. The move to Washington, the invitation to a White House social gathering and the firm handshake of the President. 'The proudest moment of our lives. A great man, Mr Bannerman, a great man.' Then the attachment to NATO and the now frequent trips to Brussels. 'A damned unfriendly place, Mr Bannerman, unless you know the right people.'

Bannerman had listened with a patience that gradually wore thin. The Schumachers' bluff harmlessness and good intent, the man's smiling adoration for his wife, his wife's misplaced belief in her husband's importance. They sketched themselves into Bannerman's consciousness like caricatures, their obvious sincerity being their only saving grace.

The panel at the front of the plane lit up. They had come down through the clouds and could see the patchwork fields below.

'What was it you said you do, Mr Bannerman?' Mrs Schumacher asked vaguely, clipping her seat belt in place.

Bannerman sighed. 'I didn't.'

She frowned and seemed surprised. 'Then what *is* it you do?'

'I sell vacuum cleaners.'

Schumacher leaned forward. 'What company are you with?'

'The Quick-Clean Vacuum and Brush Company.'

The American nodded as though he was familiar with it. 'Does it have any ties in the US? I might know someone . . .'

'I doubt it,' Bannerman said.

The plane was curling in above the airport, descending rapidly. 'I don't know how you think you're going to sell anything to the Belgians,' Mrs Schumacher said. 'They are the strangest people. Can't even make up their minds whether to speak French or Flemish. If you've never been to Brussels before you'll find it very confusing.' She smoothed down the front of her print dress. 'Looks like we're coming in to land, Henry. Have you got the passports?'

The terminal building was busy. A soulless modern structure where subliminal piped muzak attempted to lull the traveller into a false sense of security. Nonetheless, there were dark-uniformed Belgian policemen everywhere in evidence. They carried sub-machine guns and wore pistols in leather holsters on black belts. A legacy of the recent hijackings.

Bannerman watched the Schumachers drag a luggage trolley off towards the taxi rank. 'Perhaps we'll meet you again, Mr Bannerman,' Mrs Schumacher had said earnestly. 'It's been a great pleasure.'

'Yes indeed, sir, a great pleasure.' Schumacher had shaken his hand and presented him with his embossed card. 'Any time you're in the States . . .'

You can't dislike such people, Bannerman thought. He picked up his case and made his way to the telephones, where he had to wait five minutes in a queue and then decipher operating instructions in French and Flemish. He pumped the box full of Belgian francs and dialled. The phone rang twice before a receiver lifted at the other end. '*Herald*.' A girl's voice.

'Tim Slater, please.'

'Sorry, you've missed him. He's just left for the twelve o'clock press briefing. Can I help?'

'Neil Bannerman, *Edinburgh Post*. I'd arranged to meet him for lunch.'

'Ah, yes. He said you might call. You're in Brussels?'

'Yep.'

'Then your best bet is to intercept him after the briefing. You know where the Salle de Presse is?'

''Fraid not.'

'Ah. It's in the Commission building. The Berlaymont. In the Boulevard Charlemagne. Do you have press accreditation?'

'Is this an audition for *Mastermind*?'

The girl laughed. 'I'm sorry. But if you don't have accreditation . . .'

'I do.'

'Then you'll have no problems. The Salle de Presse is on the first floor. Just ask when you get there.'

'Thanks . . .' He couldn't recall if she'd mentioned her name.

She detected his pause. 'Mademoiselle Ricain. Just the dogsbody. The *Post* and the *Herald* not only share an office, they share me too – secretarially speaking.'

Bannerman laughed. 'Of course. Thank you, Mademoiselle.'

He hung up and squeezed past a fat Belgian who was anxious to secure his phone.

Outside it was warmer than it had been in Edinburgh, the sky heavy and grey, the first drops of rain beginning to fall. Bannerman felt the initial pangs of rootlessness that always came when he arrived in a strange place. The disorientation, the sense of being utterly alone. It was only then that he rediscovered his affection for home. He thought about the cluttered tenement flat in Edinburgh that he called his home. Somewhere in all its drab familiarity hid a sense of belonging. The grey routine of the *Post*, the close, dark winter streets of the northern capital, the parochial insularity of it all; gems of security to be taken out and polished during lonely nights in strange hotel rooms under foreign skies.

The taxi ride from the airport took only twenty minutes, through the industrial outskirts on the north-west fringe of the city, past the Centre Commercial on the Avenue Leopold III, down on to the Boulevard Général Wahis and the Boulevard Auguste. Streets where once German tanks had rolled in from the east, defeated Belgians watching from windows and door-ways with a quiet hatred. Now the city was being rebuilt, adapting to a new world. The hammers of the demolition workers smashing down the past – rows of grey terraces and cobbled squares, tall crumbling tenements that had known better days, and worse. Bannerman wondered what kind of future today's planners were building.

The Berlaymont stood in the heart of the commercial sector

of Brussels, a massive building shaped like a star if viewed from above, towering over the city skyline, great walls of window curving inwards. The outer wall of each office was glass from floor to ceiling, so that looking in from the outside you felt that half the building had been cut away, like a half-demolished tenement, and you at once had a private view into every room or office where people worked and fought and hatched plots. Out front was the Métro. Across the boulevard the lesser white-stone office block that housed the Council of Ministers.

The press briefing was still in progress. The five men of the Porte Parole sitting along a table at the top end of the Salle de Presse addressing a clutch of fifty or more reporters in French. The journalists were arranged along five rows of benches set in a semicircle around the top table, like a mini-conference chamber; microphones at each place, headsets linked to translation booths in galleries set high up along either side. They were empty. The journalists asking questions all, it seemed, fluent in French.

Bannerman came in at the back of the room and moved around to a bar on the right-hand side where he ordered a beer. A number of reporters were seated on stools drinking beer or coffee, chatting quietly or reading papers – *Le Monde*, the *Guardian*, *La Belgique Soir*, *Die Welt*, *La Stampa*, *The Times*. Very few of the newsmen seated round the benches seemed to be paying much attention. There was an oddly casual atmosphere. Of informality, or perhaps indifference. Two secretaries moved constantly between the rows delivering press releases in various languages. Bannerman leaned against the bar, sipping his beer. He had picked out the thin figure of Slater with his distinctive red beard. He had only once met the man, several years before when he worked on the *Evening Times*. That was before Slater had been sent out to Brussels as the *Post*'s EEC correspondent. He had aged considerably, Bannerman thought, his face pale and drawn. The long thin nose more pinched than he remembered.

The briefing broke up, and as the journalists gathered into their various nationalities, Slater caught sight of Bannerman and made his way to the bar. He was unsmiling and seemed distracted. 'You're late,' he said. 'You can buy me a beer.' He risked a smile. 'The bar's subsidized.'

Bannerman leaned across the counter. '*Deux bières*,' he said and pushed a fifty-franc note at the barman. He turned back to Slater. 'Much doing?' Green eyes in a pale freckled face avoided his.

'Not this week,' Slater said. 'The only real topic of conversation is the British election. The Germans and French are worried shitless that the government's going to lose. If the opposition get in the opinion here is that the European Union will take another backward step – not that it takes many forward.'

Bannerman sensed a hostility in Slater that made him uncomfortable in the man's presence. He thought, *and I've got to live with you for the next month.* Slater lifted his beer. 'Cheers.'

They were joined by two reporters that Bannerman had seen drifting slowly towards them. One had a tanned, creased face, about sixty, dressed in a neat dark suit. The other was younger, less formal, a shock of fair hair falling over bland cherubic features. He patted Slater on the back. 'Waste of time today, Tim. Get anything to interest you?'

Bannerman smiled. It was the game that reporters played. Seeking reassurance that they hadn't missed something. Years ago when Bannerman was starting out he had very quickly learned that reporters did not compare notes for the sake of accuracy. The instinct was to hunt with the pack rather than rely on your own judgement. As his own self-confidence had grown so he had taken cruel satisfaction in leaving the pack in confusion with a parting 'Bloody good story', while they had been busy reassuring each other that there was 'nothing in it'. Nothing was better designed to ruin their day, especially when there really had been nothing in it. But Slater just said, 'Not a thing,' and then reluctantly made the introductions. 'This is Neil Bannerman, the *Post*'s investigative reporter. Jim Willis, *Evening Standard*, Roger Kearney, *Euro-News*.'

Kearney, the fair-haired one, said, 'Ah, yes. Know you by reputation, Bannerman. What brings you to Brussels?'

'I've come to rake a little muck,' Bannerman said. 'If there's any to be raked.'

Willis laughed. 'Fertile ground for you, my old son. The place is alive with corruption. You want to take a look at the EEC system of awarding grants to the Third World. Some fantastic rip-offs there. Large backhanders to Commission officials from some of these tinpot dictatorships where half the country's gross earnings are spent on royal palaces and luxurious watering holes for the leadership. It wouldn't take much to dig something out there.'

Kearney took a slug of beer and pointed a finger at Bannerman. 'And there's the allocation of contracts to companies in member countries for infrastructure projects. There's almost certainly fraud involved. Why, for example, does France get more Community money for road building than any other member country, when a godforsaken place like Ireland gets fuck all?'

'And agriculture's another rich source of fraud,' Willis said, 'if you care to do a bit of digging.'

Bannerman made no attempt to disguise his contempt. 'Then why the fuck do some of you people not do the digging yourselves?'

Willis frowned. 'Oh, piss off, Bannerman. This is where we make our living. You don't shit in your own back yard.'

Bannerman snorted his contempt. 'Call yourselves newspapermen? You're on a right cushy number here, aren't you? Everything laid on. You should try making a living in the real world.'

Slater was eyeing Bannerman with distaste. What was his game?

'You can fuck right off!' Kearney's voice rose angrily and some heads turned in their direction. 'All right for you, floating in here, stirring the shit then buggering off. You've got no pitch to queer. Smart-arsed bastard.'

Bannerman raised a quizzical eyebrow. 'Struck a sore point, have I?'

'Let's get out of here.' Slater took Bannerman firmly by the arm and steered him away from the bar towards the door. In the corridor outside he stopped him. 'What the fuck are you playing at, Bannerman?'

Bannerman shrugged. 'Just pricking a few reporters to see if they bleed.' He looked at the distraught Slater, a small man – five feet eight or nine – painfully thin, curly red hair and beard, an open-necked white shirt, its collar out over a faded blue denim jacket. And he relented a little. 'Look, I'm sorry, I'm just a bit pissed off at being here at all. How about lunch?'

CHAPTER FOUR

Kale got his holdall down from the rack and pulled on his coat as the train braked coming into the Gare du Nord, drawing up alongside great long trolleys that stood on the platform piled high with mail bags. A sullen youth who had sat smoking Gauloises all the way from Ostend, and a fat ruddy-faced Belgian peasant woman whose knitting lay in a shapeless grey heap on her lap, both watched him curiously. He was a foreigner. They knew that, even though none of them had spoken through the hour and a half to Brussels when darkness had fallen over northern Belgium. A wordless communion had passed between the youth and the old woman, two Belgians in a railway carriage with this stranger who carried about him an air that was more than just foreign. Both felt something akin to relief when Kale slid the door open and stepped out into the corridor. A strange tension that had been a presence among them, like the clicking of the old woman's needles or the impatient tap of the youth's foot, seemed to blow away with the cold rush of air that swept into the carriage with the opening of the door. The old woman smiled at the youth, who shrugged, almost imperceptibly, and lit another Gauloise, turning his sullen stare out of the window.

Kale shivered in the cold night air and walked the length of the platform. He seemed to be the only passenger to alight here. A guard nodded and the railwayman at the barrier waved him through. Down steps into a shopping concourse and out through glass doors into a great empty marble hall, his footsteps echoing back at him. He followed a sign out into the Rue du Progrès and headed north along the dark, cobbled street past crumbling tenements with steel-shuttered windows and doors. A tram emerged from an underground tunnel that led to the prémétro and rumbled past below the railway line that ran along the top of the embankment. Three scruffy kids on bicycles raced past in the opposite direction.

Along this street one window was lit below a neon *BAR* sign. A hefty middle-aged woman in a short, low-cut dress from which she bulged at all points sat in the window looking bored and smoking a cigarette. She raised a semi-hopeful eyebrow when the figure of Kale passed, but it fell again into its set boredom when he did not stop. At the end of the street the lights from a café spilled out across the pavement. Kale pushed open the door and stepped into the smoky warmth.

Working men in grey jackets and cloth caps looked up from their beers and eyed him suspiciously. He was not a regular and nobody but regulars drank here. Kale drew up a chair at an empty table and dropped his bag on the floor. The crude wooden table rocked unsteadily, one leg shorter than the others. The barman came out reluctantly from behind the counter. 'Monsieur?'

Bloody foreigners, Kale thought. *Why can't they speak English?* '*Bière*,' he growled and lit a cigarette. The barman poured a half-litre of draught Stella and sloshed it down on Kale's table. Kale looked at the beer that had spilled across the wood and then turned his gaze on the barman. The Belgian hesitated a moment. Normally he wouldn't have bothered. But there was something compelling and slightly sinister in the stranger's dark eyes. He took a cloth off the counter and lifted the beer to wipe the table and the bottom of the glass before replacing it on a cardboard beer mat.

'*Trente-cinq francs*.'

Kale remained impassive and made no move to pay, and the barman shifted uncomfortably. Finally he took out a pad and scribbled 35F and tore it off the sheaf, laying it down in front of the stranger. Kale looked at it, nodded, and peeled a one-hundred-franc note from a wad in his wallet. The barman took it and counted the change from his pocket. The half-dozen other clients in the café watched in silence, a silence that grew increasingly obvious. A younger man turned his gaze away from Kale and began playing the pinball machine. Subdued conversations were struck up, but the atmosphere was laden and frequent glances turned toward the stranger.

Kale was oblivious. The beer tasted cool and good after the long eight-hour journey from London. It was impossible for him now to fly anywhere on a job. International airports were all equipped with sophisticated anti-terrorist equipment through which it would be impossible to carry his hardware undetected. *Fuck the hijackers*, he thought. He could not understand men who would risk their lives for political ends. And they had only made life more difficult for him.

It had been a dreary trip. The ferry from Dover to Ostend full of winter tourists heading for ski resorts in Germany and Switzerland and Austria. A girl with long dark hair and a careless laugh. Perhaps she would spend the cold winter nights in some ski lodge drinking schnapps with friends round a log fire. For she was sure to have friends. A girl like that. She had not noticed him sitting in a corner on a lower deck, listening uncomfortably to the innocent ramblings of an elderly German lady who remembered days in Paris after the war, and the death of her husband nine years earlier on holiday in Majorca. She had not been aware of his invasive presence as others always were, as maybe the girl had been and pretended not to notice. Kale had gone up on deck to escape the old lady's innocence. There was no place for innocence in his life. It troubled him.

There had been few people on deck and it suited him better. White paintwork streaked with rust, the flaking varnish on the empty rows of wooden deck benches, the lifeboats that had never left their cradles. The cold, clean air had been good to breathe, the wind stiff in his face, the strange warmth of the sun on this unusually mild winter's day. Seagulls cawed and wheeled overhead against the palest of blue skies. The wash of the sea was green in their wake, England having faded from sight, the Belgian coast not yet in view. He had remained there, huddled in his coat, a solitary figure among the empty deck-chairs, away from the warmth below where children wailed and ran between the benches, where their parents drank duty-free spirits and smoked duty-free cigarettes, and young people laughed carelessly, like the girl, and talked earnestly about life. His exile from life, their life, was self-imposed, he thought with some satisfaction, and for always. That way he could be almost at peace with himself in his empty existence.

He finished his beer and left the café with all its staring eyes, turned hard left into the Rue Masui, and walked another hundred metres to the dark little hotel where he had booked a room. The streets were as familiar to him as if he had lived there all his life. Every area of operation in the city had been studied carefully on the town-plan map. Each street and alley he might use was painstakingly etched in his memory.

Kale dropped his passport on the reception desk and watched as the clerk took him in and then glanced at the document. It had been forged by an expert in London. A small, bespec-tacled jeweller near Leicester Square who was one of the few remaining artists of his profession. Utterly discreet. Kale would have trusted no one else.

'*Ah, oui,* Monsieur Ross,' the clerk said, studiously avoiding eye contact with the foreigner. 'Sign here, please.' Kale signed the form and the clerk copied details from the passport before handing it back with a key. 'Room twenty-two. Second floor.'

Kale crossed the dark hall to the old-fashioned elevator and pulled open the wrought-iron gate. The clerk watched him disappear as the cage moved slowly upwards, and he shivered. Perhaps it was the cold air that had come in with the stranger.

Kale's room was drab and bare and smelled stale. The short narrow bed sagged in the middle. He dropped his bag by a cracked porcelain washbasin and lay back on the bed, lighting a cigarette.

He closed his eyes and smelled again the cordite and the dust that had stung his nostrils that scorching day on the Arabian Peninsula so many years before. The sergeant, a heavy ignorant man, shouting above the bursting of shells – a vivid image that had recalled itself often. The soldier beside Kale was dead, a man whom he barely knew. Soon the flies would settle on the body, feed on the wounds in the heat of the sun. Kale was sweating, pricked by fear and by heat. The whitewashed walls of the village had been reduced to rubble by the shelling from the rear. And still the rebels refused to move. Ragheads with Russian rifles. Kale crouched in the crater, his eyeline at ground level, trying to pick out the surviving figures in the smoke and dust that billowed out from the destruction. Five men from his unit had already moved a hundred yards out to his left and were trying to circle the north side of the target. The clipped tac-tac-tac of a machine gun came from not too far ahead and Kale saw two of the soldiers fall. This time the shots had not come from the enemy marksman who was so successfully keeping them pinned down.

'For Christ's sake give the bastards cover!' the sergeant was bawling. Kale moved up, head and shoulders above the crater, his mouth dry. Again the machine gun sounded and this time Kale saw the rebel, moving through a gap in the wall to his right. He sighted fast and fired. The figure dropped in the dust. The gap had been no more than three feet, maybe two hundred metres distant. Almost at once a bullet struck the rim of the crater and threw up dust and rock splinters in his face. Kale pulled his head down sharply, blinking furiously as the dust stung his eyes. 'Get that damned bloody sniper for Christ's sake!' the sergeant was shouting further along the line. 'We can't move till we get him.' But he was not firing himself.

Several rifles were cracking around Kale now and the soldier on his left fell suddenly across him, half of his head torn away. Kale kicked the man off him and watched the thick, sticky blood staining the khaki of his shirt. The shelling had stopped to allow the troops to move in, but no one stirred from his cover. The five men who had moved out earlier were all dead. And now the slightest movement brought the crack of a rifle from somewhere up ahead. Almost without fail the marksman was making a hit. Kale shifted his position slightly and picked up a dead soldier's helmet out of the dust. He threw it along to the sergeant. 'Stick that up on your bayonet so he can see it,' he shouted.

The sergeant glanced grimly at him and saw that there were only the two of them left alive in the crater. The others were sheltering behind a wall away to their left. 'Who's giving the fucking orders here?' he growled. Kale said nothing and the sergeant spat and then hooked the helmet over the top of his bayonet and pushed it above the level of the crater. Almost as soon as it appeared a bullet spun it away behind them and the sergeant heard a second shot from only a few feet away as he pulled himself tight into the rim. Kale had caught only the briefest glimpse of the sniper as the man shot at the helmet. But it had been enough. Enough for him to get in his shot and feel a tight satisfaction as the sharpshooter toppled from his cover at the end of what had once been the main street of the village. Two more figures moved in the shadows. His rifle cracked again, twice, and both fell. 'That's some bloody shooting, Private Kale!' The sergeant grinned momentarily and then thought better of it. 'You can hang in here and give us cover when we move in.'

Kale had been as accurate in training, but it had meant little to him. Strangely now there was something precious in the skill. When he saw how he could cut men down. The sergeant noticed the curl of a humourless smile on Kale's lips and frowned. What the hell was there to smile about? But in these last minutes Kale had discovered a sense of purpose. In the final event it was the only thing the army had given him. It had led him to find in himself this cold, calculated ability to kill. An ability that transmuted all his crippled bitterness into a perfect and tangible expression. Out of all those long, hot days under the relentless Aden sun, the endless, cramped, unsanitary nights among the cockroaches and the sweating bodies, had emerged a vocation, and with it an inner confidence that had finally enabled him to stand apart from a world he despised.

Kale stared up at a crack in the ceiling of his hotel room. He had one day left before the hit. He would use it well.

CHAPTER FIVE

Bannerman looked from the window of this office on the top floor of the IPC building, down into the back courts below. Mean little yards bounded by brick walls that formed geometric patterns between the terraced rows. Beyond them, against the night sky, two cranes rose high above the houses that were being swept away in the redevelopment.

He had spent the afternoon sitting in the press lounge at the Council of Ministers, drinking coffee and watching the curious rituals of the lobby men. These creatures of strange habit sat about in the lounge among the potted plants, drinking, talking, or working behind a smoked-glass screen which hid rows of desks and typewriters and a bank of telephones. From time to time groups of reporters would launch themselves suddenly from their seats as they spotted various officials whom they would follow into small rooms off the lounge, a well-practised choreography that required no apparent communication. In these tiny rooms impromptu press conferences were held. The press relations officials held court. Pens scribbled in sacred silence as the high priests delivered careful words to the scribes. The ceremonies were, without exception, performed in French. Questions were frowned upon, brushed aside. The sermons concluded, the journalists would then drift away, sometimes back to the lounge, sometimes to the press room, dependent upon whether the words were relevant to a particular country or readership. It was a strange protocol, baffling to the outsider. Only those in the inner sanctum, who could read the faces and interpret the words, were privy to its secrets.

In one corner, the Italian Minister for Agriculture, making a rare personal appearance, had delivered a diatribe to a group of excitable Italian journalists whose voices rose and fell, arms waving, frequent laughter. In another, a clutch of British reporters was gathered round a Foreign Office minister; notebooks in pockets, wary eyes on the earnest face of the minister as he spoke. Bannerman had recognised him: Robert Gryffe, Minister of State for Europe, earmarked by the Prime Minister for a senior post if the government won the election – or so it was rumoured.

Gryffe, unusually, had become a popular public figure. He had that quality, rare amongst post-war politicians, of charisma. He was an outspoken moderate, a 'man of the people'. The tabloids loved him. And the Party had capitalized on his popularity in the run-up to the election by using him frequently in party political broadcasts. Bannerman watched him with distrust. He was gravely suspicious of men of the people.

When he left the Council of Ministers it was dark, and he

had walked up the Boulevard Charlemagne, past a bar where German journalists spent their days. At the IPC building he had found Slater in his office. It was well after seven now and he turned away from the window to take in the figure of Slater crouched by the open drawer of a filing cabinet. The *Herald* man had left and the secretary, Mademoiselle Ricain, was on her break. 'I won't be long,' Slater said.

Bannerman looked around the cluttered office. Four desks were pushed together to form a square. They were strewn with discarded press releases, overflowing trays of copy, technical journals, wordy reports and empty coffee cups. The walls were plastered with charts and maps, and a door led off to an anteroom where a chattering teleprinter shared by the *Herald* and the *Post* sent copy back to the mother ships to be printed for publication in clattering machine rooms in Glasgow and Edinburgh.

The panoramic windows looked out east across the rooftops, a forest of leaning chimneys and television aerials. Bannerman pulled up a chair and sat down, and reached for an open file. It was filled with loose newspaper cuttings from various papers. He saw a grey, smeared photograph of Gryffe and picked up the cutting. He was bored already by Brussels and the EEC, depressed at the thought of spending as long as a month in this dreary place. He let his eyes wander over the cutting. *Mr Robert Gryffe, a rising star at the Foreign Office, yesterday warned at a meeting of the EEC Council of Ministers in Brussels of an impending slump . . .*

'What the hell are you doing?' Slater snatched away the cutting and grabbed the folder from his desk. Bannerman looked up, surprised, mildly irritated. Slater eyed him suspiciously, a fragile, unhealthy-looking man, all his wasted years stretching behind him like links in a rusted chain. He was a man who had started out on his journalistic career full of ambition and enthusiasm, only to have both slowly battered out of him by long, weary years of fires and murders, of knocking on doors and carving initials on court benches. There had been the anonymous pubs and reporters, drinks and stories, night shifts and fictitious expenses. And there had been, too, the moves from paper to paper until the faces had all begun to look the same, the conversations predictable, the copy more turgid.

The Brussels job had come out of the blue, like suddenly rounding a bend in a long dark tunnel and for the first time seeing light at the end of it. Old hopes had been resurrected and held out the prospect of a brighter future. But that too had gone sour, as he should have known it would, settling into an old familiar pattern. The *Post*'s interest in the EEC had been too restrictive. They wanted parochial Scottish angles on every story. And that had quickly curtailed his interest. As had the EEC itself.

Slater saw the Commission as a great, slow-moving machine whose purpose was simply self-perpetuation, self-justification. The Brave New Europe had never emerged and, he believed, never would. All its processes were too tortuous and obscure without ever being fully productive. Thousands of civil servants

sat in spacious offices dreaming up schemes for yet more intri-
cate legislation to weave into an already complex tapestry of
international rules and regulations. The only purpose served
being to complicate further already difficult relations between
member countries. And even when still no more than ideas,
they often ran into hundreds of pages of fat, incomprehensible
reports that had to go before the Council of Ministers. There
they would undergo a lengthy process of review and amend-
ment before those that survived would be sent, finally, to the
European Parliament in Strasbourg or Luxembourg. And it
too, Slater thought bitterly, was an impotent body, even after
direct elections.

Had he not met Marie-Ange there would have been no hope.
Now there was the chance of escape from it all – from the
crippling cynicism and loneliness of Brussels, the memory of
his wife, the worry of his daughter. Maybe now the child would
have a real chance too. Specialist treatment.

But Bannerman's arrival complicated things. What was he
after? Only a few more days and Slater could leave all this
behind him. Surely Tait couldn't know anything. Couldn't
have sent Bannerman to find out. Could he? Gryffe wouldn't
have talked. He wouldn't dare. Slater decided to take a chance.
'What are you really here for, Bannerman?'

Bannerman frowned. He had sensed Slater's uneasiness
at their first meeting, and now this extraordinary behaviour
over the file of cuttings on Gryffe. 'I already told you,' he said.
'What's your problem?' He watched Slater carefully. But the

reporter turned away and slipped the Gryffe file back in the cabinet and locked it. He turned again, hesitantly, to face Bannerman and seemed to consider what he should say.

'I'll tell you,' he said at last. 'I don't like you very much. Never have. And now you come over here, digging around where you're not wanted, inflicting yourself on me for the next month, insulting guys I have to work with.'

'Hey,' Bannerman snapped. 'You know none of this was my idea. The *Post* owns your apartment here, and if Tait reckons he can save the paper money by having me shack up there then that's up to him. If you have any objections you know where you can take them.'

Slater eyed him angrily for a moment, then took a deep breath and seemed to relent. 'Okay, okay, I'm sorry. I . . . well, this place gets to you after a while.'

'Really? I thought you people had it easy out here.' Bannerman's sarcasm seemed to revive some of Slater's antagonism.

'Oh, sure, if you like the idea of quietly vegetating amongst all the decaying political ideals of a generation of squabbling Europeans.' He hesitated and crossed to the window so that Bannerman could not see his face. 'This is a cold, lonely city, Bannerman. It's a God-awful place. There are more than two hundred thousand temporary or permanent immigrants in Brussels. Thousands of civil servants and politicians and jour-nalists from all over Europe who have never integrated with the local population. Most of them live in the Euro-ghettos.'

His laugh was without humour. 'Sprawling wealthy suburban areas on the edge of the city where life is divided into nationalities and private clubs and expensive social functions. If you can afford it.' He turned back to face Bannerman. 'You think *I* can? Working for the *Post*? There's no way a paper like ours can compete with the money that's being earned even by the average EEC official. These guys can make anything up to a basic eighty grand a year, with all kinds of additional allowances for home entertainment, household, family, school, cost of living.'

Bannerman felt Slater's bitterness as powerfully as if he could touch it. Something about him jarred. He was more than just a disillusioned newspaperman, more than just bitter. But it was not easy to know what more there was. Bannerman knew that Slater's wife had died shortly after the move to Brussels, that he had been left to support an autistic daughter – a girl who could not speak, who could barely write, whose terrible deficiency was her inability to communicate.

Slater was still talking. 'The Belgians are okay to work with. But there is no way you will get to know them. Not socially. A Belgian will never invite you into his home, even if you've known him for months, or years. They are a strange, introverted, suspicious people. I don't like them.'

'It seems there are a lot of people you don't like.'

'That's right.' Slater stared at him, almost defiantly, then turned to lift his coat from the stand. 'Time we went home.'

Bannerman stood and pulled on his coat, glancing at this

odd-looking man with his red hair and beard, pale face, and dark-ringed green eyes. And in that moment he knew what he had sensed in Slater. It was guilt. He had seen before how it could affect men. Perhaps it was something in his past. The death of his wife. Or maybe connected to his child.

Slater locked the door behind them and they walked in silence along the length of a hushed corridor to the elevator. There, as they waited for the lift, Slater turned to him. 'Don't expect any help from me, Bannerman.' And, almost as though he knew what Bannerman had been thinking, he added, 'And keep your nose out of my affairs.'

CHAPTER SIX

I

The child sat alone in the darkened room, the muted light from the streetlamps seeping in through net curtains. She had been sitting there for nearly half an hour and her eyes had grown accustomed to the dark. She could follow clearly the lines of the old dresser, the bookshelves and the desk. She could pick out the faded pattern of the old worn rug, the shape of the fireplace, the armchair opposite, the bed. From the kitchen came the sounds of Sally preparing the evening meal, in the street the occasional passing car.

It had been a bad day. Twice she had lost control; the screaming, the flailing arms and legs, the aimless striking out. She had tried, God how she had tried, to control it. But the frustration had been growing, taking hold of her in a way she did not know how to rein in. There had been the patient faces, the firm hands, and then the angry words. The vacant, staring faces of the other children who also knew how it was, but could never express it. Sally had talked to her on the way home; silly things, just chatter. But it had helped in a way.

Now she was at peace again, or as much at peace as she could be, and control was easier. If she closed her eyes and sat here in the dark, then she could speak, not aloud, but with some inner voice. She could walk to the window if she wanted and touch the curtain, feel its smoothness in her hand. It meant little, but it was contact with something. It was good when she could touch things, feel things, embrace things; express her love, express herself. But such moments were rare, though they had seemed more frequent recently. Perhaps as she grew older it would improve still more. They always said it would. But, in the past, as it had improved, so her frustration had increased at those times when the improvement was not there and she could not make contact. God gave with one hand and took with the other.

Still, there was always the drawing, she thought, and when that came it was like every good thing she knew concentrated in a few furious moments of expression that flowed through her arm, her hand, her fingers, through the pencil and out on to that vast white landscape of fresh, crisp paper. And then afterwards, there was such pleasure in seeing it.

She heard the front door opening and her father's voice. There was someone with him. A voice that she did not know. She listened now in the darkness, finding as she always did that the presence of a stranger in the house unsettled her. Routine was something she clung to without knowing why. There was a great security in the familiar, a devastating uncertainty in the unknown. Always she looked forward to her father's return from work. She found an odd comfort in it, though she had no love for him. She had long since been aware that he had no love for her. The memory of her mother, a pretty, smiling, caring woman, had faded quickly, leaving her with nothing more than the hollow affection of her father. He went through the motions of love, was almost always gentle with her. But he gave her so little of his time, and she felt his lack of interest with an extraordinary perception. Still, it did not affect the comfort she sought in his presence. If only it was possible to say what she felt, to tell them the things that were in her head.

Her father and the other man were in the living room now and she listened carefully. There was something oddly familiar in the stranger's voice. He spoke English with an accent like her father, but there was another quality in it that she felt, almost like a hand touching her. She had already detected the hostility in both their voices, though neither man was arguing and there were no harsh words. It was simply there, and she sensed it. She pulled her bedroom door gently inwards so that it stood slightly ajar, enough for her to see through into the living room.

Her first sight of Bannerman affected her in the same way as his voice had done. There was something more than just the man she saw; the set, sarcastic face, the hard blue eyes, the relaxed liquidity of his body in the chair. She sensed in him an aggression, perhaps frustration. Yet more, there was a feeling of contact, as though they were touching, the way she had felt his voice touch her. It was important somehow, she knew, though she didn't know why and she was seized by a sudden foreboding. Everything about him and all she felt about him filled her with great confusion and uncertainty. It was clouding her mind – thoughts that had not come in words but in some inner understanding of things that words could never make as clear. With the clouding, the frustration was returning, and the control was slipping away. She left the door and crossed to the window. Her hands were starting to tremble and then she heard her father's voice calling. The door opened and she saw him framed in the doorway against the light.

'It's all right, Tania,' he was saying. 'There's a man come to see you. He'll be staying with us for a while. He wants to meet you.' All she heard was his ersatz sincerity. He came to the window and took her hand and she allowed herself to be led passively to the door and into the living room. There she stopped and pulled back. The man had risen from his chair and was standing by the fireplace below the big framed painting. He turned to look at her. All her self-control began dissolving under the gaze of those blue eyes and she felt herself pulling her hand from her father's.

Bannerman was startled by the first shriek and alarmed when this clumsy, unattractive child, who only seconds before had appeared so passive, clutched at her hair with both hands and began backing away into the darkness behind her. The screams ripped into the quiet of the apartment. Slater became

51

quickly flushed and he tried to pull the child back towards him, coaxing, appealing with soft words that only seemed to increase her distress.

'It's all right, Tania. It's all right, little one. There's nothing to worry you.' She lashed out with a tightly clenched fist, catching him a sturdy blow on the side of his face. 'For Christ's sake!' he shouted and snatched her arm, half turning towards Bannerman. 'I knew this would happen!' As if it were Bannerman's fault.

The girl was struggling and pulling against him, tears streaming down her cheeks, her voice hoarse already with the screaming. Bannerman's confusion gave way to a stinging embarrassment. He stared numbly, sensing a great inner pain behind the child's dark eyes. And for the first time he had a glimmer of sympathy for Slater. Father and daughter were grotesquely entangled, the child's arms still trying to beat on her father who had lifted her and was clutching her to him. And still the screaming went on, filling the room, the dreadful cries of a troubled mind.

Suddenly Bannerman was aware of another presence in the room. He turned to see a dark-haired young woman, perhaps in her middle twenties, standing in the open doorway to the kitchen. She was watching in silence and Bannerman thought she looked tense. She glanced in his direction and smiled, but it was an uneasy smile. 'You never quite get used to it,' she whispered.

Slater pushed the child into the bedroom then closed the

door on her screaming. He was grotesquely pale, his lightly freckled face almost grey against the red of his hair and beard. He looked viciously at Bannerman. But the young woman stepped into the room before he could speak. 'Your dinner's in the oven, Mr Slater. It'll be about fifteen minutes. I have to go.'

Slater plunged a hand into his pocket and threw a bunch of keys to Bannerman. 'Take my car and run her home, will you?' he said curtly. 'And do me a favour. Eat out. I want the child asleep before you get back.'

Bannerman shrugged and nodded. The young woman untied her apron and lifted her coat from over the back of the settee. 'You still want me tomorrow night, Mr Slater?'

Slater nodded distractedly. 'Yes, yes.'

'Only I won't be able to make it on Sunday.'

Slater's head snapped up. 'Why the hell not?' His anger was sudden and unexpected and even she seemed surprised.

'Personal business.' She was suddenly defensive.

'Shit!' he muttered. He opened the door of the child's room and went in, slamming it behind him, leaving Bannerman and the girl in an embarrassed silence.

She tried a smile which didn't quite work. 'Well, it looks like we're dismissed. I'm Sally Robertson.'

Bannerman picked up his coat. 'Hello, Sally,' he said. 'I'm Neil Bannerman. It seems I'm taking you home.' He paused for a moment. 'Or since I'm going to have to eat out, maybe I can take you to dinner.'

Sally smiled again, and this time it was her real smile, lips spread wide across a disarmingly open and pretty face. And her green, impish eyes smiled even more than her mouth. 'Well, there's an offer I can't refuse.'

II

Outside the night air was thick and humid, great dark clouds clustering overhead, having blown in from the west during the day. There was still a winter edge of cold, but when you walked you were warm and the air felt soft on your face.

'Leave the car,' Sally said when they came out of the apartment block. 'We can walk and then take the Métro. It's a good night for walking.'

Bannerman allowed her to take his arm and they walked the length of the Rue de Commerce and turned up into the Rue de la Loi.

'I suppose you must feel pretty bad about the kid,' she said. He gave no sign that he had heard her. 'They can be that way sometimes, autistic kids. Some worse than others. A break in the routine, a stranger, or maybe a pet phobia. Any of these can set them off on a screaming fit. Sometimes it can last an hour, or two hours, or even more. But they always come through.'

Bannerman kept an even pace and did not look at her. Ill-pasted posters flapped on the hoardings, behind which workmen sweated under floodlights on excavations for the foundations of yet another office block. 'What's she like?' he asked. 'The kid.'

Sally swept her hand through a vague gesture. 'It's difficult to know. She doesn't speak, you see. It's not that she can't, physically I mean. It's just that . . . well, she doesn't. She can write a little when the mood takes her, but she can't construct sentences. She gets what she needs by gestures. A kind of sign language. But you've got to know her pretty well to understand it. The doctors say she comprehends what's going on around her, but her only positive responses to anything are the fits. She takes it all in, but she can't seem to communicate what any of it means to her.'

Bannerman tried to imagine what that might be like. To be trapped inside yourself. Your body a cage. The world can come in but you can't get out. He conjured the child from his memory of her. Straight-cut shoulder-length brown hair. A small, plain, expressionless face dominated by large, dark eyes. A grey jumper and skirt. Heavy black shoes. Clumsy limbs.

'But she can draw like I've never seen a child draw,' Sally said. 'Fantastic living drawings that she does with a pencil. Drawings that leap out of the page at you. She has this tremendous sense of depth and perspective. A compensation, maybe, for everything else she lacks. They're worth seeing.'

The streets were poorly lit and quiet here, still in the commercial sector, and they climbed the hill then in silence to the Métro at Schuman below the Berlaymont. There no longer seemed a need to speak, and the lack of words between them was an easy thing. Bannerman felt relaxed in the company of this woman with her hair cropped short like a boy's, but with a smile and touch and smell that were warm and feminine. Still, he could not shake off his distress, and she seemed to appreciate his distance and disquiet.

The child had touched some inner nerve end, a severed memory, and in his mind he kept replaying the scene in Slater's flat. Her eyes were always the focal point. Sad, appealing eyes, deceptive in their dark passivity, even at the height of the screaming. Only now, with the short passage of time, were they having their full effect on him. He knew why. Somewhere inside he knew why, but would not or could not admit it.

He remembered the small, gloomy office of the weekly newspaper where he had got his first a job as a reporter. A gauche young man full of anger at the world. Cynical already, although he had not yet fully shaken off his youthful idealism. Insecurity, however, had manifested itself as arrogance, which had not endeared him to the other reporters. They had made it hard for him there, and he had learned the toughest way you can – without friends. It was during this period, of transition from adolescence to adulthood, that he had met the girl, forming a relationship that would seal his future.

She had been a timid teenager in telesales, fresh out of school, impressed by his apparent self-confidence, starry-eyed at what she saw as the romantic world of newspapers and newspapermen. He had embodied all that she, as a young girl, might have dreamed of in a young man. And he had grasped her vision of him, as an insecure youth does, and played to it, built on it.

He had allowed her adoration to puff up his ego, and he would lie awake at night in his attic digs overlooking the canal, playing the game, making the rules and breaking them. He felt the way it gave him power to have her love him when he did not love her. Though when you play that kind of game, sometimes the division between fantasy and reality becomes blurred, and that is when it becomes dangerous.

It had been a small, cold room high up in the roof of the stone terrace, and he hated it. The dull, damp wallpaper. The miserable view across the canal, the railway line and the dark empty trees. The dirty, threadbare carpet over the blackened linoleum and the smell of stale cooking that drifted up from the floor below where an elderly woman lived in a room you could smell when you passed the door. She peed in a bucket, the students in the room below her said. They would wake up at night and hear the squirt of the old lady's urine against the side of the galvanized bucket. They hoped she had a good aim, they said. And Bannerman had lain in the darkness, hating himself for all the falseness that he needed, remembering how he had made the girl who loved him cry, how they had fought and he had made her unhappy.

And there had been his own tears in all this unhappiness, there in that room. The tears of a callow eighteen-year-old boy trying to find in himself what others always seemed to find with such ease, but resorting in the end to the hollow pursuit of self-deceit. It had never really occurred to him at the time, in the midst of his own selfish unhappiness, that it was not only himself that he was hurting, but that piece by piece he was also destroying another human being whose trust and love he was betraying.

He had thought of her as a rather foolish, if attractive, girl. And it occurred to him bitterly now that he could not even remember her face, and how he had never seen the child she bore him.

They went down into the Métro on escalators, through vast empty marble halls. Sally bought them tickets and they queued on the platform under fluorescent lights.

'Where do you want to go?' she said. 'We can ride anywhere in the city on these tickets.'

Bannerman looked at her. 'Somewhere to eat and get a little drunk and talk,' he said.

A shining orange carriage whisked them through the new Brussels Métro, along broad lit tunnels to De Brouckere, where they changed and caught one of the trams that run on the prémétro below the city centre before burrowing upwards like moles to run overground into the suburbs. They ate in a steak house on the Boulevard Adolphe Max; steak au poivre washed down with a rich Côtes du Rhône.

Their conversation was desultory, a little awkward at first, each inhibited by the other's strangeness and the memory of the scene at Slater's apartment. But Bannerman liked the smell of wine on her breath and the way she wore no make-up except on her fine lips. He found it easier to look at her than to talk.

He saw now that she was older than he had first thought. Her thick, short hair was a rich auburn flecked with the first signs of a premature grey. Her eyes, below finely stretched lids, were a deep, solemn green speckled with brown. Only the finest of lines etched out from their corners betrayed her youthful appearance. Her nose was short and a little pinched around the nostrils. It was a delicately structured face without being beautiful, and you thought you could tell from her smile and her eyes that she knew how to look after herself. She had a bright laugh, and always when she laughed she flicked back her head in a small, careless way. And Bannerman guessed she must recently have worn her hair long. She would be about thirty, he thought.

They left the steak house a little warmer and a little closer, and walked further down the boulevard towards the Place Rogier, where the towering Manhattan Centre of concrete and glass rose powerfully into the night sky. 'You're a strange, quiet sort of man,' Sally said without looking at him, her eyes fixed high up on the Manhattan building on a large *Martini* neon.

'Only when I'm strange and quiet.'

She smiled. 'You still want to get drunk?'

'Not drunk. Gently . . . tipsy.'

'We can go in here.'

The Manhattan was a small, upmarket café near the end of the Boulevard Adolphe Max, emulating the American bars of Thirties movies. A row of tall stools stood along a bar of polished mahogany, below a wooden canopy hung with beaten copper light shades. Small round tables and chairs stood in clusters in little alcoves. The walls were panelled in the same polished mahogany, and behind the bar stickers advertised Scotch, American beer and Stella Artois. It was almost deserted, and they filled two empty stools along the row. A bored waiter in black waistcoat over a white shirt and bow tie had been leaning against the end of the bar smoking a cigarette when they came in. Now he snapped to attention and approached to take their order. They asked for whiskies, which he brought in short glasses to be placed on mats on the counter in front of them. Bannerman raised his glass. '*Slainthe*.'

'What's that?'

'It's Scots for good health. Gaelic.'

She smiled. '*Slainthe* then.'

They took their first sips in silence before Bannerman said, 'Tell me about yourself.'

'There's nothing much to tell.'

'Now why do people always say that?'

'Maybe because it's true.'

He shook his head. 'No. Everyone's got a story to tell.' He took another mouthful of whisky, allowing it to slip back easily over his tongue and down his throat so that it left a seductively warm sensation in its wake. 'The editor of a paper I worked for once used to say that behind every window there's a story.'

'Can I ask a question?'

'Can I stop you?'

'Why do reporters always ask questions?'

He grinned at her. 'It's their job.'

'Is it?'

'We're a nosy breed.'

'Only you seem quite different from Mr Slater, or some of the other reporters I've met.'

'That's probably because I am.'

She tutted, partly with irritation, partly with amusement. 'Why do you always have to be so clever?'

'I don't. I'm just enjoying breaking the ice on our relationship.'

'Oh? We have a relationship now?'

He shrugged. 'Not yet, maybe.' He paused. 'So, anyway. You were going to tell me something about yourself.'

'Was I?'

'I think you owe me that, at least. We met during a scene, we've travelled together across half of Brussels, had a meal together, and all I know about you is that you're English and you keep house for Slater. Or do you?'

She sighed and gave in to a reluctant smile. 'All right. Yes, I'm English. I'm thirty-two years old, unmarried – and, no, that's not an invitation. I've lived in Brussels for two years and teach English at a private college three days a week. On the other days I keep house for Mr Slater and take Tania to and from her special school. I look after her on Sundays and sometimes babysit in the evenings when he goes out with his fancy woman. Is that enough, or would you like my life story from day one?'

Bannerman smiled. 'Quite talkative when you like. Why do you need to work for Slater when you've already got a job?'

'Because I don't make enough from teaching alone. Brussels is an expensive place to live.'

He paused. 'So what's an attractive young lady like you doing living alone in a place like this?'

'None of your business.'

Her sudden sharpness surprised him. There was an uneasy silence for some moments, then, 'Tell me about Slater's fancy woman.'

'Why should I?'

'Because I'm asking.' He drained his glass and saw that Sally's was empty too and he signalled the ever-watchful waiter to order them another two.

She shrugged. 'His lady friend is about thirty. A good-looking woman, plenty of money – or do they call it class nowadays? You get the impression she's a little out of her comfort zone with Mr Slater.'

'You mean slumming it?'

'Not exactly slumming it. They're a strange couple, that's all. Not exactly a match made in heaven. And she's not exactly what I would call affectionate.'

'She's Belgian?'

Sally nodded. 'Marie-Ange Piard. Divorced.' She half-emptied her glass then looked at him seriously. 'You know, it occurs to me that I know as little about you as you did about me. How about me asking some of the questions for a change? Like, why don't you tell me something about *your*self?'

Bannerman grinned. 'There's nothing much to tell.' He looked up and saw that she was smiling too.

'Bastard,' she said.

Bannerman raised an eyebrow and drained his second glass. 'So I've been told.'

Her smile faded slowly and there was a long silence. Then, suddenly self-conscious, she turned her eyes away.

'Do you want another drink?' he asked.

'No.' She pushed her half-finished glass away from her. 'I'd like to go home now. It's late.'

They left the Manhattan and she insisted on taking a tram home on her own. 'Will I see you again?' he asked.

She said, 'Maybe.' And he watched the tram move off along the tracks, carrying her away into the night.

III

Bannerman rode the Métro over to the east side and found the door of Slater's apartment off the latch. He went in and closed it quietly behind him. As he walked the length of the hall, he felt the quiet of the house like a presence within it, and found Slater sitting in the dark of the living room. His cigarette end glowed red as he drew on it.

'She's asleep,' Slater said. He seemed very subdued. 'Your bag's in your room. Along the hall, the last door on your right.'

Bannerman could barely see his face, but he nodded and felt all the disquiet returning through the gentle whisky haze in his head. 'I'll find a hotel on Monday,' he said.

Slater turned towards him, and his face caught the soft light of streetlamps beyond the window. 'Okay. Thanks. What will you tell Tait?' Bannerman said nothing, and Slater waited in the silence. Then he said, 'I've got to go out tomorrow night. A social function. EEC officials, some politicians, folk from NATO. Dull stuff. But you've got to keep up your contacts.' He paused. 'Well, you know that.' Then, 'I suppose you'd better come with us. I don't want to leave you here.'

'Us?' Bannerman cocked a quizzical eyebrow.

Slater shifted uncomfortably. 'Three years is a long time for a wife to be dead. A man needs a woman.'

Bannerman lay in the bed with a faint grey light creeping in through the shutters. He thought that, after all, he had no right to intrude on the private pains of a man like Slater. And then his mind turned to Sally. Her bright pretty face, her sudden withdrawal just when it seemed they were beginning to make contact. All the loneliness of the first night in a strange bed closed around him like a fist, before the drowsiness of approaching sleep scattered his thoughts and numbed his depression.

He was not sure how long he had been dozing. It might only have been a matter of minutes, or it could have been hours. And he was not certain at first what it was that had reached into the depths and forced him up to break the surface of consciousness. The moment of waking was one of confusion; the strange room, the unfamiliar bed, the smell of damp. The room was washed with the same grey light. Then beyond those first seconds of confusion came an awareness of another presence. Nothing he could see or smell or hear. He just felt it, and there was a momentary flutter of apprehension in his chest. He jerked up on to one elbow and saw the child standing in a long, shapeless nightdress, bare feet on the bare linoleum. She was only a couple of feet away, watching him. Big dark eyes. That peaceful, passive expression resting easy on her face. She seemed small, more fragile, more childlike. His first thought was that she might scream and he felt his body tighten with tension. But she just stood there.

He could hear his own breathing, loudly, clearly, and he could feel the blood pulsing at his temples. Something told him that it would be a mistake to speak, and a little of his tension slipped away. Then, as though the child sensed it, she took two small steps forward and reached out to touch his face. The fingers of her hand were icy against his skin and he felt a trembling in them. At first they rested on his cheek and then after a few seconds they began to follow the contours of his face, running along the line of his cheekbone, his nose, his lips, his jaw. He raised his own hand and placed it over hers, stopping it, feeling the coldness of it, and he squeezed it gently. A tiny smile lit her face, dark eyes staring into his, and he found himself extraordinarily moved. Then the small hand slipped away and she turned and padded to the door, opening it and closing it behind her without looking back. Bannerman remained motionless for a minute, maybe more. His head swam with the strangest feelings, the sensation that he had experienced something inexplicably precious.

A dog barked somewhere in the courtyards behind the apartment block and crashed into his thoughts. He dropped on to his back and stared up at the ceiling, and realized for the first time that he too was cold.

CHAPTER SEVEN

The blinds were drawn and the only light came from a desk
lamp bent over on a goose neck, throwing a bright pool of light
on to the scribbled blotter. Everything on the desk was laid
out neatly. A large glass ashtray, empty and clean, a long brass
letter opener, a wire tray tidily piled with dog-eared reports,
a marble pen holder, a phone, two folders and a dish of paper
clips. On the wall behind it, a large map of Brussels and a
calendar pinned to a walk-in cupboard door. The high-backed
leather armchair was set at an angle. A light came on in the
next room and spilled more light into the study through open
French windows and the glass in a wooden framework that
partitioned the two rooms. Beyond, a further set of French
windows opened out on to the back gardens. But they were
shut against the rain and the dark.

Gryffe came through to his study, an expensive camel coat
hanging on his substantial frame. The two ends of a white
silk scarf dropped to his waist. He was a large, heavy-set man,
not fat, but powerfully built. He had a face that would be
attractive to women. Smooth tanned skin below a head of

dark, thick-growing hair, neatly cut and swept back. But now he was frowning and it did not suit him. The fine arches of his eyebrows were puckered in towards the bridge of his nose and his upper lip was curled in an expression that might have been distaste. He was agitated and made straight for his desk. But then he stopped, almost as though he had forgotten what it was he had come for. Outside the rain came down, striking and running down the glass behind the blinds. Gryffe stooped hesitantly over the desk, pulling open the left-hand drawer. He seemed satisfied with what he saw and pushed it shut again. He stretched across and took a bunch of keys out of the drawer on the other side, slipped them into his pocket, switched out the desk lamp and went back to the other room. There he switched off the ceiling light and went out into the hall. The front door slammed shut, leaving the place in darkness, the quiet broken only by the sound of falling rain, the scent of his aftershave lingering in the cold, still air.

Kale saw him, from a doorway further along the Rue de Pavie, stepping into the street. He opened the door of his car, parked below one of the naked black trees set along the edge of the cobbled pavement, and slipped in. The exhaust roared and the car pulled away, heading toward the end of the street, then turning right into the Square Ambiorix, where the Saturday night traffic sped past the edge of a small deserted park. Across the street from Kale a florist's shop was closing up for the night, and a workman with a red woollen hat slouched past with his hands in his pockets, not noticing Kale standing in the shadow of the doorway. He stood there, not feeling the cold, for another thirty minutes or more, just watching the street. A row of terraces, doors opening straight on to the pavement, stone and brickwork façades with tiny stone balustrades and wrought-iron Juliette balconies. A profusion of chimney pots leaning at odd angles on the slate roofs. It was a quiet street, most of the terraces converted to offices, a modern block of flats, Residence Ambiorix, casting light from the only lit windows, at the far end of the street. Beyond the square and the park, the boulevard ran down to the Berlaymont about half a mile away.

Finally Kale moved away from the shelter of the doorway and pulled up his collar against the rain. He crossed the street and walked down to Gryffe's door. He pressed the bell-push and heard a buzzer somewhere in the stillness inside. No sound of footsteps came from behind the door, and there was no light around the edges of the blinds on the windows. He rang again and waited a further few minutes until he was satisfied there was no one at home. He glanced at his watch. It was nearly eight, and he turned and walked back, away from the lights of the Residence Ambiorix.

This was a part of Brussels that was on the way down. A seedy tobacconist's was still open on the corner of the Rue de Pavie and the Rue de Gravelines. Through the lit window Kale could see an old man with a face like a lost battle sitting on a stool behind the counter reading a magazine and smoking a hand-rolled cigarette. A half-empty bottle of beer sat on the counter. The old man caught only a glimpse of the mean face peering in at him out of the darkness, and he stared back uneasily.

It struck Kale as odd that a man like Gryffe should have chosen to buy a house in an area like this. He shrugged and took out a cigarette, cupping his hands around the end to light it. He dropped the spent match in the gutter and turned right beneath a covered stone arch that ran under the end terrace. The cobbles here were dry, and his footsteps echoed back off the wall, the light of the street receding behind him. Then he came to the end and back out into the rain, and he turned right again into a long narrow lane that ran along the back of the terraced houses, bounded by high brick walls on either side. Tall wooden gates opened off into back courts. Feeble streetlamps raised themselves above the wall every fifty metres along one side. Kale counted off the gates on his right, walking quickly over the asphalt, and stopped at the twelfth. He glanced either way and then opened it and moved into the back court behind Gryffe's house.

The yard was sunk deep in shadow, a short sodden lawn, a brick shelter for the bins, and an uneven path of cracked slabs leading to the back door. Kale eased the gate shut and then froze as he heard the sound of footsteps approaching in the lane. He pressed himself hard against the wall of the bin shelter and waited, tense, as the steps came nearer. They passed the gate without stopping and faded down the lane. A thin jet of air escaped Kale's clenched teeth and he moved back out on to the path. Silently he crossed the yard to the French windows that opened into the back room. They were locked. A lever mechanism worked from a handle on the inside. He crouched down and drew a long thin steel rod from his raincoat, working it carefully in between the two doors, before sliding it up to where the centre bolt ran through the gap. He checked the length of the rod with the position of the handle inside. It would be possible, he decided, and withdrew the rod again.

He worked quickly, shaping the end of the rod round his wrist, bending it back on itself so that it formed a hook about the size of a cupped hand. Then he gently curved the rod inwards towards the open end of the hook until it was almost a semicircle. He slipped it back again between the doors, but it stuck halfway where it had kinked slightly in the shaping. He cursed and pulled it out again and worked the rod minutely back and forth where it had kinked until it was as straight as he could make it. This time it slipped easily between the doors and he slid it up until the hook was above the handle inside, and then pulled it gently downwards. The hook slid neatly over the handle and there he stopped and let it hang. He stood up and took a pencil torch from his pocket and shone it quickly along the top of the door, standing on tiptoe. Two terminals in the cross-jamb gleamed in the light on either side of the centre gap where they made contact with metal strips at the top corners of each half of the door. Kale smiled to himself and checked his watch again. Already it was after eight-thirty. It had taken longer than he thought, and he did not know how much time he had. But it was still important to do it right. He must leave no trace. If he had opened the door without checking, the contact would have been broken and an alarm would have sounded.

He drew out a rolled black plastic bag from his inside pocket and unrolled it, searching quickly inside before taking out a small roll of metal tape, sticky on one side, a length of wire rolled tightly and tied round the middle, and a short pair of pincers. For this he slipped off his tight black gloves and worked with nimble, steady fingers, unravelling about a yard of wire, baring it at each end and attaching it to strips of tape about three inches in length. Using a nail-file, he attached one of the strips to the right-hand terminal on the cross-jamb and the other to the metal strip running along the top of the right-hand door. There was just enough space between the two to work the nail-file in and stick down the tape. The yard of wire hung in a loop down the door.

This next would be the telling move. He pulled his gloves back on and leaned his shoulder gently against the right-hand door, grasping the curve of rod that was still on the outside. It would have to be sharp and sudden to bring the handle down, but he could not afford to let the door swing in too sharply and pull the wire, or it would break the bridging contact. He felt warm and sticky and could not tell if the wetness on his face was rain or sweat. He braced himself and jerked the rod downwards. The handle on the inside came down with it and the pressure of his shoulder pushed the door in. He let the rod fall and grabbed quickly at the edge of the opening door. He caught it before the wire grew taut, and he took several seconds to regain his balance and be sure of it. Then he let go the door and retrieved the bent rod and bent it some more until it slipped into his pocket. He re-rolled the plastic bag and put it away, then brought out two plastic shoe covers. Quickly he pulled the first one over his right shoe and advanced his right leg just inside the door. He did the same with the left foot, so that now he was inside the house and there would be no tell-tale footsteps on the carpet, nothing that even the forensic people could find.

He ducked under the wire and moved quickly across the room and into the hall. Light from the streetlamps outside seeped in around blinds and shutters, providing just enough light to see by. The hall was narrow, with a small cloakroom set to one side just before the front door. That was where he found what he was looking for. An electric meter mounted in a wooden casing on the wall. Kale opened it and shone his pencil torch inside and spotted the alarm switch. He turned it off and hurried through again to the back room, disconnecting the wire on the door and the cross-jamb. Then he locked the French windows as they had been, stuffed the wire back in his pocket and went to reset the alarm. He stood then for several seconds on the parquet flooring in the hall and listened to the silence in the house.

Outside a car swept past in the direction of the Square

Ambiorix. The sound of it broke into Kale's thoughts, stirring him to action, and he climbed the stairs two at a time. Two-thirds of the way up a door led off to the bathroom from a small landing. Up another half-dozen steps and there was a small square landing with two doors leading off. The first one opened into Gryffe's bedroom. A large, rectangular room, basic and tidy. A double bed, a tall walnut wardrobe, a matching dressing table with circular mirror against the window. On a single bedside table there was a brown-shaded lamp and a book by Ernest Hemingway with a marker about halfway through. The thin beam of Kale's pencil torch picked them all out and then snapped off. He moved through to the second, smaller room. It was empty except for a single unmade bed pushed against one wall. The wallpaper was faded and old-fash-ioned, brittle at the seams where it was beginning to lift away from the wall. The room smelled fusty and unused. The whole house felt and smelled unlived-in.

Downstairs, at the end of the hall, there was a small, stone-floored kitchen. A faint odour of stale cooking. The gas stove was black and caked with grease. A porcelain sink and washtub with a wooden draining board was cracked. In a wall cupboard he found a half-empty bottle of milk, a packet of cereal, tea, coffee, sugar, cups, saucers and three plates. A wooden door leading to the back yard was bolted shut. Kale guessed that Gryffe must eat out a lot.

He moved into the back room and then through the inte-rior set of French windows into Gryffe's study. Everything in the house seemed functional, designed for convenience rather than comfort. Again Kale checked his watch. It was nine now. He pulled out the drawer that Gryffe had opened an hour earlier and found a .32 Colt automatic eight-shot handgun nestling in the dark. An old-fashioned gun. He lifted it out and felt its weight in his hand. He sniffed the barrel. It had not been fired recently. Gently, with a dexterous familiarity, he sprang the magazine out and counted the bullets through the small holes in the side of it. It was fully loaded. He snapped the magazine back in place and slipped the gun carefully into his right-hand coat pocket, allowing himself a tiny smile. Sometimes fortune favoured the bad. He had a plan.

Swiftly he went through the other drawers and found only stationery and mail, a drawer filled with pipes and empty tobacco tins. Then he spotted the door behind the desk and tried the handle. It opened into a large walk-in cupboard. Empty wooden shelves ran along the far wall. A small, battered suitcase lay in the near corner. Three battleship-grey filing cabinets were pushed against the door wall. Also empty. Kale pulled the door shut behind him and felt darkness close around him. He shivered for the first time in the cold, and with his pencil torch picked his way round the filing cabinets and squatted in the corner, back pressed against the wall, thin legs pulled in close to his chest. He leaned his left arm on the battered suitcase, though strangely it never occurred to him to check inside. He should have.

He took out Gryffe's gun and laid it on the floor beside

him, then took out another from an inside pocket and fitted its silencer. He laid it on the floor beside the Colt and let his head rest back against the wall, eyes closing, blood pulsing softly at his temples.

This was the worst time now. The waiting. Twelve hours, perhaps more. But it was all so familiar. The loneliness, the dark room. It had been that way all his life. Even now he could hear his mother in the next room, half-drunk, laughing, entertaining another customer. They came night after night. Sometimes he would recognize a voice. Any one of them might have been his father, though later his more rational self doubted it. He had lain on the cot bed in the corner below faded grey curtains, watching the line of light under the door. He had been five, maybe six years old. He never saw the faces that came and went. But he heard them, grunting, cursing. And always his mother's voice, the pretence of pleasure, the smell of the gin that fuelled her fake laughter. Then afterwards, she would come through, to stand over his bed, thinking him asleep, and bend to kiss his cheek with wet, loose lips, the smell of gin on her breath. How he loathed it. Her smell, her touch, the stink of men and sex. And how he despised her for her sobbing. Great long sobs of self-pity that he could hear through the wall when she had returned to her own room. What right had she to cry?

Finally there had been the night, long silent hours after the raised voices and the scream, when he had gone through to find her naked body. It had almost been a relief. The twist of

pain on the fleshy red lips, the wide, staring eyes, the whiteness of her flesh and the sagging of her breasts. An end to it
all. No more strange men, no more wet kisses, no more sobbing through dark, lonely nights. But he had not known then,
could not have known, that there were greater horrors in life.

CHAPTER EIGHT

I

The house stood discreetly behind a long sweep of lawn, screened from the Avenue de la Grande Armée by a row of poplars. A broad driveway opened off the road and ran around the edge of the lawn, past the side of the house to a wide double garage. Floodlights were cleverly concealed among the evergreen bushes that bordered the drive and the far side of the lawn, picking out the house against the black of the sky behind it.

It was a long, two-storey white house with green shutters and a red-tiled roof. A place you might buy if you had money and wanted people to know it. Gleaming limousines lined the avenue for thirty metres along either side, and Slater pulled his car over just beyond the house. He stepped out into the light drizzle that was drifting gently across the lawns and opened the passenger door.

Bannerman watched Marie-Ange climb out and wave aside Slater's offer of help. She was tall and elegant, long tawny hair falling carelessly across the hand-embroidered silk shawl on her shoulders. She wore a full-length white dress that flared from a band at the waist below a daring neckline.

When they had met earlier, at Slater's flat, Bannerman had realized immediately how right he'd been to interpret Sally's description of her as slumming it. She reeked of money. And breeding. And not in a good way. There was a brittleness about her, a standing on ceremony that remained a constant presence, even in her relationship with Slater. Bannerman had taken an immediate dislike to her. The condescending smile, the limp hand offered to be shaken that Bannerman had squeezed too tightly. Though if it had hurt just a little, she had not shown it. She was not a woman to reveal anything of herself.

He had to admit, however, that she was very beautiful, at least on the outside. Large cobalt-blue eyes, a long aristocratic nose and wide, full lips. A smooth, lightly tanned skin, and a distant enigmatic smile. She had a long slender body, a sexual creature, and aware of it. Bannerman recalled Sally's words – *a strange couple*. Her relationship with Slater seemed unlikely, even incongruous. And Slater himself appeared ill-at-ease in her company. Or was it just the presence of Bannerman that made him so awkward?

Bannerman carried these thoughts with him across the street and up the driveway to the door of the white house. Slater and Marie-Ange walked ahead as though he were not with them. The door was opened by a white-jacketed butler and they were shown into a large brightly lit hall. At the far end of it a staircase rode up to a halfway landing where more stairs branched off to left and right. To their right, double doors stood open, leading to a crowded reception room. It was already thick with smoke and voices, the smell of drink and perfume. The butler took their coats and tiptoed away across thick-piled carpet.

Marie-Ange looked around with a critical eye. If she was impressed she didn't show it. 'We don't have to stay *all* evening do we?' she said to Slater.

He smiled patiently. 'Just showing our faces, Marie. Appearances are everything in this town. You should know that.' He turned to Bannerman. 'Would you look after Marie-Ange for a bit? I have a little business to attend to. Shouldn't be more than about fifteen minutes.'

Bannerman glanced at Marie-Ange. She was clearly unimpressed, but seemed resigned to her fate. 'Sure,' he said.

Slater squeezed her hand. 'Back soon.' He slipped away among the dinner jackets. Bannerman lifted two glasses of champagne from a tray carried by a passing waiter.

'Drink?'

She glanced at him and then the glass, before taking it without a word.

'So where did you and Tim meet?'

She sipped on her champagne and Bannerman saw its bubbles break around her lips. She turned her head to look at him very directly. 'Not sure that's any of your business, Mr Bannerman.'

'Probably not. But I'm a nosy bastard.'

She smiled. 'And nothing if not blunt.' Then, 'You also have a very strong handshake.'

'I do.'

They moved aside to make way for another group of arriving guests. 'Shall we go in?' she said.

Bannerman nodded, and took her arm to steer her into the reception room. Immediately the sensation of being observers dissolved and gave way to the discomfort of being part of the crowd. Voices rose and fell in half a dozen different languages, socially consolidating awkward political alliances. There were too many people laughing too easily. Waiters offered smoked salmon and whisky from silver platters. A manufactured bonhomie hung in the air like smog.

'So this is how they live in the Euro-ghetto,' Bannerman said, and took his first sip of champagne.

She eyed him curiously over her glass. 'You disapprove?'

'I'm not here to judge, just report the facts.'

'And yet I sense you have already made a judgement on me and Tim.'

'Do you?' He raised an eyebrow in surprise and shook his head. 'It's not really a judgement, Marie-Ange. More an observation.'

She waited for him to elaborate. When he didn't she sighed. 'Which is?' She was doing a poor job of masking her curiosity with indifference.

Bannerman smiled. 'I think you could probably hazard a

guess.' He saw the slight puckering of her lips, the tiniest manifestation of her irritation, and he said, 'You speak very good English.'

A forced smile betrayed the realization that he was not going to give voice to his observation. So now she feigned boredom and cast her eye around the room. 'I was educated in England and Switzerland. I also speak French, Flemish and German. But English has always been my lingua franca.'

Someone nudged her elbow as they passed, and she very nearly spilled her champagne. Bannerman caught her hand to steady it and felt the lightest touch of her breast on his arm. The scent of her perfume seemed suddenly more intoxicating than the bubbles in his champagne. Her face was too close to his. She smiled, her voice faintly husky as she leaned closer. 'You're an interesting man, Mr Bannerman.'

He smiled and moved imperceptibly away. 'More interesting than Tim?'

Her smile settled like frost on her lips.

'Bannerman, isn't it? Neil Bannerman?' The voice crashed into the intimacy of their conversation. 'I hope I'm not inter-rupting.' Bannerman turned to see a small, rotund figure in a dinner suit two sizes too big, a cheap rental job badly chosen off the peg. Its wearer was in his late fifties, bald with little tufts of greasy grey hair clinging around the edges of his head. His fat, unlined face smiled amiably, a familiar smile below bushy eyebrows. A soiled red handkerchief clutched in short stubby fingers mopped at his forehead and under his chins.

His free hand was extended. 'You remember me, don't you? Platt. Richard Platt. We worked together on the *Mail*. Long time ago now.'

Bannerman heard Marie-Ange tut impatiently beside him. Of course he remembered Platt, but there was an unwillingness to acknowledge it. It was not a time about which he cared to remember. 'Yes,' he said reluctantly, and shook Platt's soft, damp hand.

Platt said, 'Must be, what, fifteen years? More. What a coincidence meeting you here in Brussels.'

'Yes, isn't it,' Bannerman said without enthusiasm.

'I've been following your career with great interest. Made quite a name for yourself.' He paused and beamed at Marie-Ange, who glanced at him with distaste.

She turned to Bannerman. 'You're not doing a very good job of looking after me, Mr Bannerman. My glass is empty.'

'Allow me.' Platt waved towards a waiter and lifted three glasses when the tray arrived. 'Sure I'm not interrupting?'

'You are, actually,' Marie-Ange said with the sweetest of smiles.

Bannerman shook his head and found a grin. 'Not at all.'

Platt shuffled uncomfortably. His smile became fixed. 'I . . . I've been in Belgium nearly ten years now. The evening paper here in Brussels. *La Belgique Soir*. Perhaps we could meet sometime, for a drink. Chat about old times. Next week if you're still here.' He searched his pockets before producing a grubby business card. 'You can get me at the office most days. And

I'm home most evenings after about ten.' Bannerman took the card and slipped it in his pocket without looking at it. Platt positively wilted under Marie-Ange's glare, and he backed off. 'Well, I'll leave you two lovebirds to it.'

'I'll call you,' Bannerman said, knowing that he wouldn't. And fleetingly wondered what a low-life journalist like Platt was doing at a gathering like this. Platt nodded uncertainly at Marie-Ange and vanished among the dinner jackets.

With distaste in her voice, Marie-Ange said, 'Lovebirds?'

But Bannerman wasn't listening. He was thinking about Platt. About how little he had changed in all the years. The same drinker's face, the same nicotine-stained fingers. The same nervous tic over the right cheekbone, the same bad teeth. Uncomfortable in his rented dinner suit, he would have been more at home in his shabby brown raincoat and felt hat. Still, all that had been a long time ago.

He replayed now what it was Marie-Ange had said on Platt's departure. He turned to her and inclined his head. 'Perhaps we make a more convincing couple than you and Tim.'

The crowd behind her parted suddenly like the Red Sea at the behest of Moses, and he saw Slater at the far side of the room in deep conversation with a man whose back was turned to them.

'Excuse me,' he said to Marie-Ange. 'I have to see a man about a dog.' He didn't wait to catch her frown of consternation, and pushed off through the crowd as it ebbed and eddied ahead of him.

A frown of annoyance crossed Slater's face when he saw Bannerman approaching, and the other man turned, running a tanned hand through thick dark hair. 'Maybe time you got back to your good lady,' Bannerman said. 'She's pretty high-maintenance, and I'm off.'

Slater could barely conceal his irritation at Bannerman's intrusion. But his companion seemed to welcome the interruption.

'Neil Bannerman, isn't it? I thought I recognized you. You were at the Council of Ministers yesterday.'

'This is Robert Gryffe, Minister of State for Europe.' Slater made the introduction grudgingly.

'Yes, I know.' Bannerman shook Gryffe's hand. 'I'm pleased to meet you, Minister. I'm flattered that you should have recognized me.'

'Ah,' Gryffe smiled. 'But Mr Bannerman, you have a certain reputation.'

'Would that be good or bad?'

Gryffe made a moue with pale lips. 'Not for me to say.'

Bannerman grinned. 'Ever the diplomat.'

All three of them shuffled self-consciously then as an uneasy silence fell among them. Bannerman had already sensed the tension between Slater and Gryffe. In the former it was patent. In Gryffe it was more subtle. Here was a man used to changing masks, as all good politicians are. The easy smile, the strong handshake. A salesman of ersatz sincerity. But Bannerman was attuned to reading the signs, peeling away the masks. He was good at it. As he had to be. As all good newspapermen had to be.

'I hope I'm not interrupting anything.' Bannerman glanced from one to the other and stole Platt's line to fill the awkwardness.

'Not at all,' Gryffe said. 'Tim and I were just chatting. Anyway, it's time I did some mixing.' He beamed at Slater, whose attempts to conceal his agitation were falling well short of convincing.

'Nine-thirty,' Slater said pointedly. And for a second Gryffe's mask slipped and his face clouded.

'Nine-thirty,' he repeated, and then the moment had passed and he was smiling once again. He turned his back on Slater and asked Bannerman, 'Are you in Brussels for anything special?'

'Just sniffing around,' Bannerman said.

Gryffe chuckled. 'Like a dog.'

'A bloodhound,' Bannerman elucidated. But his smile faded as beyond Gryffe he saw, with a sinking heart, the American couple he had met on the plane. The Schumachers. And they were heading his way. This was not his night.

'Well, Mr Bannerman. Isn't this a surprise? Just fancy meeting you here.' Mrs Schumacher was flushed from too many sherries as she barged in on the tiny gathering. Henry followed quietly in her wake. His habitual smile of embarrassment was fixed but genuine. Laura-Lee, however, was oblivious. She raised a pencilled eyebrow at Bannerman. 'I have to admire you, young man. It didn't take you long to get in with the movers and shakers.' She paused to take a breath and straighten her dress. 'Are you going to introduce us to your friends?'

Bannerman smiled awkwardly. 'Mr and Mrs Henry Schumacher, Mr Robert Gryffe, British Minister of State for Europe, and Tim Slater, European correspondent for the *Edinburgh Post*.' Slater looked positively hostile, but Gryffe remained unruffled. He shook both their hands.

'Pleased to meet you,' he said.

'And we you, I can assure you, Mr Gryffe.' Laura-Lee turned towards Henry. 'My husband is with the US government at NATO. Perhaps you'll have heard of him?'

'I'm afraid . . .'

But Laura-Lee didn't want to hear it. 'I do so think there should be more contact between the politicians of our two countries. Socially, I mean. Wouldn't you agree? Perhaps you would lunch with us one day.'

'I'd be delighted to,' Gryffe lied.

Mrs Schumacher took his arm confidentially and steered his eyes towards Bannerman. 'Has this young man been trying to sell you vacuum cleaners?'

Bannerman watched Gryffe's face with amusement while Henry Schumacher's embarrassment grew more acute. 'I think perhaps you should come and sit down, Laura-Lee,' he said.

'Oh nonsense, Henry. Don't fuss. I'm sure Mr Gryffe doesn't mind.'

'Not at all,' Gryffe said.

Bannerman noticed Platt watching them curiously from a leaning position against the far wall, a glass clutched tightly in his hand. It was time to put a stop to this. He turned to Mrs Schumacher. 'I'm sorry to break things up, but I'm afraid I have to go.' And to Slater, 'I'll see you later.' Pause. 'Goodnight.' He turned abruptly and made his way towards the door.

'Well, that's a shame,' Laura-Lee said. 'Such a nice young man. You'd never guess he was a vacuum cleaner salesman.'

'A what?' Gryffe asked, puzzled for the second time.

'A salesman. Of vacuum cleaners. What was the name of his firm, Henry?'

'The Quick-Clean Vacuum and Brush Company, I think, Laura-Lee.'

Gryffe smiled with genuine amusement. 'I think our Mr Bannerman has been pulling your leg, Mrs Schumacher.'

'Oh?' Laura-Lee glared at him. 'Who *does* he work for then?'

'He's the investigative reporter of the *Edinburgh Post*. A man with quite a reputation.'

Mrs Schumacher let go of Gryffe's arm and he took a relieved step back. 'You hear that, Henry?' She turned towards her husband. 'A reporter. Why on earth would he tell us he sold vacuum cleaners?' Henry Schumacher's face echoed Gryffe's bewilderment of a few moments earlier.

Platt watched Bannerman leave and wondered what he was up to. He drained his glass and peered at the faces of European society through a haze of alcohol and cynicism, wincing slightly as his ulcer issued the first warnings of a troublesome night. He took a tablet from a bottle in his pocket and chewed on its mintiness. It was not worth staying much longer, he thought. There was no copy in it. His news desk would be upset in the morning, but they could go to hell. It was not his kind of job anyway. Dinner suits and smoked salmon. Though he knew he could not push his luck too far. It was a long time since he had turned in a good story. But he would show them. Rémy and Clerck and the rest. There was no way he would lose this job too. He was happy in his exile. Anonymous, safe from the failed years in Scotland, safe from the single-end, the succession of hard-drinking pubs, the sole milk bottle on the doorstep and the letters of complaint from the woman across the landing. He signalled a waiter and told himself this would be the last whisky tonight. Perfect for washing down his antacid. Now he had Bannerman. An arrogant bastard, yes, but a bloody good reporter. Something must have brought him to Brussels. Something big. And if Platt played his cards right, maybe he could get a piece of the action, whatever it might be. He chuckled to himself. After all these years he might get some mileage out of Bannerman yet.

II

Sally sat listening to the slow interminable tick, tick of the clock on the mantelpiece. There was no sound from the child's room and the apartment was deathly quiet. Her book lay open on the table beside the settee. She had been unable to read, unable to watch television. She had been thinking about Bannerman ever since last night. He'd had an unexpected effect on her. His extraordinary presence, powerful, but subtle at the same time, like the taste of a good wine. There was a sense of something tantalizingly concealed behind his smile, and she found herself wanting to reach out and touch it. But then somewhere deep inside her was that same old fear of commitment that she had been unable to shake off ever since . . .

She was startled by the sound of the key in the lock and looked at the time. It was only eleven. They were early. She had not expected them back until around two. But there were no voices, only the quiet closing of the door and soft footsteps in the hall. The door opened into the living room and Bannerman stopped on the threshold. He smiled and shook his head. 'I'm sorry,' he said. 'I'd forgotten you'd be here. My mind was on other things.' He swayed slightly as he closed the door and she saw that he had been drinking. He slipped off his coat and threw it over the back of the settee.

'You're drunk,' she said.

'No.' He shook his head again. 'A little bit drunk, a little bit sad.' He walked unsteadily past her to the window where he drew back the curtains and stood looking out into the blackness. He could not have seen anything for the light in the room, but she could see his face reflected darkly in the glass.

He sank his hands deep in his pockets and she saw his eyes closing. She said nothing, and the moments of silence dragged on. Then he said unexpectedly, 'You know, there is no way of escaping the things you regret. They're always there, shaping the way you are, even when you don't know it. And then something, or someone, brings it all back and it seems all the worse for the years you've buried it.' Sally did not know what to say. He would not, she knew, say these things if he had not been drinking. 'First the kid,' he said, 'and then Platt, and maybe even you in some way.' He turned to face her.

She eased herself out of the settee and moved towards him. 'Don't say any more.' She put a finger up to his lips and he kissed it before pulling it gently away.

'I need someone . . .' he whispered.

She shook her head. 'You should sleep on it.'

'Alone?'

'Alone.' And she felt afraid again. It would be so easy. And it had been so long.

He let her take his hand and lead him out of the living room and into his bedroom. The shutters were open and the light from the streetlamps shimmered in bright yellow flecks through the drops of rain on the window, tiny needles of light in the darkness. He let her slip off his jacket and tie and start undoing the buttons of his shirt, and all the time he watched her green, speckled eyes. He still felt warmed by the drink, and the sadness had stayed with him. He felt her lips on his chest and he reached out and pressed her head close into him.

It felt small and fragile and precious in his hand, her hair soft and silky so that it was almost like touching nothing. He felt the softness of her body pressing against him. All the curves and hollows. She stretched up and he kissed her and they slipped back on to the bed so that he felt all the nakedness of her skin against his – and he could not remember her having undressed.

They lay for some time, wrapped in each other, without having made love, until Bannerman slipped away into a deep alcoholic sleep. Sally looked at his fine features and ran her finger lightly over his face, feeling the roughness of a day's growth on his jaw. She was glad that they had not made love. It made it easier to draw back, to avoid involvement.

She dressed slowly in the darkness and laid Bannerman's clothes over the chair by the bed. Something fell from his trouser pocket and landed with a light thud on the carpet. She stooped and searched about and felt a key under her hand. He'd forgotten to put the key back under the mat. Quietly she left the room and pulled the door to and slipped down the hall. She opened the front door and replaced the key beneath the mat and heard footsteps and voices on the stair below. A glance at her watch told her it was nearly two. How was it possible that three hours had passed?

She shut the door and hurried back into the living room and was picking up her book as Slater slipped his key in the lock.

CHAPTER NINE

The temperature had dropped overnight and the sky was heavy with the threat of snow from dark clouds that scraped the skyline. The cold, quiet streets were empty in the first light of this Sunday morning, milk bottles standing on doorsteps, Sunday newspapers stuck in letter boxes. The occasional taxi cruised past the grey terraces where the shutters were still closed, curtains still drawn. Brussels was not yet awake. In an hour the first sombre citizens would leave their homes and make their way darkly to early Mass among the flickering candles in ancient churches and the raised incantations of pious voices. A sheet of yesterday's newspaper fluttered across the Square Ambiorix and in the children's swing park the swings swayed gently back and forth, a rusted link squeaking in the cold air.

Slater turned his car into the square from the Chaussée Martel, his daughter seated quietly in the back staring sullenly from the window. Tania knew her father was nervous, agitated, as he had been so often recently. But this morning she felt more than that. She sensed his fear with a growing trepidation. The pressure of her own unease was building inside her and she became aware that her hands were gripping the edge of the seat so tightly that her knuckles were turning white. Slater caught sight of her face in the rearview mirror and thought, thank God she's at peace. He could not see her hands. Again he cursed Sally. Of all the mornings for her to call off. The last thing he had wanted was to take Tania with him on this of all visits. Nothing had worked out according to plan. The arrival of Bannerman, Sally's call-off. He had not been able to face breakfast this morning, and now he felt slightly sick. His heart was hammering away at his ribs and his palms were damp with perspiration.

He wiped them one after the other on his trouser legs and swung the car into the Rue de Pavie. There were cars parked below the Residence Ambiorix, but down the length of the street there was only one other vehicle. It was parked outside Gryffe's block. Slater pulled up in front of it and switched off the engine. He half-turned towards Tania. 'You'll have to stay in the car, little one.' It was foolish to have hoped that this was something she might accept, and he watched as the scream rose in her chest. Both of her hands clutched at the back of his collar as her voice filled the car. He twisted himself in the seat and took her arms to hold them firmly. 'You must,' he said, imploring her. 'I can't take you in. Please don't start.'

The strength that seemed to seize her when she threw a tantrum never ceased to amaze him, and he had to grasp her arms so tightly that he feared he was hurting her. She wriggled down in the seat and forced one leg up, her foot catching him on the shoulder. He struggled to hold her now, hindered by the back of the seat, dreading the screams that followed each series of deep, breath-catching sobs. 'For Christ's sake, stop it!' he shouted, letting go one arm so that he could slap her hard across the face. Immediately he regretted it. It did no good, he knew. And he watched the red weals spring up raw and vicious across the white softness of her cheek. Her free hand clawed at his face, nails drawing blood above his right eye. He grasped the offending hand and twisted it, holding it away from his face. 'All right, all right, all right! I'll take you in. Just stop it, please! Stop it! I'll take you in. But you'll have to stay in the hall.'

Almost at once he felt a relaxation in her arms. But it was several minutes before the screaming stopped and the sobbing subsided and she fell back passively in the seat, pale and breathless.

He turned around to face front, then dropped his face into trembling hands and wiped away the sweat. He was shaking all over, breathing in short, uneven bursts. He reached for his cigarettes and lit one, glancing at his watch. Nine-thirty. He glanced along the dead street and thought, there is still time to pull out of this. But it had gone too far now. He had passed the point of no return weeks ago. He cursed his own weakness. You have no stomach for this, he thought, and yet he knew that even this was better than the bleak despair of a future without hope. He stubbed out the half-smoked cigarette in an overflowing ashtray and stepped out of the car into the bitter cold wind that blew down the Rue de Pavie. He opened the rear door for Tania and the child scrambled out clumsily on to the cobbles, clutching at her father's arm. She sensed something dreadful and clung to the only familiar thing she knew. Slater pressed the buzzer and heard it sound somewhere far off inside. They waited a long time in the cold before they heard footsteps approaching and the door opened.

Gryffe looked dishevelled, worn and weary, as though he had not slept. He stared out of red eyes at Slater and then at the child. 'Jesus, you're a callous bastard, Slater, bringing your kid.'

Slater's words almost clotted in his throat. 'I had no choice . . .' But he stopped short of making excuses. There was no reason that he should. Where once he might have felt pity for Gryffe, he despised him now, though even hatred could not salve his troubled conscience. Gryffe moved aside to let them in and closed the door behind them. It was dark in the hall, gloomy, the only light coming from a skylight high up above the stairwell. 'She'll wait in the hall,' Slater said, and he prayed that this time she would accept it.

Gryffe nodded curtly. 'Through here.' He led the way into the back room. His suit was crumpled and Slater guessed that he had spent the night on a settee or in a chair. He glanced back at Tania as he closed the door. She seemed almost oblivious at being left on her own and was wandering into the cloakroom, attracted by the smell of coats and their softness to touch.

*

Kale had been awake throughout the night. He had heard

Gryffe return shortly after two. First he had gone upstairs and then come back down, and Kale had heard him moving around, pacing between the study and the back room for nearly an hour. At length the house had fallen silent again, though Kale had not heard Gryffe go back upstairs. He guessed that the politician had probably fallen asleep in a chair or over his desk, and he had remained crouched painfully in the darkness, cold and uncomfortable, behind the filing cabinets.

The sound of the buzzer had woken him out of a light, restless slumber and he had heard Gryffe stirring in the back room and then going out to answer the door. There were voices in the hall, and now both men were coming into the study from the back room. Kale eased himself up, straightening his stiff, painful limbs. It was still dark in the cupboard, only the faintest line of grey daylight below the door. He shone his pencil torch on his watch. Nine thirty-five. Then he located the two revolvers, grasping Gryffe's heavier Colt in his gloved right hand and slipping the lighter gun into his left-hand coat pocket. He picked his way carefully to the door, all his mental and physical energies concentrated on doing this thing right.

He could hear the two voices, raised now. They seemed to be arguing. Kale could not make sense of it. Money, it seemed, was the issue. But that was none of his concern. He tightened his hand around the handle and eased the door open about two inches, screwing his eyes up against the sudden glare of light, holding himself absolutely still until his pupils had contracted and the light no longer pained him. Gryffe was standing behind his desk, his back to Kale. Beyond him the other moved into Kale's line of vision; a thin, pale, frightened-looking man. Ginger hair and beard. Perfect, Kale thought, with an almost inhuman detachment from what he was about.

He had no thought for the men he was about to kill, their pains, their loves, all the years they had lived until now; years that he would rub out, so that only the faintest impression of their existence would remain on the pages of history. So it was with most men. What did it matter that they had ever lived? They all died, sooner or later. All the futile years. He took a single step back and levelled the Colt through the opening of the door.

'Don't be a fool, Gryffe,' he heard the ginger-haired man saying. 'I can ruin you.' Gryffe stooped and opened the top right-hand drawer of his desk and stared blankly into its emptiness. Kale squeezed the trigger, gently, fondly, almost as though he were stroking it, and then recoiled from the blast in the confined space of the cupboard. The bullet punched a hole in the centre of Slater's chest and threw him back against the wall, blood spewing from the wound. He was dead even before he fell forward on to his face.

Gryffe spun around, fingers of fear closing around his beating heart, in time to see a small, mean figure in a dark, shabby coat slip out from the walk-in cupboard behind him. The man's face betrayed nothing. He held Gryffe's Colt .32 and was pointing it at him.

'Don't move,' Kale said quietly, almost in a whisper. He

slipped out from behind the desk and crossed quickly to where Slater lay crumpled in on himself, blood spreading rich and dark on the carpet. The gun still pointed at Gryffe, Kale bent to check the dead man's jugular, just to be sure. He stood again, taking out the second gun with his left hand.

Gryffe was paralysed by a cocktail of fear and confusion. He could not believe that he was about to die. There was no need for this. Not now. Slater was dead. He clutched at straws, struggling to find his voice.

'Lamb fixed it, didn't he? It was Lamb. To get me off the hook.' Kale nodded and lowered the Colt. Gryffe felt an enormous surge of relief and almost buckled at the knees. 'Thank God,' he said. 'Thank God.'

Kale smiled. A curious, mean smile. 'Here,' he said and threw Gryffe the Colt. The politician caught the gun, a reflex action. He saw Kale switch the other gun to his right hand and level it quickly. The bullet made a small neat hole in the centre of Gryffe's forehead. There was not the same force in the second shot and Gryffe staggered back only one step before tilting sideways and striking his face on the edge of the desk as he went down.

Kale hurried over, again to check that the shot had been fatal. The man was quite dead. Then he returned to Slater, crouching to lift the top half of the body up so that he could pull the right arm out from beneath it. He took the hand. First he would need miscellaneous prints on the gun. An index print on the right side of the barrel, a thumbprint on the left side behind the chambers, two fingers on the trigger guard. They would not be totally convincing, but they would be good enough in the confusion there was certain to be. He fitted the gun carefully into the hand and bent the arm back below the body, allowing the torso to fall over it again, the way it had happened naturally. He stood up and glanced back across at Gryffe. The Colt had fallen from his hand. But that would not matter. It was his gun and it had his prints on it. He went back to the cupboard and checked that he had left no tell-tale signs, then carefully closed the door. What counted now was to get away quickly, without being seen. It was unlikely that anyone would have heard the shots. The nearest apartment block was at the end of the street. Kale took a last look round then slipped into the back room and out into the hall.

It was still and gloomy here and he waited, listening behind the front door for nearly a minute, before removing his plastic shoe covers, opening it and glancing out. The street was deserted. He pulled the door closed behind him and his footsteps receded hastily down the cobbled pavement.

It was a full five minutes before Tania stirred among the coats and felt confident enough to come out into the hall. She had heard the raised voices, the shots, and then someone moving softly around the study. She had seen the thin, dark figure emerging from the back room. The high-cheekboned face with its deep-sunk eyes and clear sallow skin. Now she stood in the hall, the silence of the house pressing around her. She was confused, afraid. She wished she could call out. She took small heavy steps from the hall into the back room. There was a strange smell of burning in here. An empty armchair by an old marble fireplace, a bookcase full of dark, bound books. A heavy, gilt-framed picture on the wall. The French windows into the study stood open, and still there was no sound. Where were they? Her father and the other man. Another few steps and she could see into the study. She stood motionless, staring, the horror of understanding what she saw growing inside with a force and a pain that she thought would choke her. And then the first cry of anguish ripped into the silence of her consciousness.

CHAPTER TEN

I

Bannerman stirred among the sheets, the thickness of sleep still in his head and throat. His mouth felt dry and furry from the drink the night before and he had the faintest pleasurable recollection of having fallen asleep with a woman beside him. But now she was gone.

His immediate inclination was to turn over and pull the sheets tightly around him and slip back into the world of dark, shallow dreams from which he had just emerged. But there was an annoying flicker somewhere in his subconscious that took several seconds to surface. Something had woken him. The sleep had not been broken naturally. He was not quite sure why that should worry him. He pulled himself up on one elbow to look at the clock and felt the cold bedroom air rush in beneath the covers. It was nearly a quarter to eleven. Slater, he remembered, had a meeting with Gryffe at nine-thirty. Was that this morning? Sally had said she couldn't babysit. Had he taken Tania with him? Bannerman frowned and listened carefully. There was someone in the living room. Perhaps Slater was back already.

He cleared his throat of phlegm and swung his legs out of bed, feeling the first throb of pain in his head. He sat for a moment rubbing his eyes then blinking and looking out of the window across the roofs of the tenements and terraces. He had forgotten to close the shutters the night before. A vague memory of Sally in the darkness of the room returned to him, bringing a rush of regret. Had he really slept with her? He had no recollection of it. He stood up and pulled on his dressing gown.

The hall was dark and he padded to the living-room door, scratching his head. 'Hello?' he called. There was no reply. He pushed open the door and saw that the curtains were still drawn. Above the fireplace a painting of hunters on a snow-covered hillside was swung out from the wall where it was fixed with hinges. A wall safe concealed behind it stood open. He had taken no more than two steps into the room when something struck him hard on the back of his head. The pain shot down his spine like long needles, and the floor swung crazily towards him, striking him with a sickening force that hammered the breath from his lungs. The moan that escaped his lips sounded strange, disembodied, as though it had come from someone else. It was far, far away in some other world into whose darkness he was now falling.

Kale looked down at the still body on the floor. He was breathless and tense. For just a few seconds it crossed his mind that he should kill this one too. But he quickly dismissed it. There was little point in drawing more attention to the incident than was necessary. Still, it irritated him. It was untidy, the only loose end in the affair. He'd been told the flat would be empty, and he had taken that on trust. He was a fool. He should have checked first. He pulled the body over to have a look at the face. It would be as well to remember it. Already the right cheek and temple were bruising where they had struck the floor. It was a wide, hard face that you would remember with little difficulty. Some blood was oozing from the mouth where the man had bitten his lip on impact. Kale let the body drop back and kicked the prostrate form viciously in the side. It was unnecessary, but there was a grim satisfaction in it, and it released a little of his tension.

He stepped over the body and crossed to the safe, lifting out the black briefcase and closing the door. He swung the picture back against the wall and pushed his gun into his coat pocket. Then he recrossed the room and slipped quickly down the hall to the front door. He closed it behind him, carefully replacing the key below the mat.

Bannerman felt the pain of consciousness slowly returning. The dull, hard ache at the back of his head increased to the point where it seemed to numb itself. He felt as though he had been kicked in the face and there was the bitter iron taste of blood in his mouth. He forced his eyes open and they hurt sharply even in the half-light. He screwed them shut, opening them again a little more slowly. A light groan escaped involuntarily from his throat as he tried to turn himself over. More pain. This time right down one side of his chest. Now it hurt even to breathe.

He lay for several minutes before he tried moving again. This time he gritted his teeth against the pain and pulled himself heavily up to his knees. Immediately the blood rushed to his head and he felt giddy and sick. He dropped one hand to the floor to support himself, and swayed slightly back and forth until the sick feeling passed. His breathing was rapid and shallow and everything about his body was, he discovered, stiff and sore to move. What the hell had happened? He fought to remember. Even that seemed to hurt. But slowly recollection returned. The dark hall, the sounds of movement in the living room. The open safe above the fireplace. He looked over and saw that it was closed now, the painting flush with the wall. He waited yet another few minutes before trying to get to his feet. Then he leaned against the door jamb breathing hard, feeling the pain wash over him time and again. With a slight shock he saw that the clock on the mantel read after twelve. He must have been unconscious for over an hour.

Then he tensed as he heard voices on the landing outside, and a key sounded in the lock. He turned to look down the length of the hall as the door opened. There were three men, one in uniform. The uniformed officer pulled a gun clumsily from a black leather holster and raised it towards Bannerman.

He shouted a warning in a language that Bannerman did not understand.

II

It was dark now, the wind battering sleet against the window. Inside it was warm and stuffy, insulated against the inhospitable night that had fallen over this grey Belgian city. The office was small and cluttered, an anonymous place in a vast building of concrete and glass that architects without a sense of history had annexed to the Palais de Justice – a building blackened by the years but still vast and impressive in its brooding grandeur. The annexe housed the police headquarters through which all life passed along drab corridors beneath glaring fluorescent lights.

On reflection, Bannerman thought that perhaps this office had a little more character than the others he had been in. A large old oak desk sat at an angle across one corner. Wire trays were piled high with ageing reports, a dog-eared blotter was scribbled with a hundred phone numbers, names, doodles. There were two overflowing heavy glass ashtrays, a fountain pen, a broken pencil. On the wall behind the desk, maps of Belgium and Brussels, charts and a *Playboy* calendar. Beside the door stood a tall, old-fashioned coat stand hung with two long dark raincoats that had seen better days, and an old tweed jacket. A broken umbrella leaned against the wall beside a pair of muddy gumboots. Along the door wall and the far wall, filing cabinets of different heights, some wooden, some a grey-painted metal, were pushed together, yet more documents piled untidily on top. The room was lit by an Anglepoise lamp on the desk.

Bannerman sat waiting on a hard wooden chair in front of the desk. He had been waiting for nearly three hours. The doctor had examined him first, dressing the wound on the back of his head. There were no ribs broken, but he was severely bruised. He might suffer the effects of concussion for some time, the doctor had warned. He should have plenty of rest, plenty of sleep.

Then he had spent a gruelling half-hour in a room with two plain-clothes policemen who spoke bad English. They had paid no heed to the doctor's advice. Who was he? Who did he work for? What was he doing at Slater's flat? Who had attacked him? What had been taken from the safe? What did he know about Robert Gryffe? Bannerman had answered everything they asked without ever seeming to satisfy them. They, in turn, had told him nothing. His curiosity had been dulled by his own discomfort and he had not pressed for information. He had been brought a bowl of soup and a cup of cold coffee, then taken to this office where he had sat watching darkness descend on Brussels.

He checked with his watch. Six-thirty. He was hungry, enormously weary, stiff, the pulsing in his head still painful. He ran his tongue over his lips where the blood had dried leaving dark brown rims. Whatever they told him eventually, he thought, would not surprise him, though he had given little conscious thought to what that might be. There was an unreal quality about everything. Like a dream. Or more correctly, a nightmare. A sequence of events through which he had passed without ever feeling that he had in any way participated.

The door opened and a lean man in a baggy brown suit stepped briskly into the office carrying a slim, beige folder. The crown of his head was bald and shiny, but dark, wiry hair grew in bushy abundance round it, and he wore round-rimmed tortoiseshell spectacles over a long, thin nose with flaring nostrils. He would be in his fifties, Bannerman guessed, with a grey, deeply creased face from which peered two small, very dark eyes behind the spectacles. His suit was well worn and fitted only where it touched. His waistcoat was open, a thin brown tie hanging from an open-necked white shirt. He carried about him an air of age and defeat, like a schoolmaster nearing the end of his career, reeking of chalk dust and blackboards and thankless years.

He closed the door behind him and nodded solemnly at Bannerman. It would have been obvious to anyone that this was his office. He dropped his folder on the desk and rounded it to sit in a leather captain's chair, resting his elbows on its arms and pressing the tips of opposing fingers together. Long, thin fingers on big-knuckled hands. He gazed through Bannerman and seemed lost in thought, and Bannerman noticed the tiny bushes of hair that grew out of each nostril.

Finally he seemed to focus and said, 'Well, Monsieur, your

story seems to check out.' The phone on his desk rang and he lifted the receiver. '*Oui?*' He spoke rapidly in French so that Bannerman could not follow him. Then he hung up and studied Bannerman again before rising and extending his hand. 'My apologies,' he said. 'Inspector Georges du Maurier of the Judicial Police. Homicide division.' His handshake was dry and firm. He sat down again and considered his next words carefully. 'Shortly after ten o'clock this morning a passer-by in the Rue de Pavie heard a child screaming in the house at number twenty-four. He rang the bell several times and knocked repeatedly on the door, but no one came to open it and the child continued to scream. The gentleman concerned called the Gendarmerie from a telephone at the Residence Ambiorix at the end of the street.

'Two uniformed officers forced entry to the house and found an eleven-year-old girl screaming hysterically in the back room on the ground floor. In the study there were two bodies. Timothy Slater, a journalist, had been shot through the heart. Robert Gryffe, a British government minister, was shot through the forehead. There were two guns. One belonged to Monsieur Gryffe. It was lying beside him and bore his fingerprints. We have been unable to trace the origin of the second gun as yet, but it was found in Monsieur Slater's right hand, which was folded beneath his body. There were no signs of a forced entry to the house, no traces of a third party, except of course for the child. Conclusion?' He paused and then answered his own question. 'They killed each other. On the face of it, everything points to that. Trajectory of the bullets, position of the bodies, prints on the guns.'

Bannerman sat in stunned silence. He had thought himself prepared for anything, but not this. For the first time in many hours he was no longer aware of the places where he hurt. He remembered Slater's file of cuttings on Gryffe, the tension between the two men at the party the night before. He leaned forward, his mouth dry. 'So, what . . . You're closing the case already?'

For the first time, du Maurier smiled. 'At present we are treating both as suspicious deaths.'

'And?'

Du Maurier raised his eyebrows but said nothing, waiting for Bannerman.

'You said everything points to them killing each other . . . on the face of it.'

The Inspector's smile broadened. 'Yes, there are other factors to consider.'

Now Bannerman waited as du Maurier lit a cigarette.

'Apart from the three or four clear prints on the gun Monsieur Slater was holding, it is otherwise clean. No other prints, no smudges. But what is more important, Monsieur Slater, it would appear, was left-handed. It is very unlikely that he would be able to place a shot so accurately with his right hand.'

The smile was gone now, and he drew distractedly on his cigarette.

'Also, the bullet that killed Monsieur Slater entered the heart centrally. Monsieur Gryffe, we discover, has owned a gun for many years but has never had any formal training in its use. A remarkable piece of shooting for two untrained men. And we must also consider that each shot would have been instantly fatal, so that unless they were fired at precisely the same moment the man who shot first would have survived. In addition we found a suitcase in a cupboard off the study. It contained two hundred and fifty thousand American dollars in used notes.'

Du Maurier folded his hands on the desk in front of him.

'And, of course, there was the assault perpetrated on you in Monsieur Slater's flat within an hour of the shooting. And whatever was taken from the safe, if anything.'

Bannerman frowned. 'So it was murder.'

'Ah, well, none of these things, either in themselves, or collectively, is conclusive. But they do raise the question. Forensics might provide a clearer insight when we get their report back from the lab.'

Bannerman tried to sort it all out in his mind through a haze of pain and fatigue. None of it seemed to make sense. 'What about the child? Tania.'

Du Maurier pulled thoughtfully at the whiskers growing from his nostrils and stared into the darkness beyond the ring of light from the Anglepoise. In the silence both men heard the soft slapping of sleet against the window. At length the policeman turned his gaze on Bannerman, and Bannerman wondered at his openness. 'The child was only brought under control finally by the use of sedatives. We brought in her carer . . . a young woman who normally looks after her.'

'Sally.'

'Yes. And one of the teachers from the child's school. We tried to question her, but as you might imagine it was hopeless. She was sufficiently drugged to keep her calm, but she was completely withdrawn. Absolutely no communication. And none likely, we're told. We provided her with a pencil and pad in the hope that she might be able to write something, anything. But she refused even to take the pencil.'

He stopped and fumbled for another cigarette.

'We left her alone in the room for, I would say, no more than half an hour while we had a brief conference. That was late this afternoon. We discussed the case with the police psychiatrist. He told us there was no hope of ever learning from the girl what had happened. In fact he suspected that the trauma of whatever she saw could well have done irreparable damage. Set her back years. It was decided that in the meantime she should be taken to a residential psychiatric hospital for children on the outskirts of the city, at least until her future is decided. Her teacher went back to fetch her and interrupted the child in the middle of this . . .' He opened the folder in front of him and slid a sheet of paper across the desk towards Bannerman.

Bannerman turned the sheet around. There was a drawing on it. A line drawing in pencil of extraordinary perspective and depth. In the foreground the figure of a thin man in a long coat was coming through a doorway. There were foreground scribblings on the wall that seemed to form a pattern. Wallpaper perhaps. Through the door, and behind the central figure, stood a large stone or marble fireplace. Part of an armchair was visible, a framed picture on the wall with the outline of a head. The drawing was vividly evocative, and yet distorted as if seen through a fisheye lens. Or a disturbed mind. There was something almost sinister about the figure in the foreground. It seemed to be stepping right out of the page. But most striking was the man's lack of facial detail. Tania had drawn only the outline of the head and ears. Everything else was observed in such detail that you would not have thought a child capable of retaining it, never mind reproducing it. But there was no face.

Bannerman was fascinated, confused. 'I don't understand,' he said.

Du Maurier lit a third cigarette from his second one and blew a jet of smoke at the Anglepoise. 'The picture on the wall in the background represents a head-and-shoulders portrait, a Rubens copy that hangs above a marble fireplace in Monsieur Gryffe's house in the Rue de Pavie. If you stand in the cloakroom in the hall and look through the open door into the back room you can see almost exactly what the child has represented in the drawing, including part of the armchair. The scribblings on the foreground wall seem to represent the patterned paper in the hall. The drawing is uncannily accurate.

I have just returned from a visit to the house to make the comparison myself.'

Bannerman thought about it for a few moments. 'And the face of the man?'

Du Maurier shook his head. 'If our meeting had lasted just a few minutes longer the child might have had time to complete the face. But she was interrupted before she had finished and nothing would make her continue. As you can see, almost everything else is so detailed. Buttons, pockets, hands. The carer, Sally, told us that the child often begins her drawings with an outline and then works inwards.'

Bannerman looked at the drawing again. It was hard to believe that it had come from the hand of an eleven-year-old. He looked up to find du Maurier watching him. 'And who is the figure in the foreground?'

The Inspector sighed. 'The man is too slight to have been Monsieur Gryffe. And if it had been her father, then surely the outline of the head would have indicated the beard.'

'So there was a third party.'

'Possibly.'

'Who didn't know the child was there?'

Du Maurier shrugged wearily. 'Perhaps. Though it's difficult to imagine how.'

Bannerman sat back and dropped the drawing on the desk. 'Maybe not. But it's clear there was a third man.'

'Then why didn't he take the money in the suitcase?'

'Perhaps he didn't know it was there.'

'Then what was his motive?'

Bannerman had no answer. But already he knew he was being drawn inextricably into this whole affair whether he wanted to or not. He wondered why du Maurier had told him as much as he had. But the policeman broke into his thoughts almost as though he had read them.

'This is not just a straightforward case of suspicious death, Monsieur Bannerman. It involves the murder of a British government minister. A diplomatic minefield at any time. But with an election in your own country less than three weeks away, and Monsieur Gryffe a high-profile poster boy for his party ... I imagine there could well be political pressures brought to bear. A tragic double homicide, each man responsible for killing the other, the reason for which will probably never be known. Case closed.'

He hesitated for a second.

'Unfortunately, Monsieur Bannerman, I have no doubt that they were murdered. And not by each other. Though by whom or for what reason, I do not pretend to know. But I don't want this taken out of my hands.' Bannerman watched him carefully. 'Political expediency, Monsieur Bannerman, can be as corrupt as murder itself. I have been a policeman all my life. Politics doesn't interest me. I believe only in the law. And justice.'

Bannerman said, 'So the men in suits are going to close down your investigation?'

'I imagine they are sitting in smoke-filled rooms right now wondering exactly how to do it.'

'Then how can you stop them?'

'By moving before they do.'

Bannerman saw determination in the set of his jaw.

'I have called a press conference to be held downstairs at . . .' He glanced at his watch. 'Seven-thirty. In just five minutes' time. I shall tell your colleagues most of what I have told you, though not everything. I have had the child's drawing photocopied and the copies will be distributed to the media. I imagine there will be quite a feeding frenzy.'

Bannerman raised an eyebrow. 'What about the men in suits?'

Du Maurier smiled. 'Politicians,' he said. 'They're too fucking slow.' He stubbed out his cigarette and got to his feet. 'We'd better go downstairs. Your colleagues await me.'

III

Bannerman sat at the back of the conference room, a small lecture theatre with rows of seats stepped back in tiers. Du Maurier took the conference, accompanied by a younger man. Both looked burned out in the glare of the television lights. A bank of microphones was mounted centrally on the rostrum for the dozen radio and television stations that would give the deaths widespread European coverage. There were more than fifty scribes straining not to miss a word, scribbling their shorthand outlines in tattered notebooks, cigarettes stuck in the corners of mouths.

Du Maurier delivered a terse statement in French and then English to a hushed silence. He covered most of what he had told Bannerman, though in less detail, and made no initial mention of Tania or the drawing. Neither did he make any reference to Bannerman.

Then came the questions. Thick, fast and confused, in French and English and Flemish.

'Are you treating this as murder?'

'At the moment we regard both deaths as suspicious.'

'What was Slater doing at Gryffe's house?'

'We don't know.'

'Do you think the motive was political or financial?'

'We don't know.'

'How were the bodies discovered?'

'The alarm was raised by a passer-by who heard a child screaming in the house.'

There were a few seconds of stunned silence, then a barrage of voices out of which no single question was distinguishable. Du Maurier raised his hands.

'Monsieur Slater's daughter was found in the house.'

'Did she see what happened?'

'We don't know. The child is autistic. She is unable to say.'

The excitement among the scribes rose like the temperature of a fevered man. The story had just got better. Bannerman imagined how tomorrow's headlines would read. Already he could see excited reporters knocking out copy on well-worn keyboards, polishing their clichés, dreaming up colour, emotive catchlines, seductive intros. All packaged and served up to be digested at breakfast along with the cornflakes.

'How old is the girl? What's her name?'

'She is eleven years old. Her name is Tania.' Du Maurier was impassive. He was making them work for it.

'Is there a pic of the girl?'

'No photographs.'

A chorus of voices raised themselves in protest. Again du Maurier lifted his hands.

'As I said, the child has been able to tell us nothing.' He paused. 'However, as a result of a drawing she made showing a man, clearly in the hall of the house in the Rue de Pavie, we are now working on the assumption that there was third-party involvement.'

Silence fell again. Absolute, if short-lived. The possibilities were turning themselves over in the minds of the scribes. Then the questions began again. But du Maurier pre-empted them all, lifting a folder from the bench and handing it to the young man beside him. 'Copies of the child's drawing have been made for your use. Monsieur Lousière will distribute them.'

Journalists clustered around the podium and Lousière fed hands that reached out like the beaks of chicks straining for food from their mother's mouth. Bannerman watched the melee with vague distaste, and yet whatever he felt, he could not detach himself from it. He was one of them. One of the vultures that gorged on the carrion of news, that fed the ugly millions their daily diet of death, tragedy, sex and intrigue. His cynicism ate at his insides, like stomach acid.

Two men had died, a child had lost her father and her future, and all any bastard could think about was the story it would make on tomorrow's front page.

Including himself.

He remembered the years of knocking on doors, cadging pics. *How do you feel about your son being killed, Mrs Smith?*

Sometimes you got there before the police, and after you'd broken the news you searched out and removed every picture of the dead boy so that the competition wouldn't get one. It was not how you wanted to work, but that's how it was. Accept it or get out. Right now he was hurting in a lot of places, inside and out, and he took the easy option by joining the pack. He pushed his way to the front and took his own copy of the drawing from Lousière. Like the rest of the carrion creatures he would do a story himself.

Only, he had a head start. He was on the inside, and knew things the others didn't.

'I am sorry. No more questions,' he heard du Maurier saying. The policeman collected his papers and headed for the door, only to be surrounded by radio and television hacks all wanting their pound of flesh; individual interviews, pics, the outside chance of an exclusive.

'*Why is there no face in the drawing?*' Bannerman heard a voice asking. Stiffly he pulled on his coat and pushed his way towards the door.

'Neil, Neil!' There was a hand on his shoulder. He turned to see Platt at his back. 'Good God!' Platt said, beady eyes examining the damage to Bannerman's face. 'You look as though you've been in the wars. What the hell happened?'

Bannerman glared back at him. 'None of your fucking business.' And he turned away.

But Platt was not to be deterred, chasing after him to grab his arm. 'Listen,' he said. 'We could work on this together. You knew Slater. I know Brussels.'

'Piss off.' Bannerman shook himself free and turned away again.

'I've got good contacts,' Platt shouted after him. But Bannerman was gone.

Platt glared after him angrily. *Cocky bastard*, he thought. *He'll come to me yet.* He wondered again why Bannerman had come to Brussels in the first place. Surely he couldn't possibly have known . . . And yet, hadn't he seen Bannerman with Slater and Gryffe just last night? He must know something. It would pay to keep an eye on him.

Outside, the temperature was still falling. The wind blew sleet up the Rue des Quatre Bras into the darkness of the Place Poelaert, to swirl around the foot of a tall black monument. Bannerman stepped out across the cobbles, pulling up his collar, and headed down towards the lights of the Boulevard de Waterloo, crossing the tramlines, past a group of people huddled below a shelter at the tram stop. The cold reached him even through the thickness of his coat. He thought about Tania and felt deeply depressed. He remembered the moment, just two nights ago, when she had come into his room, standing there in her nightdress watching him and then leaning over to touch his face.

What horrors were locked up in that little head?

Inside a large fashionable restaurant, prosperous people were seated at tables around a huge open fire, drinking wine, laughing, untouched by it all. Bannerman looked in at them through a large picture window and saw his drawn face, white and marred by bruising, reflected in the glass. He turned away and crossed the boulevard and walked up to the Métro at the Porte de Namur. He rode the underground to Arts Loi and then changed for Schuman, where he came out under the shadow of the Berlaymont. For several minutes he stood looking up at the endless rows of darkened windows, wondering if the answers to everything that had happened today might lie behind them. Then he set out with heavy steps down the Rue de la Loi towards the Rue de Commerce.

Slater's apartment was dark and still when he let himself in, and he almost expected to find Slater in his chair in the half-light of the living room where he had sat two nights before. That seemed a long time ago now. The living room was cold and empty. He went into Tania's room and stood in the darkness. An old rag doll lay in the armchair by the dead fire. He bent over and picked it up to hold against his face. Life was so unfair for those who deserved so much more. He dropped the doll back on to the chair and returned to the living room. He switched on the light and lifted the phone and began dialling wearily. The number rang three times.

'*Edinburgh Post.*' The voice was polished thin by all the miles in between.

'Neil Bannerman. Give me the editor.'

'One moment, Mr Bannerman.' A phone lifted a few seconds later.

'Tait.'

'Neil Bannerman.'

'Jesus Christ, Bannerman! Why the hell have I not heard from you before now?'

CHAPTER ELEVEN

Kale opened the shutters on the first light of morning and looked out on the grey mist that hung over the city. He had his coat on already, his bag packed and sitting on the end of the bed.

It had been a bad night with little sleep. He had dreamt of the long, cold dormitory, the voices of little boys crying beneath their covers. The harsh discipline, the loneliness of the place; both had left their mark on him. But he had never cried as others had. He had never succumbed to the authority of the housemasters. Rather, it had strengthened in him that which set him apart. The boys had known it, and so had the masters. He sensed their fear of him. They did not know how to deal with his sullen, silent rebellion against their establishment. The beatings, the solitary confinement, the withdrawal of privileges. All had been met with the same mute acceptance that so baffled them. The dark eyes that blazed their hatred; a boy who was only nine. It had all left its mark, and none of it had been without pain. But they would never know it.

Kale turned away from the window and lifted his bag

from the bed. He was unsettled, anxious now to be away. But there were still four hours to pass before he could collect the remainder of his money from the locker at the Gare du Midi. He left the room and got into a lift that hummed and clattered its way slowly down to reception. The desk clerk looked up as he swung the lift gate open.

'Your bill, Monsieur?'

Kale nodded and laid his bag on the floor beside the desk. The clerk lifted the bill off a shelf behind him and pushed it across the counter.

'Are you not having breakfast?'

Kale shook his head and the clerk shuffled uncomfortably as Kale counted out the notes from his wallet. The clerk had seen them come and go in an establishment like this, but this one was different. There was something dark and vaguely sinister about him. Nothing you could put your finger on. His wallet was amply filled, but his clothes did not suggest money. The clerk noticed these things. When there is so much time to pass in a day, you begin to look for them. The button missing from the coat, the slightly frayed cuff.

Kale lifted his bag and turned away, but stopped as he noticed a rack filled with the French-language Belgian daily, *La Dernière Heure*. 'How much?' he asked.

'Fifteen francs, Monsieur.'

Kale lifted the top paper off the pile and felt a touch like icy fingers on the back of his neck. He stared numbly at the drawing that filled the top quarter of the front page across four columns. The doorway, the painting, the chair, the figure in the foreground. There was no face, but he recognized himself with a chilling sense of déjà vu. The bold headline across a further four columns read, *L'HOMME SANS VISAGE – EST-IL L'ASSASSIN?* He looked up to see the clerk watching him curiously. He dropped the paper on the desk. 'Fifteen francs?' The clerk nodded. Kale fished in his pocket for the money. He was loath to make conversation, but he had to know. 'What's the big story?'

The clerk seemed surprised. He glanced at the paper and shrugged. 'Two men were shot dead here in Brussels yesterday. The police think the man in the drawing may have been involved. It was drawn by a child in the house where it happened. But she is – how can I say – not right in the head. The police won't say whether they think it was murder or not. But the papers don't have any doubts.' He paused and asked casually, 'What's your interest?'

Kale glared at him and dropped the fifteen francs on the counter. 'None,' he said. He lifted the paper and crossed the lobby, pushing open the glass doors and vanishing out into the street.

The clerk watched him go and frowned as a tiny nagging thought entered his mind. He rounded the desk and lifted a copy of the paper, peering closely at the drawing. The figure was suddenly familiar. There was a button missing from the coat. The same button missing from the Englishman's coat. But how could a child have noticed such a tiny detail? The clerk scratched his head and returned to his seat behind the counter, taking the paper with him. He looked at it some more, then looked at the card he had filled out with details of the Englishman's passport. James Ross was the name he had written. A salesman. Again the clerk frowned and scratched his head. But then, he thought, it was none of his business.

The Gare du Midi was busy. Passengers stood around in knots in the big arrival hall watching the boards for arrivals and departures. A thin metallic voice made announcements alternately in French and Flemish. Neither meant anything to Kale. He was seated on a wooden bench at the foot of a wide pillar from where he could see through glass doors and along a short corridor to the left-luggage lockers. It was not yet eleven-thirty, but he had been here for nearly an hour in the hope of seeing whoever might leave his money, if the deed had not already been done. The time had dragged painfully, so that all the uncertainty about what exactly was in the newspaper had grown in his mind. Over and over again he had thought about the drawing, stared at it. How was it possible there had been a child in the house without him knowing? He remembered the cloakroom. She could have been in there. But why? Still, he felt certain that no one could recognize him from the drawing. Only the child could know what he looked like, and according to the hotel clerk she was somehow mentally impaired.

He had struggled through the story again and again, trying to make sense of it from what little French he knew. But all that he had gleaned from it was the girl's name; the daughter of one of the men he had killed. He swore softly to himself. Things had not gone well. The sooner he got out of this damned country the better.

A stream of passengers emerged from platform six, partially obscuring his view of the glass doors. In that moment he saw a figure at the lockers. A figure he recognized. The white hair of a working man in city clothes. He jumped up and pushed his way through the passengers. Someone shouted at him and he stumbled and felt a hand on his shoulder. He shrugged himself free and ran towards the glass doors.

The figure had vanished.

Kale hurried down the corridor to the lockers. There was no sign of the man with the white hair. How the hell could he have got out of here without Kale seeing him? Kale looked back along the corridor towards the commuters milling beyond the other side of the glass.

Gone.

Breathlessly he took out his key and turned back to the lockers. Number thirty-nine. He fumbled at the lock and pulled open the door. The black case he had left there yesterday was gone. In its place a white envelope that was neither big enough nor fat enough to contain the money he was owed. He ripped it open with trembling fingers and pulled out a folded sheet of paper. There were three words printed across it in a tight, neat hand.

KILL THE CHILD.

CHAPTER TWELVE

The telephone woke Bannerman just after eleven. Long single rings that brought to an end the strange dreams that come just before waking. He slipped from the rumpled bedsheets, still woozy from the restless hours of shallow sleep. He had lain awake almost until dawn, unable to stop his brain from replaying the events of the last forty-eight hours. He was still stiff and his head and face still ached. The air in the flat was cold as ice and he shivered as he went through the hall to lift the phone in the living room and sit heavily on the settee.

'Bannerman.' He ran a hand over the stubble on his jaw.

A familiar voice crackled in his ear. 'That was a good piece you sent us last night, Neil.'

'That's what you pay me for, Mr Tait.' Bannerman could barely disguise his sarcasm. He heard Tait sigh.

'I'm flying out to Brussels tomorrow,' Tait said. 'For the funeral. I've been in touch with the Belgian authorities. Slater had no living relatives, so I didn't see the point in having him flown back for burial. They'll release the body after the post-mortem.'

'Save the paper money, will it?' Bannerman asked.

But Tait wasn't going to be baited. 'The arrangements are made,' he said. 'The funeral will be at the Cimetière de Bruxelles tomorrow afternoon. Two o'clock. I want you to remain in Brussels until this whole thing is cleared up. You can stay at the Rue de Commerce. We'll be making arrangements for the collection of Slater's belongings. Oh, and you'd better pick up his car. I understand it's been taken to the police car pound.' He paused, but got no response from Bannerman. 'I'll meet you at the office tomorrow around midday. We can have lunch and then you can drive me out to the cemetery.'

'What about his daughter?'

Tait cleared his throat. 'Ye-es,' he said, 'that's a bit of an unknown quantity. I suppose the paper has some kind of responsibility . . . Anyway, I'll see about that after the funeral. Meantime you stick with the story. Give me a call before the five o'clock conference and let me know what's happening.'

Bannerman hung up. It was all over already. He could read between the lines. By tomorrow night the story would be dead and buried along with Slater. The *Post* was embarrassed. There would be echoes of it in the other dailies and in the Sundays, but the *Post* would want it over and done with as expeditiously as possible. Bannerman heaved himself out of the settee and went into the bathroom to shave.

Hard blue eyes stared back at him from the mirror as he soaped his battered face. The politicians, too, would be happy to see the whole affair interred. The Belgians, like the *Post*, would be embarrassed, but for different reasons. A British government minister shot dead in the Belgian capital. They would not be relishing the publicity. And the British government would be worried about electoral repercussions. They could not afford a scandal with a general election less than three weeks away. Du Maurier's warning of political interference the previous day had been only too prescient.

Bannerman sluiced his face and neck with cold water and went back through to the bedroom to dress. He eased himself into a dark, crumpled suit and again sifted everything through his mind. He stared from the window across rooftops that shone black in the fine drizzle that drifted across the city.

He began with du Maurier's certainty that Slater and Gryffe had been murdered. If he was to work from that basic assumption then it was clear that it would be necessary to find either the murderer or the motive. Find one and you would find the other, he told himself, but without much conviction. The difficulty was knowing where to start.

He turned away from the window and sat on the bed. The murderer, apparently, had left no clues. But there was a witness. Tania had seen him, though Bannerman doubted if the child would ever be capable of identifying him. A motive might be easier to unearth.

There was the hostile relationship between Slater and Gryffe, the file of cuttings on the Minister that Slater had kept in his office, the money in the suitcase in Gryffe's study.

Bannerman got up and went through to the living room,

lifting the phone to call the *Post*. He waited uneasily as the number rang distantly. He felt a lack of commitment to this story. Tait, he knew, would not want him to unearth anything that might bring the paper into disrepute, and he felt a disconcerting lack of personal motivation. It worried him.

'Edinburgh Post.'

'Put me through to the library, please.' He waited until a receiver lifted.

'Library.' It was a woman's voice.

'Jean, it's Neil Bannerman.'

'Hello, Neil. You still in Brussels?' And without waiting for an answer, 'Poor Tim. What a terrible thing.'

'Yes,' Bannerman said. 'Look, do me a favour, Jean. Search out any cuttings we've got on Robert Gryffe, as well as anything we might have on him in his obit file. I want to lay hands on everything we know about the guy.'

'Are you in a hurry for it?'

'Yes. Just photocopy the stuff, stick it in an envelope and give it to the editor. He's flying over tomorrow. He can bring it with him.'

'Okay, Neil.'

He hung up, and drew the curtains open and stared thoughtfully down into the street. Then he turned his gaze around the living room. He might as well make a start with the apartment.

It took him less than half an hour to go through it room by room, drawer by drawer. There were extraordinarily few personal items. The safe was locked, and most of the drawers empty. It was not until he had begun his search that he noticed just how tidy the flat was. Slater had not struck him as being a particularly fastidious man. Of course the place would already have been searched by the police, and when a good cop does his job properly he almost always leaves the place he searched tidier than he found it. But still, it was more than just tidy. It was as if the flat had never been lived in. Even the child's room seemed naked, except for the rag doll lying on the armchair where Bannerman had dropped it the night before.

Here, too, the drawers were empty. Bannerman opened the wardrobe. A dozen coat hangers rattled and swung freely. Bannerman frowned as a suspicion grew in his mind. He went through to the kitchen and found the larder. There were a few cans of soup, a tin of spaghetti and a nearly empty coffee jar. The refrigerator had been switched off, and its shelves were bare. Then into Slater's bedroom, again to find an empty wardrobe, empty drawers in the bedside cabinet.

Bannerman sat on the bed and let his eyes wander about the room. They came to rest on three suitcases piled on top of the wardrobe. He took a chair from under the window and placed it below the wardrobe, then climbed on to it and reached up. The cases were heavy and he lifted them down carefully, one by one, raising a stoor from the top of the wardrobe. He opened each case in turn. Two of them were filled with men's clothing, underwear, socks, personal odds and ends. A photograph in a frame lay on top of Tania's clothing in the third, smaller case.

Bannerman turned it over and found himself looking at the

face of an attractive young woman. It was a black-and-white photograph. The woman looked to be in her mid-twenties. Bannerman knew the face. He had met her once, not long before she died. She was the mirror-image of her daughter.

Slater had taken it badly when his wife died. But still, Bannerman was surprised to find her photograph packed away for the departure that Slater had so clearly planned. Perhaps he had never quite got over her death.

He closed up the cases and pushed them against the wall. Now, at least, he knew why Slater had been so agitated by Bannerman's arrival. If he had been planning to take his daughter and slip quietly out of the country after his meeting with Gryffe, then Bannerman's appearance must have thrown a spanner in the works. But why? What had Slater and Gryffe been up to? It seemed like such an unlikely pairing.

And du Maurier? Surely he must have known about the suitcases. Why, when he had told Bannerman so much else, had he failed to mention them? Bannerman shook his head, confused, and sat again on the bed.

Finally he went through to his own room, lifted his coat and left the apartment. In the street he checked his watch. It was a little after midday. He pulled up his collar against the drizzle and brushed past a small, sallow-faced man in a shabby raincoat. He thought nothing of the brief glimpse he caught of an unremarkable face, unaware of the dark eyes that turned to watch him after he had passed.

*

He stopped at the café in the Boulevard Charlemagne where the German pressmen drink, and had a coffee and a couple of croissants before walking across the street to the International Press Centre. A girl at reception smiled at him as he went past to the lift and rode up to the sixth floor.

Mademoiselle Ricain looked up as he walked into the office. 'Can I help you?' she asked.

'Neil Bannerman. We spoke on the phone a few days ago.' He saw that she had been crying.

'Oh. Yes,' she said. 'I'm sorry. I'm still in shock.'

He nodded, uncomfortable, then tilted his head towards Slater's filing cabinet. 'Do you have keys?'

She hesitated. 'I don't know if I . . .'

'I'll be working out of this office for the next few days, Mademoiselle,' Bannerman said. 'I take it the police have already been?'

'Yes. They called me out yesterday . . . I . . . they said not to reopen the filing cabinet or touch any of Tim's stuff.'

'Well, that's all right,' Bannerman said. 'I'll take full responsibility.' She had long, fair hair and a plain face drawn by grief. Again she hesitated, before reluctantly opening a drawer in her desk and lifting out a small square key.

'How about the rest of the keys? The door, the desk?'

She looked at him coldly. 'I'm not at all sure about this,' she said. 'Maybe I should call the police for authorization.'

Bannerman kept his sigh to himself and softened his tone. 'Look, I'm sorry if I seem a bit abrupt. I'm just as shocked as you by what happened to Tim. I don't know why anyone would have wanted to kill him, but I'm going to find out. Someone cracked me on the head yesterday and played footsie with my ribs while I couldn't do anything about it. And I want to find out who did that, too.' He stopped to draw breath. 'A wee lassie who saw her father murdered has been shut away in some institution somewhere and no one seems to care. And if I don't do something about it I don't know who else will. And here's the thing, Mademoiselle, I don't have much time. They're going to bury Tim tomorrow, and paint whitewash all over this whole fucking mess. So I need you on side. Because, God knows, I've got no other friends in this city.'

Bannerman stopped to take stock. He had not meant to say any of this, perhaps unaware that it was even how he felt. But the words had tumbled out before he could stop them.

Mademoiselle Ricain managed a wan smile and took a further two keys on a ring from her desk drawer and held them out. 'I'm sorry,' she said. 'I'll do anything I can to help. Tim was a lovely man.' She fought back the tears that had stained her face earlier. Bannerman looked at her curiously. *Lovely* was not a word he would have used to describe Slater. But Mademoiselle Ricain had seen something more in him.

'You and Tim got on well, then?'

'Oh.' She got up and turned towards the window. 'He was just a nice man, Monsieur Bannerman. Considerate. About a lot of the little things that men don't usually think of. It's difficult to say what exactly. It's just the way a man behaves with you. I liked him. I knew him, I think, better than most others here did. People aren't always what they seem.' She glanced at Bannerman, suddenly self-conscious. Colour rose high on her cheeks, and Bannerman realized that she had been in love with him.

'Yes,' he said lamely, and found himself unexpectedly touched by sadness. Whatever Mademoiselle Ricain had felt for Slater had not, he was sure, been reciprocated. She moved away from the window and lifted her bag from the desk.

'Excuse me,' she said, 'I'll be back in a few minutes.' And she hurried from the office.

Bannerman stood for some moments before crossing to Slater's filing cabinet and unlocking it. He crouched down and pulled open the bottom drawer. It was half-empty, about a dozen suspension files hanging on their runners. He lifted them out and carried them over to Slater's desk and sat down. Mostly they contained cuttings of stories Slater had done on the EEC, a back reference divided into different groups – agriculture, fisheries, transport, taxation. Two of the folders were unmarked. One of them held the cuttings on Gryffe. Bannerman sifted through them.

They didn't seem to fall into any category. Altogether there were about forty pieces, not stories that Slater had written, but cut from different newspapers. They went back over two years, covering important speeches the politician had made at home and abroad, his appointment eighteen months earlier as

Minister of State for Europe, a piece from the *Telegraph* on his growing importance as a charismatic figure of influence in the party. *And* the country. It forecast his likely rise to challenge for the leadership in the not too distant future.

There were a number of photographs. Gryffe shaking hands with some African head of state, another in the Middle East. Gryffe speaking at the party's annual conference. Gryffe relaxing by a swimming pool with a bikini-clad girlfriend on holiday in Malta. He even appeared in the columns of the society diarists; best-dressed man in Britain; most eligible bachelor; a romance with Royalty (the punters would like that, though some of his party colleagues would not); a man of the people destined for the top.

Before this week Bannerman had only been aware of Gryffe in his peripheral vision. The journalist's focus had been on corruption, political and financial, in Scotland. But Gryffe, it seemed, had become a popular and fashionable figure in London social life as well as in politics. Most of the cuttings, he noticed, were taken from the English papers. He cursed himself for somehow having taken his eye off the ball.

He crammed the cuttings back into their unmarked folder and opened the other. There were fewer cuttings here. A dozen in all, clipped from Belgian newspapers, some French, some Flemish. Two names kept cropping up, Michel Lapointe and René Jansen, although they didn't appear to be connected. From one smudged, single-column pic Bannerman was able to put a face to Lapointe. A short, fat face. But the quality of the reproduction was poor and it was a face you would pass in the street without recognizing it. There were no photographs of René Jansen, although it was a name that rang a distant bell. Bannerman slipped the cuttings back in their folder, kept the two unmarked files to one side, and put the remainder back in the cabinet.

He sat for a moment in solemn contemplation before taking out his spiral-bound reporter's notebook and flicking to a fresh page to jot down four names one below the other: Tim Slater, Robert Gryffe, Michel Lapointe, René Jansen.

There had to be a common factor. Something that linked all four. Why else had Slater kept cuttings on them in unmarked folders? But the link was tenuous. There was no doubting the connection between Slater and Gryffe. However, it was possible that Lapointe and Jansen were simply red herrings. Bannerman could waste a great deal of time chasing them down. He tossed the possibilities around in his mind and looked out of the window at the heavy Belgian skies. There were times, he thought, when you had to chase red herrings, because there was nothing else to chase. He would need something before Tait got in tomorrow. Because Tait was going to want him to shut this thing down. And Bannerman would need something to convince him otherwise.

He became aware that his head was still hurting. There was a bad taste in his mouth from lack of sleep and his stomach was complaining that it needed more than the coffee and croissants he had fed it earlier. He got up and searched about the desks for a telephone directory. He found several and spent three or four minutes searching for the number he wanted.

Mademoiselle Ricain returned as he lifted the phone. Her smile was strained. 'Dial zero if you want an outside line,' she said. Bannerman saw that she had powdered her face and put fresh colour on her eyes and lips. He dialled, and a girl's voice crackled in his ear.

'*Police Judiciaire.*'

'Inspecteur du Maurier.'

'*Ne quittez pas.*'

He waited.

'Du Maurier.'

'Inspector. It's Neil Bannerman.'

'Ah, Monsieur. How are you today?'

'I'd like to talk.'

'*Bon.* Good. When?'

'Whenever it suits.'

'Hmmmm.' He hesitated. 'Five o'clock?'

'Fine,' Bannerman said.

'But not here.' Du Maurier cleared his throat. 'At the Café Auguste in the Boulevard de Waterloo. It's not far from the Rue des Quatre Bras.'

'Okay.' Bannerman hung up, then tried the keys that Mademoiselle Ricain had given him until he found the one that fitted Slater's desk drawer. He pulled it open and slipped in the two folders he had set aside. He was about to slide it shut when he saw a scarred, leather-bound notebook squeezed down one side. Slater's contacts book.

Bannerman thumbed through it, a record of all the people a dead man had known. People from whom information had been prised, or tip-offs received. Sometimes freely, sometimes under duress. A good journalist was not only good with words, he was good at getting information, research. Knowing where to look, who to ask.

As he thumbed through the pages it occurred to Bannerman to look under J for Jansen and L for Lapointe. So obvious the thought might have passed him by. There were home and office numbers listed for both. He noted them opposite the names he had written in his notebook. And then, as an afterthought, looked up Gryffe.

There were three numbers listed. One was the flat in the Rue de Pavie, another was Gryffe's London mews house. The third was a Belgian number with an H in brackets beside it indicating *Home*. Bannerman frowned. Had Gryffe possessed two homes in Brussels?

He noted all three out of habit and replaced the contacts book in the drawer. Mademoiselle Ricain was watching him over her typewriter.

'Anything I can do . . .?'

Bannerman shook his head. 'Thanks,' he said. 'Not right now.' He was distracted. The day was slipping away from him. After his meeting with du Maurier he knew the night would stretch emptily ahead, lonely hours in Slater's flat or in some bar getting drunk. Depression settled on him like dust. Then an idea came, forming slowly, a burgeoning light in the darkness. He said to Mademoiselle Ricain, 'Tim had a young woman who came in to look after Tania sometimes. Any idea where I can get in touch with her?'

She thought about it. 'Sally Robertson. Her number's probably in Tim's contacts book.'

'Oh, yes.' Why hadn't he thought of that? He took the book out again. The number was there, of course. He got an outside line and dialled. He let the phone ring several times before hanging up. No one home. He saw Mademoiselle Ricain watching him and tried not to show his disappointment. Carefully he made a note of the number in his own notebook.

The door opened behind him and Bannerman swivelled to see a middle-aged man shuffle in, accompanied by a rush of cold air and the smell of alcohol. He had a weary face as crumpled as his raincoat, and an untidy mop of greying hair that tumbled over heavy eyebrows. A dog-eared notebook was clutched between the ink-stained fingers of his right hand. He threw his coat over the remaining free desk, and half a dozen pens and pencils revealed themselves in the breast pocket of a jacket of indefinable shape and colour. He raised his abundant eyebrows when he saw Bannerman.

'Neil Bannerman, I presume,' he said in a voice gravelled by years of drink. He rounded his desk and slumped into a creaking chair to kick his feet up and rest them on the edge of it. 'Someone been having a go at you?' He screwed up beady eyes to examine the bruising on Bannerman's face and took out a match to stick in one corner of his mouth. He allowed himself a small, humourless grin.

'An accident,' Bannerman said. 'And you are . . .?'

'Eric Palin.'

'Ah, yes. Sent out to grass by the *Herald* and to pickle what remains of his liver, I heard.'

Palin was unimpressed. 'Smart bastard!' And he moved the match from one corner of his mouth to the other. 'I heard about you, too. Shooting your mouth off the other day at some of the boys, like you were God Almighty.'

Mademoiselle Ricain looked uncomfortable and busied herself with some paperwork. Bannerman was in no mood for exchanging wisecracks with a drunk. All the same, he said, 'Maybe I am. And maybe some of the boys need a good kick up the arse.'

Palin snorted, and his amusement seemed genuine. 'Aye, maybe they do.'

Bannerman said, 'And maybe when you're sober you can tell me what you know about Tim Slater. And his relationship with Gryffe.'

Palin snorted. 'What makes you think I would share information with the opposition, Bannerman? You might figure I'm just some drunk. And I won't deny I enjoy a dram or three. But I'm still a fucking good reporter . . .' He glanced towards Mademoiselle Ricain. 'Apologies for the French.' Then back to Bannerman. 'This is the hottest story that's broken in this shithole of a city in all the time I've been here, and I'm not about to give you a head-start on it.'

Bannerman leaned forward and said, 'It doesn't matter how good you are, if you're drinking you're no damned good to any-body, Palin. You can't be trusted. By anyone. Your editor knows that, so he's taking a calculated short-term risk in sending you out here. A fresh challenge. A new start. And you'll probably do okay. Keep it up for a year, maybe two. Then you'll start slipping, because people like you always do. And then you'll be out of a job so damned fast you won't know where your next half's coming from.'

Palin was sharp enough to know the truth when he heard it, a truth that he might never admit to himself. And it hurt, because the truth usually does. 'Fuck off!' He dropped his feet to the floor and took the match from his mouth. 'Think you know it all, don't you?' Amid the anger, there was a smugness in his voice. 'Well, you don't know half of it, Mr God Almighty Bannerman.'

Bannerman got up and slipped his notebook into his pocket. 'See you around.'

'At the press conference, no doubt,' Palin said.

Bannerman turned. 'What press conference?'

Palin's grin widened. 'Tomorrow at the Rue des Quatre Bras. Minister of Justice on the Slater deaths. Didn't you know?' He knew Bannerman didn't. The announcement had only just been made. Mentally he notched one up.

'I do now,' Bannerman said. 'Appreciate you sharing with the opposition.' He nodded at Mademoiselle Ricain and left.

In the corridor he took his time walking along to the lift, replaying his joust with Palin. Something worried him. Something in Palin's demeanour. Smugness betraying knowledge. Something he knew that Bannerman didn't. And not just the news about the press conference. Palin had worked in the same office as Slater for nearly a year. You don't work as closely with someone for that length of time and not get to know something about them. However obnoxious Palin might be, he was still a good journalist, even if he was just a shadow of the man he might once have been.

Palin watched the door close, anger and alcohol hardening the line of his mouth. He took out a cigarette and lit it with an unsteady hand before turning to Mademoiselle Ricain and catching the pity in her eyes. 'Jesus Christ!' he said. 'What are you looking at?' She flushed deeply, lowered her head and started to type. But he wanted her out of there. 'Take a hike, love,' he told her, and without a word she abandoned her typewriter, lifted her bag and left.

When she had gone Palin sat for several minutes, undecided. Then he went to Slater's filing cabinet, unlocked it and crouched down to open the bottom drawer. He riffled quickly through the suspension files before realizing that the unmarked folders were gone. Fuck! Bannerman must have taken them. He stood up and felt the blood rush to his head. He took a moment to steady himself and looked quickly around the room. Then he crossed to Slater's desk and yanked open the top drawer. He expelled a sigh of relief. There they were! He took a flask from his hip pocket, took a quick snort and smiled his satisfaction.

He lifted out Slater's contacts book, shut the drawer and picked up a phone. He got an outside line, found the number he wanted and dialled. A woman answered and he spoke in slow, clear French. 'I'd like to speak to Monsieur Jansen.'

'Who shall I say is calling?'

'He won't know me,' Palin said. 'Just tell him I worked with a man called Tim Slater and that I have some information to sell him. I think he'll speak to me.'

CHAPTER THIRTEEN

I

The Boulevard de Waterloo was thick with people wrapped in heavy coats and brightly coloured rainwear. They clutched umbrellas and briefcases and shopping bags. Hurrying, heads bowed, through the darkness and the big white flakes of snow that fell brightly through the lights from cafés and shops. The snow was wet and was not yet lying on the pavement. It came drifting lazily over the tops of tall buildings that stood dark against the orange glow reflected in the thickly clouded sky, turning white in the light of the streetlamps, slapping softly against faces like the merest touch of icy fingers.

The rush-hour traffic on both sides of the boulevard crawled noisily in frustrated fits and starts, carrying weary breadwinners home after long, noisy, dissatisfying days in anonymous offices. It was just another dark winter evening in Brussels.

Bannerman walked west from the Métro at the Porte de Namur, brushing the shoulders of people hurrying the other way, getting wet from the snow and catching the drips from passing umbrellas. It was odd, he thought, how you were no more a stranger in a busy street at the rush hour in a foreign city than you were in your own home town. They were the same faces you passed anywhere. The same people you didn't know that lived the same lives in which you played no part. He might have been just like them.

There was a time when perhaps he would have married, raised a family, mortgaged a house in the suburbs, taken a safe job in the city, and been hurrying home like everyone else with nothing more to worry about than what TV show he would choose to while away the evening. There had been that time, but it had long since passed. He had made his choices, and some of them had been made for him. He hardly ever regretted them, though there were times when he lay alone in the dark listening to dogs barking in the night and wondered how it might have been if he had followed the well-worn path, how it might have been to have had someone to come home to, someone to share a life with. But thoughts like those came only in the darkest hours, and usually he would decide it was as well things had turned out the way they had.

A newsboy was standing under the awning of the Café Auguste, a bundle of evening papers under his arm. He had no need to shout. Business was good. News was bad. They were still carrying the story of the shooting and the girl's drawing. People liked to sit back in comfortable armchairs in front of warming fires after their evening meal and read about the horrors of life from the safety of their own little boxes. So long as it didn't touch them directly.

Bannerman bought a copy of *La Belgique Soir* and glanced briefly at the front page. There were pics of the death house, single-column pics of Gryffe and Slater and a reproduction of the drawing. The byline was Richard Platt's.

He folded the paper under his arm and walked into the steamy warmth of the café. The place was full of people and noise, a strong aroma of coffee and cigar smoke. It was a big barn of a place, crammed with tables and chairs, mirror tiles behind the bar, and big, scarred pillars supporting an ornately corniced ceiling almost obscured by a fog of smoke and damp. Two waiters in white jackets and black trousers darted among tables conveying endless orders of coffee and beer on brightly coloured trays.

Du Maurier was sitting at a table at the far side of the café, behind a square-panelled pillar. He raised an arm to wave Bannerman over.

'What will you drink, Monsieur?'

Bannerman eased himself into a chair opposite. 'Whisky.'

Du Maurier barely moved his head and one of the waiters was at his arm, a thin, dark-skinned man with a small black moustache and a permanent scowl.

'*Inspecteur?*'

Du Maurier ordered a whisky and an absinthe. When the waiter had gone the policeman tugged at his nostril hair and lit a cigarette. He sat back and regarded Bannerman with sharp, watchful eyes. 'Well?'

'So they're going to pull the plug on you tomorrow.'

He smiled sadly. 'They already have. This case is consigned to history. Tomorrow is just an exercise in public relations. The dirty work is done. I have to admit, I did not expect them to move quite so quickly.'

Bannerman thought about it. 'Then there is more to it than embarrassed politicians?'

Du Maurier seemed so relaxed he was almost liquid. 'For them to know and you to find out.'

'And you?'

Du Maurier leaned forward and placed his elbows carefully on the edge of the table, clasping his big-knuckled hands below his chin. 'Not me, Monsieur Bannerman. The case is closed.'

'Is it?'

'Officially I can do nothing.'

'And unofficially?'

Their waiter arrived with drinks on a tray and left the bill in a saucer. Du Maurier reached for a jug on the table. 'Water?' Bannerman shook his head and the Inspector poured some into his absinthe and watched it turn cloudy. He picked up his glass and took a sip. 'The case,' he repeated very deliberately, 'is closed.' He took a mouthful, then, of his absinthe and studied Bannerman thoughtfully. 'What do you need to know?'

Bannerman took his first sip of whisky and kept the glass close to his mouth. 'Michel Lapointe and René Jansen.'

Du Maurier shook his head sadly. 'You are on the wrong track, Monsieur. Like you, we found those cuttings yesterday. But there is no connection that I can discern with Monsieur Gryffe, or what happened in the Rue de Pavie.' He paused to consider his words. 'René Jansen is a very powerful man in this country. His business interests are extensive, as is his bank balance. He wields influence, yes, but not *that* much. He is a big man, but not *that* big. The decision to close this case is political, and Jansen is not a political animal. This is not his affair.'

'And Lapointe?'

'A company lawyer. Look, Monsieur, there is no connection here.'

'But any connection could do them harm?'

Du Maurier sighed. 'Perhaps.'

Bannerman emptied half his glass. 'So why are you trying to protect them?'

Du Maurier was annoyed, and his annoyance seemed genuine enough. 'Perhaps I have made a mistake,' he said curtly. 'I thought you were an intelligent man.' He drained his glass.

'Me too,' Bannerman said. 'But I'm just naturally suspicious. Like you. And I can't for the life of me think why you are talking to me at all.' He put a hand on du Maurier's arm to stop him from standing up. 'Oh, I know what you told me yesterday. Justice, morality, the law. All very noble. But I'm just a little too cynical to believe all that. Forgive me. As I said, I have a suspicious mind.'

Du Maurier's years seemed deeply etched in the lines of his

face. He sighed and sank back in his seat. 'Okay. There's no reason you should believe me, Monsieur. My motives are my own. And perhaps they are not very noble, but they are real enough. And I don't see why I should share them with you.' A mantle of what looked very much like defeat settled heavily upon his shoulders. 'Of course I was not mistaken. You are a very astute young man. But you should know that the last thing I would want to do is protect someone like Jansen. He would fit neatly into the category of what one of your political leaders once described so nicely as the unacceptable face of capitalism.'

He sighed deeply.

'I am no socialist, but I believe in democracy, Monsieur. Men like Jansen make a mockery of that. Political parties do not run on fresh air. They need money to survive. And it is men like him who provide the cash. And surely none of us is naïve enough to believe that it is done for love of party.' He chuckled humourlessly. 'Of course not. Such benefactors seek influence, a return for their investment, benefits if not power itself. Jansen's business interests sail very close to the wind when it comes to the law, and sometimes he will steer a course that is discreetly outside it. But he has influence, you see. He has paid for it, and so he survives. I would dearly love to bring such men down, but that is not the way of things. Who am I? Too old and tired, that's who. But I have no reason to protect him. Even if I thought Jansen were involved there is little I could do about it. You would be well advised to take my advice, Monsieur Bannerman. Don't tangle with either of these men.'

Bannerman nodded slowly. 'I believe you,' he said. 'But my instinct is a journalist's instinct. If Slater went to the trouble of putting together a folder of cuttings on Jansen and Lapointe and filed it along with his cuttings on Gryffe, then there was a reason for that. They might be connected with what happened, and they might not. But my instinct is to check it out.'

Du Maurier shrugged. 'Then you'd better follow your instinct.'

'I always do.'

The Inspector smiled wearily and finished his drink. He pushed back his chair. 'I must go.'

'There's more,' Bannerman said quietly.

Du Maurier's face set. 'What more?'

Bannerman signalled the waiter and ordered another two drinks. A group of working men in the far corner raised their voices in laughter. Some bawdy joke. Du Maurier set fire to another cigarette. 'Slater was planning to leave,' Bannerman said.

Du Maurier looked at him with resignation. 'You have had a busy day.'

Bannerman nodded. 'You didn't tell me.'

'There are many things I haven't told you. Things I am not going to tell you. Things you will have to find out for yourself. Things that only I could have told you – and there are people who would know that. I am prepared to help you, for reasons of my own, but I am not going to be your sacrificial lamb.' He paused as the fresh round of drinks arrived then leaned across the table again. He lowered his voice. 'Slater had a flight booked Sunday evening for himself and his daughter. London, and then a connecting flight to New York. Tickets and passport were in his inside jacket pocket.'

Bannerman felt needles of shock prick his skin. For the first time he began seriously to doubt that there had been a third party. Doubt the interpretation of the child's drawing. 'It is just possible then that Slater went with a gun to the Rue de Pavie intending to kill Gryffe, take the money and skip the country.'

'Possible,' du Maurier conceded, 'but I doubt it. It is a theory with very little to support it. Don't forget all that I told you yesterday. Before I was instructed to drop my investigation, we found no way of connecting the gun to Monsieur Slater. In fact, I don't think we ever would. The registration number had been filed off, and I'm sure that ballistics would have told us that they have no record of it. It was a professional's gun, Monsieur. A once-only job. And Monsieur Slater was not a professional. Neither was he stupid. A man is shot dead, a man who others knew was meeting Slater in his house that morning. Slater disappears. Those are the actions of a stupid man. And Slater's flight to London was not until Sunday evening. Even if he had meant to murder Gryffe and run, he would not have waited nearly twelve hours. He would never have reached the airport.'

Bannerman conceded du Maurier's logic with something like relief. Since finding the packed cases there had been a niggling doubt in the back of his mind about Slater. At no point until then had he thought the man capable of murder. Du

Maurier's confirmation of Slater's intention to flee the country had brought that seed of doubt to flower. But now it withered as quickly, leaving a greater clarity. 'Then we are left with the original question of what business Slater had with Gryffe.' He thought about it. 'Blackmail?'

Du Maurier smiled. 'Go on.'

'If Slater was blackmailing Gryffe then there would be no need for him to make a hurried departure. Maybe,' his mind was working overtime, 'maybe if Slater had been blackmailing him for some time, Sunday was to have been the final pay-off. A quarter of a million dollars is a lot of money, but I wouldn't have thought it was enough to make Slater give up everything here. Certainly not overnight. People win more on the Pools.'

Du Maurier poured water into his absinthe. 'It's all possible,' he said. 'Personally I like the idea of blackmail. It answers many questions. Though not all of them. If, for example, Slater had been blackmailing our friend for some time, where is the rest of the money? He certainly didn't bank it, either here or in England. There was no money in the apartment, though it is possible that money was removed from the safe by your intruder. But somehow I don't think so. It seems to me that if blackmail was the motive for murder, then the evidence is what was removed from the safe. So, if there was more money, where is it?'

'A numbered account in Switzerland.'

'Again, possible, but I think not. There would have been records somewhere among his personal belongings.'

Bannerman took a slug of whisky. 'Seems like you've been busier than me.'

Du Maurier smiled and ran a hand through the remains of black, wiry hair. 'More importantly,' he said, 'blackmail does not furnish us with any motive for murder by a third party.'

'Someone else who felt threatened?' Bannerman suggested. 'If Slater had dirt on Gryffe, then perhaps some of that dirt might have stuck to others.'

The policeman scratched his chin. 'Assuming that was true,' he said thoughtfully, 'would the murderer have left the money behind?' He sighed. 'There is little point, Monsieur Bannerman, in speculating. We could talk around the subject all night and only create for ourselves more questions that we cannot answer.' He emptied his glass.

Bannerman placed a hand on his arm once more. 'One final question. Gryffe had another place in Brussels. Where?'

The Inspector frowned. 'He had no other apartment in Brussels, Monsieur Bannerman. Only in the Rue de Pavie.'

Bannerman shook his head. 'Then you are not as thorough as you might have been,' he said. 'Slater lists two home numbers in Brussels for Gryffe. They are in his contacts book. Presumably one of them is the Rue de Pavie.' He took out his notebook and flipped through to the page where he had noted the numbers, and pushed it across the table at du Maurier.

The other man's frown deepened. 'The first number is the Rue de Pavie,' he said. 'What makes you think the second number is Belgian?'

'It was preceded by the Belgian country-code, thirty-two.'

Du Maurier looked again at the number. 'It is not a Brussels area code. Somewhere provincial, perhaps.' He took out a small black notebook and a pen and copied the number into it. 'I will check.' He scribbled another number on a fresh page, tore it out and handed it to Bannerman. 'If you need to call me, phone that number. Speak to no one else but me. Do not come to the Rue des Quatre Bras.'

Bannerman took it and folded it into his top pocket. He said, 'I'll want Slater's car from the pound.'

Du Maurier stood up. 'I will arrange to have it taken to the Rue de Commerce.' He nodded. '*Au revoir*, Monsieur.'

When he was gone, Bannerman stared at the remains in his whisky glass. He knew more now than when he had come in, but still not enough. He drank the last drop of whisky and noticed that du Maurier had left him to pay for the drinks. He drew out a 500-franc note and dropped it in the saucer, and left the warmth of the Café Auguste to brave the snow.

The newsboy was still selling papers. The news was still bad and business was still good.

II

Bannerman ate alone in a bistro off the Avenue de la Toison d'Or, a small, cheap eating house where they served good steak and Bordeaux wine by the carafe.

It had stopped snowing when he left. He headed back along

the Boulevard Waterloo toward the Porte de Namur. Over the meal he had thought again about Palin with some disquiet. He had known plenty of drunks, abusive ones at that. But with Palin it was something else. Bannerman checked his watch. It was after eight. He had been unwise to leave the cuttings in the office, and he decided it would be safer to stop off at the International Press Centre and pick them up. They would be more secure at the apartment. He didn't want to risk Palin getting his hands on them.

At the Porte de Namur he rode the escalators down into the Métro and spent twenty-five francs on a ticket to Schuman.

There were only a few lights still burning in the windows of the IPC building. A bored telephonist sat behind the reception counter. Up steps and beyond the desk, across a wide, thickly carpeted lobby, the sound of voices oiled by alcohol came from the press bar. Bannerman took the elevator up to the sixth floor.

The corridor was dimly lit, every second light switched off for reasons of economy. He watched his shadow overtake him, fade like a giant and then drift by him again as he passed under the next light. All the offices were empty and the floor was quiet as death except for the distant rumbling of traffic that came along the Boulevard Charlemagne from the Rue de la Loi. Bannerman looked out his key and thought about phoning Sally again from the office. The key wouldn't turn in the lock. He swore softly and tried another key. The same again. 'Shit!'

He tried the handle and the door pushed open. Someone had forgotten to lock it.

Perhaps because the hours of darkness are the hours of fear and danger, or maybe because of something he heard, or the slightest movement registered in the half-light, he stopped on the threshold. It might even have been some intrinsic sixth-sense warning of another presence that triggered the reflex action that raised his crooked arm to take the full brunt of a blow that would surely have cracked his skull. The pain spiked up his arm to his shoulder and his knees buckled. He staggered into darkness, falling, tangling with the legs of his unseen attacker. The other man lost his balance and toppled on to Bannerman's back, grunting as he fell. A foot caught Bannerman's throat. Bannerman choked back vomit and felt fire in his head and chest. His right arm and hand had gone numb already.

The other man was struggling to disentangle himself from Bannerman's legs. Then he was up and running, heavy steps beating their retreat down the length of the corridor towards the lifts. But Bannerman had no interest in pursuing him. He rolled over and spat blood and saliva on to the floor. His head cleared a little, but his throat hurt like hell. He pulled himself up to his feet with the help of the edge of a desk, and took several unsteady steps to the light switch.

The glare filled his head with fire and he pulled up a chair and sat down heavily. His mouth tasted of blood and sick. 'Shit,' he whispered softly to himself. This was getting to be a bad habit. *You're going to have to take more care, son,* he told himself.

He let his head drop between his knees for several minutes while he breathed deeply. Then he sat upright and saw a narrow-necked water jug and glass on Mademoiselle Ricain's desk. He reached over and filled the glass left-handed. He rolled the first swig around his mouth and gargled in his throat before spitting it out on the carpet. Then he took a long draught and felt the smooth cold water track all the way down to his stomach. He turned his attention to his right arm. It was the fleshy bit of the forearm that had taken the blow. He slipped his jacket off and rolled up his sleeve. Already the arm was swollen and bruised. But nothing broken. His fingers seemed to have locked, and his arm was bent at the elbow and hurt badly when he tried to straighten it. *Must have got a nerve,* he thought.

The next few minutes he spent slowly, painfully, making fists with his right hand and working his arm straight and then crooking it. Gradually the muscles and the nerves eased and he got a pins-and-needles sensation from shoulder to fingertips. But that passed and he leaned back in his seat to look around the office. It seemed much as it had earlier in the day. There was no evidence of an intruder. He got up and crossed to Slater's desk, pulling open the drawer. The folders were gone. So was the contacts book. Someone had known what they were looking for and exactly where to find it. That narrowed the field considerably. He sat for a few minutes more, then took out his notebook, flipped over several pages, picked up the phone and dialled. He wasn't sure why he was calling her. A cry in the dark. The number rang out and he hung up.

He stood up and swung his head to either side to ease the stiffening in his neck. He switched out the light and closed the door behind him, making sure it was well and truly locked.

III

A light shone from the window of the top-floor flat in the apartment block in the Rue de Commerce. Bannerman might not have noticed it except that there were only two other lights showing in the entire block. Slater's car, a dark blue Volkswagen, sat at the kerbside. Bannerman paid off his taxi and watched the vehicle move off down the street. It was only a fifteen- or twenty-minute walk from the IPC building, but he had not felt like walking.

He shuffled about on the pavement, unsure what to do. He looked up again at the light in the window, weighing the possibilities. But he was too tired and too sore to think too much about it. It was cold out here, his breath billowing yellow in the street lights, melting the big snowflakes that were falling all around him. Inside he started up the stairs, listening to his footsteps clattering back at him off the walls. It seemed even colder in the stairwell than it had outside. The landing lights were mercilessly icy in the chill of their glare. But the light they cast on the stairs was feeble.

At the door of the apartment he fumbled with his keys and then carefully opened it, standing well back and letting it swing inwards. The landing light spilled into the darkness of the hallway, and at the far end he could see a crack of light framing the door of the living room. He stepped inside and closed the door behind him. The air was warm and dusty and touched with a faintly familiar scent. He stood perfectly still as the crack of light widened ahead of him and a long shadow reached out across the hall as if to touch him. The figure in the doorway was silhouetted against the light behind. Bannerman couldn't see her face, but he knew who it was.

'Hello,' Sally said. Her voice sounded very small. 'I've been waiting for you. Quite a long time. It's kind of scary sitting alone in a dead man's house.'

Bannerman slipped out of his coat and dragged it along the length of the hall behind him. He stopped in front of her and looked down into her shadowed face. 'How did you know I would be here?'

She was disconcerted by his closeness. 'I didn't know for sure. I've still got a key, so I came up. I found your clothes in the bedroom, so I guessed you'd be back. I . . . I was frightened I might not see you again.'

'Why? Would that matter to you?'

'Maybe.'

He smelled her perfume, warm and musky, and sensed her reserve. 'Why is it so difficult to get close to you?'

There was a very long silence. 'I don't know,' she said at

last, knowing that she did. Then she looked up a little more brightly. 'I brought some wine. I put the refrigerator on and left it in there to chill.' Bannerman lowered his head and let his lips brush hers. It was what she had wanted, and yet still she drew back. 'I'll get some glasses.'

He followed her into the living room, puzzled, disappointed, wondering why she had come, and yet glad that she had.

She went into the kitchen. He heard her open the refrigerator then the sounds of her searching for glasses. He switched off the overhead light, turned on a table lamp and sat back in the settee staring at the painting over the mantelpiece. The browns and blacks, blues and greens, their starkness against the white of the snow that covered the scene. A group of weary hunters returning from the kill, mean-looking dogs slinking at their feet, a fire being lit at the inn on the hilltop. Through the trees they looked down on to two square frozen lakes where tiny figures wrapped in winter coats were skating. There was a great peace about the painting, a strange sense of satisfaction in it, men and women frozen in the painter's mind below the palest of winter blue skies that faded almost to yellow.

Sally came in with the bottle uncorked and set it down with two glasses on the stained wooden coffee table in front of the settee. She sat down beside Bannerman and followed his eyes to the painting. 'Brueghel,' she said. 'So gentle by comparison with the horrors and madness of his later work.'

Bannerman wondered if the choice of painting reflected

anything in Slater. It was a curious choice for such a man. Perhaps it had come with the apartment. He dragged his eyes away from it and turned his head to watch Sally pour the wine. The bottle was misted, and the glasses misted too when she filled them. Now she raised her glass to her lips. 'It hardly seems right to toast anything,' she said, and took a sip. Bannerman lifted his glass and took a mouthful. It was dry and a little fruity and was cool in his throat, which still hurt where he had been kicked. Sally put her glass down and without looking at him, asked, 'What happened to your face?'

He told her. About the assault in the apartment, and the assailant who'd attacked him in the darkness of his office. She turned in amazement.

'You mean there was someone in here waiting for you?'

'Not waiting for me. He was after something in the safe. I disturbed him. I suppose he got what he was looking for, but he must have thought the house was empty.' He hesitated. 'Let me ask you something. You normally came on Sundays. Why did you not come yesterday?'

She looked at him curiously, a hint of uncertainty, suspicion, in her green eyes. 'You don't think I . . .'

'I don't think anything. I'd just like to know.'

'I had a lunch engagement with a professor of English from a very exclusive language college in Rome. There's a post available and I have applied for it. It's a full-time job and it pays well.' There was a hint of hostility in her voice. 'Usually I took Tania out on Sunday mornings. To Mass. They were Catholics, you know. I'm not, but I took her anyway. She seemed to get something out of it.'

Bannerman nodded. 'And that's why whoever it was that clobbered me expected the house to be empty.'

She picked up her glass and half-emptied it. 'I'm sorry,' she said. 'I thought that maybe you thought I . . .' She stopped. 'It doesn't matter.'

'No.' He leaned forward and refilled both their glasses, a slight, sharp intake of breath as the pain returned to his outstretched arm.

'Why would anyone want to kill Mr Slater?' she said suddenly.

Bannerman passed her the glass. 'Because he was blackmailing Robert Gryffe. Because someone else felt threatened and decided that the best way out was to kill them both. Then he came here to get whatever it was that gave Slater a hold over Gryffe. And maybe cash, if there was any in the safe.' If he said it often enough he might believe it. He took in her look of incredulity.

'But how can you possibly know that?'

He shrugged. 'I don't. But it fits with the known facts.'

She shook her head. 'I don't believe it.'

'It's easier to believe than what you're going to read in tomorrow's evening papers.'

She frowned. 'What do you mean?'

'The Interior Minister is going to make a statement tomorrow announcing that the police are satisfied that Slater and Gryffe shot each other during some private quarrel. The case is already closed.'

She said nothing, raising her glass slowly to her lips and sipping at it several times. She got up and walked to the window, and stood tracing patterns with her finger in the fine condensation. Outside the snow still fell, brushing the glass, lining the ledge. 'A cover-up?' Her voice was quiet and the words were almost lost.

'Perhaps.' Bannerman replaced his glass on the table and went to the window, standing behind her, his hands resting lightly on her shoulders.

'But why?' she asked.

He sighed. 'I have no idea. But I mean to find out.'

She turned then to face him, her eyes turned up to meet his. 'It's so unfair.'

'Nothing in life is fair,' Bannerman said, and she was stung by the bitterness in his voice. 'Right now there are tens of thousands of children with swollen bellies who haven't eaten in days, or even weeks. Arms and legs so thin they might break if you so much as looked at them. We've all seen those pictures in the papers. Staring, hopeless eyes. Some of them have days, maybe only hours left to live. There is no food for them. Only disease and despair. And we sit sipping our wine and warming our anger because two men have died and someone doesn't want us to know why. Is that fair?'

She saw the intensity in his face as he paused to choke back his emotion.

'A little girl was born with autism. She lost her mother to cancer and saw her father shot to death yesterday. Maybe she'd like to tell us how it was. Maybe she'd like to say, "I loved my Daddy." But she can't, because her autism won't let her. Do you care? Do I care? Does anybody care? That doesn't really seem very fair either, does it? You can't go through life expecting it to treat you fairly. God, if He exists, either had an off-day when He put us on this planet, or else He's playing some ethereal game of chess where we're all pawns, expendable in the greater scheme of things, whether we think it's fair or not. You can talk about right and wrong, and even that is different for each of us . . . But nothing is fair.'

She listened in silence to his rancour. 'Maybe,' she said. 'And, God knows, I should know about fairness, or the lack of it. But wouldn't it be sad if we all thought the way you do?'

Bannerman looked at her thoughtfully. 'Was it a man?' he said.

'Isn't it always?' She turned away.

'No, not always.' He turned her back to face him and cupped his hands either side of her face, tilting her head upwards. 'It needn't be,' he said. And he bent to kiss her. She responded, soft lips, the smell of wine on her breath. She pulled her head away and pressed it into his shoulder.

'It's hard,' she said, 'not knowing if you can ever really trust anyone again.'

'Do you want to talk about it?'

She shook her head. 'No.' And she pushed away from him, turning again to the window.

He stood for a moment, then crossed to the coffee table and retrieved his glass. 'I'd like to see Tania,' he said, and drank what was left of his wine.

'I'll take you. Tomorrow?'

'Evening. If it's possible.'

She nodded. 'Okay.'

'You'll be going to the funeral?'

'When is it?'

'Tomorrow afternoon, two-thirty at the Cimetière de Bruxelles.'

'Oh, I didn't know. Yes, I'll be there.' She paused. 'Why do you want to see her?'

He looked up sharply. 'I don't know.' And he had no idea why. He knew there was very little chance of her communicating anything he didn't already know. And it was only then that he realized she had been flitting around the edge of his consciousness all day. A small, clumsy, barefoot child whose cold hands had touched his face in the darkness. Then he remembered something else.

'The other night, when I came back drunk. Did I . . . Did we . . .?'

She smiled at his unusual bashfulness. 'No,' she said. 'We didn't.' She hesitated, then, 'I could stay tonight.'

'No, I'll take you home.' He said it a little too quickly and it hurt her, and he realized too late his mistake.

'Fine.'

'Look, I didn't mean . . .'

'You don't have to apologize.'

There was an awkward silence, then Bannerman asked, 'You want some more wine?'

'No, it's getting late.'

He fumbled absently in his pocket and then frowned. 'The police brought Slater's car back. I saw it outside. But I guess I don't have the keys.'

'They're on the mantelpiece.' Sally crossed the room. 'They must have put them through the letter box. I found them lying on the floor in the hall when I came in. But don't bother, I'll phone a taxi.' He would have argued, but he saw in her face that she would not be argued with. And he thought, *I could love you.*

It was fifteen minutes before the taxi came and parp-parped down in the street. They'd had time to finish the wine and say many things. They had done neither. 'I'll come down with you.'

'Don't bother.'

'I'll come down with you.'

He helped her on with her coat and they walked down the stairs in silence. The taxi was revving impatiently at the kerb, clouds of exhaust fumes rising into the darkness. She stopped in the doorway and relented, turning to kiss him quickly on the lips. He held her arm to stop her from going. 'Did you . . . did you get the job in Rome?'

She looked at him quizzically for a moment. 'I don't know. They said they'd be in touch. See you tomorrow.'

He watched her climb into the taxi. The car purred off down the Rue de Commerce, leaving black tyre tracks in the thin layer of snow, and he wondered if she would always be leaving.

Back in the apartment all that remained of her were lingering traces of her perfume and the faintest smear of lipstick on her empty glass. He finished the wine, drinking slowly, listening to the clock ticking in the silence and feeling the dull ache in the stiffening muscles of his right arm.

IV

A silent figure stood in the snow, pressed against a gable end, the eaves too high above him to afford any protection from the thickly falling flakes. The tyre tracks of the taxi had vanished already, only a slight, slightly whiter impression remaining in the whiteness of the road. The man shifted his feet, but the feeling in them had long since gone. Even the muscles of his face seemed to have frozen. His hands, pushed deep in his pockets, were raw cold and stiff. His eyes were dull and sunk deep in shadow, and yet still they watched. It was a pointless vigil now, but perhaps for the first time in his life Kale was afraid of the loneliness of his hotel room, locked away in the dark listening to the throbbing early morning music that came drifting up from the basement nightclub in the adjoining block. There would be too much time to think during the sleepless hours. There were things that would trouble him, dark thoughts coming like strangers in the night to blacken the blackness in him.

The light in the top-floor apartment went out, and still he could not bring himself to move. The woman had been gone twenty minutes and there was no way the man would lead him to the child tonight. And yet he stood on, like a punishment. A mean, lost soul in a foreign city where people spoke words he could not understand, where he had killed two men without a second thought. Only now it was a prison. There was no escape. Every eye watched him, every voice accused him. There was a dreadful inevitability about it all, like death itself.

Of course, there was a way out, but somewhere beyond his grasp, there just to torture him. He had only to leave. By morning he could be in Ostend, by teatime in London. But it was not to be. A child had seen him commit murder, a child with a troubled mind, a child who would probably never identify him. But she might. He knew that, his employer knew that, and there were others who knew it too. It was expected of him to negate that possibility. He expected it of himself. He had killed before. It was easy, it was necessary, and yet standing there in all the cold and snow on this black winter night, he did not know if it was possible.

It was the uncertainty that trapped him here. He had thought he knew all the dark territory of his mind. Had no illusions about who or what he was. It was something he accepted, like life or death. But somewhere in that inner darkness he had stumbled on something unfamiliar, something he could not come to terms with. To kill a child with his secret locked somewhere in her head. A note in a locker, three words on a scrap of paper, and he had discovered in himself the seed of destruction that is in the souls of all men.

To kill the child would be to kill himself. He knew it with a dreadful clarity. You choose your own road to hell and you think you know every twist and turn in it. Then you discover that hell is not the end of the road. He was a human being, after all, and there was a point beyond which you could not go. *It is no use*, he thought. *I will think about it whether I stand here punishing myself, or whether I lie awake in my room.* The man whose head he had cracked, whose ribs he had kicked, would lead him eventually to the child. He was no longer in control of his own destiny. He was being drawn towards his own destruction as helplessly as the man being swept into the vortex of a whirlpool. For somewhere in all his lack of humanity, he had discovered a conscience.

He moved stiffly away from the wall against which he had sought some shelter and began walking along the Rue de Commerce. Somewhere he would find a bar to spend time in before he could face the room he had taken across town, and the long hours before morning.

CHAPTER FOURTEEN

I

People hurried by without even glancing at the solitary figure sitting at one of the red-painted metal tables under the awning. The market stalls were being removed. The early morning trade had been poor because of the weather. Piles of snow were dotted about where it had been swept up to make way for the stalls. Lines of cars stood at the far side of the square gleaming in the morning sunshine, and snow was melting on the black flagstones where great slabs of sunshine fell between the buildings. The sky was a clear, pale blue and reminded Bannerman of the sky in the painting over the mantelpiece back at the apartment. It was still cold, though, out of the sun.

He sat at one of the tables near the end of the awning, where the sunshine still splashed in beneath the yellow canvas, warming the air. The coffee, too, warmed him inside. He wasn't thinking too much about anything, just watching the men and women moving the stalls.

The Grande Place was dominated on one side by the ornate

splendour of the Town Hall, with its tower and tall tapering spire. It was an impressive square, the heart of the city, full of life and colour and gaiety. The old guild houses, medieval gabled buildings, lined the other three sides. Now they were fronted by souvenir shops, restaurants and cafés, though you could still tell which trades they had once represented; the boatmen's guild house with its roof shaped like the stern of a seventeenth-century vessel; the archers' house with its carved statue of St Sebastian holding a bow; the weigh-house with a pair of scales above a balcony supported by two figures.

Across the square, several workmen on ladders were washing down the walls of one of the houses, and repainting its gold decoration. Bannerman took it all in, enjoying it. The sun had lifted him and he felt almost relaxed for the first time in forty-eight hours. He might have been a tourist basking in the winter sun without a care in the world.

But now, as the sun rose higher, the shadow of the awning moved across the table and he felt the cold creep over him. He finished his coffee, then stood up and checked his watch. It was a little after ten. He dropped some francs in a saucer and stepped out across the square. His day seemed clearly mapped out for him. The press conference at the offices of the Judicial Police at eleven. Then his meeting with Tait at the office, and the funeral in the afternoon. And in the evening he would go and see Tania. He found himself thinking about the child often, and with an odd affection.

Then there was Jansen, and of course Lapointe. He would

have to decide about them today. And there was some unfinished business with Palin. He thought, too, about Platt. It did not please him to have to think about Platt. For here he might be forced into an alliance. And he preferred to work alone. But on this, he would need someone who knew his way around.

II

There was a great expectancy in the conference room. Reporters and photographers, television crews, radio journalists with recorders slung over their shoulders. Television lights, and the pall of smoke that hung above it all, caught in sunlight that slanted through narrow windows along the back wall. Many of the journalists had been here on Sunday night, their numbers swelled now by newsmen who had arrived from all over the world.

Bannerman pushed his way through the crowd and found a seat. A uniformed gendarme stood by swing doors beyond the podium through which bureaucrats and their boss from the Ministry of Justice would shortly enter. A small, rotund figure plumped itself into the seat next to him.

'Hello, Neil. Any idea what this is all about?' Platt was flushed and perspiring. His grey flannel suit fitted no better than his dinner suit of the other evening. The grubby collar of his once-white shirt was curled up at one side and the knot of his tie was too tight. Short stubby fingers fidgeted endlessly with the corners of his notebook. 'I thought I might be late.'

He seemed breathless. Bannerman glanced at his watch. It was ten past eleven. He said nothing. 'Well?' Platt persisted.

'Well, what?'

'Any ideas?'

'Uh-huh.'

'And?' Platt was impatient.

'You'll learn soon enough.' Bannerman hesitated. 'I'll let you buy me a drink afterwards, though. There are some things I think we should discuss.' Without looking at him, Bannerman was aware of a change in Platt's attitude. The older journalist turned himself in his seat.

'What things?'

Bannerman was saved from replying by the entrance of the ministerial entourage. Three pinstriped civil servants flanked the Minister of Justice. The Minister himself was a slight-built man, but gave a bigger impression. Power could do that, especially on camera. Bannerman guessed he was about sixty. Remarkably unlined skin on a thin face, dark hair cut short and greying at the temples. His eyes in the television lights seemed black, and shone as they raked across the gathering of journalists.

He seated himself centrally behind the rostrum, and Bannerman was annoyed that he was unable to see his hands. The things a man did with his hands were often a reflection of what was going on in his head. His face was implacable. The pinstripe immediately to his right sat beside him while the others remained standing. There were some moments of hesitation as journalists settled in seats. Reporters without them stood or sat in the aisles.

One of the civil servants who had remained standing cleared his throat and began in French. He spoke for less than a minute in short, rapid bursts. Then paused and said in English, 'Good morning, gentlemen. I am happy you could attend. The Minister regrets that it has been necessary to convene this meeting today. He wishes to make a brief statement regarding the unhappy events of Sunday past. His statement will be delivered in both French and English. There will be no questions. Copies of his statement have been prepared in both languages and will be available immediately after the conference. Thank you.' He bowed towards his boss. 'Minister . . .' And he sat as the Minister rose to his feet.

The man the Belgian Prime Minister had appointed to oversee the country's justice system produced a pair of horn-rimmed glasses, slipping them on with a single easy movement. His voice was unexpectedly sonorous for so small a man. A smooth, persuasive voice, rich in its French fluency. Bannerman watched him carefully, but there was nothing to be gleaned from his demeanour. He read from a prepared statement, eyes lowered, spectacles perched near the end of his long nose. When he completed his delivery in French he raised one hand to still the buzz of incredulity soaring among the French-speaking journalists.

Platt squirmed excitedly beside Bannerman, scribbling furiously in his notebook all through the statement, then glancing at Bannerman. But Bannerman kept his eyes on the Minister as he began again in English. Bannerman did not bother to take notes. He watched and listened as the politician peddled his platitudes:

'I have been advised by the Judicial Police . . . no evidence to suggest . . . after close consultation with the British government . . . who are in complete agreement . . . regret that the press should have made such an issue of this drawing . . . mentally disturbed . . . all parties are in no doubt . . . full and frank discussions . . . decision . . . the case has been closed. Thank you, gentlemen, for your patience.'

He turned at once, stepping down from the podium to head for the swing doors, followed by his entourage. A number of journalists were already on their feet and he was mobbed even before he could reach the doors. The single gendarme was hopelessly outnumbered, and the pinstripes had to push and shove to clear a way through for their master.

There wasn't a journalist in the room who didn't understand that this was a blatant whitewash. They also knew there wasn't a hope in hell of getting the Minister to add anything to his statement, though it wouldn't be for want of trying. Flashlights fizzed and dazzled. TV cameramen jostled for position. This, they knew, would look good on-screen. *Minister of Justice mobbed by pressmen following controversial statement on the deaths of Gryffe and Slater.*

At the centre of the undignified scrum Bannerman caught a glimpse of the Minister's face, tight and grey. Angry. Maybe even frightened. His head was bowed, his hand raised defensively, before finally he disappeared through the doors.

Platt was on his feet and could no longer contain his impatience. 'You knew, didn't you?'

Bannerman rose slowly. 'More or less.'

Platt stared at him, his face flushed with excitement. 'How?'

'What about that drink?'

The big clock on the wall behind the counter at the Café Auguste showed eleven forty-five. The press conference had lasted a remarkably short time. It had seemed longer. And the walk from the offices of the Judicial Police to the café in the Boulevard de Waterloo had taken only a few minutes.

Platt wore a battered old checked hat well back on his head, and a dark blue Burberry that had seen better days. He sat uncomfortably in a chair opposite Bannerman and began chewing dirty fingernails. Bannerman infuriated him. He had said nothing during their walk from the Rue des Quatre Bras and now he was flicking abstractedly through his notebook. No doubt he would say what he had to say in his own good time. But Platt did not have time. His second-edition deadline was pressing. By now his news desk would know everything about the Minister's statement. It was hard to beat radio for instant news. He was going to get his ear chewed when finally he called in. The waiter from the previous day approached their table and nodded acknowledgement to Bannerman.

'Monsieur?'

'Two whiskies.'

'I am sorry, Monsieur, it is forbidden to sell spirits in cafés.'

Bannerman raised an eyebrow in surprise. 'But you served me whisky last night.'

The waiter permitted himself a stiff smile. 'Last night, Monsieur, you were drinking with the Inspector. Today you are not.'

Bannerman looked at Platt. 'Beer?'

The reporter nodded, a smile dawning on fat lips.

'Two beers.'

'Thank you, Monsieur. I am sorry, Monsieur.'

Platt watched the waiter go and his smile broadened. 'So you were drinking with the Inspector last night. Du Maurier?' Bannerman made no reply, which Platt took as a yes. 'And that's how you knew what the Minister was going to announce today. What else did the Inspector tell you?'

Bannerman sat staring at his hands. He was annoyed that Platt should have discovered his source of information so easily. It had been a mistake to come here. Finally he looked up and said in a hushed voice, 'Quite a bit, Platt, quite a bit.' Then leaned forward on the table. 'But that's confidential. Just between you and me.'

Platt shrugged. 'We'll see.'

'You'll see fuck all if you start getting clever!' Bannerman paused for emphasis. 'The only reason I'm talking to you at all is because I need someone who knows this city and the people who make it tick.'

'In return for . . .?'

'A share of the story. If I can make it stand up.' He sat back as their beers were delivered to the table. Platt was containing himself with difficulty. He took a mouthful of beer and waited for Bannerman to go on. But Bannerman kept his own counsel and enjoyed Platt's discomfort.

'Well?' Platt barked finally. He was like a dog anticipating walkies.

'Well what?'

'What's the story?'

'Ah, well, that's between me and me.'

'Jesus Christ!' Platt almost knocked over his glass. 'What do you mean, between you and you?' He glanced anxiously at his watch.

Bannerman lifted his beer and took several long, slow pulls. He drew the back of his hand across his lips. 'When's your second edition go to bed?'

Platt's face was a mixture of misery and frustration. 'Twelve.' He glanced again at his watch. It was ten to.

'I'll make it brief, then,' Bannerman said. But he was in no hurry. He took another mouthful of beer. 'You work in the dark until I start putting things together. I will need certain information on certain individuals. The facilities you have here and your knowledge of Brussels could save me a great deal of time. If and when the story stands up I'll consider sharing it with you – if you have contributed anything of value.'

Platt glared at him angrily. 'What kind of deal is that?'

'The only one I'm prepared to make.'

'You've got a bloody nerve, Bannerman. Suppose I provide you with all this information.' He glanced towards the clock behind the bar. 'What's to stop you from cutting me out? I'm supposed to take you on trust, is that it?'

Bannerman smiled. 'I don't know anyone else I would rather put my trust in.'

Platt gulped down the remainder of his beer then wiped his mouth with his sleeve. His hat seemed to have slipped even further back on his head. 'No deal.'

Bannerman stood up. 'Suit yourself.'

'No, hold on! Wait a minute!' Platt was lost in an agony of indecision, and the imminent passing of his midday deadline. 'Sit down, for Christ's sake.'

Bannerman sat down.

'All right. Okay. You're a real bastard, Bannerman, you know that?' He hesitated and stole yet another glance at the clock. It was now two minutes to twelve.

Bannerman said, 'You're going to hold up your second edition.'

'Get on with it!'

'All right. I want to know all about a man called René Jansen. Anything and everything you can get. Personal life, business interests. Also a man called Michel Lapointe. Give me a call first thing tomorrow at the IPC building.'

Platt was confused, curious, but also conscious of the time.

And anticipating the fury of his news editor. He stood up, aiming his most contemptuous look in Bannerman's direction. 'Bastard!' he said again, and hurried off to find a telephone. Bannerman took his time finishing his beer, then settled up and made his way to the door.

When he stepped out into the boulevard the sun was no longer shining. Dark clouds had rolled in from the east, heavy with the threat of more snow.

III

Mademoiselle Ricain looked up from her keyboard and smiled when Bannerman came in. Bannerman wondered what it was she always seemed to be typing. Palin was slumped at his desk, still in his coat, going through his shorthand notes. He had not been at the press conference in the Rue des Quatre Bras and must only just have returned from the midday press briefing at the Salle de Presse. Palin glanced at him, then buried his head again in his notes. Bannerman sat down and threw his notebook on the desk.

'Your editor telephoned,' Mademoiselle Ricain said. 'His flight's been delayed and he said for you not to expect him before one.'

Bannerman looked at his watch. It was a little after twelve-thirty. 'Fine. Thanks.' He paused. 'Listen, could you pop down to the bakery on the corner and get me a sandwich? Seems like I'm not going to get lunch.'

'Of course.' She smiled and stood up, apparently happy to run an errand for him. 'What filling would you like?'

Bannerman shook his head. 'Doesn't matter. Whatever they've got.' He drew out a note. 'Thanks.'

She took it from him, smiled again, then lifted her bag and coat and was gone, leaving a swirl of perfume in her wake. He had not been aware of the perfume yesterday, but it was making its presence felt today. He frowned.

He sat for a full minute after she had gone and then glanced at Palin. 'You and I need to talk.'

'Do we?' Palin pushed himself back in his seat and looked at Bannerman coldly. In eyes clouded by alcohol there was a hint of apprehension which he was doing his best to disguise. 'What about?' He stuck a match in the corner of his mouth and began chewing on it.

Bannerman waited, allowing Palin's apprehension to take root and push out shoots. 'About the phone call you made to René Jansen yesterday.' Palin paled visibly and Bannerman knew he'd guessed right. It could easily have been Lapointe. Fifty–fifty. He'd struck lucky.

'What the fuck are you talking about?'

Bannerman retained a studied calm. 'I don't know if it's possible to see that you never work in newspapers again, Palin, but I'll make damn sure your editor is in full possession of the facts. I can only imagine what his reaction will be. As for the union, well, they're not quite as predictable, but I would think there's a good chance you'll be expelled. And then there's the

Judicial Police. I wouldn't swear to it, but it's quite possible that you've actually broken the law.'

A deathly pallor washed across Palin's face. He was silent for a very long time. Then, 'You can't prove anything.'

So he was not even going to deny it. Bannerman kept his anger in check. 'Maybe. Maybe not. But you and I both know that Slater was blackmailing Gryffe.'

Palin's face gave nothing away. Did he really know that? Bannerman watched him switch the matchstick to the other corner of his mouth and the chewing became more agitated.

Bannerman said, 'The way I read it, Jansen and Lapointe were also involved somehow.' Although he had no idea how, or even if it was true. Platt was still wearing his implacable face. Bannerman pressed on. 'I don't know who murdered Slater and Gryffe, but it's not unreasonable to assume that it might have been on the orders of someone like Jansen. Or Lapointe. Or both. And whatever you knew, or didn't know, it was enough to figure out that one or the other might be interested in a folder of cuttings that Slater had compiled on them.' He was flying a kite here, without the least idea of which way the wind was blowing. 'What were you after, Palin? Money?' He shook his head. 'Doesn't matter. It makes you an accomplice after the fact. An accessory to murder.'

Palin fought to maintain a façade of calm. 'I heard they'd dropped the case.'

'Maybe *they* have. But *I* haven't. And you know I'm going

to get to the bottom of it, Palin, don't you? You know you're in deep shit.'

And finally Palin cracked, professionalism and morality eroded by drink. He leaned forward on his desk, dropping his head into ink-stained hands, and Bannerman watched him with indifference. A man of ability diminished by addiction, and finally succumbing to his own stupidity.

Palin looked up, and Bannerman was shocked to see tears leaking from the corners of his eyes. A pathetic figure teetering on the brink. He reached into his back pocket for a hip-flask and flipped it open with unsteady fingers. He tipped his head back, and the neck of the flask disappeared between pale lips while he suckled on it like a baby at its mother's teat. Then he banged the flask on the desk and looked wretchedly at Bannerman. 'I really don't know anything,' he said, his voice breaking somewhere in the back of his throat. 'Only that Slater had something on Gryffe. Little things I picked up. The tail end of telephone conversations. The file he'd been putting together.' He took another pull at his flask from a shaking hand. 'Then I found the cuttings on Jansen and Lapointe. I reckoned he must have had something on all three. But I never thought it was blackmail. Just a story he was doing. Something big. Something he was trying to hide from me. And that got me interested.' There was an appeal for understanding in his eyes, and when none was forthcoming, he heaved himself out of his chair and turned away towards the window.

Bannerman watched him impassively. 'So what did you

really hope to achieve by tipping off Jansen about Slater's file?'

Palin couldn't bring himself to turn and face his accuser. His voice was drawn thin by anxiety. 'I thought . . . I thought he might pay for the information.'

'And did he?'

'Not exactly. He said he would need proof. That he would get in touch when he had it.'

'And you agreed?' Bannerman could hardly believe that Palin could have been so stupid. The man, or what was left of him, returned to his desk and picked up his flask. He took a long draught, and a little of its liquor crept out at the corner of his mouth to run down his chin. He wiped it away with the back of his hand.

'What you said yesterday . . . about my appointment here being short-term. You were a damn sight closer to the truth than you thought.' He paused. 'I . . . I've been recalled.' And he almost choked on his words. 'Next month. New position. Second man on the night news desk. After all these years, put out to pasture. To sit like some stookie through the early hours. Deskbound. Paperwork. A glorified nothing. A has-been with a title. And Glasgow? I don't want to go back to Glasgow. To some shabby bedsitter reeking of damp and stale cooking. I'd rather die. When you've been on the road all your life . . .' He looked at Bannerman very directly, accusation now in his eyes. 'Someday you'll know it, too. When they don't want you any more, and they stick you somewhere out of sight and wait for you to retire. Or die.' His mouth twisted in a bitter little smile. 'Only consolation I can think of . . . that some day even smart bastards like you will get put out to grass.'

The alcohol was fuelling a revival of his aggression, the flask empty now. He opened a drawer and drew out an unopened bottle of whisky, twisting off the cap to thrust the neck of it to his lips. He sucked freely, all restraint vanishing.

'Yeah, even bastards like you.' He was swaying a little now, and Bannerman guessed there must have been another session earlier in the day. Palin looked at him. 'I suppose you're going to tell everyone.'

Bannerman sighed and stood up. 'No, I'm not going to tell a soul, Palin. You're not worth the trouble. But maybe Jansen will think that you are. Maybe he'll send someone looking for you, like he sent someone up here last night.'

Fear blackened Palin's eyes. 'He wouldn't . . . I don't even know anything.'

Bannerman stood up and advanced on the other man. 'I hope he does,' he said. 'I hope someone puts a hole in your head so that maybe some brains might leak in.' And he swung a tightly clenched fist into Palin's face. Palin staggered backwards and sat heavily in his chair, blood spurting from his nose and mouth. Bannerman ran a hand over his knuckles. That had hurt more than he expected. 'That was for last night,' he said in a voice that sounded strange even to himself. Palin pulled himself up in his chair, drawing a handkerchief from his pocket to press to his face. A gurgling noise came from his mouth.

All the anger drained out of Bannerman then as he looked at the wretched figure, and he regretted having hit him. He had thought it might make him feel better. It didn't.

He handed Palin the bottle. 'Here. You'd probably better take some of this.' Then turned as the door opened, to see Tait standing glaring at them. 'Jesus Christ, Bannerman!'

Mademoiselle Ricain appeared at his shoulder clutching a half-baguette filled with cheese and tomato. And her mouth fell open.

CHAPTER FIFTEEN

The day had not fulfilled its early promise. Snow was falling. This time there was a wind driving it in. And this time it was not a wet snow. It would lie. And if it snowed for some hours it would lie deeply. People in the street retreated into their winter shells. Hats, coats, scarves, boots. Heads bowed, tilted against the wind.

Bannerman and Tait could see them passing outside the window from where they sat in a small bistro in the Rue des Patriotes. It was less than half a mile from the Berlaymont, and just around the corner from the Sacré Coeur church in the Rue le Corrège. Hams, and gourd-shaped cheeses, and sausages and chitterlings hung from the ceiling. Enormous flat loaves lay piled up in the window. It was quiet and darkly lit here. They were eating late, and very few other tables were still occupied.

They had not intended to eat at all. Time was pressing. But Tait had spotted the bistro as they drove through quiet streets trying to find the church where the service was to be held. He had kept his own counsel since leaving the International Press Centre.

A time-worn old waiter in shirtsleeves and a pair of baggy black trousers handed them menus. Tait ordered for both of them without reference to Bannerman. *Plat du jour*. Fillet of veal with lentils and two glasses of Moselle. Bannerman watched him light a cigarette before finally turning his eyes towards his reporter. 'I ought to have sacked you on the spot.'

Bannerman said nothing.

'Don't you care?' Tait seemed exasperated.

'Not particularly. I could survive without you or the *Post*. And besides, I think the union might have something to say about it.'

Tait blew out his cheeks. 'I think the union might have something to say about you assaulting a fellow member.' He paused. 'And, anyway, when did you start allowing the union to fight your battles for you?'

Bannerman shrugged.

Tait puffed at his cigarette and thought about it for a while. 'Okay, tell me what it was all about.'

'Palin's a drunk. His paper's pulling him out of here, promoting him sideways so he can die quietly in some dark corner somewhere. He knew I was interested in a man called René Jansen, someone Slater had been keeping a file on. So the bastard tipped him off, thinking it might be worth money to him. Jansen sent someone to disappear it from the office.'

'Did he get it?'

'He did. And he also got me.' Bannerman pulled back his

190

sleeve to reveal the bruising on his right forearm. 'Nearly broke my fucking arm!'

Tait was frowning. 'Jansen . . . I know that name.' He seemed to have forgotten about Palin, and showed no interest in Bannerman's injury.

'A bright light in the Belgian business world, apparently. A man with influence as well as money.'

'And why were you interested in him?'

Much as he disliked it, Bannerman told him. About the folders of cuttings that Slater had been compiling on the three men, about his conversations with du Maurier, and the conclusion he had arrived at that somehow Slater was blackmailing Gryffe.

'Jesus Christ!' Tait barked, then quickly lowered his voice. 'Blackmail! For fuck's sake. How do you think it's going to look for the *Post* if it comes out that one of its journalists was blackmailing a government minister?'

It was no more than Bannerman had expected, but still it made him angry. 'We're journalists, Mr Tait. Or have you forgotten? We're supposed to report the truth. And if it's true, then people ought to know it. They also ought to know who murdered Slater and Gryffe and why people in high places are trying to stop us from finding out.' He drew a breath. 'I take it you do know about this morning's statement by the Minister of Justice?'

'Of course.'

But Bannerman thought, how could he know? He was in flight when the statement was being issued. 'Since when?'

'Since last night. They told me, off the record, since one of
our people was involved. On the understanding, of course, that
we adhered to the embargo.'

'And you agreed?'

'I did.' Tait was getting uncomfortable.

'And it never occurred to you to put me in the picture.'

'As it turned out, you knew already.'

'No thanks to you.'

The old waiter arrived with their veal and began pouring
their wine. Bannerman checked the time. They would have
to make this quick. The funeral service began in less than
twenty minutes. Tait took a mouthful of wine and they ate
in silence. The old man watched them from behind the bar
and wondered at two men sharing a meal together and saying
nothing. Especially when they had been so animated just a
few minutes earlier.

Tait finished first and emptied his glass. He lit another cigarette and looked coldly at Bannerman. 'I want you off the
story,' he said quietly. 'Whatever I might think as a newspaperman, as an editor there are other things I have to consider.'

Bannerman ate on without looking up. When finally he
washed down the last mouthful with the remains of his wine
he leaned back without a trace of emotion and said, 'If you are
prepared to allow other considerations to take priority over the
basic principles of good journalism, then in my very humble
opinion that makes you a pretty shit editor.'

Tait angrily stubbed out his half-smoked cigarette and

stood up. 'I don't have to take that kind of crap from you, Bannerman. I'm telling you now, you're finished here. There is no story. You'll fly back to Edinburgh tonight.'

'I won't,' Bannerman said, his face still impassive.

'You'll do what I fucking tell you!'

Bannerman shook his head. 'I don't work for you any more.'

'Like hell you don't.'

'I just resigned.'

Tait's laughter lacked any trace of humour. 'You've got a contract of employment, Bannerman. Requiring you to give me three months' notice.'

'Fine. Let's take it to an employment tribunal. See how you feel when I start explaining in open court just why I quit.'

Tait's face had lost all its colour now. His hands were trembling at his sides. The old waiter watched them with interest, although he had no idea what they were saying. A couple of workmen at a nearby table turned their heads. Tait became suddenly self-conscious and sat down again.

Bannerman leaned forward and said in a low voice. 'Here's the thing, *Mister* Tait. I've never taken shit off anybody, and I'm not about to take any off you. Whatever Slater may or may not have done, however that might tarnish the image of the *Post*, it's going to look a hell of a lot better for the paper if it comes out with it first. Make no mistake, if you force me out, it's not going to stop me. And when I break the story, you can be sure the *Post* will be the last paper on this earth to get it.'

Tait was ashen, and just for a second, Bannerman thought

he was going to hit him. Then quite suddenly he seemed to lose the will to fight. He'd lost this round and he knew it. But pride was sticking in his throat. In a voice that was barely a whisper he said, 'All right, Bannerman. You follow the leads where they take you. And when you deliver, if you deliver, then we'll run it. Then you can empty your desk and fuck off. You have no future with this paper.'

Bannerman nodded. 'One other thing,' he said. 'Slater's daughter . . .'

Tait interrupted. 'Whatever you might think of me, Bannerman . . .' He stopped himself. 'We are making arrangements for her to receive the best possible care back in Scotland. Until the arrangements are made she will be staying where she is in Brussels. A few days at the most.' He looked at his watch. It was almost two. 'Time to go. I'll walk to the church. You can pick up the bill and bring the car round.' He stood up abruptly and headed out into the snow, pulling his coat collar up around his neck.

Bannerman sat on, letting his heart rate slow. It had been inevitable really, and he had known from the first day Tait arrived that his days with the *Post* were numbered. He thought of it with only a little sadness. *'Garçon! L'addition, s'il vous plaît.'* And he thought how absurd it was to address such an old man as 'boy'.

CHAPTER SIXTEEN

It was many years since Bannerman had stood at a graveside. It seemed such an anachronism in these days of conveyor-belt cremation. There was something almost primeval about it. Dust to dust, ashes to ashes.

The priest was a small man, bald, silver threads of hair plastered sparsely across his pate, gown flapping in the wind, a flash of purple in the lining. His face was pink, stung by the snow. He read from a Bible whose pages were wet and he laid one of his big hands across the lower half to stop the pages from lifting in the wind.

Around the grave stood a handful of mourners. More pink, solemn faces. Pressmen with whom Slater had worked. The black of their suits and coats and ties under black umbrellas a stark contrast against the backdrop of snow. Hovering at a more discreet distance were a number of reporters covering the funeral for their papers. A television crew was sheltering beneath a knot of naked trees, the cameraman using a long lens. This would look particularly evocative on tonight's television screens. A black and white funeral filled with all the bleak imagery of death.

But if you were someone who had known the dead man, and not particularly liked him, you were probably standing in the cold out of a sense of duty, and the aesthetics would be lost on you. You would get little more out of it than cold feet, and maybe a lingering depression brought on by your own heightened sense of mortality. If you were here to report it, you would go first to buy a drink and then you would write fine words about a man you never knew, before contriving indignation at the way the case had been handled by the Judicial Police. If you were the priest, then you were doing God's work.

And if you were Slater you were dead and none of it could touch you.

Tait shuffled impatiently beside Bannerman as the coffin was lowered into the hole that had been dug for it out of frozen ground. He had not spoken a word during the drive from the Sacré Coeur to the Cimetière de Bruxelles, smoking one cigarette after the other. The dreary, almost pagan, ritual of the Mass had done nothing to improve his humour.

Bannerman no longer cared. He was watching Marie-Ange Piard, who stood at the far side of the grave. She was wearing a three-quarter-length black dress beneath a black cape and wide-brimmed hat with the obligatory black veil. Bannerman could not see her face and so could not discern what emotions it might be concealing. But she did not have the bearing of a woman in mourning. She appeared almost bored, standing very still and upright, and perhaps if her face had been visible it might have borne no expression at all. Bannerman could not imagine that Marie-Ange was a woman who would shed tears for anyone. He found it hard to believe she'd had feelings for Slater, and yet she had been his lover. Apparently. The incongruity of their relationship came back to him. He had not thought about her at all since Slater's death, and now she was resurrecting his curiosity. She was, it seemed to him, yet another ill-fitting piece in this strange jigsaw.

Sally stood beside her in a long dark coat and beret. She had glanced towards Bannerman once or twice, but not approached him either at the church or the cemetery. Perhaps she had sensed the antagonism between Bannerman and his companion and decided not to encroach. Or maybe she was simply struck by the sadness of the occasion and did not feel it appropriate.

The priest uttered his final words as he threw a handful of dirt over the coffin. Much of it was whipped away in the wind. The remainder rattled across polished wood. Then the mourners and the rest abandoned the graveside to the diggers who had been skulking among the gravestones beyond the path like lepers. And as the little group trod through the snow towards the gates they heard the first shovelfuls of earth clatter on to the coffin.

Bannerman became aware of Marie-Ange walking at his side. Tait was two or three yards ahead of them. 'I did not expect to see you here, Mr Bannerman,' she said. She pulled back her veil to reveal a pale, quizzical face.

'They do a nice line in funerals. I wouldn't have missed it for anything.'

She sighed. 'Are you ever serious?'

Bannerman said, 'Why are *you* here?' He saw annoyance flash momentarily in her eyes, then it passed.

'Oh,' she said, and looked away as if she had lost interest, 'one has to keep up appearances. And anyway, I was sure you would be here.'

'I thought you were surprised to see me.'

She turned a tiny smile on him. 'We never finished our conversation the other night. You left rather abruptly, and without saying goodbye. It was very rude of you.'

The mourners had reached the gates now and stood in little groups indulging in desultory conversation, stamping their feet against the cold and wishing they were gone. Bannerman saw Sally watching him from a distance. Tait was scuffing his feet impatiently in the snow by the car.

'You don't seem particularly grief-stricken,' Bannerman said. Marie-Ange looked surprised.

'Do I not?' She shrugged. 'Appearances can be deceptive.'

'So you are?'

'Of course, Mr Bannerman. Death is always sad.' She paused. 'Look, Tim and I had an understanding of sorts. A relationship of convenience. There may even have been a little affection between us. But poor Tim, I'm afraid, had begun to take it all a little too seriously. Which doesn't mean I'm not shocked by his death.'

'And no idea why someone should want to kill him?'

She raised an eyebrow. 'I understand the police have satisfied themselves that he and the politician shot each other.'

Bannerman shrugged. 'A curtain of convenience that those in power have drawn on the affair.'

She seemed surprised. 'Why on earth should they wish to do that?'

'I have no idea. One thing is clear, though. Whatever the authorities might say, Slater and Gryffe were murdered.' He watched closely for her reaction. Was there the slightest colouring of her face? The moment passed too quickly to be sure.

'Really?'

'I suppose you have no idea what Slater and the Minister were discussing that night at the party?'

She smiled and opened her handbag, taking out a small memo pad and a pen. 'Not a clue,' she said. And when she had scribbled something on her pad she tore off the top sheet and handed it to him. 'I take it you are playing detective. And I do so love mysteries. When you have a free evening call me at this number. We can get together and you can tell me all about it.'

Bannerman folded the paper into his top pocket without looking at it. He pushed his hands into his pockets and said, 'I'll call you.'

'Make it soon.' She turned and walked briskly away towards a black limousine parked further along the line of cars.

Bannerman watched her go and thought he was probably wasting his time. Sally touched his arm and he turned, a little startled. He hadn't heard her approach. She turned her eyes in the direction of Marie-Ange's car. 'Interested?'

Bannerman laughed and shook his head. 'Absolutely not.'

'Good.' She looked down, embarrassed. Then, 'Is seven-thirty all right? For going to see Tania?'

'Sure. I'll pick you up.'

'No, I'll come to the Rue de Commerce. Around seven.' She hesitated for a moment. 'By the way, I forgot to give you my key to the flat last night.'

'Keep it.' Bannerman looked at his watch, then glanced at Tait still standing impatiently by the car. 'I have to go.'

'Who is he?'

'My editor. I'm not exactly his golden boy at the moment. I'll see you at seven.'

In the car Tait retrieved a folded foolscap envelope from his overnight bag and handed it to Bannerman. 'I almost forgot,' he said coldly. 'The stuff from the library that you wanted on Gryffe.'

Bannerman took it, and looked inside at the photocopied sheets. There were about two dozen of them. Various obituary pieces on Gryffe that had appeared in the important British papers, plus a selection of the cuttings from the *Post*'s obit file on him. He chucked the envelope into the back seat.

'You can drop me at the airport,' Tait said. 'I'm catching a flight to London. I'll be back in Glasgow the day after tomorrow. I might require you to put Slater's kid on a plane. At any rate, I'll be in touch.' He lit another cigarette.

Bannerman sat for a few moments then started the car. As he pulled away from the kerb he saw a taxi in his rearview mirror pull out from the line of cars behind him. Even had he noticed the face of the passenger in the back seat he would almost certainly never have recognized it as the one he had passed in the Rue de Commerce the day after the killings. A face he had only glimpsed, without any particular reason that it should have left an impression.

He had not noticed that same taxi sitting outside the church during the Mass, and then again at the cemetery. If he had, he might have wondered why its passenger had never stepped out. But there was no reason that he should have given it a second thought. The streets were full of taxis.

For Kale, drawn and fretful in the back of the taxi, none of this had been easy. There had been problems making the driver understand what it was his fare wanted of him. But money was a language all men understood, though Kale was only too aware that money would not erase the driver's memory. The man kept looking at him in the rearview mirror. These were risks that he would never have taken before. And he knew he was making mistakes.

An inch of ash fell from the end of his cigarette and burned a tiny hole in his coat. Unaware, he drew more smoke into his lungs.

The driver caught sight of Kale's face in the mirror and felt a slight chill run through him. He did not like this fare. If it hadn't been for the money . . . Perhaps, when he had finished the job, he would go to the police. But what could he say? That an Englishman with a face that disturbed him had paid over the odds to have him run around after a blue Volkswagen? More than likely they would laugh at him. Was he in the habit of running to the police every time he took a dislike to the face of a passenger?

What was it about this face whose still, dark eyes stared out from the back seat? What could he tell them? He was being stupid, and yet he could not shake himself free of disquiet. He turned his attention to the road and the Volkswagen ahead of him.

CHAPTER SEVENTEEN

The office was empty when Bannerman got back to the IPC building. It was just after five and already it was dark outside. He was frustrated and tense. In twenty-four hours he had got exactly nowhere. The office was warm and stuffy and he threw open one of the windows, allowing cold air to rush in. It brought with it the odd flake of snow that landed on the sill and melted almost immediately. Twenty-four hours ago he had been sitting with du Maurier in the Café Auguste. What had he accomplished since then? He had been attacked here in this office, punched a colleague in the face, done a deal with Platt, fallen out with his editor and attended a funeral. But he had achieved nothing.

He turned from the window and found a note on his desk from Mademoiselle Ricain. Inspector du Maurier had phoned twice. There was a number to call back. It was the same number the Inspector had given him the other day. There was also an invitation to British press correspondents to attend a dinner at a Brussels restaurant that night where the Foreign Office would announce its arrangements for shipping Gryffe's body back to London. There was an embargo until ten a.m. tomorrow when an official government statement would be put out on the wires. Dress was informal.

Ironically, the invitation was addressed to Timothy Slater Esq., EEC Correspondent, *Edinburgh Post*. Bannerman crushed it in his fist and chucked it in the bin. One more exercise in government PR. The tragedy was that their attempts to draw a veil over the affair would probably succeed. Most journalists were susceptible to good food and drink and the gentle persuasions of contacts they were almost certain to need in the future. Correspondents based here in Brussels, like the two he had met the day he arrived, would be reluctant to dump in their own backyard. It was the staff men sent over from London who would be harder to convince. But how many of them would stay here long enough to get to the truth?

Bannerman sat down and examined his swollen knuckles. His hand had stiffened up. He wondered where Palin had gone. Was he getting drunk somewhere? And Mademoiselle Ricain. She would not understand why he had hit his colleague. The world was filled with people who would not understand, who would never understand. Bannerman took out the envelope Tait had brought him and began reading his way laboriously through every article.

It took him half an hour to read them all twice. But there were no sudden revelations, no blinding lights on the road to Damascus. Just the bare bones of a man's life. Not much more than he'd known already from the file of cuttings Slater himself had compiled.

Gryffe had been forty-four years old when he died. Born in a London suburb, the son of a wealthy lawyer, he had been educated at a lesser-known public school before going on to academic distinction and an honours degree in economics at Cambridge. His background did not suggest that his politics would fall on the side they did.

It was while at Cambridge that he'd first become involved in the youth movement of the party he would later represent, initially in the Commons and then in Government. He was an enthusiastic convert to begin with, but on leaving university his first choice had not been a career in politics. He had taken up a lucrative job as a junior executive with a US-based company that built tractors in seventeen countries. During his ten years with that company he travelled widely, rising quickly in the firm, latterly establishing new plants in a number of African and Middle Eastern states.

At the age of thirty-three he had finally joined the party with which he had first flirted in his early twenties. A year later he was nominated as a parliamentary candidate for a safe constituency and was elected the following year with a majority of fifteen thousand. Almost from the start of his political career he had fallen under the influence of the party's ageing chairman and guiding light of the previous thirty years, Lord Armsdale, becoming something of a protégé. Which had earned him both respect and influence.

It was obvious, even then, that he was destined for great things. He was appointed private secretary to the then leader of the opposition. During the next five years he gained experience in a number of important positions before finally winning his coveted post as Minister of State at the Foreign Office, shortly after his party won the general election. However, within a year of that appointment his mentor, Lord Armsdale, had suffered a coronary and was forced to retire from active political life. Many commentators seemed convinced at the time that Gryffe's meteoric rise in the party would come to an end. Armsdale, they said in their columns, had been the real architect of his success. Without him to pull the strings Gryffe would slide back into obscurity. But he had proved them all wrong, not only by retaining his job but by extending his circle of influence, and expanding his status as a public figure. A populist, he seemed to have brought a breath of fresh air to the tarnished domain of British politics – a grey world bereft of character and charisma.

Even the commentators appeared to have been converted, and within two years they were describing him as the natural successor to his boss at the Foreign Office. Some even went so far as to predict that he might one day lead the party itself – a future prime minister.

Bannerman rubbed his eyes and leaned back in his chair. Gryffe had not only been an astute politician, but a manipulator of the media, climbing to political success initially on the back of the party's former chairman, and then demonstrating to his critics that he could have done it on his own anyway.

It was now nearly six. Bannerman looked again at the note Mademoiselle Ricain had left for him, and picked up the phone. He dialled and leaned forward on his elbows listening to it ring. This would be a direct line to du Maurier's office. He was about to give up when the receiver was lifted from its cradle.

'Du Maurier.'

'Bannerman. You were looking for me.'

'*Oui.*'

'I was at the funeral.'

'Ah yes.' He sounded tired. 'Can you meet me?'

'When?'

'Now.'

'No, I'm going to see the child.'

'Later then.'

'Okay. At the Café Auguste?'

'No. In the Place Poelaert. At the far end of the Rue des Quatre Bras. At the far side of the Palais de Justice. We should not be seen together.'

'Can you tell me what it's about?'

'No. When can you be there?'

Bannerman thought for a moment. 'Eleven?'

He heard du Maurier sigh. 'All right. Eleven.' The line went dead and Bannerman hung up. He swung round in his chair and saw the invitation to the Minister's dinner lying crumpled in the bin. He lifted it out, smoothed it on the desk and stuffed it in his pocket.

CHAPTER EIGHTEEN

The hospital was set back from the road and screened by trees and thick evergreen shrubbery behind a high stone wall. The poorly lit road that ran around the side of the hill overlooking this outlying suburb was narrow and treacherous in the snow. A steep drop on its left side fell away to a disused railway line. Set in two acres of its own grounds, the hospital was housed in one of several large stone villas that perched precariously on the slope of the hill. This had once, perhaps, been an exclusive part of town, a retreat for the rich. Now the large ornately carved stone gateposts were blackened and chipped. Rusted wrought-iron gates opened on to driveways where weeds poked through the light covering of snow beneath the trees.

From the road, most of the houses simmered in darkness. They might have been derelict. The only building that showed signs of life was the hospital itself, light from its windows divided into fragments by the naked branches of winter trees. The whole street huddled in the shadow of the hill, an air of hushed decay falling with the snow. They came upon it unex-pectedly as Bannerman's car whined up the steep curve of the road from the housing estate below, tyres slipping in the snow. It was a corner of the city forgotten by time.

The polished brass plaque on the gate seemed quite incongruous. *HÔPITAL DES ENFANTS*. Very discreet. A residential psychiatric clinic for children. Bannerman swung the Volkswagen into the driveway and they wound up through the trees to where the drive broadened into a parking area in front of the house. From here there was a stunning view over the city, which lay swathed in snow below them.

Thick flakes were falling around them as Bannerman and Sally stepped out of the car. Half a dozen other vehicles sat close to the house, ledges of snow accumulating on their roofs. The house looked better cared for than its neighbours. Sandblasters had restored the stone to its original honeycomb yellow, window sashes and shutters a freshly painted green. It was an impressive building with turrets at each of its four corners, and steeply pitched grey-slate roofs.

They mounted the steps to double swing doors and pushed into a bleak tiled hallway, a staircase to their left climbing to the next floor. The air here was warm and heavy with a sour smell that reminded Bannerman of the school dinner hall. A nurse in a starched white uniform came out of a room at the far end. She was preoccupied with charts on a clipboard and didn't notice them at first. When she looked up she seemed momentarily taken aback. She approached and spoke to them in French. Sally replied, and Bannerman wondered why he was surprised by her fluency. But, of course, if she taught English she must speak French. The nurse smiled and nodded and asked them to wait.

The two stood in the hall shuffling impatiently, neither inclined to conversation. In the still of the house, the only sounds to reach them were distant. Muffled voices, the opening and closing of doors, the chatter of a typewriter. Then the clatter of footsteps on the stairs and a man in a dark suit came down to greet them. He shook both their hands solemnly and addressed himself to Bannerman in English. 'You've come to see little Tania. I am Doctor Mascoulin.'

Bannerman nodded. 'Neil Bannerman.' And he turned towards Sally. 'This is . . .'

Mascoulin interrupted. 'Yes, we've already met.' And Bannerman glanced at Sally, surprised to learn that she had been here before. He realized how little he really knew about her. Mascoulin said, 'Tania's with some of the older children still in the playroom. Perhaps you would like to observe her first. She has not integrated well, but maybe that is to be expected.'

He led them upstairs and down a cream-painted hallway. Halfway along it he opened a door that led into a small observation room. A dozen seats were gathered around a one-way mirror that allowed for observation of the children without being seen. They found themselves looking into a large, brightly lit room where eight or ten children were involved in various stages of play. Paintings and drawings, clearly done by the children themselves, covered its walls. Games were spread out on a long, oblong table and two of the children sat on tubular steel chairs playing with a pile of wooden bricks. Other pieces of apparatus and more chairs lay scattered about the floor, seemingly at random.

Tania sat alone on one of the chairs, watching the others. There was not the least flicker of interest in her eyes. She clasped her hands in her lap, her face wooden, dispassionate. Distant, as though she were somewhere else. A nurse in jeans and a white T-shirt encouraged the children in their activities and from time to time spoke to Tania. But Tania appeared not to hear her. No sound reached Bannerman and the others from the playroom. It was like watching a silent movie.

Doctor Mascoulin said, 'We employ an integrated team approach here. A nurse will work with the children in the play-room and attempt to introduce various methods or approaches by which both she and we in the observation room can learn about the child. In here our sessions normally involve the par-ents, and we learn from their experience, too. Unfortunately, in the case of little Tania there are no parents.' He turned toward Sally. 'But Mademoiselle Robertson has proved most helpful in this respect already.'

Mascoulin might have been talking about bacteria observed through a microscope for all the empathy he showed, and Bannerman found his apparent disinterest irritating. And yet it was easily possible that this clinical detachment was simply a manifestation of professionalism born of compassion. It was too easy to judge people too quickly.

'As you can see, Tania has not adapted well to her new environment. To an extent this is to be expected. She has been traumatized, and there is a language barrier. We do not know how much French, if any, she understands. Naturally, for the other children and the staff . . . well, French or perhaps Flemish is the native tongue. We cannot upset the routine for one child, though several of our nurses do speak English and have spent some time with her. Individual attention. But I'm afraid there are limits to what we can do for her here.'

Bannerman was looking at Sally, who seemed intent on the children. He wondered again at her interest in Tania. It had not occurred to him that her feelings for the child might have gone beyond that of an occasional carer. Had she visited more than once? It was odd, he thought, how the child had affected them both.

'The sooner she can be taken back to Scotland the better,' Mascoulin was saying. 'I understand your paper is trying to get her a place at the Brook Clinic in Edinburgh.'

'Yes,' Bannerman said. It was the first he'd heard of it.

'Doctor Brook has some interesting, if rather unusual, approaches to treatment across the autistic spectrum. Of course, there is no general agreement on any one approach . . .'

Bannerman had returned his gaze to Tania. She had not moved. Nor, it seemed, had she so much as blinked. Her eyes were dark, mysterious pools that gave no hint of what might be going on behind them. Bannerman remembered the touch of her cold fingers on his cheek and he was disturbed by the affection that stirred in him. 'What kind of future does a child like that have?' he heard himself asking. And he turned to look at Mascoulin's square, ugly face.

'It is difficult to say. Only time will tell. But there is a great danger in such cases that lack of responsiveness to treatment will lead eventually to confinement in a mental institution. There they tend to resort to drugs to maintain some kind of equilibrium, in some cases leading to schizophrenia.' He scratched his head thoughtfully. 'You see, autistic children grow up to become autistic adults. In bad cases, and where there is no one else to look after them, they are unable to look after themselves. They are unpredictable and sometimes violent. There is little else that can be done.' He saw the alarm in Bannerman's face and added quickly, 'That is only in extreme cases, of course.'

The session in the playroom came to a close. Another nurse led the children away, but Tania was the last to go. The nurse who had spoken to her earlier took her hand and the little girl followed with that same passive serenity that Bannerman had seen in her before.

'She has a room of her own,' Mascoulin said. 'She likes to be left to her own devices. Sometimes she draws, but never in the playroom. Athough we always provide pencil and paper there. She regards our attentions as . . . well, as an intrusion, I suppose.'

'Can we see her?' Bannerman said.

'She might react.'

'I know, I've seen it.'

Mascoulin shrugged. 'Just one of you, then.'

Sally said, 'On you go. I'll see her next time.'

Tania's head snapped around abruptly when the door opened. She was sitting at a small desk pushed against the wall. It was covered with sheets of paper. She clutched a small pencil in her hand. The weary, pained face of Christ looked down from a crucifix fixed to the bare white wall above her. Her bedsheets were a mess, as if she had spent a tortured night in them. A dark wooden dresser stood against the far wall. A threadbare square of carpet covered black-painted floorboards. It was an austere, functional room, like a cell.

The first thing that Bannerman noticed was the bars on the window that looked out from the first floor on to the driveway below. Beyond, the lights of the city twinkled in a snowy distance.

Then he was drawn by her eyes.

In the first moment, before she recognized Bannerman, her eyebrows puckered towards the bridge of her nose, eyes flaring with anger. Then, just as quickly, her forehead unfurrowed and her eyes became once more those dark, placid pools. Mascoulin satisfied himself that there would be no tantrums. 'I'll leave you for a moment.' He closed the door softly and Bannerman stood awkwardly, looking at the child. In the silence he could hear his own breathing, like the scraping of chalk on a blackboard.

The child remained motionless, half-turned in her chair, staring back at him. The seconds dragged interminably. 'Hello,' Bannerman said at last, and his voice sounded feeble. Still she made no movement, and he took two or three steps towards her and looked at the drawings spread on the table. Even though he had seen her drawing of the man in the house, he was startled by their brilliance. Seldom had he seen so much expression conveyed in such simple lines. Movement and perspective accurately observed by the merest stroke of her pencil. There were horses and riders, a dog, a bird in flight. 'They're beautiful,' he said, and thought how inadequate that was to express their genius.

She had turned her head around so that she could watch him. What was she thinking? He crouched down suddenly, on an impulse, so that his eyes were on a level with hers, and took one of her hands. For a moment there was something on the tip of his tongue, something he had been going to say. But it vanished as quickly and he lost his grasp of what it was. Everything he felt about her, all the strange emotions she awakened in him, were hopelessly elusive, impossible to define. He was at a loss, foundering in a sea of confusion, and he felt a sudden urge to take her into the protection of his arms. But scared of the reaction it might provoke, he let the moment pass.

He was embarrassed without knowing why, and lowered his head. He sighed and felt the soft warmth of her small fingers in his. How could he explain it to her when he could not explain it to himself? He wanted to protect her, to keep her safe from harm, the way a father would a daughter. An instinct foreign to him, and yet completely natural.

He raised his eyes and saw that she was smiling. A gentle smile that showed in her eyes and at the corners of her mouth. There was a great serenity in her face that made its plainness almost beautiful. He squeezed her hand and stood up, still touched by his embarrassment, but a little easier within himself. 'I'll come and see you again.' But her hand clung obstinately to his and he felt her distress. 'I must go.'

Still the hand held his. And then suddenly she seemed resigned to his leaving and her hand fell away. He wanted to go, but his feet would not take him. Her face was still turned upwards, looking at him with sadness now. That hint of a smile long gone. He bent over and kissed her gently on the forehead, catching a glimpse of his pale, bruised face in a mirror on the wall opposite. He looked tired, and he turned his eyes away from the reflection. The kiss was a simple thing that seemed to come without thinking. But still it surprised him. 'I'll come back,' he heard himself saying. And then felt the cold of the metal door handle in his hand as he stepped out in the corridor, shutting the door behind him.

Mascoulin emerged from the room next door and looked at him strangely. 'She has a marvellous talent,' he said.

Bannerman nodded, not trusting himself to speak.

They walked the length of the corridor together, and on the stairs Mascoulin said, 'Children have an almost unlimited capacity for love, Monsieur Bannerman. Most autistic children find that kind of connection with others very difficult. It frustrates them, almost as much as it frustrates their loved ones. It's hard to keep loving someone who cannot love you back.'

Bannerman nodded.

The doctor went on, 'Every child needs a love to return. Just a little goes such a long way and is returned manyfold. Perhaps little Tania has missed out in that respect.'

Bannerman didn't doubt it. He looked at the doctor. It was almost as though he had been witness to the events in Tania's room. Then he remembered the mirror on the wall. He felt momentarily annoyed, spied on. But the anger passed quickly.

'You were watching,' he said.

Mascoulin nodded. 'We like to be able to keep an eye on the children.' He paused. 'I must admit that the way she responded to you was quite exceptional. She's been like an automaton since she arrived. Even with Mademoiselle Robertson.' He hesitated. 'How long have you known the child?'

Bannerman shook his head. 'I hardly know her at all.'

Sally was waiting in the hall. She looked up as she heard them on the stairs. 'I do hope you will come again,' Mascoulin said. He shook both their hands and watched them pass through the swing doors, out into the snow. And wondered at the curious scene he had witnessed in the child's room.

Outside, Bannerman stopped at the foot of the steps, breathing in the cold night air, and turned his face slightly upwards so that the snowflakes cooled the heat of his skin.

He felt Sally's arm slip through his and she guided him slowly towards the car, her feet scuffing in the soft snow. 'Why did you really come?' she asked.

He shrugged. 'I don't know.' He searched absently in his pocket for the car keys. 'The first night I stayed at the apartment I woke in the small hours to find her in my room. She was just standing watching me, and then she put her fingers on my face. Stood there a while, just gazing at me, then left. It touched me. Touched my soul, Sally. I don't know how else to explain it.' He glanced at her, self-conscious. Then away again. The keys were cold in his hand and he unlocked the passenger door. 'Would you like to go somewhere?'

'You could take me home,' she said. 'I'm very tired.'

CHAPTER NINETEEN

Kale told the driver to go on past. The brass plaque flashed briefly in the headlights of the taxi, a flicker of information caught in a moment of light and time that told him he need look no further for the child.

Beyond where Bannerman's car had turned into the hospital, the taxi made virgin tracks in the snow and its gears whined as the tyres fought for grip. The vehicle pulled slowly towards the top of the hill. Here there were a few trees where the ground levelled off and the road swung away to wind itself down around the other side. Kale stopped the driver and counted out a thick wad of notes. He was not sure how much it would be in English money. Perhaps two hundred pounds. It seemed extravagant, but then it hardly mattered any more.

The driver took the money and felt its thickness in his hand. He dared not count it then, but he knew it was a lot. Many times more than the fare he had clocked up. He stuffed it hastily in his pocket and half-turned, a stiff smile on his face, and muttered words of thanks. The cold eyes of his passenger flickered briefly over him, each eye reflecting a pinhead of light from its darkness. The mouth, pinched and pale, said nothing. Only the eyes spoke, a silent warning, before their owner turned to open the door and slip quietly out.

The driver wasted no time in pushing into first gear. He turned the car out from the kerb to head down the hill and glanced in the rearview mirror. But already his passenger was only a shadow, barely visible among the trees. He let out a deep breath, one that he seemed to have been holding in his lungs all day, and allowed himself a smile of satisfaction as he fingered the wad of notes in his jacket pocket. All his fears and doubts of earlier melted as quickly as the snowflakes that landed on his windscreen. The thoughts he had entertained only a few hours before, of going to the police, seemed ridiculous now. Who cared why this sullen foreigner had wanted him to follow the blue Volkswagen? He pulled the flap over his pocket. Perhaps he could take a few days off.

Kale watched the red tail lights of the taxi vanish from view where the road turned down through the trees. He stood for some minutes. At first he felt nothing. Not even the cold. In a few hours it would all be over and then nothing would matter any more. Back the way they had come he could see the lights of the hospital through the branches of trees. He barely noticed the view of the city below him to his right.

He turned and walked back down the hill until he reached the first of the villas standing darkly behind its high stone walls. There a solitary streetlamp rose above its own pool of feeble yellow light, and he stopped to light a cigarette and turn up the collar of his coat. His every movement seemed remote to him, mechanical, as though he had stepped outside of his body and was simply an onlooker. He had surrendered himself completely to the job in hand.

He smoked only half of his cigarette before throwing it away and carried on down the road to the gates of the clinic. Already the tyre tracks of Bannerman's car where it had turned into the hospital were covered by fresh snowfall, leaving only the merest of impressions. Kale hesitated for just a moment in the gateway, then moved silently from the drive into the trees. Here the snow lay in patches, the thick layer of dead leaves spongy under his feet. There was a smell of decay, damp and cold, among the evergreen foliage. He scrambled up the slope, his sleeves and trousers snagging on bushes, and then waited, breathless, at the top, crouched below the cover of the wall that bounded the terrace. A fine cold sweat beaded his forehead.

For several minutes he remained there before pulling himself up so that he could see beyond the wall, across the terrace to the house itself. A number of cars, including the one he had been following all day, stood in its shadow, the light of the lamp above the main door streaming out across the terrace towards him. More lights shone in windows on all floors, casting reflections in the snow. He crouched down again and made his way below the wall to where it cut away at the end of the terrace. From here he had an oblique view across the front of the house beyond where the light fell in long yellow slabs. He eased himself in against a short flight of broken stone steps to watch and wait, silent and unseen, with an infinite and chilling patience.

He could not tell how much time had passed before the man and the girl came out. They came down the steps and crossed to their car, damp snow creaking beneath their feet. Their voices drifted with the snow and he registered only a little surprise to hear them speaking English.

'Would you like to go somewhere?'

'You can take me home. I'm very tired . . .'

When the car had gone the silence returned and Kale stretched his stiffening legs. He glanced up and saw a small face pressed against one of the lit windows on the first floor, watching through bars as the lights of the vehicle travelled back down the hill towards the housing estate below.

Suddenly he felt the cold, the pain in his legs and the numbness of his fingers. He no longer stood apart from himself. The face at the window was just a shadow, a small head silhouetted against the light behind it. A tiny hand came up and pressed against the pane before sliding slowly, hopelessly, down to the sill. Kale knew with a frightening certainty that this was the child who had seen him in the house at the Rue de Pavie.

Still he did not move. Another figure appeared in the room. A nurse who came to the window. The child turned and they both moved out of vision. Several more minutes passed before the nurse reappeared at the window and drew the blind so that the light behind it showed only around its edges. Then the light went out.

It was after midnight when the last lights went out around the house and its grounds lay in darkness. For the last hour Kale's attention had been focused on the child's window. He had been surprised, sometime after the light was extinguished, to see the blind slowly rise and reveal the paleness of her face in the light reflected by the snow. And there she remained, staring into the dark, head pressed against the glass.

He had found himself thinking about her. Alone in the world without parents, without love, separated from others by something in her head, something that set her apart, condemned to exist in the loneliness of her own mind. There was an affinity between them. Her life was no more, no less, than his had been then, or than it was now. How much pain might he have been spared if some stranger with a gun had ended his life thirty years ago? No loss to anyone. No one to miss him. But, he knew, he was only seeking virtue in evil. Self-justification. Such a bitter irony. It was something he had never needed before.

Now, with all the lights out, he could no longer see her at the window. But she was still there, he knew. He eased himself painfully to his feet and felt for the gun in his pocket. The cold of the barrel burned his fingers. With a heavy heart he began up the steps to the terrace. It was time.

*

Her skin was burning as though with a fever. Occasionally she moved her forehead on the glass so that it was cold again. She did not feel sleepy. She would wait at the window, she had decided, until Bannerman's car returned. Maybe tomorrow, or the day after. She wanted to see the car come up the driveway. She wanted to see him standing in the snow. Perhaps he would glance up and see her at the window and wave. And perhaps she would smile and wave back. It might be difficult, but she wanted to do it. She wanted him to know all the things she couldn't tell him. Why was she so drawn to those startling blue eyes? Maybe it was what she saw behind them.

The lights of the city twinkled and shone in the valley below in seemingly random patterns. He was out there somewhere. Doing what? Did he think about her as she thought about him? Of course not. Her reasoning was clear and sound. She constituted only a tiny fraction of his life, of his thoughts. It was only in the great void of her own existence that he was so important to her, filling the emptiness, bringing light into darkness. There was no reason that he should think of her at all. And yet he had come here, hadn't he? And so clearly felt something for her, something that he too was unable to express. He would come again. He had told her he would.

The clinic had been in darkness for some time now. The others would be asleep. The doctors, the nurses, the other children. Strange mirror-images of herself. Prisoners within themselves, prisoners in this house with bars on the windows.

She gave a slight start as a door slammed somewhere in the

depths of the building. Not everyone was asleep. A light came on downstairs, throwing a broad wedge of light out across the snow on the terrace. Something was moving down there, something dark and huddled that froze as it was caught in the sudden light. The shadow of a man fell away from the house, long and thin. A face turned up towards the window, sickly pale, whiter than snow. Tania did not move. It was a face she knew, a face in which she saw a reflection of her own fear. Eyes in which she recognized the same hunted look she had seen in the Rue de Pavie. Then the light went out and she could no longer see him, but knew he was still there. And knew, too, that he had come for her.

CHAPTER TWENTY

The night was empty and yet still young. Bannerman had dropped Sally outside a block of tenement flats in the old part of town. She had not asked him up, returning alone to an empty apartment. He had sat for a few minutes in the car watching her light go on three floors up. She was so unpredictable. Someone must have hurt her very badly.

He remembered the girl from telesales, the night that he had finally taken her to bed. Clumsy and inexperienced. A moment spoiled by youth, ignorance and fear. The final disillusionment of the angry years. Nothing in his life had been sacred since. It was a night when he should have grown up. But that was not to come until six weeks later, when she came to him one night after work and told him that she was carrying his child.

Though even then he had failed to learn. It was ironic that she was the one who would teach him, that it was she who grew up in that time much more quickly than he.

Bannerman turned the car away from the kerb. A curtain on the third floor fluttered and a face appeared momentarily at the window. But he did not see it. He glanced at the time. It was not yet nine, and he recalled the crumpled card in his pocket and took it out. He stopped the car under a lamp post and held it in the light. *Her Majesty's Minister for Foreign Affairs extends an invitation . . .* Nine o'clock at the Restaurant Noir in Rue des Bouchers. He rummaged in the glove compartment and found an indexed street map. The Rue des Bouchers was about a hundred metres from the Grande Place where he had sat that morning under the yellow awning enjoying the winter sunshine. He allowed himself a grim smile and slammed the glove compartment shut. It was about time he began stirring things.

The Restaurant Noir was set back from the street. In the window, thick red curtains hung on rings from a polished brass rail. Menus were displayed outside beneath elaborate imitation gas lamps. Expensive fare. You did not eat here unless you had a fat wallet. And HMG had plenty of taxpayers' money at their disposal. It was in a good cause, after all. Wasn't it? What price the goodwill of the press? A commissionaire in maroon uniform and gold-braided cap held the door open for Bannerman and he stepped inside.

The muted sound of voices, of knives and forks on plates, of bottles kissing the rims of glasses, drifted softly from a dining room set behind stained-glass screens of medieval knights and gracious ladies. Less muted voices came from an adjoining bar.

A face hovered darkly behind a cloakroom counter away to

his left and a flunky in a black suit and white starched collar approached on tiptoe. He smiled with the ease of a professional smiler.

'Monsieur?' Bannerman held out the battered invitation card which the flunky took between thumb and forefinger as though it might somehow be contaminated. '*Ah, bien.* May I take your coat?'

The newspapermen were in the bar with the Minister, a junior member of the Foreign Office staff and a government press officer. There was a distinct lull in the conversation as Bannerman came in. Without exception every face turned in his direction. But it was a moment that passed quickly, and afterwards everyone pretended not to have noticed him. All except for the press officer who pushed forward to shake his hand in greeting. 'Neil Bannerman, isn't it?' His well-practised smile widened and his dimples threatened to swallow the rest of his face.

'I'll have a whisky,' Bannerman said.

'Of course.' The PR man scuttled off to the bar.

A few of the faces in here were familiar to Bannerman. Others were not.

'Here you are.' The press officer handed him his whisky. 'My name's Holt, Harold Holt.' He was young, with thinning mouse-brown hair. No more than twenty-five, Bannerman thought. He oozed confidence and the ersatz camaraderie that was the hallmark of his profession.

'Well, Harold, how would you like to tell the Minister I'd like a word with him?'

Holt's face darkened, though his smile never wavered. 'I don't think the Minister will want to discuss . . .'

'Just a chat, that's all. Off the record, of course.'

He watched the reluctant Holt approach the Minister, touch him lightly on the shoulder and utter a few words close to his ear. The Minister half-turned and smiled in Bannerman's direction, raising one finger to indicate that an audience would be granted in just a few moments. Holt scurried off to the bar to fetch more drinks. Bannerman took a mouthful of whisky, swilling it slowly before swallowing.

'Well, Mr Bannerman. I don't believe we've met before.' The Minister approached with an outstretched hand. 'You have quite a reputation. It seems such a pity that you spend most of your time buried away up there in Scotland.'

Bannerman smiled. 'Maybe you ought to put it on your list of countries to visit. I'm sure it wouldn't be beyond a man of your capability to reopen diplomatic relations.'

'Very amusing, Mr Bannerman. Another drink?'

Bannerman shook his head. 'No thanks. I'd like to talk.'

'Depends what you want to talk about.' He smiled easily. A man who had shaken the hands of presidents and prime ministers could take someone like Bannerman in his stride any day of the week. He was a good sixty years old, and not a man to use words carelessly. Gryffe was being groomed to succeed him. Which is why, perhaps, the two men had never got on. Or so the gossip columnists had hinted.

He had a good head of steel-grey hair and shrewd brown eyes that held you in their wryly condescending gaze. A man of gentle but firm persuasion, the ultimate diplomat. He had a reputation as a hard man, but fair, and good at his job. At a glance you could see why, and Bannerman thought, there was no point in staying for the meal.

'I'd like to talk about Robert Gryffe and Tim Slater.'

The Minister smiled patiently. 'Off limits I'm afraid, Neil. Unfortunate, of course, the whole affair. After the meal I shall be releasing details of our plans for having Robert's body flown back to England. And the memorial service.' He put a friendly arm around Bannerman's shoulders and steered him gently towards the bar. 'Of course, after the election, when' – he smiled – 'when my party is returned to office, we can perhaps have lunch together.'

Bannerman shook his head and returned the Minister's smile. 'Not really good enough, sir. Of course, I understand your reluctance to say too much before the election. A nasty business. Can't have the voters getting the wrong idea. All the same, I'm sure many people would like to know why the assassinations of Gryffe and Slater have been hushed up by the Belgian authorities.' He paused. 'And whether or not Her Majesty's government had any hand in it.'

The diplomatic smile was becoming a little frayed around the edges. 'Oh, come now, Mr Bannerman.' Gone was the friendly 'Neil'. 'There is no evidence to suggest that either man was assassinated. A quarrel . . .'

'With all due respect, Foreign Secretary, you know as well as I do that is bullshit! All the evidence points quite clearly to murder by a third party.'

The Minister began steering Bannerman away again from the bar.

Bannerman said, 'The trouble is that most of that evidence hasn't been made public. Yet. But you and I both know, don't we? The left-handed Slater with the gun in his right hand. The quarter of a million dollars in the suitcase. Slater's air tickets to the States. The break-in at Slater's apartment within half an hour of the murders. Perhaps you forget that I was there.'

The Minister dropped his voice, and his smile had vanished. 'You have no evidence to support any of this, Bannerman . . . It's just journalistic fantasy.' Gone too, now, was the 'mister'. 'You'd do well to be very careful what you put in print.'

Bannerman almost laughed. 'Or what? You'll sue me? For writing the truth? Last thing you'd want to do is wash all that dirty linen in public, surely?'

It was Bannerman's turn now to place a friendly arm around the shoulder of the Minister. He steered him ever further from the bar and spoke in hushed tones. 'You know what I think, Foreign Secretary? I think that Robert Gryffe was up to something that might have proved very embarrassing to the government. I think Timothy Slater knew what that was. And to put it bluntly, was blackmailing him.'

The Minister was frowning, but superficially he had lost none of his composure. He had donned his mask of sincerity and now adopted a different tack. 'Just how good is your information, Neil?' He looked searchingly at the reporter.

'Good enough.'

'Because if what you say is true then it may well be that we shall have to take another look at the whole thing. It may be that the Belgian authorities have kept vital information from us. We should get together, you and I, and discuss the source of your information.'

Bannerman smiled. 'Now, Minister, you know I would never discuss my sources. And if you are really so misinformed, then you will be of little help to me.' Pause. 'But I'll tell you what. When I've got my story together I'll call you and you can give me your on-the-record reaction. Hopefully I will have things tied up and out of the way before the election. Either way, I promise, you'll be the first to know.'

Bannerman almost admired the Minister's ability to prevent his facial expressions from betraying what lay behind them, particularly after the somersaults he had been forced to make in the last few minutes.

The journalist leaned over to lay his glass on a table. 'By the way, I must apologize,' he said. 'I'm afraid I shan't be able to stay for dinner. I do hope it goes well, though.' He extended a hand to shake the Minister's. 'Goodbye, sir.' And he headed out to the cloakroom to retrieve his coat.

Before stepping outside once more into the snow he glanced

back towards the bar. Everyone in there knew something had passed between Bannerman and the Minister, though no one knew what. In the competitive world of newspapers, the cardinal sin was not knowing what the story was. None of those pressmen would enjoy their meal tonight. Nor would the Secretary of State for Foreign Affairs.

CHAPTER TWENTY-ONE

I

The stairwell seemed colder than it had on previous evenings, the landing lights more muted, the stairs darker. Outside the snow was falling ever more thickly. Winter seemed determined to tighten its grip on the city. As Bannerman trudged up the stairs someone coughed on the landing above. A man's cough. A deep retching cough. Bannerman could smell cigarette smoke. Whoever was there was making no attempt to conceal his presence, and he must have heard Bannerman's footsteps.

Bannerman climbed the next flight cautiously before he saw Platt's face, round and fat, peering down at him. 'Is that you, Bannerman? I've been hanging around here for more than half an hour. I'm bloody freezing.'

Platt's face was blanched white and touched with blue around the eyes. He was wearing a thick coat, a scarf wrapped tightly round his neck. His battered checked hat was pulled down low over his forehead. He made an exaggerated show of stamping his feet for warmth.

'What do you want?' Bannerman asked. He turned his back on the other man to unlock the door to the apartment.

'Oh, that's nice,' Platt said, his voice dripping with sarcasm. 'I've been knocking my pan in all afternoon trying to get background on Jansen and Lapointe and then most of the night trying to track you down . . .'

'I told you tomorrow would do.' Bannerman paused and looked at the pathetic figure on the landing and relented. 'You'd better come in.'

Platt followed him down the hall to the living room slapping his hands together and blowing into them. Bannerman took a bottle wrapped in brown paper from his pocket and laid it on the table, then threw his coat over the back of the settee. He switched on the fire and saw Platt eyeing the bottle.

'Malt,' Bannerman said, but made no effort to open it. 'Let's see it.'

'What?' Platt looked confused.

'Your stuff on Jansen and Lapointe.'

'Oh. Yes.' Platt struggled out of his coat and draped it over a chair before drawing a large folded envelope from his inside jacket pocket and passing it to Bannerman. He crossed to the electric fire and rubbed his hands together in front of it, before easing himself into a chair. He ran a dry tongue over wet, purple lips and glanced longingly again at the bottle of malt. 'I got most of what I needed on Jansen from a series the *Soir* ran on him about six months ago. I've done you a précis of the relevant details in English. There was some stuff on Lapointe as well, but not in the same detail. He keeps a much lower profile than Jansen.'

Bannerman sank into the settee and looked at his watch. It was just after ten. He dropped the envelope on to the coffee table without looking inside it. 'Tell me the salient details. I haven't time to read this stuff just now. I'm going out again shortly.'

Platt made no attempt to hide his irritation. 'When are you going to come clean with me, Bannerman?'

'All in good time, Platt.' He paused. 'Did you make your second edition?'

Platt's lips tightened. 'Yes, I made it. But the paper was fifteen minutes late going to press and I got a right roasting.' Bannerman couldn't resist a smile, which only annoyed Platt further. The old reporter glanced again at the bottle. 'How about a drink, Bannerman? You owe me that much at least. Take the chill out of my bones.'

Bannerman said, 'Alcohol accelerates loss of body heat. Help yourself.'

'Glasses?'

'In the kitchen.'

When it became clear that Bannerman wasn't going to go and get them, Platt heaved himself reluctantly out of his chair and went in search of them himself.

Bannerman listened to the sound of Platt clattering noisily in the kitchen and remembered encountering him for the first time all those years before at the weekly paper where he had got his first job.

Platt had been there for years. He knew it all, or thought he did, and breathed whisky and contempt on a succession of keen young news-hounds passing through on their way to better things. He had been a lonely individual even then. A widower. Embittered by all the opportunities in life that had passed him by. At first he had poured his scorn on this new-comer too, but as he had come to recognize that Bannerman was different, and set on a career trajectory that would leave Platt wallowing in his wake, he had done everything he could to make life even more difficult.

Bannerman had hated him for it. And wasn't it Platt who had mixed things for him with the editor over the business of the girl from telesales? Wasn't it Platt who had taken such delight in his hurt, and set off a whispering campaign among his colleagues? Bannerman had always suspected that Platt might even have been responsible for him losing his job. Anger at that had lived in him for a long time afterwards. Only the passing of the years had diminished the humiliation of that time before finally dispatching Platt to the mists of a painful and half-forgotten past.

And now, all these years later, here they both were, reluc-tant collaborators on a murder case in a cold winter city far from home. Bannerman had no idea what ebbs of fortune had brought Platt to his exile in Brussels, still chasing the dreams that had escaped him in his youth, but his antipathy towards the man remained undiminished.

Platt came out of the kitchen with two cups. 'I can't find

any glasses.' He set them down on the coffee table, opened the bottle of malt and poured two large measures. Clutching his own cup he dropped back into his seat and raised it towards Bannerman. 'Cheers.'

How he detested Bannerman. His success, his arrogance, his self-assurance. He took a gulp of the smooth malt and grimaced as he felt the first twinges of pain in his stomach. Bannerman was watching him.

'Ulcer,' he said. 'First mouthful always gets me that way.' *Still,* he thought with some comfort, *there are one or two things that I know about you.* He grinned. 'Where should I begin?'

'At the beginning.'

Platt shifted in his chair and took another gulp of whisky. 'René Jansen might well be the richest man in Belgium. His pedigree's spotless. He comes from one of the oldest and most influential Flemish families in the country. An only child. Wealth and privilege lavished freely upon his fair head. Education, breeding, money – he's got the lot. When his father died he inherited the Jansen empire. But he didn't just sit back and enjoy it, he built on it, made it more than it ever was when his father was alive. He's into everything. Owns the biggest private aerospace concern in Europe, supplying not only the bulk of the fleet for the Belgian airforce and the national airline, but also for half the major airlines in the world – and exclusively to a number of smaller Third World airlines.

'He's also into construction. His companies are almost single-handedly rebuilding Brussels and some of the bigger provincial towns. Nearly half of that is on government contracts, the other half in the private sector. Those are the two biggies. But he's got fingers in lots of other pies. Property, department stores. He even owns a couple of provincial newspapers. He's got interests in a shipping line and owns a brewery.'

Bannerman knew now why the name Jansen had seemed familiar. He was one of that two per cent who own ninety-five per cent of the world's wealth. Men who exist in billionaire bubbles, lavishing themselves with private jets, executive suites and country estates. Their pictures appear on the covers of fashionable magazines, dining with Royalty, on safari with film stars. They are never seen without a beautiful woman at their side. Jansen's was the kind of lifestyle to which Robert Gryffe had aspired.

'How does he structure his companies?'

Platt filled his cup again. He offered the bottle across the table but Bannerman shook his head. 'Everything comes under the umbrella of the parent company, I.V. Internationale, which is headquartered in the Boulevard Bischoffsheim.' Platt paused. 'If you're trying to find skeletons in his cupboard you'll be hard-pushed. It's been tried before. Everything's above board. All I.V.'s activities are on record and can be checked. Business registration in this country is as accessible as it is in the UK. Companies are registered at the Tribunal de Commerce and there is one of those in every commercial court in the country. They are all linked to a central register held here in Brussels by the Ministry of the Middle Classes. And you or I or anyone can examine that register. You can find out the names of a company's directors, its capital holdings, just as easily as you can obtain the same information at Companies House in London or Edinburgh.'

'Financial state? Shareholders?'

Platt shook his head. 'Companies are not required to divulge that information. But that's hardly important, is it?'

Bannerman shrugged. 'We'll see. Go on.'

Platt drained his second cup. A little colour had returned to his cheeks. 'He's not married, he's in his late forties and lives with his mother in a vast mansion in its own estate just outside Brussels. He's got no overt political affiliations, although it's said he contributes funds. Generally he keeps a pretty low profile, but he's widely known as a bit of a philanthropist. Apparently he contributes large sums every year to worthy causes. But his private life is private.'

Bannerman frowned. It was not necessarily what he had been expecting. The philanthropic billionaire who steers clear of public politics and jealously guards his spotless reputation by keeping it out of the glare of publicity. All very virtuous. And yet this same man had sent a hoodlum to break into the *Post*'s office in the IPC building and steal an innocuous folder of newspaper cuttings. He checked the time and then drained his cup quickly. 'And Lapointe? Make it quick. I have to go.'

Platt was in no hurry, remembering how Bannerman had made him late for his deadline that morning. He filled his cup for the third time and sank back again in his chair. 'Lapointe,' he said at length, 'is the legal brain behind I.V. Internationale. He's a short, stout man in his middle fifties. Very grey and very proper. Wears neatly tailored suits and carries his wealth discreetly. Old-fashioned, conservative. A widower with one grown-up daughter. Divorced, I believe. He began his career in criminal law and went on to specialize in company and commercial law. He worked for Jansen's father before he died and has been associated with the family for many years. He's not a man in the public eye in any way, but a key figure in the company.' Platt sipped his whisky. 'And that's about it. Although perhaps a little surprisingly he's a Walloon, a French-speaker.'

Bannerman stood up suddenly and Platt blinked at him. 'What is it?'

'I've got to go. You can let yourself out.' He lifted his coat and headed out into the darkness of the hall.

Platt heard the front door closing, and a few minutes later Bannerman's car coughing to life in the street below. He smiled, satisfied with his day. And the whisky was having its effect. He would show them! Especially Bannerman. His eyes wandered towards the Brueghel snow scene, reminding him of how it was outside. That, and the dull ache of his ulcer, were the only things that troubled him now. He took a tablet from his pocket, crunched it between bad teeth, and prepared to pour himself another whisky to wash away the taste.

II

The Palais de Justice took on a sinister air at night. During the day it was one of those vast blackened buildings whose pillars and ornate façades seem somehow eternal, if now a little shabby. Odd pieces of scaffolding had been erected by artisans on a crusade to restore its original dignity with limited civic funds.

Through a small window Bannerman saw a night watchman pouring himself coffee from a flask at a desk pushed against the wall of a tiny office. Behind him a stove glowed brightly and warm yellow light fell out across the snow.

The Place Poelaert was deserted. Night traffic rumbled past in the Boulevard de Waterloo two hundred metres distant. At the far side, where Bannerman waited, snow crusted along the top of a high wall beyond which the city shimmered below him in the cold. A floodlit church, steeply sloping snow-covered roofs. The tail lights of traffic on the boulevards. And in the misted distance, the *Martini* neon on the Manhattan Centre at the Place Rogier.

Footsteps on cobbles echoed in the silence, coming from the shadowed lee of the courthouse where the snow had not fallen. Bannerman turned to see the tall, slightly stooped figure of du Maurier step from the shadows and into the feeble light of the streetlamps. He seemed older, his coat hanging loose on his lean frame. A cigarette glowed at one corner of his mouth and his breath billowed around his head like smoke in the cold.

His hat, tilted forward, threw a shadow over the top half of his face. Hands pushed into his pockets, he walked slowly to the wall, brushed away the crusting of snow and leaned on it to stare out across the city. Bannerman smelled drink on his breath.

Without looking at him du Maurier said, 'Five years ago I was up for promotion. Principal Commissaire. One of my contemporaries, a Fleming, got the job.' He paused. 'You see, Monsieur, this great country of ours is really an uneasy alliance of two very different cultures. Two countries, you might say. The Flemings in the north and the Walloons in the south. The language of the north is Flemish and in the south it is French. But our differences go much deeper than language. They are cultural, historical. Brussels may have been crowned the new political capital of Europe. A great cosmopolitan city.' He snorted his derision. 'But it is pure veneer, Monsieur Bannerman. All the old hatreds, all the old prejudices fester still beneath the surface. They say that Belgium is bilingual. It is not true. Outside of Brussels, where we all pretend, we are a nation of two one-language communities. The language and culture of north and south prevail over the nation. It is expected. In the schoolroom, in the boardroom, the officers' mess, the law courts, the tax office, the Church.' He lit a fresh cigarette from his old one and seemed lost in thought. Bannerman shuffled impatiently, but said nothing.

'It was my misfortune to reach the point of promotion at a time when the balance of power was shifting. For years

French-speakers held sway. It was they who had power and influence in government and all its institutions. Then a conscious political decision was taken to reverse the tide, to bring about what they called balance. It was the turn of the Flemings.' His mouth tightened. 'Ironically I had always been opposed to discrimination against the Flemings. I had always believed that a man should be judged on his abilities. But you see, I lost my chance because I spoke French at a time when the political climate was against me. Not because I didn't merit the job.' He turned to Bannerman. 'Why should I feel any allegiance to such a system?'

Bannerman wondered how many absinthes the policeman had consumed. He said, 'You didn't have me meet you here in the middle of the night to complain about political discrimination, I hope.'

Du Maurier pursed his lips. 'No-o.' He stretched the word out thoughtfully and then lowered his head. 'I had information for you.'

Bannerman's breath billowed into the night air. 'But now you're having second thoughts.'

The Inspector looked up and searched Bannerman's face. 'What makes you say that?'

'Because you've been all fired up since they passed you over for promotion, and when the politicians descended to take away your murders at the Rue de Pavie you saw your chance to hit back. You saw that they were vulnerable. Now you're not so sure if you're doing the right thing.'

Du Maurier wished he had not drunk so much, for his head was fuzzy and he found it difficult to think clearly. He felt foolish for having unburdened himself like this to the Scotsman. He had only made himself vulnerable.

Bannerman said, 'The trouble is, you've already committed yourself. There's no going back now, Inspector. I could blow the lid on our little tête-à-têtes any time I choose.'

The years sat heavily on du Maurier's bony shoulders and he seemed to age twenty years. 'And would you?'

Bannerman let that hang for several long moments. 'No.'

Du Maurier stared at him. 'Why not?'

Bannerman shrugged. 'No self-respecting journalist would ever reveal his sources.' Then he said, 'So what you want to say to me tonight is that you've changed your mind? Is that it? That you no longer feel able to pass me information from the inside?' Du Maurier nodded.

Both men stood in silence then, one staring out over the city, the other with his back to the wall staring across the darkness of the cobbled square. Neither spoke for several minutes. Finally Bannerman said, 'What *was* the information you had?'

Du Maurier turned his head slowly. '*Mon Dieu!* You really expect me to tell you now?'

'I believe in what I'm doing, Inspector.'

The other man shook his head. 'I wish I had that kind of belief in anything any more.' He closed his eyes and hesitated for several long seconds before drawing a folded sheet of notepaper from his coat pocket and pushing it at Bannerman.

Bannerman opened it up and squinted at the paper in the bad light. There was an address written across it in a tight, neat hand. 'That's the address linked to the phone number you gave me. A country house in West Flanders near Torhout, about seventeen kilometres south-west of Bruges. Monsieur Gryffe, it seems, had been renting it for about two years. The property is owned by a Brussels-registered company, a subsidiary of I.V. Internationale.' There was irony in his smile.

Bannerman said, 'Jansen's outfit.'

'Perhaps you were right after all, Monsieur.'

Bannerman's fingers tightened on the slip of paper. No matter how tenuous, it was the first real lead to emerge from this whole bloody mess.

Du Maurier said, 'What will you do?'

Bannerman let his head fall back so that he was staring up into the falling snow, big flakes catching cold light. 'I shall go to Flanders.' Pause. 'And you? What will you do?'

Du Maurier surveyed the chewed wet end of his cigarette. 'I don't know,' he said. 'I will need to think about that.' He threw the cigarette over the wall. 'Goodnight, Monsieur.' And he turned away to cross the cobbles and start down the narrow steps to the Rue des Minimes below.

Bannerman watched him disappear into the shadows before pushing himself away from the wall. He stood for a moment, lost in thought, then set off across the Place Poelaert.

CHAPTER TWENTY-TWO

I

The first grey light of dawn hung in the sky. In the waiting room the electric light burned white and hard. Slatted benches were cold and uncomfortable. The sounds of the train station drifted in the open door with the fog that smothered the city. An elderly couple sat close and quiet, staring bleakly through the windows at porters passing with their trolleys of luggage and mail. Occasionally they exchanged a word or two in whispers. There was no reason for anyone to speak in whispers, but a voice more raised would have seemed somehow inappropriate.

A plump businessman, prosperous in his navy coat, camel scarf and dark homburg hat, stood puffing impatiently on a long cigar. He kept wiping the window where it was misting and staring down the line for signs of the train. It was not due for another five minutes. His premature impatience was annoying Bannerman.

The journalist's eyes were gritty and stinging from lack of

sleep. His mood brittle. He was tense without knowing quite why. The weather had changed overnight, the snow turning to rain, and a fine drizzle was drifting down the tracks towards the platforms that stretched away on either side. The damp seeped into everything, chill and raw.

Bannerman had risen early, the sound of his alarm drilling into a confused dream that dispersed with waking consciousness. The windows of the bedroom were milky white with condensation, and outside it had still been dark. In the living room the smell of stale smoke and alcohol hung in the air, the bottle of malt standing empty on the table like a reproach. The first cup of coffee had been good.

He shoved a few items into a holdall to see him through, in case he had to stay overnight. When he was in the hall the phone began to ring. He frowned and checked the time. Just after seven. He hesitated briefly before deciding not to answer. It was still ringing as his footsteps echoed down the stairwell. Had he taken the call he would not have been sitting in this station waiting room.

More than a dozen people stood now on the platform below the mist that eddied in the lamplight. It was still dark, despite the traces of light in the the sky. A tall man with short, sandy hair stooped to peer into the waiting room. His eyes lighted on Bannerman for a second and he turned away quickly as the reporter became aware of him. The lights of the train came out of the blackness of the tunnel beyond the station, and with a clatter and grinding of metal on metal, it came to a halt along the length of the platform. Doors were flung open and people who had travelled through the night from Germany stepped down pulling suitcases behind them.

Bannerman left the waiting room, pushing past several people on the platform, and climbed up into the train. At the far end of the corridor he caught sight of the man with the sandy hair. He was carrying a polished wooden case. Bannerman slid open the door of an empty compartment and slipped into its welcome warmth. He threw his holdall into the overhead rack and took a seat by the window with his back to the engine. He watched figures pass in the corridor. The elderly couple who had been in the waiting room, a thin man in a dark suit with a Gauloise clamped between his lips and a briefcase under his arm. They all passed. There was no sign of the man with the sandy hair. Bannerman wondered why he had expected to see him, anticipating that he might even step into the same compartment. Something about his rabbit eyes, perhaps, or the way he'd looked at Bannerman through the window in the waiting room.

The raised voice of the platform guard sounded in the dark, and then the slamming of doors. A whistle breathed hoarsely into the morning and with a slight groan the train began dragging itself out of the station, gathering speed, wheels clattering across a confluence of rails at the junction.

II

The early afternoon air was clear and bright, sunlight lying in patches on snow that stretched away across the flatness of West Flanders. The distance was broken only by the occasional hedge or row of poplars. The mist had lifted and the heavy grey of the sky was clearing to reveal a pale blue behind it. The road was wet and black, a dirty slush piled along its verges where it had been thrown up by the wheels of cars. The snow was still wet, but if the sky continued to clear then it would freeze again tonight.

A deep silence lay across the land. Only the birds could be heard greeting the return of the sun. The road was deserted, stretching emptily away towards a belt of trees. Beyond them the spire of a village church rose sharply against the clearing sky. Bannerman had walked nearly two kilometres from where the Bruges–Kortrijk bus had dropped him on the main road. In that time he had not seen a single vehicle or a single human being. The small town of Torhout lay somewhere to the east, but whatever town or village lay beyond the belt of trees, it was not important enough to appear on the Michelin map.

The house was set on its own, surrounded by a few gnarled trees, leafless and black, their branches crusted with white. The track that led off the road across half a kilometre of open field to the house was obliterated by snow. Only two crooked wooden gateposts gave clues to its existence. A crow sat one-legged on the faraway post, grooming black feathers beneath its wings. It stopped and watched suspiciously as Bannerman approached. It had seen him coming for some time, waiting until he was within a few metres before taking clumsily to the air with a loud caw-cawing. Somewhere across the fields another crow answered its call, and then silence descended again.

Bannerman paused for a moment before turning on to the track and ploughing through snow that had drifted two to three feet deep along the ridge. It took him nearly ten minutes to reach the house. It was a long, narrow building with a steeply sloped red-tiled roof. A greying whitewash flaked off the walls and the green of the shutters had faded and cracked. A rusted rone pipe had stained the wall blood-red down one side where it ran from the guttering. It was an old house, a survivor of the last war, and it bore the scars of neglect.

Against the north wall the snow had drifted several feet deep, and on the protected south side weeds poked up through the patchy skin of snow that covered the gravel path. In summer it would be a fine place to live. Bannerman stood staring up at it, listening to the quiet. Sunlight fell at an oblique angle through the trees, dappling the south wall. All the shutters were closed tight and the storm doors locked.

He walked around the house trying each of the shutters in turn. At the back there was a yard and a crop of crumbling outbuildings. A slab of snow slid from the glistening tiles on the roof and fell with a thud behind him. The stab of fright that shot through him made him conscious for the first time of a growing uneasiness. He cast his eyes over the surrounding countryside, looking – for what? He didn't know. There was nothing to be seen. Not a movement, not a sound. And yet he had the strangest sensation of eyes upon him. Watching him. It was foolish, he knew. He was just tired.

He went around to the south side. Here the windows were set just above head height, and he saw that the shutters on the first of them were not properly closed. Where one half met the other the wood was splintered and broken. He reached up and pulled them open. The steel-framed windows behind them were opened inwards, the glass on one side broken, jagged shards still caught in the frame. Bannerman felt a rush of both excitement and disappointment. Someone had been here before him, though not within the last twelve hours. For there were no tracks in the snow, and it had stopped snowing the night before.

He stepped back, and on the wall below the window he saw the marks left by the intruder's boots where they had sought a grip to push him up and into the house. Again he turned and looked out across the fields. Still nothing stirred. He threw his holdall into the house, took another two or three steps back and then ran at the window, jumping to get his hands up over the sill. His soles scraped on the wall below him as he pulled himself up, first straddling the window ledge and then dropping down into the semi-darkness. He crouched for a while, waiting for his eyes to grow accustomed to the gloom.

The room took shape around him. A small bedroom, sparsely

furnished. A bed, a dresser and a short bedside table with a lamp. The sheets had been torn from the bed and discarded on the floor. The pillows and mattresses had been cut open and searched. Horsehair and down lay in clumps all around the bed. The drawers had been pulled from the dresser and piled untidily on top. Bannerman, still squatting on the floor below the window, accepted even then that his trip to Flanders had been a waste of time. Gryffe's country house had been thoroughly searched. He would find nothing here. He could not even tell when this search had taken place. It might have been yesterday, a week ago, or even a month before Gryffe was murdered. But no! He revised that thought. The broken wood on the shutters was too fresh. Within the last couple of days perhaps.

He stood up, laden with disappointment, and the glass from the broken pane crunched on the floor beneath his feet. He picked his way across the room and out into the darkness of a short hallway. He fumbled along the wall until he found a light switch. Nothing. The power must be off at the mains. He moved carefully across the hall and opened another door.

Tiny chinks of sunlight leaked around the edges of the windows where the shutters fitted badly. But they shed enough light to see that this was a big room, windows on two walls. There was a sofa, a working desk, several wall cabinets, bookcases, a coffee table. Two large armchairs and an old wooden rocker stood arranged around a huge open fireplace. The debris of the search was here too. Papers and books, whole drawers and their contents cast carelessly across the floor. Bannerman opened one of the front windows, unhooked the shutters and pushed them out.

Sunshine streamed in and a rush of fresh, cold air invaded the smell of dust and damp that pervaded the house. A few papers stirred in the breeze. Bannerman stared thoughtfully across the fields towards the road. What had they been after? Had they found it? Who were *they*? He turned and walked across the room to sit in the rocker. It creaked as he pushed it gently back and forth, and he let his head fall back on the wooden rest. This was a dead end. He could see no way past it. He would seek interviews with Jansen and Lapointe. But even if they would see him, what would they tell him? That they knew nothing, of course. He had given Tait the ammunition he needed to get rid of him, and without a story he had no bargaining power. The future lay ahead like a desert. The words of the drunken Palin came back to him like a bitter reproach. *Someday even bastards like you get put out to grass.*

Bannerman sighed and leaned forward on his elbows. The contents of a wicker wastebasket were strewn across the stone slabs of the hearth. Even it had been searched. Bannerman bent down to pick up a crumpled envelope, smoothing it out to look inside. Empty. The stamp was Swiss, the postmark December. He was about to throw it away when he noticed the address. P.O. BOX 139, BUREAU DE POSTE, PLACE DE LA MONNAIE, BRUXELLES. Bannerman frowned. It had almost slipped his notice and its significance did not immediately dawn on him.

He stared at it for some time before crouching down to search for more envelopes. He found several. All but two were addressed to Gryffe at his London home. The others were addressed to the same PO box number in Brussels. He got up and started looking around the room for more. Within a few minutes he had found seven. All empty. He clutched them in his hand and cursed softly. So Gryffe had been receiving letters which he picked up from a PO box in Brussels. Private correspondence that he didn't want anyone to know about.

Bannerman dropped the envelopes on the floor. Whoever had gone through the dead man's papers had been careful to remove all his letters. But he had overlooked the tell-tale address on the envelopes. If Gryffe had kept a private PO box then he would almost certainly have had a *poste restante* card. It was just possible that the intruder might have overlooked that too, if it was here. But it had to be. For surely if it had been among his personal possessions in Brussels, du Maurier would have told him.

It did not occur to him until after nearly an hour of fruitless searching among the chaos in the house that it might be among Gryffe's things in London. The thought stopped him as suddenly and effectively as if he had walked into a stone wall. He righted the upturned desk chair and slumped into it, hot and frustrated. Through the open window he saw that the sun had become a big red globe hanging over the distant horizon. The room had sunk into a deep pink gloom. He felt drained and disappointed. The card would have given him access to the box. It was just possible that there would still be mail there for Gryffe that had never been collected.

The drawers down either side of the desk had been pulled out and then not replaced. They lay about the floor where they had been dropped or thrown. Instinctively Bannerman felt under the leaf of the table and found the small round knob of the tray drawer that slides in and out above the top drawer of most office desks. He pulled it out. The card lay in the tray section among a scattering of paper clips and pins. Carefully, Bannerman lifted it out and examined it before slipping it into his jacket pocket and allowing himself a tiny smile. 'Got you,' he said softly, and the whisper seemed thunderous in the still of the room.

He leaned back in the chair then and everything slowed. His thinking, his breathing, even time itself. It would have been impossible to say how long he sat there, allowing time to wash over him.

He saw a face peering through a misted waiting-room window. A little girl was shouting, but there were no words. She ran towards him, arms outstretched, but she seemed to go through him and was gone. A hand wiped away the mist from the other side of the window and another face appeared. Bannerman tried to see it. There were features: eyes, a nose, a mouth. They were there, and yet he could not discern the face itself.

He awoke with a start and blinked in the darkness, momentarily confused and a little frightened, until he remembered where he was. He was cold. The room was like ice. Moonlight slanted through the window he had opened. He stood up and found his legs and arms stiff with the cold. He picked up his holdall and stumbled across the room in the darkness to find the door. He crossed the hall and returned to the bedroom he had first entered through the window. Here the moon rising in the south flooded the room with a light that reflected no colour and threw deep shadows across the floor. The sky was a chaos of stars, and frost was already glistening on the snow.

Bannerman threw his bag out of the window and then pulled himself up on to the sill. A small spot of red light fluttered momentarily on the wood of the architrave beside his head. As he saw it, the architrave split and threw jagged splinters into his face. The crack of a rifle shot echoed away into the night. An owl in a tree just outside the window screeched and flapped off into the dark. For just a moment Bannerman was confused. He drew his hand from his face and saw his fingers running with blood. He had no time to register that someone had just shot at him before he felt another bullet whistle past, no more than two inches from his left cheek, to smash into the plaster of the wall at the far side of the room. The gap between the two shots might only have been seconds, but it felt like hours. It was the full realization that came with the second shot that brought the fear. He recoiled instinctively and fell backwards from the sill.

He landed clumsily in the darkness and felt the broken glass from the window cut through his trousers and into his right knee. He rolled clear of it and lay on his back on the floor, listening to his breath coming hard and fast. And there, on the wall, was the same spot of red light, no bigger than a halfpenny. It moved slowly along the broken plaster then vanished. Some kind of infrared sighting device, reinforcing for Bannerman the intent of someone somewhere set on killing him.

A jumble of thoughts tumbled through his mind. Those that stuck brought no comfort. They were miles from the nearest village. There was no one to hear the shots. He was on his own.

He turned over and scrambled to his feet, keeping in the shaded part of the room. His hands were shaking, but he felt no pain from his injured face and leg. He searched about the room for something he could hold up at the window. A pillow lay at his feet. It had been cut open and some of its down scattered across the floor. The sniper must have chosen a position that gave him maximum coverage, the south, west and east sides of the house. The north side had to be blind.

Bannerman thought it out carefully, but he could not bring himself to move. He remained crouched for fifteen, twenty, thirty minutes until his teeth began chattering with cold and fear. The perspiration formed like ice on his face. Maybe he could sweat it out until daylight. What was the bastard waiting for? In the silence a twig snapped. It didn't seem far off. Bannerman's nerve broke. The yell ripped out from his throat as he threw the pillow up at the window. Almost immediately the rifle cracked in the moonlight beyond and the pillow was flung back in a cloud of feathers. The room seemed filled with them. Bannerman's indecision was stultifying. Surely he would be safer to hold out. His chances of success in trying to escape across the snow seemed less than remote. And yet he was inexorably drawn to that alternative.

But the luxury of choice was quickly gone. The first thing he heard was movement in the snow outside, and a small, dark object hurtled through the window and into the room. It clattered across the floor and immediately began issuing a thick vapour that spread quickly in the stillness. Bannerman coughed, tears springing to his eyes as the stink and acrid vapour stung his nostrils and burned his throat. He made a lunge for the door, pulled it open, and stumbled blindly across the hall and into the room opposite.

There was still a little light here from the window he had left open and the air was fresh and cold. He tripped as he made for the other wall and struck his face on the edge of the desk. The pain filled his head, but the instinct to get out was stronger. He pulled himself up and reached the far wall. His fingers fumbled infuriatingly with the window catch. It seemed to him that he was taking hours to unsnib it and he felt dizziness overtake him. He took long deep breaths to clear his head.

Finally the window pulled open and he unhooked the shutters to push them out. As he pulled himself up so that he filled the frame it struck him, with a kind of gripping horror that for a second almost paralysed him, that there might be more than one shooter out there. That any moment a man lying in wait to cover the north side of the house would gently squeeze a trigger and snuff him out with a single simple shot. He almost felt it. But it did not come, and he jumped down into the cold and was almost buried in the snow that had drifted against the wall.

For several seconds he floundered in it before staggering clear of its burning cold and sprinting towards the fence that bounded the house. He felt the friction of icy air on his skin and was aware of fragments of snow flying from his coat as he ran, like sparks in the night. Most of all he felt the crushing vulnerability of being out in the open.

The dizziness he had shaken off a few moments earlier was returning. He was over the fence now and running across the field as fast as the foot-and-a-half of snow would allow. All the time he was waiting for the bullet in his back. Surely he would fall into the sights of his assailant at any time. He glanced back. He had covered several hundred metres and there was no sign of movement behind him. Ahead, maybe a kilometre or more distant, lay the dark belt of trees he had seen earlier in the day. At least they would provide some kind of cover. And beyond the trees, he knew, there was a village. He had seen the spire.

But already his strength was waning. The dizziness was intensifying. Perhaps from the gas he had inhaled. Was the snow getting deeper, or was it just that he found it harder to drag his feet through it? He was no longer cold, but burning hot, his face wet and glistening with sweat. And still he pushed on as hard as he could. He might have been running for ever. His lungs and throat on fire, tears streaming from his eyes.

A drystone wall, three or four feet high, divided the fields ahead of him. Beyond that lay another three hundred metres before he would reach the comparative safety of the trees. The thought was fatal. He slowed to a stagger. About a metre in front of him, fractionally to his right, the red spot appeared as if by magic and began searching the ground. It was strangely elongated. A small plume of snow lifted up from the rest. The sound of the gun followed a fraction of a second after. The red spot zigzagged ahead of him and the second bullet struck the stone of the wall, throwing off splinters in the moonlight. Again the now familiar crack of the rifle.

He almost fell into the wall, scraping knuckles and tearing fingernails in his eagerness to be over it. A crippling numbness overtook him as he sprawled in the snow on the far side. His heart hammered painfully against his ribs, each breath tearing at the next as his body fought to recover the oxygen it had burned in flight.

He had no idea how long he lay like this, and he was not sure he cared any longer. He was not hot any more. The cold had crept back. It was wrapping itself around him in a welcome mist of growing unconsciousness. Somewhere in his head a voice was screaming its warning. *Don't let it take you! Keep going, keep going! Don't succumb to it, it'll kill you!* It took a supreme effort of will for him to roll over and get up on to all fours. He blinked furiously to stop his eyes from closing on him. The lids felt heavy, as though weighted by lead. His fingers found the wall and he pulled himself up so that he was looking back the way he had come. He could see his tracks in the snow as clear as day. He followed their line back several hundred metres until his eyes fell on the dark shape of a man walking towards him. The silhouette stood out vividly against a rich red glow in the sky behind it.

For some seconds Bannerman was confused. The sun had set some time ago. He wiped the back of his hand across his eyes and saw that the house was ablaze. Flames licking fifty feet into the air. Through the glow he could see the black, crumbling frame of the building. Bannerman refocused on his assassin. He was tall and lean and wore a heavy jacket over jeans and thick boots. His rifle was held across his chest and he was moving relentlessly closer. But he was still just a shadow, a shape in the night. He had no face that Bannerman could see. And Bannerman felt hope and life slipping away.

He slid back down behind the wall and knew that he could not last much longer in the open. He had expended all his reserves and now, if this man with the gun did not finish him off, the cold and the open would. 'Fuck you!' he shouted defiantly at the night. But his voice sounded feeble. *Keep going, keep going*, the other voice in his head was screaming. He heard himself sobbing, but he was on his feet again, though he was not sure how, and staggering towards the trees.

Afterwards, there was no recollection of how he covered the ground between the wall and the trees. He was certain there'd been no further shots. All he knew was that overhead the protective boughs of many trees spread themselves between him and the stars. He threw his arms around a trunk, the bark scraping his cheek. His legs were liquid. Looking back he could see the man with the rifle no more than twenty metres away, coming through the line of the trees. Bannerman pushed himself off and felt the ground falling away beneath him. He fell for what seemed like an age, down and down until suddenly all his senses became sharply focused by the ice-cold water that soaked his clothes and burned his flesh. He heard the sound of running water and felt it wash over him. Chunks of snow and stone were rattling down the bank after him. Oh, how easy now just to slip off into blessed unconsciousness. But the shock of the water had brought back some of his awareness, as well as his determination to keep going.

His fingers scrabbled in the dirt until he found a hold, and he pulled himself clear of the water and clung to the bank. He had never realized how quickly the cold could steal away your will to live.

A sudden roar filled Bannerman's ears. For a second the night seemed alive with fire. Then almost as quickly it was over, a softness of earth showering down. The silence that followed was extraordinary. It was the last thing he would later recall with any great clarity. He had no memory at all of how he clawed his way to the top of the bank, and only a broken recollection of seeing the crater among the tree trunks. A whole tree half torn up by its roots. Scorch marks on the surrounding trunks. The remains of the man with the rifle, a white face, wide eyes, sandy hair matted with blood – the rest barely identifiable as human. And all he could remember of the next minutes was the urge to run, and keep running. He had not understood then, or now, what had happened. All he could hear was the voice in his head, glancing back at the trees behind him, the flames of the burned-out house dying in the distance, the sound of his feet dragging through the snow. The fence. The road. And then the lights that came out of a darkness that fell on him like a shroud, stealing him away, at last, into a black unconsciousness.

III

Light came slowly into his world of darkness. But just before light came sound. Distant at first, then jumbled, unrecognizable. Until gradually it grew clearer. Feet moving across wooden floorboards, the rustle of cloth on cloth, a woman's voice. Words he could not understand. As awareness increased he began to register smells, odours evocative of distant memories. The musk of a woman's perfume, the smell of hot food, cigarette smoke.

He opened his eyes and light flooded his head in a startling, swimming brightness. He screwed them tight shut and then eased them open more slowly. Where was he? He felt warm and stiff, and all around a delicious softness caressed his skin. Above him he saw a white plaster ceiling supported by black painted beams. A woman's face peered down at him and smiled. It was a round, pleasant face. She spoke to him, but he could not understand. Her head turned away and she spoke to someone else that he could not see. Consciousness had fully returned now, and with it came a pounding pain in his head. His body ached and he found it almost impossible to move.

With a great effort he pulled himself up on his elbows to lower his horizon. Beyond the end of the bed du Maurier sat on a hard-backed wooden chair, watching him. He wore the same hat and coat as when he'd last seen him, the same weariness etched deeply in the lines of his face. His dark eyes stared sadly back at Bannerman.

The woman bent over Bannerman, blocking the policeman from view, and she plumped the pillow behind his back so that he was supported to sit half upright in the bed. Then she had a bowl of hot soup at his lips. He accepted it gratefully and took rapid gulps of the hot, thick liquid, allowing a little of it to spill from the corners of his mouth in his haste. It tasted good in a way that nothing had ever tasted before. It filled him with a core of warmth that seemed to radiate outwards to reach every part of him. He finished it and let the bowl drop away from his mouth, suddenly self-conscious of the eyes that were on him. And with that self-consciousness came memory, of the events of . . . he knew not how long ago. The red dot, the choking gas in the moonlit bedroom, the agonizing chase across the snowy wastes, the remains of the man in the crater.

The rest was hazy. Staggering through the snow, the lights on the road. He held out the bowl and the woman took it.

'Thank you,' he said.

She was a plain, plump woman in her middle forties, long thick hair drawn back and held with an elastic band. She smiled.

'Are you strong enough to talk?' du Maurier said. Bannerman glanced at him and nodded. The Inspector spoke briefly to the woman, whose face clouded. There was a terse exchange between them which du Maurier cut short with an authority Bannerman had not seen in him before. The woman stopped mid-sentence, colour rising on her cheeks, and left the room without another word. Silence fell in her wake.

This was not a big room. Bare floorboards covered by a small square of rug. Rough plaster walls painted white. The old brass bedstead in which Bannerman lay was pushed against the wall opposite the window. A big wardrobe dominated the room. A dresser and two chairs took up the remaining floor space. The light-bulb dangling from the ceiling was unshaded and threw its unrelenting light into every corner. Du Maurier took off his hat and leaned forward. Elbows on knees, he ran the rim of the hat round and round between his fingers.

'So,' he said, 'I've driven all the way from Brussels and I've sat up most of the night.'

'I didn't know you cared.'

Du Maurier glared at him. 'If I had not come you might have been in a great deal of trouble. I want to know what happened.'

'And if I don't tell you . . .?'

'You could still be in a great deal of trouble.'

Bannerman considered this. His head hurt, his body ached. He didn't have the strength to fight. So he told du Maurier exactly what had happened, or as much of it as he could remember. Leaving out only his discovery of the PO box in Brussels and Gryffe's *poste restante* card. Somehow, in the telling, that seemed like such an obvious hole. But du Maurier appeared oblivious. He sat listening, his face blank.

'I don't know what happened to the shooter,' Bannerman said. 'There was an explosion. I have no idea why, but there was not much left of him.'

The Inspector nodded. 'I've seen his remains for myself. You were very lucky, Monsieur. You were saved by a land-mine. The woods are riddled with them, a legacy of the last war. There are warning signs every hundred metres or so. It is quite common in this part of Flanders.' Bannerman shivered suddenly as though someone had walked over his grave. Du Maurier sat back now, his eyes fixed on Bannerman, fingers still turning the rim of his hat. 'The red spot you saw was a laser beam. These things can pinpoint a target at over one thousand metres. A new American rifle, the B120. The high-powered laser sight enables the marksman to line it up on any target. Even I couldn't miss.'

Bannerman frowned. 'But *he* did.'

'Yes, he did.' The policeman paused and placed his hat carefully on his thighs. 'Let me tell you something, Monsieur

Bannerman. The B120 is a highly specialized weapon. There are very few of them around. To be in possession of one you'd have to be somebody pretty . . . special.'

Bannerman considered the implications. And du Maurier's use of vocabulary. 'Like . . . Special Forces, you mean?'

Du Maurier shrugged. He was not going to commit himself. 'Let's just say a professional marksman.'

Bannerman said, 'So he wasn't trying to kill me.'

Du Maurier inclined his head in silent acquiescence.

'Well it sure as hell didn't seem like it at the time. What about the gas?'

'Tear gas, probably. Or something a little more toxic. But you were never in danger, Monsieur Bannerman. He left you a way out and you took it. Though neither you nor he could have foreseen how it would all end.' He took a pack of cigarettes from his pocket and lit one. 'How long was it since you had eaten?'

'I had a coffee and croissant at the station before I caught the train.'

'And nothing after that?'

Bannerman shook his head.

'So you hadn't eaten all day. You spent several hours in a freezing-cold house. You had lacerations to your face and leg. You inhaled a toxic or semi-toxic gas, then ran nearly two kilometres in sub-zero temperatures before falling into a half-frozen stream. You must have the constitution of an ox, Monsieur!'

Bannerman raised a wry eyebrow. 'They breed us tough in Scotland.'

Du Maurier was unimpressed. He blew smoke at the naked bulb and watched how it clouded the light. 'When the Police Communale found you in the road you were very nearly dead. They got fluids into you last night and a doctor from Torhout dressed your wounds. His recommendation is that you remain in bed for two or three days.'

Bannerman glanced at the window. There was no sign of light beyond the shutters. 'What time is it?'

Du Maurier glanced at his watch. 'Just after eight. It should be getting light soon.'

'Where are we?'

'A small auberge in the village of Smoelaert. Just a few kilometres from Monsieur Gryffe's house – or what's left of it.'

'Are you going back to Brussels?'

'In an hour or so. I have to square things first with the local police.'

'Will you give me a lift back?'

Du Maurier shook his head. 'Monsieur, you are in no condition . . .'

But Bannerman was dogged. 'Will you give me a lift?'

The Inspector sighed. 'If you insist.'

'I do.'

They fell silent then, and there was not a sound in the place. Bannerman rubbed the stubble on his chin and saw for the first time that he was wearing an old woollen dressing gown with a faded checked pattern. He looked up to see du Maurier drawing on the last of his cigarette.

'Who was he?'

The policeman said, 'An Englishman going by the name of Michael Ritchie. Almost certainly an alias. He had been staying here at the auberge for the last couple of days, and I have no doubt it was he who searched Gryffe's house before you. The night before last he checked out in a hurry, apparently after getting a telephone call at the inn. He made inquiries at reception about train times to Brussels.'

An ugly little thought wormed its way into Bannerman's mind. He pushed it aside.

Du Maurier lit a fresh cigarette. 'You'd never seen him before, I take it?'

Bannerman said, 'Yes, I had. Yesterday morning at the Gare du Midi. He was waiting on the platform, and got on the same train as me.' He remembered the face peering at him through the waiting-room window.

'So he caught a train from here to Brussels, then came straight back on the same train as you.'

'A lot of trouble for someone to go to *not* to kill me.'

Du Maurier said, 'Perhaps he just wanted to frighten you.'

'They did that all right. Scared the shit out of me!'

'They?'

Bannerman said, 'He was just the piper, Inspector. Someone else was calling the tune.' And when du Maurier frowned

Bannerman smiled. 'A Scottish idiom. Just means somebody else sent him. Someone who'd rather I dropped this story.'

'Perhaps.'

The policeman drew Gryffe's *poste restante* card from his jacket pocket and held it up.

'You forgot to tell me about this.'

'So I did.'

'And do you want to now?'

'Not really.'

'Then you'd better take it.' He held it out.

Bannerman pulled back the covers and very gingerly swung his legs over the side of the bed. He took the card and looked at du Maurier with genuine surprise.

'It's of no use to me,' the policeman said. 'And in any case, my superiors would only bury it.'

'I thought you'd had a crisis of conscience about feeding me information.'

Du Maurier's head fell a little and an odd melancholy washed over his face. 'Things have changed since then.'

Bannerman frowned. 'What's changed?'

The policeman sighed. 'The night before last, just a few hours after you visited her, Tania Slater went missing. An alarm was raised after an apparent break-in at the clinic and her room was found empty.'

CHAPTER TWENTY-THREE

I

The afternoon editions of the evening papers were on the streets. The sounds of traffic, of people laughing, of the paper-boy calling headlines, floated through the doors of the café. Tucked away in a side street off the Boulevard Adolphe Max, this place felt removed from the life that flowed around it like a stone in a stream.

Kale sat in the farthest corner from the door. Here he sought refuge, alone in a dark place where his face was unknown. He would be neither noticed nor remembered. The only light came through grimy windows that faced on to the street. The floor was unswept, tables and chairs rocked on uneven legs. Half a dozen people sat alone, staring gloomily into drinks that they made last for hours. Or gazing sightlessly at the flickering screen of a TV set on the far wall. The sound was set to mute, but the second-hand images of other people's lives held a mindless fascination. Company for lonely souls.

An old woman with short grey hair sat behind a scarred

zinc bar, staring into space, puffing periodically on an evil-smelling cheroot. Kale stared despairingly at the newspapers in front of him. He had bought them all. This day and the day before. Scrutinizing every column inch of words he did not understand. Searching but never finding. There was nothing that even remotely suggested a story about a missing child. Not even anything on the shootings at the Rue de Pavie. It was as though none of it had ever happened. He was discovering a quiet, alien desperation in himself, a need to know that his existence made a difference, that the things he did had consequences. Here in this strange foreign city, where he knew no one and no one knew him, it was as though he did not even exist.

The nightmare quality of the last days haunted him. He had discovered things in himself that he never knew were there. Things that confused him, frightened him. His values, if he'd ever had any, his relationship with the life that ebbed around him, had altered beyond his understanding. It was as if he had thrown a pebble into a pool and seen the stone vanish without breaking the surface of the water. There were no concentric rings radiating out to infinity, no evidence that the pebble had ever existed. Would such a man, perhaps, begin to doubt his own existence? Would he then dare to look into the pool for fear that there might be no reflection?

He pulled on the last inch of his cigarette and blew grey smoke through nicotine-stained teeth. Why had he not killed her? The opportunity had been his for the taking. And why,

after only two days, had the killings in the Rue de Pavie vanished from the front pages? The papers, surely, should still
be full of it. As they should be full, today, of the disappearing
child.

He had bought English newspapers, too, at a newsagent's in
the centre of town. Front pages had been given over again to
the election; the Prime Minister speaking in Edinburgh; the
Leader of the Opposition making an important policy statement on immigration.

Why had he not killed the child?

His mind drifted back to the hospital in the snow, to the
sudden flood of light from the downstairs window which had
trapped him like a rabbit in the headlights of a car. He had seen
the child looking down at him, seen the recognition in her
eyes. Even then, after the light had gone, it had not crossed his
mind to draw back. Neither had he fought against the irresistible pull of the currents that drew him towards the vortex. He
had moved around the house, forcing a window and climbing
into the pitch darkness of the kitchen. It must have been then
that he had heard the first whispers of guilt. Something in
the warmth of the place, the stale smell of cooking, a scrap of
blue ribbon lying on a work surface by the door. Something
reminiscent of his childhood.

In the hallway, night lights glowed faintly along the ceiling
and his heart leapt at the sight of a figure watching him from
the far end. It took several seconds before he realized he was
looking at his own reflection. A mirror on the far wall. He had

stood staring at the mean and furtive figure that was himself, unable to move, unable to draw his eyes away from it. And for just a moment he thought he saw his mother's face staring back at him out of the darkness. He had never seen the resemblance before. It was uncanny.

The spell had been broken by the sound of footsteps coming from somewhere in the house, falling softly like blows upon his conscience. Was it fear that had made him turn on his heels and run? Back through the kitchen, out again into the cold night, the window left swinging behind him.

In the darkness he had stumbled through the snow in despair. And as he came around the house he saw her. A shadow in the night running down the steps, a coat clutched tightly, a woollen hat pulled down around her head. She had glanced in his direction, but hadn't seen him, and had run away across the terrace. She slipped and fell. He heard her sobs as she picked herself up and ran on, out of sight down the driveway. He might have followed. It would have been easy then. But he had not.

A gendarme came into the café, a black cape across his shoulders, and Kale tensed. The policeman cast an eye around the tables. Was it only in Kale's imagination that his eyes had rested longer on him? He stared back out of sullen, hateful eyes and the policeman turned away to buy a pack of cigarettes. He exchanged a few words with the grey-haired woman and left without a backward glance.

Kale finished his beer, left fifty francs in the saucer, and went out into the street. He scuffed along the pavement close to the wall, away from the boulevard, turning left into the Rue Neuve and along to the Place de la Monnaie. A great weight had settled on him. He stopped to light a cigarette and looked up to see the man he had followed to the hospital.

Bannerman was crossing the square only fifty metres away. Kale stood transfixed, watching as the man climbed the steps to the heavy swing doors of the Post Office. It all came back to him. The knowledge of what he must do. He might almost have cried. Something he had not done since childhood. But then, that would have shown weakness, and he could not afford to find yet more fault in himself. He slipped his right hand into his coat pocket and felt the slip of paper he had drawn from the left-luggage locker. Just three words. They very nearly burned his fingers.

II

Some time later, Bannerman stepped into the warmth of the IPC building. There was still an ache in his bones and he felt a slight shiver raise goosebumps on his skin. A fine, cold sweat crawled across his forehead. He passed the reception desk. The telephonist did not look up from her magazine. In the press bar he sat on one of the high stools and leaned forward on his elbows, breathing heavily. The barman raised an eyebrow. 'Monsieur?'

'Whisky.'

He clutched the glass with trembling fingers and poured its golden warmth over his throat.

'Another.'

We are making every effort to find her. Du Maurier's words came back to him. They had been walking across the street from the auberge to the car, the sun rising over the tops of trees that were sculpture against the palest of skies. 'But there has been none of the attendant publicity you would expect. People in high places are afraid it could resurrect the entire case. And God forbid such people might put the welfare of a child above their own survival.'

Bannerman's breath had drifted like mist into the early morning. 'Is there any chance, do you think, that they will find her alive?'

Du Maurier said, 'You want my honest opinion?'

Bannerman nodded, knowing what the answer would be.

'No.'

'And I suppose nothing of what happened here last night will reach the papers either.'

Du Maurier cast him a cynic's glance. 'Monsieur Bannerman, it never happened.'

'And if I choose to go public?'

'Someone will stop you.'

'But not you?'

'Not me.'

Bannerman drained his second glass, dropped some coins on the counter and limped back out to the lifts. The whisky had restored some of his strength and numbed a little of his pain.

Mademoiselle Ricain looked up in surprise as he came into the office.

'Monsieur Bannerman . . .' She seemed embarrassed. 'What happened to your face?'

He just shook his head.

She said, 'Your office in Edinburgh has been trying to reach you for nearly two days. And' – she fumbled among some papers on her desk – 'a man called Platt. He has phoned several times. As has Mademoiselle Robertson.'

Bannerman sat down and glanced across at Palin's empty desk. 'Where's Palin?'

Mademoiselle Ricain blushed. 'He . . . he's gone back to Glasgow.' She hesitated. 'You really look terrible, Monsieur.'

'Flattery will get you nowhere, Mademoiselle.'

She blushed again and slipped a sheet of paper into her typewriter.

Bannerman took an envelope from his pocket. It had been easy. After du Maurier dropped him off he had gone straight to the Post Office at the Place de la Monnaie and presented Gryffe's card. The girl behind the counter had not given him a second glance, returning after a moment with the envelope he now held in his hand. Perhaps he should have felt more excitement than he did, but Tania still filled his thoughts.

He tried to detach himself from his emotions. Why should it matter to him? But it did. And then he thought, *Let it feed your anger. Let it make you angry so that you want all the more to get the bastards.* If he could not channel it into something positive, then his sorrow and his anger would become self-defeating.

He looked at the stamp and postmark on the envelope. It had come from Switzerland, posted at the beginning of the month. Nearly two weeks ago. He slit it open. There were two sheets of paper clipped together. The top sheet was letter-headed, a firm of chartered accountants in Geneva – Fouquet, Maxim and Schmidt, 50 Rue des Quartiers. It was addressed to M. Robert Gryffe, and the letter was brief and in English.

'Dear Sir, please find enclosed, as requested, a quarterly statement of accounts for Machines Internationale S.A. for the three months ending the immediate past year. Your servants etc.'

The sheet attached listed purchases, sales and overheads in columns of figures down the right-hand side. They showed a pre-tax profit for the previous three months of five million pounds, with a rolling total for the first six months of nearly fifteen. Further returns were expected.

Bannerman was stunned. He ran his eyes up and down the figures. Just numbers on a sheet of paper. But now, he knew, he was starting to make real inroads into finding a motive for murder. Sales, purchases and overheads were not itemized, but that would come. Here was a beginning, the first inkling of what it was that Gryffe had been involved in. He was oblivious to Mademoiselle Ricain's typing, to the late afternoon sunshine slanting across his desk, to the fine film of sweat on his forehead. He reached for the phone and dialled quickly.

'*Edinburgh Post.*' It was a good, clear line.

'News desk.'

When the phone on his desk rang, George Gorman was preparing the schedule to be typed up for the five o'clock conference. He was harassed. It had been one of those afternoons. Five dead in a fire in Glasgow; the Prime Minister's press conference to be held before his election rally at the Usher Hall; a ScotNat MP claiming a political motive behind a burglary at his home. Important documents on the SNP's election strategy were missing, he claimed. There were the diary entries for the daily round of press conferences each party insisted on giving in the run-up to polling day. And he had two reporters off sick. But if he were to stop and think about it, this was how Gorman liked it.

'Dave!' he barked, as a copy boy dropped long, ragged-edged sheets of pink paper on his desk. A young reporter with a thick dark moustache and a broken nose ambled across the newsroom. Gorman held out the pink sheets. 'Press Association copy on the fire. Better check we've got it all.'

'Course we have!' The reporter grinned and ambled back to his seat.

Finally Gorman picked up the phone. 'News desk.'

'George?'

'Neil?'

'Listen, I'm in a hurry . . .'

'Hold it, hold it! Where in the name of the wee man have you been, Neil? Tait's been looking for you for the last two days. Ever since Slater's girl went missing.'

'You know about that?' Bannerman was surprised.

'They told Tait. But he won't run anything. He's been going spare, and I've been getting the shit end of the stick all day every day. Where *have* you been?'

'I don't have time to go into it. I want a number from my contacts book.'

Gorman interrupted. 'Fuck sake, Neil, you've got to talk to Tait.'

'I'm through talking with Tait, George. I guess he didn't tell you I'm on notice?'

Gorman's mouth fell open 'You're joking.' Then, 'Yours or his?'

'Probably both. We had a little disagreement in Brussels. But I don't suppose he would tell you about that either. When I've filed this story, George, I'm through.' Gorman heard him draw breath. 'But that's neither here nor there. I need that number. A guy called Hector Lewis. He's got a small enterprise in Geneva which does company searches, among other things. I need to get in touch with him tonight. The book's in my desk drawer.'

Gorman was still in shock. He and Bannerman went back a long way. 'Hold on.'

He made his way across the newsroom. In the last week he

had missed the familiar sight of the cantankerous Bannerman sitting at his desk, shouting at copy boys and being thoroughly objectionable. It didn't seem possible that he might not be back. And he wondered when it would be his turn.

He lifted Bannerman's contacts book from its drawer and riffled through it as he returned to the news desk. He picked up the phone. 'Got it.' He read out the number and then hesitated. 'What will I tell Tait?'

'Tell him to go fuck himself.'

'Can I quote you?'

'Please do.'

'Good. I'll enjoy that.'

As he hung up, the door behind him flew open and Tait stood in the doorway, shirt sleeves rolled up above the elbows, clenched fists on his hips. 'Any word from that bastard Bannerman yet?'

Bannerman had begun dialling before Tait had even stepped from his office. He listened to the shrill single rings in his left ear and became aware that Mademoiselle Ricain was still typing at the desk opposite. What *was* she typing? There were only he and Palin working out of this office. And Palin was gone.

'*Vous cherchez?*' The voice crashed into his thoughts.

'Hector Lewis, *s'il vous plaît.*'

'*Moment.*' A line got plugged through the switchboard.

'Lewis.'

'Hector, it's Neil Bannerman.'

You could almost hear Lewis running the name through his head in the split second before he responded, 'Neil! Good to hear from you. How are you?'

'Let's skip the formalities, Hector. Do you still do company searches?'

Lewis guffawed heartily. He was a man you could not easily offend. 'Same old Neil Bannerman. Yes, I still do the occasional search for old customers like yourself. But I've been branching out a bit lately. Doing a nice line in PR now.'

'Another martyr to presstitution?'

'Haha, that's a good one. Must remember that.'

'It's not exactly original, Hector.'

'Nothing is nowadays, Neil. Who have you got under the microscope this time?'

'A company called Machines Internationale. I have reason to think it might be registered in Switzerland. Possibly Luxembourg, but probably Switzerland.'

'A pleasure, sir, a pleasure. What do you want to know?'

'Everything. Director, associated companies if any, capital, line of business. And if you do turn up any related companies I'd like the shit on them too.'

'Something big?'

'None of your business.'

'Haha. You're quite right. Mum's the word. But it'll cost you. My time is valuable these days.'

'You mean the time you spend on your backside while you delegate the donkey work to your little army of diggers?'

'Exactly right, Neil. Why keep a dog and bark yourself? Where can I reach you?'

Bannerman gave him numbers for the office and the apartment in Rue de Commerce.

'What are you doing in Brussels, Neil?'

'Shelling sprouts.'

'That's good. Haha. Very droll. It wouldn't be anything to do with those shootings, would it?'

'What was it we agreed, Hector?'

'Oh, yes. Mum's the word. How soon do you want this stuff?'

'Just as soon as you can get off your fat arse and start digging.'

'Haha. Right, good. Give my love to, eh . . . well, whoever. I'll be in touch.'

Bannerman hung up and leaned back in his seat. He would rather have gone to Switzerland himself, but there was no time. And Lewis was good. But he was a vicious bastard. Somewhere behind all that ersatz affability he hid a sack of poison.

The sharp ring of the phone startled him. He lifted the receiver. 'Bannerman.'

'Neil, it's Sally. I've been trying to reach you for days. God, I've been so worried. You know about Tania?'

'Yes, I know.'

'Where have you been? I thought maybe you'd gone back to Scotland. They phoned me the morning after she went missing. I tried to get you at the Rue de Commerce, but there was no reply. You haven't heard anything, have you?'

'No.' There was a silence on the line that seemed longer than it was.

Then Sally said, 'Can we meet?'

Bannerman wiped the perspiration from his forehead. 'I'm tired, Sally. Maybe tomorrow.' There was another silence and he heard the phone go dead. He hung up and leaned forward on his elbows, rubbing his eyes with the palms of his hands. The typing stopped and he looked up to find Mademoiselle Ricain watching him. He stared back, almost without seeing her. Suddenly he said, 'Would you do me a favour, Mademoiselle?'

'Well, yes,' she said hesitantly.

'It's all right, I just want you to phone Richard Platt at *Belgique Soir* and tell him I'll be in touch tomorrow. I'm going home now. When you've done you might as well knock off too.' She nodded, expecting Bannerman to go. But he sat on, still looking at her. She grew more self-conscious and dithered before reaching for the phone. 'I'm sorry,' he said at length. 'About Palin. I embarrassed you.'

'Oh . . .' she said, not sure about how to respond. 'He . . . he probably deserved it. He wasn't a very nice man.'

'No.' Bannerman stood up and crossed to her desk. 'What are you typing?'

She blushed. 'Nothing. That is . . . nothing important.' Bannerman leaned over and pulled the sheet of paper from the typewriter. The typing was neat and accurate. *The quick brown fox jumped over the lazy dog.* About thirty lines of it. Bannerman smiled and laid it on her desk.

CHAPTER TWENTY-FOUR

The muffled ring of the telephone reached Tania on the landing. It seeped through her drowsiness like light on a foggy night. She was only vaguely aware of it, although it was not until it stopped that she awoke fully to the gnawing ache in her belly and the cold that gripped her like a vice in the dark.

Another night. Was it the second or the third? She was losing track of time.

She looked up at the skylight and saw stars in the blackness of the sky. She thought she heard Death on the stairs, saw its dark shadow lengthening on the steps. But there was no longer fear in her. It didn't matter any more. She would have welcomed it. Escape, finally, from the prison of her mind.

She was not certain how she had got here. Her memory of the face caught in the light below her window was fading. Her flight from the house into the deserted road, the snow that fell through the street lights, the empty bus terminus. The fingers of her memory had numbed and were no longer able to hold such things in their grasp.

Suddenly the landing lamp blinded her. And the shock of

it brought back the horror of that moment on the bus when she could not pay, when the conductor had begun to shout and she could not say what it was she wanted to say. The memory came like the sudden flare of a struck match and died as quickly, leaving only a slow flame to flicker hopelessly and make little impression in the vastness of her misery. That first night, though, remained vivid in her recollection. The brick bin shelter, the cold, the smell of decay, the sound of rats scurrying unseen.

She closed her eyes against the glare of the light and heard slow, heavy footsteps on the stairs. Perhaps this, at last, was Death.

Bannerman had asked the driver to slow down as they drove past the house in the Rue de Pavie where Gryffe and Slater had been murdered. It lay in darkness, empty and neglected, like the street itself. At the far end he got out and went into a general store on the corner. An old man sold him a loaf, some cheese and two litres of red wine. As an afterthought he also bought a carton of milk. The old man gave him a brown paper bag to carry his purchases back to the taxi, which whisked him off through the snowbound city as the stars came out hard and clear overhead.

In the Rue de Commerce, Slater's car stood by the kerb where he had left it. Three inches of snow lay on the roof, its coat of frost glistening in the lamplight. He climbed out of the taxi, paid the driver and watched it slither cautiously away down the street. The weight of his fatigue and the burden of his pain were enormous. How could he even think about things or put them in their proper perspective until he'd had some sleep? He would have a hot bath, and then something to eat, washed down with wine. And more wine. And more. Until both his mind and body were numb. Then he would sleep for ever.

Each flight of stairs, each landing, was depressingly familiar. He had never wanted to be here in the first place. And it was a long climb for weary limbs.

He almost didn't see her huddled in the corner opposite to the door. It was only the slightest sound that made him turn as he was slipping the key in the lock. Her eyes were open and staring up at him. There was no hint of recognition, nothing. He opened the door and slid his bag inside and crossed the landing to crouch beside her. The face was drained of colour, dark eyes ringed and sunk deep in her head. He lifted one of her limp hands and was shocked by its coldness. 'My God!' The words came in a breath like mist in the lamplight.

Very carefully he lifted her in his arms and carried her across the landing and into the house. He kicked the door shut and staggered through the half-light in the hall and into the living room. He laid her gently on the settee and lit the fire before switching on a small table lamp and drawing the curtains. Her breathing seemed shallow. He sat on the settee beside her and unbuttoned her coat. All the time her eyes never left him. He took each of her hands in turn and rubbed them briskly between his.

'I'll get a doctor,' he said. But in her first response since he had found her, her hand clutched at his sleeve and she shook her head. 'You need a doctor,' he said firmly. She shook her head again and he saw that look in her eyes that he had seen before.

He sighed and thought about it.

'Have you eaten?' Again she shook her head. 'All right, I'll give you some hot milk to start with. Will that be okay?' This time she nodded and he thought he saw a tiny smile on her lips.

He was anxious and confused and again stricken by the uncertainty that this child produced in him. He knew he should get a doctor, but understood that she would not have it. At least not right away. He pushed the coffee table aside and dragged the settee nearer the fire. 'I'll heat your milk.'

In the hall he gathered the bag where he had dropped it by the door, and took it into the kitchen. He found a saucepan in a cupboard, poured some milk from the carton and placed the pan on a high gas. Perhaps she should have a hot bath. The worst was not knowing the right thing to do. When it was just you, you didn't care too much. You mistreated yourself. You did all the wrong things. You drank, you ignored your doctor's orders. But when it came to someone else, you felt a responsibility that you never felt for yourself.

He found the switch for the water heater on the wall by the kitchen door and turned it on. Then he remembered the suitcases in Slater's bedroom. She should change into fresh, warm clothes. Her coat and dress had been cold and damp to the touch. He found her suitcase and delved inside it. There was a heavy woollen dressing gown and a pair of pyjamas. He found a small pair of slippers and took out a pair of socks.

Tania felt warmth only superficially. It was on her skin, but inside the cold was still there. It dulled her thinking, misted the window through which she looked out on the world. Only a tiny corner of it was clear, and through it she saw Bannerman, smelled him, felt him.

She'd never really had contact with the world outside herself, been always just an observer. Somehow Bannerman bridged that gap, or at least it seemed to her that he might. That somehow he could provide what she had longed for so much from her father. The love that had never come. Thoughts drifted in her mind like mist. When she reached for them they simply dispersed and she gave up trying. She heard Bannerman in the kitchen and was aware of him going into her father's bedroom. Presently he returned to the kitchen, then he was there beside her, helping her up into a sitting position.

She tried very hard to raise herself out of the mist. The glass was in her hand and he was bringing it up gently to her lips. Its hot milkiness washed away the bad taste in her mouth and she felt it going down, warm and soothing. Its warmth spread inside her and she felt the cold receding. For the first time in many hours she shivered. The gnawing in her stomach retreated, and she grew acutely aware of her hunger. At last the mist was clearing. She looked up to find Bannerman watching her with concern.

'That better?' His voice was close and soft. She nodded. He held up a bundle of clothes and she recognized her dressing gown. 'I've had these warming in front of the fire. If you feel able, you should change out of the clothes you're wearing. They're damp.' He paused, waiting for a reaction. She managed a feeble smile and nodded. 'I've put the water heater on. The water should be hot enough for a bath in about fifteen minutes. I think probably a hot bath would do you good, don't you? Then we can eat.'

They sat eating in silence in front of the fire. The bread and cheese was dry, but the wine was good. He'd heated up more milk for Tania and she was gulping it over after wolfing down several slices of bread. Now Bannerman's own fatigue was catching up with him. In all his concern for the child, he had forgotten his own weariness, his own desperate need for food and sleep. His bath would have to wait until tomorrow.

When he'd finished eating he drank more wine, watching her over the rim of his glass. She was searching in the pockets of her dressing gown. Finally she drew out a paper handkerchief and stood up to draw it softly across his forehead and mop away the fine beads of perspiration.

He caught her hand. 'I'll have to tell them you're here.'

Almost immediately there was fear in her eyes and she shook her head vigorously.

He said, 'It's all right, little one. Just so they can stop searching. It's only fair. No one's going to take you away tonight. I won't let them.'

He did not wait for a reaction, but stood up and crossed to the phone. He began to dial.

'*Police Judiciaire.*' A woman's voice.

'*Inspecteur du Maurier.*'

'*Ne quittez pas.*'

A phone lifted. 'Du Maurier.'

'You're still there. I didn't really expect to get you at this time. Have you no home to go to?'

'What do you want?' Du Maurier sounded irritable.

'The child is here. At the Rue de Commerce. God knows how or why. She was waiting on the landing when I got back.'

Tania watched Bannerman darkly. She would not let anyone take her away again. She wanted to be with Bannerman always. She examined him closely as he spoke. She saw his weariness, the perspiration that had broken out again across his forehead, the lacerations on his face. A hard face, something a little frightening about it. But she knew that behind the façade lay an unexpected gentleness.

'And next time I want one of your men at the clinic night and day till she leaves,' she heard him saying, and became aware of her heart pounding.

He hung up and smiled at her. 'It's all right,' he said and he returned to the table. She detected his hesitation. 'Tomorrow,' he said. 'Sometime tomorrow . . . you'll have to return to the clinic. It'll only be for a day or so and then we can go back to Scotland together.'

She had known this would happen. That she couldn't have him to herself. That they would take her away again. But knowing did not stop the flood of anger and hurt. It was always what *they* wanted. Never what *she* wanted.

She flew at him, clenched fists beating against his chest, a cry of anguish on her lips. Bannerman had not been prepared for it. The fists hurt him, tiny blows raining across his chest and shoulders and face.

He tried to catch her arms, but fear of hurting her made it hard. Finally he got his arms around her so that hers were pinned to her sides, and he hugged her, feeling the sobs that racked her body. 'It's all right, it's all right,' he heard himself saying. Then felt sick as he remembered hearing her father utter the selfsame words.

She was still struggling, but her strength was waning rapidly.

'Tomorrow,' he said breathlessly, 'we'll talk about it. We'll work it out.'

The struggling subsided with a whimper and her head fell on to his shoulder, her face turned away from his. He rocked her gently to and fro.

'I don't want to hurt you,' he whispered. 'God knows, I don't want to hurt you.'

Something inside him broke. A kind of iron self-control that had made him invulnerable for so long. But it had grown brittle with the years. His own voice sounded odd to him.

'Somewhere,' he said, 'there's a little girl . . . Just three or four years older than you. My . . .' He couldn't even bring himself to say it. 'I'm her father. Never even seen her. I'd pass her in the street and not know it. She probably thinks someone else is her daddy. I don't know. All I know is that somehow she's the part of me that's missing.' He turned his head a little and saw that she was asleep. She hadn't heard any of it. As no one else had, or ever would. And probably that was best.

CHAPTER TWENTY-FIVE

The morning had almost gone when Bannerman turned over and opened his eyes to the sunlight that filled his room. He craned his neck around to see Tania standing by the window staring out across the rooftops. She turned and smiled.

'Good morning,' Bannerman said, returning her smile.

She looked vastly improved from the previous evening. He checked his watch. It was nearly midday.

'Jesus! I've been asleep for hours!' He sat upright. 'Have you been awake long?' She shook her head and held up one finger. 'An hour?'

She nodded. She was dressed and there was a little colour in her cheeks.

'You must be starving.' She grinned and walked, almost ran, to the door, then stopped and beckoned him to follow. 'I'll be with you in a minute,' he said. 'I need to get dressed.' But she just shrugged and stood her ground. He felt the pleasure of unaccustomed laughter. 'On you go. I'm not a pretty sight first thing in the morning.' She smiled and nodded her agreement.

He threw his pillow at her and it hit the door with a thud as she closed it quickly behind her.

There was still a stiffness in his limbs as he climbed out of bed and felt the cold air brush his skin. When he had dressed he went through to the living room and saw a lump of bread and a piece of crumbling cheese set out for him on the coffee table, with the last half-litre of wine and a glass. A plate of crumbs next to it betrayed her hunger. She had been unable to wait for him.

'Well, thank you, Tania.' He stooped to tear off a hunk of bread with his fingers and pop it in his mouth. He looked at the wine and smiled reproachfully. 'The wine was a nice thought, but not first thing in the morning. Would you like coffee?' She nodded and followed him eagerly into the kitchen.

There was milk enough to make coffee half and half. He spooned sugar and instant coffee into two mugs and watched the milk and water come to the boil in a pan over the gas. Despite the aches and pains he felt good. He couldn't remember having slept so well in a long time. It was the first morning in many that he had risen with a lightness of heart, and without his usual ambivalence about the day ahead. But beyond the next hours, he knew, the future still lay brooding ominously on the horizon. The good things in life never lasted. This was the false peace, the calm before the storm. Or perhaps the eye of tranquillity at its centre. An ephemeral thing. He shook his head to clear the thought. He did not want its impermanence to spoil it while it lasted.

'Here.' He handed her a mug and they drank in silence,

enjoying its hot sweetness. He said, 'Later we'll have to talk about the future.' He saw her face cloud. 'But right now we're not even going to think about it. We can just spend the next few hours finding out a little bit more about each other. What do you say?' She tilted the mug back to hide her face and he could not detect her response. When she lowered it again she smiled, as though he had not spoken, and he wondered what on earth was in that little head of hers.

The doorbell rang and brought a sudden tension crashing into their world. They exchanged glances and her eyes said, *Don't answer.* He sighed and turned away so that he did not have to see them. He placed his mug on the work surface and went out into the hall.

He felt something like relief when he opened the door to find Sally standing smiling uncertainly. But there remained a residue of annoyance at the intrusion. 'What is it?'

The smile left her face and it coloured with anger. 'I came to apologize,' she said coldly. 'For being short with you on the phone last night. But now I don't think I'll bother.' She turned quickly and Bannerman grabbed her arm.

'I'm sorry. I've got company.'

Her eyes flashed with a strange dark emotion. 'I see. I'll not disturb you then.'

Bannerman held on to her arm. 'Not that kind of company.' He opened the door wide for her. 'Tania's here. She was waiting on the landing when I got back last night.'

All of Sally's antagonism dissolved. 'Is she all right?'

'Come and see.'

When they went into the living room Tania was standing at the kitchen door cradling her mug.

'Hello,' Sally said. 'I see you two have made friends.'

Tania stared at her impassively and Bannerman wondered if she resented Sally's presence. He took the mug from her hands and laid it on the table, then he crouched down and took her hand in his.

'Listen, little one. The whole world isn't against you. Even if sometimes it seems that way. We all need a bit of courage to deal with the things life throws at us. But you have to start by trusting the people who love you.' She stared back at him, her face a blank mask. Impossible to know what was going on behind it. Bannerman stood up. He glanced at Sally and wondered if she'd thought his words were meant for her, too. 'How about we all go for a walk?'

It was a day full of promise, the sun pale and round in the washed-out blue of the sky above the city. The air was crisp and so cold it stung your eyes and made them water.

The three of them walked briskly to keep warm, wrapped in coats and scarves. Along the Rue de Commerce and into the Rue Belliard. They crossed the Boulevard du Régent where the road shone wet with the salt, and the traffic threw up a spray of black slush. Down Lambermont and into the Parc de Bruxelles. The seeds of happiness lay in them all. But lost in the darkness, where they would have trouble germinating.

Sally suggested they build a snowman, but the snow was too crisp and dry. It was Bannerman who gathered a handful of wet snow where the sun had lain for some hours and threw the first snowball. Sally was still trying in vain to build her snowman while Tania stood watching uncertainly. She saw Bannerman put his fingers to his lips before throwing his snowball to catch Sally on the shoulder. It burst in a spray of fine snow over her face and she wheeled around angrily. Bannerman was grinning, and Tania unable to stop the smile from creeping across her face.

'All right,' Sally said. 'If that's the way you want it. Come on, Tania, we're not going to let him get away with that, are we?'

She stooped quickly to grab a handful of snow that broke into a white cloud as she threw it.

Bannerman laughed. 'You need to get it where the sun's been shining.' He scooped up another handful and threw as Sally ducked to see it fly over her head. She grabbed Tania's hand and they ran to where the sun slanted down between the trees on virgin snow.

'Like this,' she said, showing Tania how to cup it between her hands and compress it into a ball. Then she yelled as another burst on her back. She stood up quickly and hurled her snowball at Bannerman. He sidestepped easily, slipped and fell heavily on his side. He felt snow in his shoes and burning the side of his face. The black railings of the park, the outline of biscuit-coloured buildings against the sky. Trees overhead and the sound of laughter. Sally's fine clear voice, and Tania's.

He rolled over to see the child's face reddened by the cold and bright with the laughter that came tumbling from her lips like music, joyous and unrestrained. He thought he had never heard anything more beautiful in his life.

A snowball burst on his forehead, stinging his skin and bringing tears to his eyes. He heard footsteps crunching across the snow and Tania was there, standing over him, her laughter very nearly hysterical. She raised a hand and threw her snowball. It broke on his chest and he yelled as she dropped on her knees, her arms around his neck, life and laughter pulsing through her small, clumsy body. He hugged her and got to his feet, lifting her clear of the ground and spinning her round and round until the world swam and he had to stop.

They both fell into the snow and Tania lay on her back breathing hard and laughing at the sky. Bannerman saw Sally crouched a few yards away in the snow. She grinned at him and tilted her head to one side. He scrambled to his feet, brushing snow from his coat and trousers. 'I'm soaked. What do you say we eat?'

Tania had stopped laughing and he saw that she was gazing up at him with a clear, bright light in her eyes. And his own happiness muddied a little as he wondered if he was capable of condemning her to life in an institution.

Two hundred yards away, across the snow and the gravel path beyond the trees, the figure of Kale, clad in a dark coat, stood watching. The skin of his face was taut and shiny in the cold, touched by yellow and blue, thin lips compressed in a hard line. It was a face without expression. Only the eyes betrayed his melancholy. The same dark eyes which had watched life pass them by, concealing more than they ever revealed. All the regrets of a life less lived.

At first Kale had shrunk away from his new reality, like a man coming out of a dark place into the light. He had been temporarily blinded. But awareness was returning, slow and painful. Things were clearer now, resentment replaced by sadness.

Everything had changed with those three words on a scrap of paper.

Through the trees he stood watching the figures in the snow. He heard them laughing, their voices raised in the still of the winter morning. He felt drawn to them, wanted to share their laughter. But he had long since passed out of their world into his own dark place. He could look back, but never return. A single tear ran from the corner of his eye.

He would not, could not, kill the child.

CHAPTER TWENTY-SIX

I

Platt battered out the final page of his copy, checked it, and called for a copy boy. A spotty youngster with a shock of red hair snatched it from his tray and headed for the news desk. Had there been a hint of contempt in the boy's cold, green eyes?

The newsroom was buzzing with activity in the last minutes before copy deadlines for the final edition.

Platt lit a cigarette and puffed on it nervously. He was through for the day and felt badly in need of a drink. But there were still things to be done. He was both excited and a little edgy. It worried him that Bannerman should simply have disappeared for two days. Then last night there had been the phone call from Mademoiselle Ricain. Bannerman would phone him today. The call had not come. It had crossed his mind more than once that Bannerman would not keep his word, that when it came to the bit he would not share the story. Why should he? After all, Platt had contributed little or nothing so far. He also knew that his guilty fears about Bannerman's intentions derived from the hatching of his own shabby plots. Still, he smiled at the thought of putting one over on the bastard.

Bannerman had asked him for background on Jansen and Lapointe. But Platt had gone further than that. The hours he'd spent searching through records at the Tribunal de Commerce had repaid him handsomely. At last he had something to trade with Bannerman. He had bargaining power.

He felt the first grumblings of his ulcer. With fumbling fingers he opened a bottle of antacid tablets and shoved two past his lips. And in a gesture that had become second nature, he took out the red handkerchief to mop his brow.

Hesitantly he reached for the phone and dialled.

II

Tania kept her eyes fixed on Bannerman's face as he flicked through her drawings, averting them only when he looked up. It had been Sally's idea to show him the drawings. Slater had omitted to pack them and she had found them still in the folder beneath her bed.

They all sat around a small desk by her bedroom window where the late afternoon sun streamed in, warm and soft, to suffuse the room with gentle light. She could not remember ever having felt such inner calm.

She noticed the way that Bannerman and Sally looked at

each other. Something in their eyes. She was not jealous, even though she realized that they had feelings for each other. But with the extraordinary perception that was her gift, she was aware that neither was ready to admit it.

Today had been the best day of her life. None of that frustration that grew and grew inside her until it exploded from the inside out, stealing away control. It was wonderful. She glowed within.

They had lunched at a bistro not far from the park in the Boulevard de l'Empereur, where they had been served cold chicken salad. Tania had watched the adults drink dry white wine. All their faces glowed red from the cold and the exertions of the snow fight, and they ate in silence, pleased just to look at one another and smile. Afterwards, they walked back through the park to the apartment.

Bannerman gathered all the drawings together. 'They're just amazing,' he said. He looked at Tania, waiting until she lifted her eyes to meet his. 'You have a marvellous talent,' he told her. 'Maybe we can get these published when we get back to Scotland. Would you like that?'

If that meant showing them to other people she wasn't sure. They were such private things. She only wanted those she loved to see them.

Bannerman sensed her uncertainty. He said softly, 'They say everything that you cannot say with words, little one. They can tell the whole world about you, all the things that you see and feel and need, just like everyone else.' She smiled and reached for his hand. He took it and squeezed it and tensed inside as he made a difficult decision.

With his free hand he reached into the inside pocket of his jacket, slung across the back of his chair, and took out a folded sheet of paper.

'I have a copy of one of your drawings.'

Without turning his head he was aware of Sally's sudden anxiety. She had remained quiet since the meal, but now her presence beside him was very powerful. He stole a glance at her and saw the doubt in her eyes. He was not sure himself. A fine perspiration moistened his palms as he let go of Tania's hand to unfold the paper and smooth it out on the table. The child looked at it and nodded slowly. Her face was blank.

'Do you remember this?' Nothing. He waited a long time before asking, 'Do you know who it is?' Again nothing.

Sally put a hand on his arm. 'Don't,' she said.

But still he persisted. 'Look at me, Tania. It's important that I know.' Her eyes seemed to look straight through him. 'This is the man that killed your dad, isn't it? And the other man.'

In the hush that fell across the room he could hardly bring himself to breathe. The bedside clock ticked solemnly in the silence. Tania nodded suddenly and turned her head away.

'All right, all right,' Bannerman said, and he took her hand again, squeezing it tightly. It felt limp and small. 'Just one more thing. Just one. Would you . . . would you know him if you saw him again?'

He felt her hand tighten around his and saw fear in her eyes. And he misunderstood.

'It's okay, little one,' he said. 'He can't harm you now.'

But still her fingers pressed into his hand, nails digging into flesh, and she shook her head in savage frustration. How could she tell him? *I have seen him, I have.* She pulled her hand free and stabbed her finger several times at the drawing he had spread on the table. Then nodded. Two, three, four times and felt something like despair as she saw Bannerman's confusion.

It was Sally who realized. 'Oh my God, she has! She has seen him again.'

Bannerman glanced at her, and then back at the child, and he saw that it was true. He took Tania by the shoulders – 'When? How?' – before it dawned on him, and he felt a sense of horror pricking his skin. 'At the hospital.' Where else could she have seen him? 'Is that why you ran away?' Her lips parted as though she were about to speak.

The telephone rang in the living room and startled them all. Not one of them moved, but all three hearts were pounding. The spell was broken.

Bannerman stood up, infuriated by the interruption, and strode through to the living room.

Sally smiled with false cheer and pushed her chair back noisily. She said to Tania, 'How about coffee? I'll go and make some. Do you want to help?' Tania didn't move. 'That's all right, I'll get it.' She bustled quickly off to the kitchen, and from the other room Tania could hear Bannerman's voice in irritable conversation with someone on the phone.

The glow of her day was fading now, like the sun setting behind the rooftops. She knew that Bannerman would take her back to the hospital now. She'd known it all day, but had buried the thought. Out of reach, out of sight, out of mind. Wasn't that the key to survival? The ability to grasp happiness when it came without looking beyond it.

Whatever the future held for her, nothing could erase the memory of today. Somehow she felt that this man who had come into her life would always be there for her. She'd seen it in his eyes, felt it in words he thought she hadn't heard last night. Knew that each of them could fill an empty place in the other's life. He would keep her safe from . . . she glanced at the drawing on the desk . . . from *him*.

She wondered then why she had not drawn the face. She had no recollection of the interruption that prevented her from finishing it. Would Neil be pleased, she wondered, if she drew the face now? But she had a better idea. Something that would say more. She tore a strip of paper off the foot of one of her drawings and reached for the pencil. It was always difficult for her to come to terms with words on paper. She squeezed the pencil until her fingers went white and she began, with great difficulty, to sort out letters in the right order.

It was strange how, when she drew, the pencil rested easily between her fingers and flew across the page with such fluidity. Now the letters formed themselves clumsily, and the effort of it drained her. When she had finished, it felt as though it had taken hours. Just three words.

Quickly, nervously, she folded the paper and slipped the note into the right-hand pocket of Bannerman's jacket. Then she ran her hand over the softness of the brown cord and put her face close to it. It felt soft and smelled of Bannerman.

III

When he left Tania's bedroom, Bannerman was depressed and irritable. He felt guilty about confronting the child with her drawing. She deserved better than that. And yet it had confirmed things now beyond doubt. There might even have been more to come. He snatched the phone.

'Bannerman.'

'It's Platt. I've been waiting for your call.'

Bannerman had an immediate picture of the fat little man sitting at his desk, sweating and dabbing his brow with that infernal red handkerchief, his hair falling in greasy ringlets about his thick neck. 'Well?' he said.

Platt was taken aback. 'Well, I thought you might have something for me. You just vanished for two whole days. I thought maybe . . .'

'Then you thought wrong. I've got nothing new.'

He could hear the dryness in Platt's mouth as he spoke. 'Well, maybe I have. Been doing some digging of my own.'

'And?'

'I've come up with something quite interesting.'

Bannerman sensed his tension. 'Which is?'

'Perhaps,' Platt said, 'we should get together and, you know, compare notes. Don't you think it's time you came clean with me? I'm sure we can work out something to our mutual advantage.'

Bannerman sat down. It was just possible that Platt had something. Although it was equally possible that he was simply trying it on.

'Hello. Are you still there?' Platt sounded anxious.

Bannerman decided to call his bluff. 'I don't think there's much point in our meeting, Platt. If you've got something to tell me, tell me now. Otherwise forget it. I've got more important things on my mind.'

Platt said quickly, 'Look, Bannerman, it's time we laid this thing on the line.'

'Goodbye.'

'No, no, wait.'

Bannerman had the impression now that Platt was cupping his hand around the mouthpiece to make this confidential. His voice was very close and slightly hushed.

'I've been looking at company records. It's an absolute jungle, Bannerman. Took me ages to piece together how it all works. That's Lapointe's handiwork. The man's a genius. He can put companies together and take them apart again like a kid with Lego. It all looks legit on the surface, but if you start from the basic premise that nothing is really what it seems, and start picking at all the loose threads, then the whole thing starts to unravel.'

'Get on with it!' Despite his tone, Bannerman was interested.

'Okay, okay. The way Jansen got fat was by buying up the competition. He'd squeeze them financially, forcing them to borrow. Then when things got tough and loans got called in they would go into administration. Almost invariably they would then get snapped up by a holding company called La Trasque, which in turn sold them to Jansen. Turns out that La Trasque, and the finance companies that put up most of those loans, were all owned by a nominee company called Corniche S.A., which traded on behalf of unnamed clients. It wasn't until about two years ago when Corniche shut up shop and reregistered in Liechtenstein that it became apparent who was really behind it.'

'Who?'

'No one seemed to notice at the time, but it's all there if you check back through the records.'

'And?' Bannerman could barely conceal his impatience.

'It was Lapointe's law firm. Not directly, but through another company he'd set up.'

Bannerman sighed. 'So where's all this going?'

'Well, don't you see? It was actually Jansen who was lending cash to his competitors. They had no idea. He turned the screws then called in the loans. And when they couldn't pay, bought them up for a song. He may have had to pay off their debts, but in reality he was just repaying himself. All indirectly, of course, through the cobweb of companies that Lapointe had spun for him.'

Bannerman sighed. 'Well, is that illegal?'

Platt was confused. 'I . . . I don't know. But it's a bloody good story.'

Bannerman said dryly, 'Maybe you should stick to writing up fires and press releases on the price of butter. How Jansen built his empire is of no fucking interest to me at all.'

Platt was clearly stunned. 'But I thought that's what you wanted. Something on Jansen and Lapointe.'

'A bit of background is all I needed. You already got that for me. Look, Platt, I don't know what the law is in this country, but I doubt very much if what you've described is illegal. Unethical, perhaps, but not illegal. You've been wasting your time, pal. I'll call you.' He hung up.

Platt replaced the receiver with a trembling hand. His breath came in rapid bursts, his mind ablaze with anger and humiliation. His face had paled to the colour of yellowed ivory. He rose unsteadily, picked up his coat and hat and headed for the door.

Bannerman sat for a few minutes thinking about what Platt had told him. It might be of value, it might not. It was impossible to know yet. He reached for the notepad beside the telephone and scribbled down the names of the companies while they were still fresh in his mind. Platt said that Corniche S.A. had shut up shop and reregistered in Liechtenstein. Technically, then, it was a new company. Why, he wondered, would that have been necessary? And as if to lodge the thought firmly in his mind, he underlined the name in his notes.

He stood up as Sally emerged from the kitchen with a tray full of steaming mugs of coffee. 'No time for that,' he said. 'We need to take Tania back to the clinic.' Immediately he saw her hurt and realized he'd been unnecessarily blunt. He backtracked, but too late now, and he knew it. 'She's tired, I'm tired. I need time to think.'

Sally laid the tray on the table and looked at him wearily. His mood had changed again with the phone call, and she felt dismissed, bewildered, angered by his sudden indifference, annoyed at herself for caring. And then she needed to say the thing she'd been keeping bottled up since this morning. The whole day she had been careful to remain discreetly in the background, not to intrude on the relationship she saw flowering between Bannerman and Tania.

'I got the job,' she said. 'I'm leaving tomorrow for Rome. This is my last night in Brussels.'

Bannerman was startled. He had taken it for granted that she would still be around, at least in the short term. To discover that in a matter of hours she would be gone from his life, probably for ever, left him suddenly bereft. No chance to sort out his feelings for her. The very thing that he'd been putting off, in the belief there would always be time. Or because he was afraid to ask himself the question. Had he not learned by now how often love was gone before you even knew it was there? But how could he love her? He hardly knew her.

She said, 'Could we go somewhere tonight? I'd like to talk.'

He nodded, barely trusting himself to speak. 'All right,' he said, and he turned away to the bedroom.

CHAPTER TWENTY-SEVEN

I

It was a cold, clear night. There was a splash of light above the entrance to the café, and across the cobbles taxi drivers sat picking their teeth in empty cabs waiting for fares.

Bannerman crossed the square weighed down still by the memory of the child. The sense of betrayal in her face as he left her at the clinic had haunted him afterwards, all through a solitary meal in some anonymous restaurant. And now, his rendezvous with Sally on this dark Brussels night. A meeting, it seemed, that would be their last.

She was waiting for him at the bottom end of the square, her face pale and sad when they met and then flushing quickly in the sudden warmth of the café as they stepped inside.

The café was Eastern European, run by a small fat exile from communism. A four-piece Hungarian orchestra played by the light of candles that flickered dimly on the tables. A pianist who never smiled sat at a grand piano, and a tall thin creature wrestled with a double bass. The clarinettist sat on a high chair by the piano, and a gaunt middle-aged man stood out front by a microphone which hung by its lead from the rafters. He played haunting melodies on his violin. The music was soft and pleasant, and wrapped itself around them. Walking into this place was like stepping into the past.

The wooden tables were rough-hewn, and the stools hard and uncompromising. The stone walls were whitewashed and a wooden staircase led to a gallery crowded with more tables. People leaned on the rail and gazed down on the orchestra, faces flickering in the candlelight, tiny mobile pinpoints of light shining in their eyes.

Bannerman and Sally sat at a table by the big window that looked out on the Place du Grand Sablon, and although the café was busy they felt safe and anonymous in its darkness. A waiter with a black shirt and trousers and a white napkin over his arm came to take their order. Sally's face brightened. 'You must try their speciality,' she said. And to the waiter, '*Deux thés Slaves.*'

Bannerman looked around. The clientèle was mostly middle-aged. There were one or two young couples holding hands below tables and watching the orchestra, or gazing at each other as though just discovering love for the first time and believing that somehow it was unique to them.

'The place never closes,' Sally said. 'Open twenty-four hours a day. I used to come in for a drink sometimes after college, and occasionally when I'd been babysitting for Tania.' She was talking for the sake of talking. 'On Sundays the square is transformed into a marketplace for antique dealers. The stalls are set out all the way up to the church. You can see the antique shops across the other side there.'

Bannerman smiled and reached for her hand. 'You don't have to talk,' he said.

She took a deep breath and tried to smile. This was difficult for her. She said, 'I think, perhaps, I could have feelings for you, Neil. I barely know, but maybe it's worth finding out?' He felt her hand tighten around his. 'It's been too easy just to put it off, not to think about it. But now I've got to decide, haven't I?'

'I thought you already had. I thought you were going tomorrow.'

The violinist had begun to wander among the tables and he stopped now at theirs to play for them. It seemed as though every eye in the café had turned in their direction. Bannerman looked at him and shook his head almost imperceptibly, but the maestro did not miss it. He was too experienced. He smiled and moved on to the next table. Sally's smile was strained. 'God, it's embarrassing when that happens.' She hesitated, then for the first time faced him with it. 'Help me, Neil. Please. If I only knew how you felt. If . . . if you wanted me to, I'd stay.'

There had been a time when she had vowed never to make that kind of commitment again. To any man. And she remembered the horror of that night before the wedding. *I'm sorry*, he'd said. Just that. *I'm sorry*. And she had shed tears of hurt and humiliation. Before gathering herself to break the news to all those who'd travelled for the ceremony. So many presents to be returned. The embarrassment of her friends who didn't know what to say. The false comfort of relatives who told her they had never liked him anyway.

But things had changed. She was thirty-two now. Ahead lay a lifetime of loneliness. And with Bannerman, somehow, it seemed different in a way that had caught her unawares. Yet, as she had just acknowledged, she hardly knew him, and within her still lay the seeds of doubt and mistrust sown that night three years before.

The *thés Slaves* arrived in glasses wrapped around with paper napkins, a mixture of tea and some kind of spirit that the waiter set alight at their table. The flames licked up over the rims of the glasses, soft and warm. Bannerman looked across the table at Sally's downturned face. The flames softened it and he thought she looked almost beautiful. He felt a tremendous weight of responsibility. It would be too easy to say yes, that he wanted her to stay. But he knew she would make demands on him that he was not sure he could fulfil. And his was the kind of life into which relationships did not easily fit. There was a space inside him, big and empty, that badly needed to be filled. But in that way he was like Tania. So often it was those who needed love the most who were the most difficult to love. And what kind of life could he give her?

'It's not for me to say,' he said, knowing that he didn't want her to go. 'You really *don't* know anything about me. Nor I about you.' He blew out the flames in their glasses. 'Drink,' he said. 'You'll feel better.' And he thought what an empty thing it was to say.

They lifted the scalding liquid to their lips and drank it in tiny sips. It was strong, and the spirit filled their mouths like burning breath, before slipping over to glow inside them. She stared into her glass.

'Is that just a roundabout way of saying that you don't want me to stay?'

Bannerman said nothing. If that was what she wanted to think then perhaps it would be easier for her.

Then suddenly she said, 'I'd like to spend just one night with you, Neil. Something' – she hesitated – 'to remember you by.'

So, she had decided. And he knew now that it was beyond recall. He was going to say he didn't think it would be a good idea, but a voice interrupted before he could speak.

'Well, Mr Bannerman, isn't this a surprise. Come on, Henry. You don't mind if we join you, Mr Bannerman?' Mrs Schumacher sat herself down without waiting for his reply.

Bannerman turned in astonishment. Mrs Schumacher grinned at him, her face flushed in that way he had seen at the party. She had been drinking. Again. Behind her Henry Schumacher hovered apologetically. He nodded politely at Bannerman and the girl. 'Perhaps they want to be alone, dear,' he said.

'Oh, nonsense, Henry, sit down.' Then to Bannerman, 'Well, Mr Bannerman, this is unexpected. Aren't you going to introduce us to your young lady?' And confidentially, 'You certainly are a fast worker. Does she speak English?'

Bannerman smiled indulgently. 'She *is* English. Miss Sally Robertson – Mr and Mrs Schumacher.'

Sally was taken aback by the sudden arrival of this garrulous American woman with her big bosoms and timid husband. She took a moment to collect herself. 'How do you do?'

'It's a pleasure to meet you, my dear.'

A waiter arrived promptly at the table and Mrs Schumacher flashed him a winning smile. 'How are you tonight, Jean?'

'I am very well, Madame. Have you had a good evening?' He looked almost as though he might be genuinely interested in her reply.

'Why, yes, Jean, as always. We took your advice about that little restaurant in the Grande Place. Exquisite.'

'I'm very pleased, Madame. You will have a sherry?'

'Well, yes. But just a very small one.'

'And Monsieur?'

'A whisky-soda, please.'

Jean bowed and dematerialized into the gloom.

Sally and Bannerman exchanged looks. 'Actually we were just leaving,' Bannerman said.

Schumacher leaped self-consciously to his feet to allow Sally out from behind the table. 'Perhaps you would join us for a drink tomorrow night,' he said. 'We are going home on Sunday.' He seemed so eager for their company that Bannerman was almost sorry to turn him down.

'I'm afraid that won't be possible.'

'That's a pity,' Mrs Schumacher said. 'Tomorrow's our last

day, and I would so have liked to hear all about the exciting world of newspapers. We're flying back to Edinburgh on Sunday morning to spend a few more days there before going back to the States. It is *The Times* you work for, isn't it?'

'The *Post*. The *Edinburgh Post*.'

She frowned as the myth she had been constructing in her mind crumbled. She would no doubt rebuild it over the next few days. 'Wasn't it just terrible about that poor Mr Griffin?'

'Gryffe,' Bannerman corrected her.

'And to think we were speaking to him just the night before he was killed.'

'Yes,' Bannerman said. 'Goodbye. I hope you have a good journey.'

'Why thank you, Mr Bannerman. Goodbye, young lady.' Schumacher shook their hands solemnly. 'It's been a pleasure,' he said. 'If you should change your mind, about the drink I mean, give us a call. We're at the Hotel Regent in the Avenue Louise.'

'I'll do that.'

And when they had gone Mrs Schumacher said, 'They haven't even finished their drinks. He seems a very strange young man, doesn't he? You don't think he's trying to avoid us, do you, Henry?'

'They struck me,' Schumacher said thoughtfully, 'as two young people with rather a lot on their minds.'

II

Bannerman watched her undress in the moonlight that flooded in through open shutters. The room was cold and he shivered. He knew this was a mistake. Afterwards, it would only be all the more difficult. But he wanted her, with every fibre of himself.

'Let me,' he said.

She had slipped out of her jeans and panties and stood only in her T-shirt. Bannerman ran his hands over its intimate softness, over the swellings of her small breasts. Then behind her, pulling her to him, feeling the smoothness of her buttocks and lifting the shirt up over her head. He dropped it on the floor and kissed her, his tongue in her mouth, seeking out every part of it. Then he lifted her and carried her to the bed.

Afterwards they lay still for a long time, curled up in one another's arms, each reluctant to be the one to break the spell. Finally it was Bannerman who rolled over and turned on the bedside lamp. They blinked in its sudden brightness. She pulled the sheet up to wrap around herself and lay on her side watching him. 'I wish . . .' she said. But her voice trailed away and she never said what it was she wished.

But Bannerman could guess. 'It probably wouldn't have worked out,' he said. 'It's probably as well that you're going.'

And for the first time she knew for certain that he *didn't* want her to go. But somehow it was all too late. They would go their separate ways though neither of them wanted it. Neither of them had been able to summon the courage to face the alternative.

She reached up and pulled his head down so that she could kiss him, taste him again, reassure herself about what had gone before. 'It was perfect,' she whispered. 'You and me. It's never been like that before.'

Bannerman pulled away, rolling over on to his back and staring up at the ceiling. 'Perfection,' he said, 'comes only once. It's never the same a second time. Or a third. You spend the rest of your life trying to recapture a lost illusion.'

She was silent then for a very long time. Before finally she said in a tiny strained voice, 'Doesn't it mean anything to you?'

He thought about it. 'Yes. It probably means more to me than you'll ever know. But that's now. What it will mean next week, or next month, or next year – I don't know.' She lay quite still. 'A week ago,' he said, 'there was no one in my life. Now there are two people.' He heard her head turn but he didn't look. 'You and . . . Tania. And you are leaving. Sometimes life is like that.'

'Yes.' And somehow that one word was the final acceptance of their parting, that whatever they might feel now there was no real future in it. Then she asked, 'Why does she mean so much to you?'

And he wanted to tell her. He knew that tomorrow she would be gone and it wouldn't matter any more.

'Somewhere' – he gestured vaguely in the moonlight – 'there is a child.' His laughter was hollow and laced with bitterness.

'Not even a child any more. Very nearly a young woman. A part of me. My daughter.' He turned to look at her, but there was nothing in her face. 'I've never seen her. Not even a photograph.'

'You were married?'

'No. Her mother was a girl I knew a long time ago. She was just seventeen. Worked in telesales on my first newspaper. I was eighteen. She was a shy girl. Didn't know much about anything. Least of all sex. She thought she loved me, and maybe she did. I used to pretend that I loved her too, even to myself. It was a kind of growing-up game I played. Testing her, testing myself, playing with both our emotions to see what would happen. I was just a stupid boy who thought the world had given him a raw deal. Anyway, I took her virginity. Led her into it when she really didn't want to. I had to promise that I loved her, you know, the way kids do. And it was easy to say it; it's always easy to say when you don't mean it.' He paused. 'Much harder when you do.'

For several long minutes he was lost in recollection. All the finely etched memories that would be with him always. 'She got pregnant, of course, and I thought the whole world had fallen in on me. Didn't give her feelings a second thought. It was all about me. How *I* felt. How it would affect *my* future. I tried to persuade her to get rid of it, but she wouldn't. She just cried and cried and said she would have to tell her parents. So I said I would marry her.' He shook his head sadly, and the flicker of an ironic smile crossed his face. 'She turned me down. No great fuss or anything. Just said, no. Didn't want to marry me. She would have the child and stay with her parents if they would have her.'

Sally heard the catch in his voice.

'And still, all I could think about was me. *My* feelings, *my* confusion, *my* hurt. She would rather go through the pain of being a single mother than marry me. The mist was gone from her eyes and she saw me for what I was. A liar and a coward.' He shook his head. 'And then once I'd got over my injured pride I realized I was free. I didn't have to marry her. There'd be no paternity suit. She didn't even want my money, because that would have given me rights.' He snorted his self-contempt. 'It lost me my job, though. Word got around. My editor called me in and told me he didn't want someone like me on his staff, and that I'd better start looking for another job. I was pretty sore at the time, but I did get another job. In England. I heard later she'd had a baby girl, and then I lost contact. It didn't seem to matter then. I was just glad to have escaped.'

He turned to see Sally's dark unreadable eyes gazing into his. He couldn't meet them, and turned away.

'Then,' he said, 'well, then I had time to think about it. The years pass. You get a little older, a little wiser, and you become more aware of consequences. I find it difficult now to reconcile myself with who I was then. I ruined two lives. Stole a girl's innocence, and robbed a child of her father's love. I didn't discover my own wounds until later. Perhaps not until now.'

In the silence that followed, he felt no better for having told her. What had he expected? And suddenly he was embarrassed at having opened his soul to her. This was only making the moment of parting worse.

He rolled away and climbed out of bed, crossing to the window, standing naked in the darkness with his back to her.

'Neil . . .?' Her voice trailed after him.

'You'd better go,' he said, his voice muffled against the glass, breath misting it.

She rose and dressed slowly. He heard her moving about behind him. Then he heard the bedroom door opening and closing. From out on the landing came the sound of a door shutting, and footsteps echoed distantly on the stairs.

When he could no longer hear them, he let his face rest against the cold glass and whispered, 'Goodbye.'

CHAPTER TWENTY-EIGHT

He woke with a bad taste in his mouth. It had been a restless night and the sheets were wrapped around him like a shroud. He was cold, but didn't get up immediately. He lay staring at the rectangle of blue sky he could see through the window.

She was gone. All that remained was the lingering traces of her perfume.

He got up and dressed himself slowly, with an empty feeling inside. He made coffee in the kitchen and sat drinking it in an armchair in the living room where the sun slanted in and warmed the air.

Closing his eyes he pictured her at the airport. Or perhaps she hadn't yet left her apartment and was still packing. He allowed the thought to flicker through his mind only briefly. It was over, a thing of the past, already a memory that he would lock away with all the others.

The phone rang, a long single ring, then an interminable wait before it rang again. He rose reluctantly and crossed the room. 'Bannerman.' His voice caught on the phlegm that had gathered in his throat overnight and he coughed.

'A heavy night, Neil?' A pause. 'Hector Lewis here.'

'What have you got?' Bannerman sat down on the edge of the settee and wiped the sleep from his eyes.

'I thought I'd call you early in case I missed you. I tried yesterday evening, both at your office and at this number, but you were out gallivanting no doubt.'

Bannerman repeated irritably, 'What have you got?'

'Now hold on just a minute, my old friend, not so fast.' His smarminess oozed across the telephone lines all the way from Switzerland, and it occurred to Bannerman that Lewis would not have been trying this hard to reach him if he hadn't hit on something worthwhile. 'It's going to cost you.'

'You said that already.'

'Yes, but that was two days ago, and I was talking about the search fees. Now it's going to cost you to keep the information exclusive.'

'What the hell do you mean, Lewis?' Bannerman fought to stay calm.

'I mean I've just unwrapped a time bomb that's going to blow up in a lot of faces in London and Brussels. It's meaty stuff, Neil, and in column inches alone I could make thousands.'

'I could be on a plane for Switzerland within the hour and break your fucking neck by lunchtime.'

'Haha, yes, that's good, Neil, but by lunchtime I could have sold the story halfway around the world, and you wouldn't want that, would you?'

Bannerman felt his grip tighten around the phone. He

should never have trusted this to Lewis. But he'd had no choice. Now he was being screwed. 'So?'

'So I have a certain reputation for confidentiality to maintain, and since you came to me in good faith, I'm offering you first option – in good faith.'

'You bastard!'

'It's how I make my money.'

'How much?'

'Ten thousand.'

Bannerman was stunned. 'You've got to be out of your mind, Lewis! You think the *Post*'s going to pay ten grand for a company search?'

'They will for this one.'

Bannerman's thoughts were racing. 'I would need to know what I'm buying.'

'But of course. I have no objection to giving you the broad outline over the phone. But you'll require documentary evidence to back it up before you run the story. And before you get that, I'll require the money.'

'Let's hear it.'

'You agree to my terms?'

'Not until I know what you've got.'

Lewis sighed. 'The company, Machines Internationale, is owned jointly by René Jansen, Michel Lapointe, and . . . ah, the late Mr Robert Gryffe.'

Bannerman felt the skin tighten across his scalp.

'Not directly, of course. That would have been too easy. No,

Machines Internationale is ostensibly owned by another company which in turn is an offshoot of another company, and so on. All shell companies of course. A cobweb of deceit, if I may lapse into cliché, to disguise the identity of the man to whom the number one company is ultimately responsible.'

At last it was the link between Gryffe, Jansen and Lapointe that Bannerman had been looking for. But not worth ten thousand. 'What is its business?'

Lewis waited and then replied with calculated melodrama, 'Armaments, my friend. Guns and bombs and landmines, and God knows what else. Machines Internationale buys arms, mostly from the US, and sells to the Third World, some of the Arab states, and one or two of the South American republics. Not in itself a crime, of course. But when a minister at the British Foreign Office is involved, then it starts to get interesting, doesn't it?' Lewis chuckled to himself, and when there was no response from Bannerman, he added, 'So I got my boys to dig a little deeper in the company records, and it would appear that Machines Internationale have also been selling their wares to a number of pirate companies which operate out of several small states in Africa and the Middle East – companies which, it seems, are supplying arms direct to South Africa, in open defiance of the UN embargo on the apartheid régime there. And perhaps even more interesting, to Rhodesia – during almost all of the time that sanctions were being imposed against the illegal Smith regime.'

'Jesus Christ!'

'My sentiments exactly, Neil. So much so, in fact, that I even did a quick trace on the origins of a couple of the pirate companies. Each of those I checked out is owned by a Liechtenstein-registered company, Corniche S.A. Corniche, unfortunately, is one of those naughty little nominee companies that can act for unnamed clients whose anonymity is protected by law. Of course, you'll know about nominee companies. This one is owned by a very respectable Swiss lawyer and businessman, so it's unlikely we'll ever know who's actually behind it, or the companies it controls. Worth it though, eh? Ten grand? Cheap at the price. *British government minister murdered in Brussels was selling arms to Rhodesia and South Africa.* Neat headline wouldn't you say, Neil?'

Bannerman felt the muscles in his throat contracting, and the fingers of his free hand trembled slightly as he reached for the notepad by the phone. One glance showed the name of the company he had underlined in the notes he had taken after Platt's phone call. Corniche S.A.

'Hello, hello? You still there?'

Bannerman was fighting to piece it all together. Corniche S.A., formerly a Belgian-registered company belonging to Lapointe, had uprooted and reregistered in Liechtenstein, and was now a new company listed to a Swiss lawyer. But wasn't it just possible that Lapointe, who had used the original company to buy and sell other companies for Jansen, was still pulling the strings, still providing the cash? That this Swiss lawyer was just his front man? It occurred to Bannerman that he

330

didn't even need to prove that. A plain statement of the facts would make the connection by implication. Gryffe, Jansen and Lapointe had not only been selling arms to pirate companies who were in turn selling to the white-ruled African states, they also owned the pirate companies themselves. It wasn't indirect selling, for Christ's sake! They were doing it direct. The implications for the British government were incalculable. And for Jansen and Lapointe. International pressure would be bound to force the Belgian government to take action against the Jansen empire.

'Bannerman, you haven't died on me, have you?'

No wonder Lewis was seeking his pound of flesh. 'I'll call you back,' Bannerman said.

'No, no, no. You just wait one minute. None of this is for free. I want a certified cheque within twenty-four hours. When that cheque is in the hands of my bank you will get your documentary evidence. And if the cheque hasn't shown by nine o'clock Monday morning, at the latest, I'll sell the story elsewhere. You understand?' The tone had changed. This was a hard statement of terms.

'How the hell can I get that kind of money to you over a weekend? The banks are all shut.'

'Just do it, Bannerman. Cash in bank before the records office reopens on Monday morning.'

'I'll call you.'

'I'll be here till midday.'

The line went dead and Bannerman dropped the receiver

back in its cradle. 'Shit!' His voice resounded in the stillness of the room.

In Edinburgh it was raining, as it nearly always does. The grey and red sandstone tenements were dark and streaked with wet. The wind blew and rattled empty washing lines against rusted poles. In suburban Morningside big houses stood silent and solid behind long sloping lawns and trees that bent in the wind.

Tait lay safe and warm in his bed listening to the rain battering against his window. Outside, the streets were empty and only a few sodden leaves, remnants of the autumn, stirred in the gutter. He liked to lie in on Saturdays, though he had been awake for some time. Now he heard the phone ringing distantly in the house and he cursed. When the phone went it was always for him.

He lay listening for his wife's footsteps on the stair, but he missed them and was surprised by the gentle creak of the door as it opened.

'Are you awake?' Her voice came in a breath.

'Yes. Who is it?'

'It's someone from the paper.' His wife seemed distressed. 'A Neil Bannerman. Long-distance. I told him you were still asleep, but he was very rude.'

'There's no need to whisper. I *am* awake.' He threw back the covers and sat up. What the hell was Bannerman after?

He pulled on his dressing gown, pushing his feet into

slippers, and followed her downstairs to take the call in the living room. The children had their own playroom at the back of the house, and as he lifted the phone he heard his wife telling them to keep the noise down. 'What in God's name do you want, Bannerman? You realize it's only just gone nine, and it *is* Saturday!'

'I need ten grand. Today if possible, tomorrow at the latest.'

It took several seconds for Bannerman's words to sink in. 'Jesus Christ!' Tait's first reaction was anger. But then he realized that Bannerman would not phone and ask him for ten thousand pounds at nine o'clock on a Saturday morning unless he had a bloody good reason. He almost resented the fact that Bannerman was as good as he was. It made it all the harder to get rid of him. Although it made no impression on his resolve to do so. No one could speak to Tait the way Bannerman had. 'Why?'

'To prove that Robert Gryffe, René Jansen and Michel Lapointe were selling arms to Rhodesia and South Africa.'

Tait ran the implications through his mind with a practised professional detachment. Then he felt the first buzz of adrenalin. 'Who gets the pay-off?'

'A guy called Hector Lewis. He has a business based in Switzerland. Does company searches, among other things. I got hold of some information and asked him to check it out. When it turned up what it did he got greedy. He wants a certified cheque in his bankers' hands by nine on Monday morning at the latest, or he'll sell the story elsewhere.'

'Fuck!'

'Ditto.'

'How reliable is he? Can you trust him?'

He heard Bannerman's bitter chuckle. 'Oh, I think so. He's good, very good, a real pro. The fact that he's a twenty-four-carat bastard is merely incidental.'

Tait felt the irresistible creep of a smile. So Bannerman was fallible too, and it hurt him like it hurt anyone else.

'Well?' Bannerman was impatient.

'Where does Slater fit into all this?' The question was inevitable. To Tait it was almost more important than the story itself. Just how embarrassing was it going to be for the *Post*, even if they were the ones to break the story?

'I don't know yet,' Bannerman said.

'Good.'

'But I will.'

'For fuck's sake, Bannerman! Can't you just leave Slater out of this?'

'Do I get the money or not?'

'Yes, you get the fucking money. But how the hell are we supposed to do it when the banks are shut?'

'That's your problem. I'll call you back with the relevant details when I've spoken again to Lewis.'

'Hang on a minute. What arrangement have you come to about Slater's kid?'

'Arrangement?'

'For getting her on the plane tomorrow.'

Bannerman frowned. 'I don't know anything about that.'

'Oh, for Christ's sake! I had a telex sent yesterday to your office asking you to put her on the Edinburgh flight on Sunday morning. The Brook Clinic in Edinburgh has agreed to take her.'

For the first time Bannerman was confronted by what he had known all along. That whatever he might feel, Tania was going to spend the rest of her life in an institution. His mind swerved away from the thought. 'I didn't go into the office yesterday.' Some protective barrier raised itself. He had taken enough of an emotional battering already. 'I'll arrange it.'

'Good. Someone from the clinic will meet her at the other end. At least no one can say the *Post* is shirking its responsibilities.'

Bannerman hung up and then immediately redialled. Lewis answered promptly. 'Well, well, that was quick, Neil. Good news I trust?'

'You've got your ten grand.'

'Excellent. I knew you'd come through.'

Bannerman's voice was very controlled. 'I'll not waste my breath telling you what'll happen if you fuck me over on this, Lewis.'

'Neil, Neil, would I do a thing like that?'

'All we need are your account details. You'll get your cheque. Just make sure the results of that search are telexed to Edinburgh by midday on Monday.'

'It's as good as done, Neil. Just as soon as the money's in the bank. Do you have a pen handy?'

'No. You can arrange the details with my editor.' He gave him Tait's home number. They deserved each other.

He hung up and sat for some minutes trying to resolve his conflicting emotions, the struggle between his personal feelings and his professional instincts. He needed a clear mind to steer him through the day ahead, and his thoughts turned to Platt. Platt was a problem. Bannerman had promised him a share of the story. He would have had no scruples about welching on that promise, but for the material Platt had unearthed on Lapointe's nominee company. He needed Platt. It would take him too long to collect the data himself and the pressure was now on to run an early story. He couldn't trust Lewis to sit on it if he held it back, even for a few days. And the stuff Platt had so diligently compiled completed the circle. It was within his grasp to prove beyond doubt that Gryffe had been involved in selling arms to rogue states in contravention of UN sanctions.

Even now he found it difficult to grasp the full enormity of the story. One thing he didn't yet know was who had ordered the execution of Gryffe and Slater. Or who had shot at him in Flanders. There was also the riddle of Slater. That he had been blackmailing Gryffe seemed beyond doubt, but Bannerman had no proof. And how had Slater come by his information? It was not the kind of thing that you stumbled on by chance.

Again Platt wormed his way into Bannerman's thoughts. There was no escaping it. He would have to take Platt into his confidence. With great reluctance he dug out the grubby business card Platt had given him at the party – how long ago that seemed now – and dialled.

'Platt.' The voice was thick with phlegm. The call had clearly woken him.

'Bannerman.'

'Oh . . .' Platt was wide awake now and fumbling for his bedside clock. 'What time is it . . .?'

'Time you and I had a talk.'

'What about? What's happened?'

'I'm at the Rue de Commerce. I suggest you get over here. I'll expect you.' The line went dead on Platt's confusion.

Bannerman thumbed through his notebook until he found the unlisted number he had copied from Slater's contacts book. There was a sense of urgency bubbling to the surface now. He picked up the phone again and dialled. It rang three times before a voice answered in Flemish.

Bannerman said, 'Do you speak English?'

'A little.'

'I'd like to speak to René Jansen.'

'Who wants him?'

'Neil Bannerman.'

There was a long wait before the voice returned. 'Herr Jansen is not available.'

Bannerman said calmly, 'Tell him I intend to expose a company which is selling arms in breach of UN sanctions. I think he knows who I am.'

'I don't think . . .'

'No one's asking you to think. Just tell him.'

There was another long wait before the voice returned. Then, 'Herr Jansen will speak to you at his home this evening. If you will be here for eight-thirty.'

Bannerman hung up and wondered fleetingly if the toxic information now in his possession made him the next target. He shrugged the thought aside and turned his mind elsewhere before reaching for the telephone directory. He found the number of the Hotel Regent in the Avenue Louise in a matter of seconds.

Schumacher picked up the call, then handed over to his wife when Bannerman told him why he was calling. She seemed surprised, but pleased. He said unnecessarily, 'I thought that since you were flying to Edinburgh on Sunday anyway you wouldn't mind. It's just that she can't travel alone.'

'Mr Bannerman, there's no need to apologize. Of course we'll take her. That poor, poor child.'

He spent an uncomfortable few minutes on the phone with Laura-Lee sorting out the details and wondering if he was right to entrust the child to these eccentric Americans. Was Mrs Schumacher's concern for Tania genuine, or was it just one more story of European adventure with which she could regale her social circle back home?

When, eventually, he got her off the line he called the airline and booked a seat for Tania on the Schumachers' flight.

Now it only remained for him to inform the clinic here in

Brussels. The news would have to be broken to Tania herself. For a long time he sat looking at the phone. It would be too easy simply to phone Dr Mascoulin and ask him to tell the child. He knew he owed it to her to tell her himself, but didn't know that he could face the consequences. He sighed deeply, closing his eyes, and sat back to wait for Platt.

It was almost half an hour before he heard footsteps on the stairs. He eased himself out of the settee and went through to the hall. Platt stood flushed and breathless on the landing.

'I got a taxi straight over,' he said, and followed Bannerman through to the living room. 'What's happened? I thought after yesterday . . .'

'You're back in business, Platt,' Bannerman interrupted and sank back into the settee.

Platt stared at him. 'What do you mean?'

'I mean that the stuff you dug out on Lapointe's Corniche company has turned up trumps – in the light of further evidence. And I'm prepared to do a swap. Documentary evidence. Your information for mine. A simple exchange, and then we've both got a story.'

'But . . . but what have you got?' Platt was suspicious. Why the sudden change of heart?

Bannerman sighed. He knew that he would have to tell Platt everything; his conversations with Lewis, the information unearthed in Switzerland, the deal he had been forced to make.

Platt sat down on the edge of a chair and listened in aston-
ished silence as Bannerman spelled it out. He was barely able
to conceal his excitement, mopping his fat flushed face repeatedly with his soiled red handkerchief.

'What about Jansen?' he said when he'd had time to process
it all. 'We'll have to put it to him.'

'Yes.'

'When?'

'Tonight. I've already fixed a rendezvous. But I'm seeing
him alone.'

Platt didn't argue. In fact he was quite relieved. He would not
have relished a confrontation with a man like Jansen. He knew
his own limitations. And, anyway, why not let Bannerman do
the dirty work? Hadn't he dismissed Platt's efforts so dispar-
agingly only yesterday? Let him do it on his own and then
make him eat dirt. Finally he had Bannerman right where he
wanted him. Platt could hardly believe his luck. The euphoria
of the day before returned and he beamed happily. 'How about
a drink to celebrate?'

Bannerman shook his head and looked at Platt with faint
distaste. 'I agreed to share the story. I don't feel obliged to
drink with you.'

Platt's smile never wavered. *I'll show you*, he thought. 'Can I
borrow Slater's car?'

Bannerman was surprised. 'What on earth for?'

'There are things I need to do. I'll have to go to the office
and take copies of my notes from the Tribunal de Commerce,

and then I can bring them round to you tonight. After you've seen Jansen.'

Bannerman felt in his pocket for the keys and threw them across to Platt. 'Don't wreck it.' This way, at least, he had an excuse for not going to the clinic.

Platt scurried off with his happiness and his dark secrets, leaving Bannerman to face the phone call he knew he must now make. An image came to him of Tania standing at the window, watching for him to come. She would be expecting him today, and he did not have the courage to face her, or tell her of the plans other people were making for her future.

CHAPTER TWENTY-NINE

Across the city Kale lay fully clothed on his bed as he had done throughout the hours of darkness. At first it had been the thump of music from the nightclub next door that kept him awake, pounding through his head until after five. But by then he had been beyond sleep. He had left the shutters open, and a neon sign in the street outside flashed every few seconds to bathe the room in a warm red glow. Now, many hours later, the smoke from his cigarette drifted lazily towards the ceiling where a thick pall from all the cigarettes that had gone before hung in the grey light of late morning.

He had reached a decision. All these days of torment, of discovery and self-doubt, were behind him. Tomorrow he was leaving. Tomorrow he was walking away from all this. He didn't care about the remainder of his fee, or his reputation. He didn't care about anyone or anything. He was simply leaving. It seemed so easy now. Now that he had finally admitted to himself that killing the child in cold blood was not an option. He had discovered in himself, quite unexpectedly, a potential for love. Or, at least, a hate less corrosive. No longer was he haunted by the compulsion to follow her, to confront himself with the failure that was his own humanity.

Tomorrow morning a taxi to the airport, a flight that would take less than an hour, and he would be back in London. Safe and sound.

CHAPTER THIRTY

You could not see the house from the road. It lay somewhere behind a high stone wall in secluded darkness. The avenue was broad and well lit, sloping gently uphill, past the mansions that wealthy men had built here in this exclusive quarter of the city over more than a hundred years.

The taxi drew up at the gates of the Jansen place and Bannerman climbed out. It was a cold night and the sky was hard and clear.

'Wait,' he told the driver. He pressed a buzzer set into the carved stone gatepost and leaned forward to the speaker grille. 'Neil Bannerman for Monsieur Jansen.'

Almost at once a soft hum filled the air and the gates swung soundlessly inwards. Bannerman climbed back into the taxi and they drove through the gates along a driveway that ran between ancient trees whose intertwining branches formed a canopy overhead. There was nothing to be seen in the darkness beyond this tunnel of trees and the reach of the headlamps.

Then, quite unexpectedly, they came out into a wash of naked moonlight lying across a flat snow-covered lawn. The

344

drive divided the grass into two squares beyond which the arched windows of a three-storey mansion rose into the night sky. Not a single light showed in any one of them. This, Bannerman thought, was the end of the road. And he felt his excitement rising. A tiny stab of apprehension.

The driveway opened on to a gravel strip that ran the length of the house, and the driver pulled in at the foot of a short flight of steps leading to a grand porticoed entrance. Again Bannerman told him to wait, and as he climbed the steps double doors swung open ahead of him. A soft yellow light split the darkness, throwing his shadow back down the steps and across the gravel. An elderly man wearing a neatly pressed suit and starched white collar beckoned him into a vast circular hall panelled in oak. Bannerman's shoes resounded on mosaic tiling and he found himself facing a broad marble staircase that swept upwards in a curve to the first floor whose balcony repeated the circle before yet more stairs spiralled to the floor above. He craned his head up to see a dome of stained glass crowning the atrium. It would be magnificent in sunlight, showering shards of coloured light on to the stairs and landings. Dark, anonymous portraits stared down at him from the walls.

The man at his side coughed discreetly. 'Your coat, sir.' Bannerman slipped it off and Jansen's butler draped it carefully over his arm. 'Please follow me.'

The sound of their footsteps on the marble stairs echoed off into the vastness. The first-floor balcony was carpeted in a rich, dark blue. They walked around half of its circumference before the butler stopped to open one of the many doors leading off it. Why, Bannerman thought, when a man has all this, does he need to sell illegal arms?

He walked into a high-ceilinged room, its windows hung with velvet and looking out on to gardens at the rear of the house. An enormous marble hearth simmered in darkness. There was no fire in it, although the room was not cold. A crystal chandelier threw its almost perfect mirror reflection on to the surface of an oblong dining table of highly polished mahogany. There were places set at either end of it. A tall man in a claret smoking jacket stood waiting by one of them. The door closed behind Bannerman and the man extended his arms towards the place opposite.

'Have a seat, Mr Bannerman. I take it you have not eaten?'

'No.' Bannerman moved towards the nearer end of the table and both men sat down to face each other along its length. Jansen was not as Bannerman had imagined. He seemed much older. There was a fullness still to his dark hair, but it was shot through with grey. His face was drawn, cheekbones high and angular, large eyes brown and watery as if he were on the verge of tears. His long, straight nose was almost aristo-cratic. But the line of the jaw was weakened by a loosening of the flesh at his neck, and skin that had turned the tex-ture of crepe. Yet Bannerman knew that this was a man still only in his late forties. It showed only in the way he held himself, eyes gazing steadily back at Bannerman. His smile lacked warmth and he spoke with a voice that was clear and without accent.

'My father built this house,' he said. 'And my mother still lives in it. You will have something to drink before we eat?'

'Whisky.'

Jansen lifted a small bell from the table and rang it. A young man entered from an adjoining room. Without turning his head Jansen spoke to him briefly in Flemish. The young man disappeared and returned with a decanter of whisky and two glasses. He poured the drinks at each place and left. Jansen raised his glass.

'Your very good health, Mr Bannerman.' They drank in silence before Jansen said, 'Shall we talk before we eat?'

'I'd prefer that.'

Jansen clasped his hands together on the table in front of him and waited. They were like two chess players, and Bannerman had the first move.

He made his opening gambit. 'You knew a man called Robert Gryffe.'

'Is that a question or a statement?'

'Both. But it is a question only out of politeness.'

Jansen smiled the same cold smile. 'Yes,' he said, 'I knew him. But not well. I met him on only a handful of occasions.'

'And Tim Slater?'

'I did not even know he existed until I read about him in the newspapers.' He shook his head. 'I know what you are thinking, Mr Bannerman. But you are wrong. The assumption from what you and I both know is clear. That Mr Slater came into possession of certain knowledge with which he was blackmailing Mr Gryffe. But that is a conclusion we have both come to in hindsight. If that *was* the case, then I knew nothing about it. And I certainly had nothing to do with their deaths. Even if I had known . . .' He paused to smile again. 'You see, I can weather the storm of a scandal over illegal arms sales.'

'You don't deny it then?' Bannerman had been absorbing the other man's words with a growing unease.

'Why should I? You are obviously in possession of the facts. Naturally I would prefer to avoid such a scandal, but if necessary I will ride it out. It will hurt me only a little. Heads will roll, but not mine. The burden of guilt will fall upon others, though it is I who shall accept the ultimate responsibility for the indiscretion of certain employees. In six months it will be forgotten. The government will be embarrassed, but then they need me more than I need them. As I have said, it is a storm I can weather, Mr Bannerman. Murder, however, is something else. One would not entertain murder lightly, and I not at all. Not from any moral standpoint, you understand, but simply because it is far too risky an enterprise.'

Bannerman stared thoughtfully at the man opposite. This was not what he had expected. And yet everything he said had the ring of truth about it. Men like Jansen never took the fall. They had all the advantages that money, power and influence afford. Effective buffers against retribution. Would he really need to resort to murder? But there were still too

many questions left unanswered. He said, with sudden reso-
lution, 'You sent someone to recover files of cuttings from
Slater's office.'

Jansen nodded. 'Yes,' he said. 'But at that point it seemed as
though our secret might yet remain intact. Lapointe attended
to the details. Perhaps it was a mistake.'

'And the house in Flanders?'

'Ah, yes, it was burned down, I believe. I am told there will
be problems regarding the insurance.'

Anger rose quickly in Bannerman. 'Someone tried to kill me
there, and damn nearly succeeded.' He caught himself, and
reined in his emotions. 'I'm not at all sure I believe that you
had nothing to do with the murders in the Rue de Commerce,
Mr Jansen, or the attempt on my own life in Flanders.' He drew
a deep breath. 'You set up a network of companies to sell arms
to Rhodesia and South Africa in defiance of the United Nations
embargo. That makes you just as responsible for the deaths
of the people those guns kill as those who pull the triggers.
So why would you be squeamish about killing your business
partner and his blackmailer if you saw that as a threat? Morally
there is no distinction.'

Jansen laughed. 'How refreshingly naïve. Morality is not
a word in my lexicon. Do you think I give a damn about UN
embargoes and human rights, or Gryffe and Slater? Or you
for that matter? Self, Mr Bannerman, is what life is about.
Self.'

He ran a hand back through thick, steely hair.

'Not even the ones we love, or like to think we love, are as important to us as ourselves. It is the true human condition, you see. It's what we all feel but are ashamed to admit. Why, I don't know. For selfishness is the essence of existence.'

He spread his hands to either side as if dispensing reason.

'What, for example, determines the way we vote in an election? Of course, we vote for the party we judge will bring us the best advantage. Why do we weep when a loved one dies? Because of our own loss. All motivation is selfish, even religious motivation where the reward for a life lived piously on earth is eternal life in Heaven. And so am I motivated. When I think of selling arms to anyone I weigh up the advantages and the disadvantages. If the rewards are high, and the risks low, I proceed. But, as I told you, when it comes to murder . . . well, I would have decided against it. While the advantages might have been considerable, they would certainly have been outweighed by the risks.' He raised his eyebrows. 'Do you see?'

Bannerman nodded. He saw only too well. 'Yes,' he said, 'I see that you are a man who cannot ever have known love, either as something given or received. Of course people are selfish. That is an instinctive thing, self-preservation, perpetuation of the species. But we have other qualities too. Or at least, most of us do. There is a balance in our design. For each personality trait necessarily there must be an opposite. As in all natural things. Night and day, light and dark, summer and winter. In people the contrasts are more subtle, but they are there if you look for them. Love and hate, anger and forgiveness, greed and generosity, selfishness and compassion.'

He leaned forward with his elbows on the table in front of him.

'The thing is, Jansen, that without one the other can't exist. Without night there is no day. Without hate there is no love. Without compassion there is no self. What you are is an aberration. One of nature's rare mistakes. My problem is that I'm not quite sure whether I believe you or not.'

Jansen listened in silence, his face drawn and expressionless, before presenting a pale imitation of his earlier smile. 'Most unfortunate,' he said. 'I had hoped you might be corruptible. I should not have asked you here otherwise. Perhaps I was wrong. A man like you can't be bought . . . can he?' He paused expectantly and Bannerman stared at him for a moment.

'Is that a question or a statement?'

Jansen smiled his first genuine smile. 'You think you are very clever, don't you, Mr Bannerman?'

Bannerman said, 'I don't think I'll bother with the meal.' He stood up and drained his glass. 'Good whisky, though. Scotch, of course.'

Jansen's gaze followed him all the way to the door. But he didn't speak until Bannerman opened it. 'Of course you realize that everything I have said here tonight was off the record.'

'Then you should have made that clear before you said it.'

'I'll sue.' There was an edge to Jansen's voice now.

Bannerman held the door half-open. 'I doubt it. It's amazing how much unsubstantiated shit can get flung around in open court. And I doubt if you would risk all your splendid isolation to refute it.'

Outside the night was a little colder and the glitter of stars seemed a little harder. The frost glistened on the snow as the taxi's headlights swept through the tunnel of trees. Bannerman glanced back and the receding house remained in darkness. The gates were open when they reached the end of the drive, and when they had passed through them, shut again with a soft electronic hum.

Inside Jansen's vast mansion the billionaire climbed stiffly to the second floor and walked around the landing to his study without looking down. The room glowed faintly in the moonlight and he crossed to his desk to switch on a small reading lamp. It threw a bright pool of light on the desk, plunging the room beyond its halo into obscurity. Jansen lifted the phone.

CHAPTER THIRTY-ONE

Platt was waiting in Slater's car outside the apartment block in the Rue de Commerce. He had been sitting with the engine running for nearly half an hour, his stomach aflutter with nerves and excitement. And a strange, gnawing fear.

He saw Bannerman's taxi draw up in the rearview mirror. He switched off the engine and jumped out on the pavement.

'Well, did you see him?' He hurried up the stairs after the younger man. But Bannerman said nothing. 'I've been waiting for ages.'

In the apartment, Bannerman drew a bottle of whisky from his pocket and threw his coat over the settee. He screwed off the top, got two glasses and poured stiff measures into each. Platt watched him apprehensively and snatched the proffered glass. He didn't drink it immediately, but watched as Bannerman knocked his own back in one then poured himself another.

'Well?'

'I saw him.'

'And?' Platt felt the dull ache of his ulcer and sipped gingerly at his whisky.

'First the company stuff.'

Platt laid his glass on the table and took out a folded Manila envelope which he thrust at Bannerman. Bannerman opened it and glanced over the photocopies of clumsily typed sheets inside. He dropped them on the table and poured the second whisky over his throat.

'He wouldn't say anything.'

'What do you mean?' Platt glared at him suspiciously. 'He must have said something.'

'What did you expect?' Bannerman glared at him. 'That he would break down and confess all? The man is untouchable, Platt. He has all his protective layers of power and bureaucracy and money to hide behind. And any number of scapegoats to take the fall. He's just going to sit quiet. No comment. Why don't you phone and ask him?'

Platt sat down on the edge of the settee. What *had* he expected? Of course the man wasn't going to say anything. He should have known that. Still, 'No comment' can be expressed in many ways. *Last night Belgian billionaire René Jansen remained tight-lipped.* He looked at Bannerman. *Bastard.* He was holding something back. And Platt had no intention of missing out. 'So that's it?'

Bannerman nodded.

'I don't believe you.'

'Then maybe you should leave.'

'Now look here, Bannerman . . .' He was unprepared for the speed with which Bannerman suddenly grabbed his lapels and lifted him bodily out of the settee.

'Get out!'

Platt pulled himself free and straightened his coat with as much dignity as he could muster. In that moment he hated Bannerman as much as he had hated anyone or anything in his life. But he controlled himself. His time would come.

'When do I get my copy of the stuff from Lewis?'

'Whenever I get it. Monday or Tuesday.' Bannerman turned away towards the window, and Platt allowed himself a smile. By then it would all be over. And yet, somehow, that didn't seem revenge enough. He wanted to hurt Bannerman now.

'You don't care about anyone, or anything, do you?' he said.

'Get out!' Bannerman still had his back to him.

'That girl, all those years ago. You didn't care about her either. It was me that got you the sack you know. I told the editor what you'd done to that girl. And I was right, wasn't I? You never even turned up for the funeral. You just didn't care.'

Bannerman wheeled round. 'What are you talking about?'

Platt frowned. 'That girl, the one from telesales, the one you got in trouble. My God, don't you even remember?' He stared at Bannerman in disbelief before realizing, quite suddenly, that Bannerman didn't know, had never known. 'She killed herself. Just a few months after the baby was born. Her parents threw her out. She drowned the baby and then killed herself. Didn't you know?' He felt a great inner joy. At last he had found the place where he could hurt him most.

Bannerman's face betrayed nothing. 'I'll call you.'

Platt stood for a moment then turned and went out through

the hall. Bannerman poured himself another drink and when he heard the car start up in the street below realized he would have to take a taxi again in the morning.

The whisky burned his throat this time, and he felt his tears hot on the cool skin of his cheeks.

Bannerman could not have said how long he had been dozing, but it felt like forever. His jacket lay in a crumpled heap on the floor and there were only three fingers of gold left in the whisky bottle. He was lying face down on the settee, one arm hanging over the side so that his fingers trailed loosely on the carpet. He did not hear the bell, and it took several minutes before the hammering on the door forced its way through the undulating folds of sleep and alcohol.

Slowly he pulled himself up into a seated position and tried to wipe the sleep from his eyes. He was still drunk and found it difficult to focus on his watch.

'Christ,' he groaned. It was after two. A fist hammered again at the door. 'Just a minute!' he shouted, and his head felt like it had been split by an axe. He made his way unsteadily through the hall and opened the door. Du Maurier pushed his way in and switched on a light. Bannerman blinked blindly.

'Get yourself sober,' the policeman said. 'We're going for a drive.'

'What the fuck . . .' Bannerman heard his own voice slurring in the half-light.

Du Maurier gripped his arm firmly and pulled him into the

bathroom, filled a toothglass with cold water and threw it in Bannerman's face. Bannerman tried to swing at him, but the policeman caught his fist and held it fast. 'Take a cold shower. I'll wait for you downstairs.'

When Bannerman came down ten minutes later the world was still swimming, but he was sober enough to realize that du Maurier must have a damn good reason for dragging him out at two in the morning. He slipped into the passenger seat and du Maurier turned his car away from the kerb.

'Where are we going?' The car drifted noiselessly through dark, deserted streets. 'It's not Tania . . .?'

'No, it's not. We'll be there soon.'

They stopped outside a dark, anonymous building, with only the odd light burning in windows rising through two storeys. Du Maurier took him by the arm and they climbed steps into a dingy reception hall, before descending to the basement in an elevator. Light shone through the windows of double doors at the end of a long gloomy corridor. Du Maurier propelled him towards the light, and Bannerman screwed up his eyes as they pushed through swing doors into a large, white-tiled room. The stink of formalin filled his nostrils and did more to sober him up than any amount of cold water. A man in a white coat leaned out from an adjoining room and nodded them through.

The body that lay on the stainless steel table was naked beneath the glare of surgical lights. The stench of death and acid preservative was nauseating, and Bannerman felt his stomach heave.

There was a look of serenity on Platt's face, but his chest was open, like a carcass in a butcher's shop. The white flesh around the wound was tinged with blue, all blood drained from the body.

'Jesus, Christ! Where's the toilet?'

The man in the white coat took Bannerman across the hall to the men's room, leaving him to kneel on the floor and vomit into the pan. Bannerman remained doubled over it, breathing hard for several minutes, before pulling himself to his feet and staggering to the washbasin. He turned on the cold water to sluice his face and swill his mouth, before taking a long, cool drink.

Du Maurier was waiting in the corridor and they went back out to the car. The two men sat in silence while the policeman rolled down a window and lit a cigarette.

'So,' he said. 'Can you give me a formal identification?'

Bannerman answered mechanically. 'Richard Joseph Platt.'

'What was he doing with Slater's car?'

'He borrowed it. Give me a cigarette.'

Du Maurier lit it for him and watched him screw up his face at the taste.

'What happened?'

The policeman sighed. 'Someone used both barrels of a sawn-off shotgun. Close range. We found the body in Slater's car. It was parked in a side street near the Gare du Nord.'

Bannerman tried to make himself feel something, but couldn't. His only thought was why had Jansen done it. The man had played it smart until now. The Inspector held out a folded wad of paper. Bannerman took it. There were about a dozen sheets, all clumsily typed.

'It's in French,' he said. 'I can't read it. What is it?'

'You don't know?'

'Maybe I can guess.'

'And what do you guess?'

'I guess maybe it's a story about how René Jansen, Michel Lapointe and Robert Gryffe formed a consortium to sell arms. Knowing Platt he'll have dressed it up a bit. He probably paints a picture of Gryffe as a high-powered salesman with access to heads of state. Lapointe as a kind of wizard of company law who set up a network of companies that enabled them to sell to whomever they liked from behind a veil of anonymity. And Jansen as the quiet power behind it all who supplied the money and creamed off the lion's share of the profits. Of course, he'll have made the biggest play of the sales to South Africa and Rhodesia.'

'Is it true?'

'Yes.'

'Then why in God's name did you not tell me?'

Bannerman shook his head sadly. 'I would have. Probably today. I only found out yesterday. I had a deal with Platt, but it looks as if he meant to jump the gun. Screw me over.'

'My God, you are a fool, Monsieur! Who else knew about this?'

'Only Platt, myself, my editor, and the man in Switzerland who did the company searches. Oh, and Jansen, of course.'

'Jansen?'

'I confronted him with it last night.'

Bannerman heard the air escape from between du Maurier's clenched teeth.

'And who knew about your deal with Platt?'

'No one, as far as I know.'

The Inspector lit another cigarette. 'Then it is you that they meant to kill.'

Bannerman closed his eyes. Still drunk, still in shock. 'Yes.'

'You're taking it very calmly.'

'Appearances can be deceptive.' Bannerman was right on the edge. He could not remember having felt this bad at any time in his life. He had failed. Failed in everything. 'Will you arrest Jansen?'

'How can I arrest him?'

'Because who else could be responsible?' He was thinking how easily he had been taken in by Jansen, how easily he had been led to doubt Jansen's involvement in the killings of Gryffe and Slater.

Du Maurier shook his head. 'There is no proof. Not yet, anyway. One thing is clear, though. Whoever pulled the trigger on Monsieur Platt, it was not the same man who killed Gryffe and Slater.'

Bannerman turned to look at the policeman. His face seemed pale, almost yellow, in the light of the streetlamps. 'How can you know that?'

'Because the man at the Rue de Pavie was a professional.

Meticulous in every way. Monsieur Platt was killed by some underworld hoodlum. A hired gun. Effective, but crude. Messy, not a pro. We have a better chance of catching him and so we have a better chance of finding out who hired him. We do not know that it is Jansen. Besides, I think your obsession with that man is perhaps blinding you to other possibilities.'

Bannerman shivered. 'What do you mean?'

'I am very tired, Monsieur.' Du Maurier sighed. 'I should like to be home in my bed. You will be required to come to my office later today to make an official statement. Perhaps we can discuss it then.'

Bannerman folded Platt's story and held it out to the Inspector.

'No, you keep it. It is better that we never found it. I shall wait until you have published. You see, Monsieur, public pressure will have a greater influence on my superiors to reopen the case than an uncorroborated story found on the body of a dead journalist. And we would not want to give them advance warning, would we?'

CHAPTER THIRTY-TWO

Sunday. The change in the weather overnight was marked. It had rained steadily for some hours before dawn, and when the first light misted the rain-sodden air much of the snow had gone.

In the taxi that swept east through the city along the Boulevard Leopold III to the airport at Zavantem, Bannerman and the child sat in silence. He had barely been able to speak to her and saw the hurt in her eyes. She had been expecting him yesterday, and now he had come to put her on a plane that would take her away from him. He had not even tried to explain it, except to say that a lady and gentleman from America would be with her on the plane, and that he would come and see her when his business in Brussels was finished.

She was wondering what it was she had done to offend him, and she felt that ache inside her that was the seed of frustration. A bubble that was growing. She was afraid of it, afraid that it would take control and that when finally it burst he would not understand. She slipped her hand into his. It felt warm and big and it responded with a little squeeze. *Please let me control it*, she was saying inside. *Please let me control it.*

Bannerman gazed out at the same buildings he had passed on his arrival ten days before, and thought how ten days can change your life.

At the Hotel Regent the Schumachers had risen early and Mrs Schumacher had fussed and gushed with excitement. 'Which dress should I wear, Henry?' She had held up two dresses, one cotton print with a colourful pattern, the other plain blue wool.

'I don't know, dear. You look good in both.'

'Oh, Henry, don't be so infuriating.'

'Perhaps the print dress, then.'

She looked at it and then the other. 'I think I'll wear the blue. More sombre for the occasion. Poor child. Oh, but isn't this exciting, Henry?'

'Yes, dear.'

'No, no, don't wear that tie, Henry, it clashes with your suit. Yes, that one. Now that looks so much better.' She struggled breathlessly into the blue dress. 'Zip me up, please, Henry. Do you think maybe we could stay on in Edinburgh an extra day?'

'Well, I do have to be back in Washington . . .'

'Yes, yes. Of course, you're right.' Pause. 'I wonder what she's like. I certainly hope she won't throw one of her tantrums on the plane. That, I could do without.' Then she added, 'Poor thing. We must do what we can, Henry.'

'Yes, dear.'

'Hurry now, or we'll miss breakfast.'

But as the car sped them towards Zavantem she was curiously quiet. Henry Schumacher stared morosely from the rear passenger window, and his wife wondered why she felt so nervous. A touch of indigestion, perhaps. She had eaten breakfast much too quickly. Or it might be the change in the weather. The weather could do that to you. Tomorrow the damp would bring that rheumatic stiffness back to her joints.

Kale felt a lightness in his heart. He liked the rain. It reminded him of London. He liked the feel of it on his face and the dampness in the air where people gathered for a drink with their steamy wet coats and hats. For him this was the day of release, the day when the nightmare of the past week would end. All the questions about his future remained unanswered, but they could wait. The prison sentence of his past was drawing to a close. The only conscious reminder was the weight of the gun in the holster strapped across his back and over his left shoulder. He had decided not to leave it at the hotel, though he could not take it with him – it would never pass the security checks at the airport. But it was at the airport, he had decided, he would dispose of it. In one of the flush tanks in the toilets, after he had wiped it clean of prints.

His taxi drew up outside the terminal building and he stepped out into the bluster of wind and rain. Through sliding doors, head down as he passed the security policemen with their hip holsters and machine guns. Rows of airline desks, and people with cases milling around, a mechanical voice announcing flights over the tannoy. Kale breathed a sigh of relief and glanced at his watch. He had half an hour before his flight would be called.

He checked in at the BA desk and left his case, and then looked for the *Toilet* signs. They led him up a flight of steps on to a concourse on an upper level. He saw the toilets at the far side, brushed past a group of travellers sharing a joke, and stopped with a feeling like death inside him.

The child was not looking his way, but he saw her head turning. Perhaps she sensed that he was there. Beside her stood the man he had followed to the clinic, and an elderly couple. He could hear the woman's voice. An American.

'Well, Mr Bannerman, I don't think you need have any fears about leaving little Tania in our custody for the flight. She is such a darling girl. I know we're going to get on just great . . .' Her voice trailed away sharply as the scream tore from the child's lips.

Heads all around them turned. Bannerman looked at Tania, at the terror on her face, and followed her eyes. He saw a man in a shabby coat, a man in a drawing without a face.

Kale panicked. Suddenly the prison door had slammed shut and he was still on the inside. The screaming went on and on, and yet it must only have been seconds. Everything was happening in slow motion. It wasn't a conscious decision to draw the gun from his holster, but the instincts that had kept him alive all these years. He was aware of the gun trembling in his hand as he raised it with the speed and efficiency of training and practice. And for just one more second there was an enormous battle between will and instinct, before he squeezed the trigger and saw the child thrown backwards.

Now there was screaming all around him and he glanced to either side, still unable to move. The elderly American was advancing slowly towards him, his wife yelling at him hysterically. 'Henry . . .!'

'Okay, son, give me the gun,' the American was saying. 'You've done what you came to do. No need for anyone else to get hurt now. Just give me the gun.' The voice was soothing, relaxing, its effect almost hypnotic. Kale felt his gun hand dropping.

Then there was a voice shouting at him above the noise of all the others. He looked round and saw the dark uniform of a security policeman. He looked back helplessly at the American, and for a second Schumacher thought he saw the hint of a tear in the man's eye.

Kale ran, bodies scurrying to either side, squealing like rats in a panic. Again he heard the voice of the security officer and he seemed to be running into a vast emptiness. The guard levelled his pistol and fired one, two, three times.

Kale's head hit the tiles with a smack and his body slithered on for several metres across their shiny surface, carried by its own momentum, spraying blood in its wake. He came to rest, twisted and ugly, with a pool of blood spreading rapidly around him. His eyes were open and staring through the walls of glass across the runway. But he saw nothing.

CHAPTER THIRTY-THREE

I

The sound of voices echoed mechanically along the corridor, footsteps on a hard floor, unseen doors opening and closing. They seemed remote, disconnected. A nurse in white uniform wheeling a trolley from one ward to the next, the sound of an orderly laughing, cut short by doors swinging shut.

Bannerman stood in the emptiness of the glass-walled reception hall. The lights above reflected off the polished floor. He glanced across at the bowed head of Henry Schumacher sitting on one of the red vinyl seats, and thought of the man's courage in stepping forward to face the gunman. He thought, too, of the child's blood on his own hands, and he glanced at them now. They were pale and white, the blood all washed away.

He looked at his watch. Anything to stop him from thinking. It was only a little over an hour since it had all happened. Still Sunday morning, still grey and wet outside.

He looked again at Schumacher and scuffed his feet. 'I'm

sorry I got you involved in all this,' he said. 'I hope everything will be all right with your wife.'

Schumacher waved his hand carelessly. 'She's all right. Just shock. It's the child . . .'

A doctor pushed through swing doors. He looked tired. 'She is in the operating theatre.' His accent was thick and clumsy. He glanced at Schumacher and then back to Bannerman. 'It could be hours. And even if the operation is successful, there is no guarantee she will survive it. You can wait if you like.' He paused, awkward and embarrassed, before disappearing again behind the doors. They swung back and forth for some moments before coming to a standstill.

'I'll be back,' Bannerman said and set off towards the elevator.

Schumacher looked at him in surprise. 'But the police . . .'

'Tell the Inspector when he gets back that I'll be in touch with him.' He pressed the down button.

'Where are you going?'

Bannerman hesitated. He was trembling. 'To get the bastards.'

Even in daylight you could not see Jansen's mansion from the road. The rain was falling steadily as Bannerman's taxi drew up at the gates. Bannerman got out and crossed to the gatepost. He pressed the button and spoke into the grille. 'Neil Bannerman for René Jansen.' Silence. He pressed the buzzer again and kept his finger on it for several seconds. Then repeated his message.

The speaker grille crackled and a voice said, 'Herr Jansen is not at home.'

'Like hell he's not!'

The gates were nearly seven feet high and spiked. The taxi driver watched Bannerman with astonishment as he scaled them, wobbled unsteadily as he straddled the spikes, and then dropped down to the other side. Somewhere in the grounds a siren began wailing through the trees. Bannerman started running, his feet smacking on the tarmac, the trees locked in around him. All he could think of was Tania. All he could feel was his anger.

The driveway seemed longer than it had the previous night. At last the two squares of lawn opened out before him and he emerged from the damp, dripping tunnel of trees. The wailing of the siren intensified as he reached the house, and now he could hear bells ringing in the building itself. He ran through the slush that lay in patches on the lawn, across the gravel, and glanced up at the rows of arched windows. For a moment he caught the glimpse of a pale face watching him from behind a window-blind on the second floor, but when he looked again it was gone.

The moulded iron knocker on the great door was heavy and thundered against its metal block. He could hear the sound of it echoing away inside the big circular hall behind it. He hammered for a full minute before the door finally opened a crack. The butler who had let him in the previous night peered out.

'The police will be here any moment,' he said coldly. 'I would advise you to leave now.'

Bannerman put his shoulder to the door, pushing the old man backwards into the hall. 'Where is he?' The butler's face was drained of colour.

'I told you. He is not here.'

Bannerman swept past him and up the marble staircase two at a time. He remembered the face on the second floor and went on up to the second landing. There were nearly a dozen doors leading off it. He opened one after another. A drawing room. A bedroom. A study. A library. Another bedroom. All empty. The sixth door opened into darkness. He was about to move on to the next when he sensed a presence in the room. Perhaps the slightest movement, or a warm scent. He stopped and peered into the gloom. All the blinds were drawn and only a little yellow light crept in around their edges.

Suddenly a light came on to his right. A small table lamp that lit up an old woman in a wheelchair. She stared at him out of a white, bony face with empty grey eyes. Her hair was the purest silver pulled back in a tight bun. She wore a black shawl around her shoulders and a rug draped itself over her knees. Twisted, arthritic hands lay in her lap, clutching a small glass of red wine. The remains of a log fire smouldered in the hearth. She spoke in a high, clear voice. 'My son is not here.'

Bannerman hesitated for a moment as the door swung shut behind him. He had not expected this.

'Where is he?'

The old woman sighed and her slight, fragile frame drooped

a little. 'You are Mr Bannerman, are you not? My son has told me about you. But you are quite wrong about him.'

Bannerman felt uncomfortable, caught in the gaze of those pale grey eyes.

'Where is he?'

'He left early this morning. For the Bahamas. We have an estate out there. I do not expect to see him for another six months.' There was a smugness in her tone. The bells and the siren stopped and the awful silence that followed was broken only by the slow tick of an old clock on the mantelpiece. The door opened behind Bannerman and the old butler appeared.

'The police are here.'

'Send them away,' said the old woman. 'I don't believe Mr Bannerman will cause any further trouble.' The old man stood for a second and glared at Bannerman. Then he turned, shutting the door softly behind him. 'Have a seat, Mr Bannerman.'

'No thank you.'

'As you like.' Her eyes flickered briefly beyond him and then returned with that same empty stare. 'You see, if my son had been involved in the things of which you accuse him, I would have known. There is nothing I do not know about him. He is a good boy. He will do nothing without his mother's approval. He has never married. For you see, it is me he needs. Me he depends on. My only fear is what will become of him when I have gone.' She smiled. 'I'm afraid he will fall prey to vultures like you.'

'So you are the power behind the Jansen empire?' Bannerman was sceptical.

Now she chuckled. 'Yes,' she said. 'It is the way my husband wanted it. He knew that René would never be the man *he* was. Of course, René liked to play the part, to pretend. But then, he knows that he must always answer to Mama, as when he was a child. He doesn't love me, I think. But he fears me. It was I who sent him away.' She paused. 'I'd like you to leave too now, please.'

Bannerman shook his head in disbelief. He found that he was still trembling. 'Well, I don't really care what you'd like me to do,' he said. 'There's a little girl lying in an operating room in a hospital not very far from here that I care about a great deal more.' He paused. 'So you can start by telling me all about Michel Lapointe.'

'Ah, Michel,' she said, quite unruffled. 'He is a genius, Mr Bannerman, but a man of little breeding. My husband trusted him implicitly.' She took a tiny sip of her wine. 'He is a man I have never liked. I am afraid I have used him unscrupulously. He has remained loyal only because the rewards are high. And I fear that he does not hold me in as high regard as he held my husband. But perhaps he is just a little afraid of me, as René is. It is unfortunate that he must be sacrificed. A sop to public opinion, you understand. He really did overstep the mark by initiating this distasteful arms business. On his own initiative, it must be said. I cannot, you understand, allow my son to fall victim to any scandal.'

'Where is he?'

'Who? Monsieur Lapointe?'

'Yes.'

'At his office, I imagine. He likes to work on Sundays.'

Bannerman moved towards the door. As he opened it the old woman said, 'Who is the child you spoke of?'

'Tim Slater's daughter. She was shot this morning at the airport. But then, you'll know all about that.'

'No,' she said. 'I know nothing at all about a child. I am sorry.'

'Of course you are.'

She raised one of her withered hands. 'Before you go, Mr Bannerman, let me warn you that should you attempt to harm my son I shall fight you.'

'Then you will lose,' Bannerman said, and he shut the door behind him.

II

Lapointe dialled the combination with trembling fingers and the door of his safe swung open. There was no money in here, just large Manila folders tied around with red ribbon to contain their bulging contents. These were all his secret records. The companies, the deals, statements of account going back nearly twenty years. It was a large safe, but his records filled it. He had been meticulous, his memory such that he could pinpoint almost any deal, any company, within minutes. It would take someone unfamiliar with his system hours, perhaps days, to make sense of it all. There was nothing here that would convict him in a court, but in the wrong hands they could destroy him.

As he transferred them one by one to the suitcase he had opened on his desk, he felt the sick fear he had lived with for the past fifteen hours turning again in his stomach. Why had Jansen been so feeble? Surely he could have bought Bannerman off. Lapointe blamed the old lady. He conjured an image of her, frail and delicate in her wheelchair. He heard her voice, supercilious and condescending. What power was it she had over them all? She was, after all, just an old woman. But it didn't matter any more. He would not have to see her again. Or her weak, ineffectual son, who had, as usual, left him to clean up his mess. Now it was all over. When Jansen came back from the Bahamas he would be gone. To live out his last years in comfort and warmth on his farm in Malta, enjoying the fruits of his years of labour. The Jansens would be all right, but to hell with them, he didn't care any more. He had committed his final act of loyalty, as much for himself as for them, and now he was going.

He was nearly finished packing when the phone rang. 'What is it?'

'Security at reception, sir. There is a gentleman here who wants to see you. A foreigner. He says he has a message from Madame Jansen. Shall I send him up?'

'No. Ask him to leave his message with you and have someone bring it to me.'

'I've already suggested that, sir. But he's most insistent that the message should be delivered personally.'

What was the old lady up to now? 'All right, send him up.'
Lapointe was nervous. Surely the fool hadn't told his mother.
He hurriedly finished packing his case and checked the time.
His flight was not until late afternoon.

There was a knock at the door.

'*Entrez.*'

A stocky, powerful-looking man with a mop of curly dark
hair and cold blue eyes stepped into his office.

Bannerman looked quickly around him. The large
mahogany writing desk with its three phones and clean
blotter. An ashtray stuffed with fat cigar ends. A suitcase
packed full of large Manila folders open on the desk. The
carpet was thick and soft underfoot and the walls were hung
with copies of old Flemish masters. Or perhaps they were
originals. The windows, along one side behind the desk, rose
from floor to ceiling and looked out on a breathtaking view
over the city from this tenth floor.

Lapointe himself was a short, thickset man, probably in
his late fifties. A few strands of grey hair were plastered back
across his bald pate. His face was flushed and he stared inso-
lently at Bannerman from behind steel-rimmed glasses. He
spoke abruptly in French.

'Well, what is it?'

Bannerman did not reply, but took his time strolling across
the office to look out over the damp mist that obscured the
distance.

Lapointe's voice rose with irritation: 'For God's sake, man!'

Bannerman turned and looked boldly at the Belgian. 'You had better speak English. I don't speak French or Flemish, and I don't want there to be any misunderstandings between us.'

'What do you want?' Lapointe was growing uncomfortable, and regretted now having the man sent to his office. 'You have a message from the old lady?'

Bannerman drew a folded morning paper from his coat pocket. It was damp from the rain. He threw it on to Lapointe's desk with a front-page story face up and ringed in red ink. Lapointe glanced at it and felt a stab of fear.

JOURNALIST SHOT DEAD IN CAR.

He looked up abruptly. 'What has this got to do with me?'

'Take a look at the name,' Bannerman said. Lapointe's hand shook as he lifted the paper to read of the discovery early that morning of a dead man in a car near the Gare du Nord. A journalist called Richard Platt. The paper fell from his hands and he looked up again at Bannerman.

'Who . . . who are you?'

'My name is Neil Bannerman.'

The colour drained from Lapointe's face and he began backing off. 'It . . . it was Jansen. It was his idea. I swear.' Then he steadied himself. 'You can't prove anything.' But his defiance was fragile.

Bannerman walked slowly around the desk. 'Let me tell you something, Monsieur Lapointe,' he said. 'I am sick of playing the game according to the rules. Rules that protect rich bastards like you. I am way beyond caring about what happens to me any more, and I'm going to break you into little pieces and feed you to the fucking dogs.'

Lapointe yelped as Bannerman grabbed his lapels and banged him up against the window. The reporter's face was very close to his. Lapointe could smell his hatred. 'It's a long way down. You're going to make a hell of a mess on the pavement.' The glass bowed as Bannerman pushed him harder against it.

'No!' Lapointe screamed. 'I'll tell you. Anything you want to know!'

'You tried to have me killed last night.'

'Yes, yes. It was Jansen. He phoned me last night, after you had been to the house. He said we had to get rid of you and I should attend to it. He was going to the Bahamas until things cooled off.' He broke into French and Bannerman slapped his face.

'English! Speak in English! Did the old woman know?'

'No.'

'She told me her son tells her everything.'

'She . . . she's an old fool. He only told her what he wanted her to know. There are lots of things she knows nothing about.' But he knew that was only half the truth.

'Who killed Gryffe and Slater?'

'I don't know.' Bannerman pushed harder and the glass creaked. 'Jesus, God, I don't know! I swear. We knew nothing about it until we heard it on the news. My God, please believe me.'

'I don't!' Bannerman felt his frustration coiling up inside him. His raised voice seemed to fill the room. He pushed again and the glass cracked from top to bottom. He was within a fraction of an inch of killing this man.

'I swear!' Lapointe screamed in terror and was then reduced to a pitiful hysterical sobbing. Bannerman eased off and let him go, and the man slumped to his knees. Bannerman's voice cracked as he spoke and he felt tears welling in his eyes. He thought about the child lying bleeding on the concourse at the airport, her hand slipping into his in the car. He needed someone to take all that out on. A target for his hate and anger and bitterness. But not even Lapointe could provide that.

'What about the gunman in Flanders?'

Lapointe's head came up slowly, tears coursing down his face. It was plain that he had no idea what Bannerman was talking about. 'I'm sorry,' he sobbed. 'Please, I'm so sorry.'

The door opened and Bannerman looked round to see the weary figure of du Maurier standing in the doorway.

'Madame Jansen said you might be here,' he said. He looked at Lapointe. 'What has he told you?'

'That Jansen got him to arrange to have me killed last night.'

'And what else?'

'Nothing!'

The Inspector moved across the room and helped Lapointe to his feet. He turned back to Bannerman. 'Do you still believe that Jansen was responsible for what happened at the Rue de Pavie?'

There was a long silence. Then Bannerman sighed. 'No,' he said reluctantly. 'I don't.'

Du Maurier nodded. 'It is time we talked.'

III

Bannerman sat alone in du Maurier's office. It was almost exactly a week since he had last sat here, on the same hard seat in front of the same cluttered desk. The same broken umbrella leaned against the wall beside the same pair of mud-spattered gumboots. In this little world, at least, nothing had changed.

Outside it had grown dark. The rain battered against the window. Bannerman was drained. His whole being was numb. The Anglepoise lamp spread its small circle of light in the darkness so that everything on the desk seemed hard and so finely focused that it hurt his eyes to look at it. Just as it hurt inside to think about the child.

The door opened and du Maurier came in, the habitual cigarette hanging from his wet lips. He rounded the desk and sat down, flicking ash carelessly at the ashtray and missing it. He let the cigarette burn in one hand while pulling with the other at the whiskers that grew from his nostrils. He regarded Bannerman for some moments. Then finally he said, 'They finished operating two hours ago.'

Life flickered briefly in Bannerman's eyes.

'And?'

'They say the next twelve hours will be critical. The surgeon gives her a fifty–fifty chance.'

Bannerman subsided into his gloom.

'First, Monsieur,' du Maurier went on, 'we should deal with Lapointe. He has made a very full statement which has implicated both himself and René Jansen in the murder of Monsieur Platt. We should have the actual gunman in custody before the day is out.' He lit another cigarette from the end of his old one and drew deeply. 'I think we can safely rule out either man from involvement in the murders of Gryffe and Slater. I am quite certain that the man hired for that act was the one shot dead at Zavantem this morning. The child's drawing was uncannily accurate. Unfortunately, one of the few things we do not know is who hired him or why. But I shall return to that.'

He blew smoke at a nicotine-stained ceiling.

'On the basis of what I have learned from Lapointe I think it can be safely assumed that Slater was indeed blackmailing Gryffe.'

Bannerman leaned forward. 'How?'

Du Maurier smiled wanly. 'Lapointe has a daughter. She is divorced and until recently lived with her father before moving into an apartment of her own. They were quite close, father and daughter. She knew about most of his activities. According to Lapointe there were few secrets between them. Then . . . they had a row, she moved out. Her name is Marie-Ange. But she has kept her married name.'

'Piard.' Bannerman shook his head. He should have

guessed. What was a woman like her ever doing with a man like Tim Slater? 'Slater's girlfriend,' he said, laden with self-recrimination. 'Why did I not think of her before?'

Du Maurier smiled again. 'It is something we both over-looked, Monsieur.'

'So she provided the dirt, Slater made it stick, and they shared the spoils. A very cosy arrangement.'

'Unfortunately,' the Inspector sighed, 'I do not think it is something we can ever prove.'

Bannerman felt anger welling inside him. It rankled that she might be the only one to remain untouched by any of this.

As if he'd read Bannerman's mind, du Maurier said, 'In my business there are always the ones who get away. In yours too, no doubt.'

'Yes, in mine too.'

Du Maurier clasped his hands on the desk in front of him, his mouth set in a grim line. Both men knew there were many things they could never hope to know or understand. The power and influence of old Madame Jansen. She had come as a surprise to them both. How much did she really know? And how had the arrangement between Gryffe, Jansen and Lapointe ever come about? Why had Gryffe risked an outstanding career in politics to deal in illegal arms? Was it really just greed? So many questions that would remain forever unanswered. Why men do the things they do. Bannerman knew they could only ever hope to scratch the surface.

'It won't go away, will it?' du Maurier said at length.

Bannerman looked at him curiously. 'What?'

'The question of who had Gryffe and Slater killed – if it wasn't Jansen.'

'No, it won't.' An ugly little thought had been burrowing into Bannerman's consciousness since the episode in Flanders. And now it returned. He remembered his conversation with the Foreign Minister the night before he left for Flanders, the sandy-haired man at the Gare du Midi, the professional's specialist military rifle with the laser sight.

He was hardly surprised when du Maurier said, 'The man who shot at you in Flanders was an SIS field man. British Secret Intelligence Service. Our own people have him on their files.'

Bannerman could not bring himself to believe the implications. He dropped his head into his hands and rubbed his eyes with the heels of his palms. He looked up. 'I find it difficult to accept what you are saying,' he said. 'I know that in one sense it seems logical. I agree that the British government stood to lose much more than Jansen and Lapointe. With a general election at the end of the month they would have been annihilated if it had leaked out that the understudy to their Foreign Minister was selling arms to apartheid South Africa and Rhodesia's Ian Smith. But there's nothing to suggest that they ever knew. And even if they had, I just can't accept that they would have had him murdered. I know that governments do questionable things, but to assassinate a Minister of State, and a journalist . . . All they needed to do was remove Gryffe from office, pressure him to resign his seat, even the party. Why kill him?'

Du Maurier looked at him solemnly. 'Sometimes,' he said, 'I wonder if perhaps I am too old and too cynical. Your reasoning is sound, but I am not convinced. Maybe if it was my own government I would see it your way, be prepared to give them the benefit of the doubt. But was it not my own government that forced me to close this case when it was clear two men had been murdered? Why? To protect diplomatic relations? Because of pressure from your government in London? Your people moved too quickly not to have known.' He paused to consider his next words. 'For me the only real doubt arises from the fact that they did not kill you in Flanders. That they never meant to. And then, of course, there is the man shot dead at the airport. There appears to be no connection.'

'Who was he?'

'An Englishman. William Francis Kale. That, of course, was not the name on his passport. We put out a fingerprint check through Interpol, who tracked him down through his British army record. He served in the armed forces for three years in the early nineteen sixties. Then did nine months in a military prison for assaulting an officer. He had no police record, but he was known to police in England. Suspected of a number of contract killings. Though nothing was ever proved.'

Bannerman felt crushed. He thought about what du Maurier had said. There were so many conflicting bits and pieces, of fact and assumption. All that was clear was that someone had hired a man called Kale to kill Gryffe and Slater, and to make it look like a quarrel. When it became apparent that Tania had witnessed the murders, she had become the next target. But if you eliminated Jansen and Lapointe, and if you ruled out the government in London, who else had a motive? And then, why did the man, Kale, not kill Tania at the clinic when he had the chance? Or at almost any other time? Why choose a busy airport where he had little or no chance of getting away with it?

'Is there anything among Kale's belongings . . .?'

Du Maurier shrugged. 'Nothing that means anything to me.' He opened his desk drawer and pulled out a large polythene bag full of Kale's personal effects. 'He was carrying these about his person. There was nothing in his case but clothes.' He emptied the contents on to his desk and Bannerman pulled his chair closer.

There was a holster, a wallet with some money and a cheque-book. A passport, a pen, keys, some loose change, a pack of cigarettes, a tattered map of England, a lighter and a scrap of paper. Du Maurier lifted the piece of paper and handed it to the reporter. Bannerman read the three words and dropped it on to the desk as if it had burned his fingers. And in that moment he thought perhaps he understood why Kale had not attempted to kill her sooner.

'We've checked it for prints. Clean, except for Kale's.'

Bannerman surveyed the killer's personal items with a stultifying hopelessness. He might have carried any of these items himself. Except for the holster. Du Maurier opened out the map and spread it on the desk. 'You may want to take a look at this.'

It was a large-scale map, well thumbed, tearing at the folds. Bannerman's eyes were drawn by a red line connecting two circles drawn with a felt pen. The first encircled a small Lancashire town near Southport, from which the red line followed the A565 north past a place called Crossens, before veering off in a short stroke to the west and the second circle. The words 'big house' were written in small letters beside it, followed by 'farm track' and 'bridge over water'. In the margin, written in green ink, was the word 'Lamb', followed by a large question mark. For a few seconds Bannerman stared at it without understanding. Then suddenly he made the connection. His heart quickened and his face flushed. He looked up at du Maurier, who raised an eyebrow. 'It means something to you?'

'Can I use your phone?' He needed to double-check.

'By all means.' The policeman got him a line.

Bannerman dialled, du Maurier watching him with interest. 'News desk,' he heard him say. Then, 'George. Neil Bannerman. Do me a favour. Dig out a copy of Who's Who and look up Lord Armsdale. Armsdale is a place name. I want to check his family name, before he got the peerage.' He glanced at du Maurier, but each man kept his own counsel. 'Hello. Yes.' He drew out his notebook and began writing. 'Lamb. Thomas Walter Lamb. What's his address? . . . Armsdale House, Lancashire . . . That's near Southport, isn't it? . . . Yes . . . No . . . I'll be in touch.' He hung up and sat back in his chair, adrenalin pumping. There was a wild look in his eyes. Everything, quite suddenly, had fallen into place. And it left him feeling strangely empty.

'Well, Monsieur?'

Bannerman slumped in his chair, almost overcome by weariness. 'Thomas Walter Lamb, or Lord Armsdale as he is now, is the retired chairman of Gryffe's political party. In many ways he is, or was, the party. Its chairman for nearly thirty years. He, more than anyone, made it the electoral force it is today. Gryffe was his protégé, his golden boy. Being groomed by the old man for future leadership. The intellectual that Armsdale never was.' He thought about the cuttings he had read in Slater's office and wondered why it had not occurred to him before.

Du Maurier sighed and lit yet another cigarette, leaning back in his seat and gazing at Bannerman with big, watery eyes. He understood the implication. 'Are you sure?'

'Pretty much so.'

'And how will you prove it?'

'I don't know. But I will. I'll get the first flight to London tomorrow.'

The policeman seemed to be staring into space. Finally he broke the silence between them. 'I feel sorry for you, Monsieur. You are bearing a burden that no one man should have to.'

Bannerman's head dropped a little. He knew it.

'When you write your story you will bring down your government, whether they were involved in it or not.'

Bannerman clenched his teeth. 'Yes,' he said.

CHAPTER THIRTY-FOUR

Sally watched how her fingers trembled as she toyed with her cup. She was waiting for the Brussels flight to be called. Some coffee had spilled into her saucer and it dripped across the table from the bottom of the cup as she lifted it to her mouth. The coffee was sweet and dark and strong, and its hotness filled her mouth. It took some of the edge off her tension. She shivered, though the airport cafeteria was hot and airless. All around her, voices prattled gaily in that melodic, aggressive way that Italians speak. Rome. Monday morning. Mild and sunny, only a little chill in the air outside.

She had slept badly, and her face was pale, the skin drawn tightly across her cheeks. The morning had come like a relief, the sheet damp and twisted around her. The hours of darkness had tormented her with all the questions, all the doubts. But she knew she had made a mistake. Even as she had left the apartment in the Rue de Commerce with the silent tears on her cheeks she had known it.

But it had taken a headline on the front page of one of the Rome dailies to make her turn back. Back to the man she should never have left. The job, the money, the security meant nothing now.

The paper had been lying on her table at breakfast at the Hotel Vittoria in the Piazza Mastai where she had booked in only the night before. For a moment the headline had meant nothing to her. Then she realized. *GIRL (11) GUNNED DOWN AT BRUSSELS AIRPORT*. And in smaller type, *GUNMAN SHOT DEAD BY SECURITY POLICE*.

Du Maurier felt the heat of the sun through the glass. Its warmth seemed such a deceit when outside it was still bitterly cold. He was down to his shirtsleeves, and he screwed up his eyes against the sunlight that streamed in the window of his office and fell across his desk.

In front of him lay Lapointe's statement, typed and signed. The boys in the commercial branch had already begun going through the suitcase full of Manila folders. He had put in his request to start extradition proceedings to bring Jansen back from the Bahamas. That might prove difficult. At least the examining magistrate, Judge Markelbach, was sympathetic for once. But a man like Jansen would be difficult to convict, especially with friends in high places. And doubtless the old woman would have a few strings she could pull. How much, he wondered again, did she really know about it all? How much control had she really exercised over her son, over Lapointe? She was something of an enigma.

The phone rang and he snatched the receiver, anxious

for some distraction. 'There is a young lady here to see you, Inspector. A Mademoiselle Sally Robertson.'

'Send her in.' He leaned back in his chair to light a cigarette and wait for the knock on his door. When it came he said, '*Entrez.*'

She came in, pale and hesitant, the cold winter air still clinging to her clothes. Du Maurier stood up and indicated the seat at the other side of his desk. 'Bonjour, Mademoiselle. I am happy to see you again. Please take a seat.' Sally sat gingerly on the chair opposite and saw the weariness etched into the face of the old policeman. He said, 'What can I do for you?'

'I . . .' she began self-consciously. 'I only heard this morning about Tania.' She hesitated. 'I've just come from Rome. Is she, will she . . .?'

'Still in the balance I'm afraid, Mademoiselle,' du Maurier said. 'I'm expecting a call at any time.'

She nodded. 'I tried to phone Neil . . . Mr Bannerman . . . from the airport. He's not at the apartment or his office. Do you know where he is?'

Du Maurier smiled sadly. 'I'm afraid, Mademoiselle, that you have missed him. He took the ten o'clock flight to London this morning.' The phone rang and he lifted it quickly. She watched him closely. The droop of his shoulders. 'When?' he said, his voice thick with emotion. And she feared the worst.

CHAPTER THIRTY-FIVE

London was blowy, a light rain carrying spots of city smut in the wind. A wind that gusted into Sally's face as she hurried down Fleet Street from the tube station. Past the rising glass windows of the *Daily Express*.

There was a quiet desperation in her now, a disturbing sense of confusion and uncertainty. Perhaps, she thought, she was just compounding her original mistake. There was a sad hopelessness in her pursuit halfway across Europe of this man whom she might or might not love. How would he react? What if he did not want her? Why had she ever left him in the first place? And then there was Tania. She felt an ache inside her.

After leaving du Maurier's office she had taken a taxi back to the airport in time to catch the two o'clock flight to London. Despite the months she had lived in Brussels, the city seemed strange to her, almost alien. She felt nothing in common with the people she passed in the street and they, in turn, barely seemed to notice her existence.

She found the *Post*'s London office at the bottom end of Fleet Street, a grey sandstone Victorian building rising into the late afternoon sky. Heads in the newsroom turned as she came in. She looked helplessly about her for a familiar face.

'Can I help you?' a young man at the nearest desk said.

'I . . .' She broke off to catch her breath. 'I was looking for Neil Bannerman.'

'You've just missed him, love. He left about an hour ago to get the Glasgow train from Euston.' A pause. 'Stood you up, has he?' But she was gone, the door swinging behind her.

In the street below she had to wait nearly five minutes for a taxi. 'Euston station,' she told the driver. 'Please hurry.'

'I'll do me best, Miss. But you picked the wrong time to get through London in a hurry. Traffic's bloody diabolical at this time of day.'

It took over half an hour to get to the station, and she ran up the steps from the covered rank and across the concourse towards the barriers, searching frantically for the Glasgow train on the departure board. She grasped a porter's arm. 'The train to Glasgow,' she said breathlessly. 'Has it gone yet?'

'Fraid so, Miss. About ten minutes ago. But there's another one at quarter to six.'

She turned away, the weight of her case – the entire contents of her life – straining her arm. She felt disappointment bring tears to her eyes. And for a moment she wondered if perhaps it was a sign. That she should just give up and turn back to the future she had left only eight hours before.

CHAPTER THIRTY-SIX

The car bumped and rattled its way over the rough, rutted mud track, headlights picking out the grass verge and the blasted wooden fence posts. In the distance the lights of the house twinkled intermittently through the branches of tall, dark trees that swayed in the wind. It was a wild night.

Bannerman turned the wheels over a small humpbacked bridge across a narrow gushing stream. The track broadened a little, lined by trees along one side. He did not know what to expect, or what he was going to say to the old man. But he felt, somehow, that this time it really would be an end to it all. The car clattered over a cattle grid and Bannerman pulled up on a gravel courtyard.

He had left the train at Preston and hired a car to drive the ten or twelve miles south-west on the A59 and A565 to Armsdale House near the tiny Armsdale landfall. He switched off the lights and stepped out into the blustering wind that drove in across the Irish Sea. But there was a softness in the air that was mild and smelled of rain.

The house itself was a big, stone, turreted affair that stood dark and impressive in its own grounds. The door was opened by a thickset man with a crop of white, wiry hair. His face was tanned and leathery with age. He wore a heavy tweed jacket over a thick sweater and moleskin trousers. He stared at Bannerman suspiciously and the journalist noticed that his big working-man's hands were weathered and calloused.

'Yes?'

'I've come to see Lord Armsdale.'

'And who is it that's wanting 'im?'

'My name is Neil Bannerman. I'm the investigative reporter of the *Edinburgh Post*.'

There was a pause as the man considered this. 'Does 'e expect you?'

'Not that I know of.'

'Then you'd better come and wait in the 'all and I'll see if 'e'll see you.'

Bannerman waited in the big hall, worn flagstones beneath his feet, a staircase rising to an unlit floor above. It was cold here. He thought about Tania and felt guilty. Not knowing if she was alive or dead. He should have been there . . .

A door opened on his left and a shaft of warm yellow light fell out at his feet. 'In 'ere.' The white-haired man beckoned. Bannerman went through the door and found himself in a sprawling, cluttered sitting room filled with cumbersome articles of old-fashioned furniture. A sofa, two well-worn easy chairs, a writing desk, bookshelves, walls hung with landscapes and portraits. A fire burned in a large stone fireplace and Lord Armsdale sat beside it, languid and relaxed, in one of the easy chairs. He was pulling gently on the stem of a pipe, blue smoke lingering in the air above him. The eyes that gazed out from his lean, lined face twinkled sadly as they turned towards Bannerman.

'Take a seat, Mr Bannerman. Will you have tea?'

'Thank you, no.' Bannerman sank into the softness of the chair opposite and felt strangely at home in this warm and friendly room. It was a lived-in place. Nothing pretentious here. Just comfort. Lord Armsdale surveyed Bannerman shrewdly for some seconds.

'Would I be right in thinking I know what you are here to talk to me about?'

Bannerman nodded almost imperceptibly. 'Probably.'

The old man glanced beyond him towards the white-haired man who had remained by the open door. 'That'll be all, Arthur, thank you.'

Arthur turned reluctantly and pulled the door shut behind him. Lord Armsdale went on puffing on his pipe, lost in a gentle euphoria of smoke and thought. At length he said, 'He has been with me a long time, my Arthur. Almost from the start. A good man. Gardener, chauffeur, general factotum. He carried my messages for me, found the right men for the right jobs. Trusts me implicitly. Always has. In a way I suppose I have let him down, too. He worked in the mines when he was a boy. I wonder how he will manage without me. I think, perhaps, he needs me as much as I have needed him.'

He looked at Bannerman as he emerged from his reverie. 'I have been expecting someone since I heard the news yesterday. I had no idea who it might be, but in a way I suppose I should have guessed it would be you. I have heard that you are very good.' He paused again to take comfort in his pipe. 'At the beginning I took a great many precautions, you know. I thought it was foolproof. But then, when it went wrong, the business of the child, I think I knew that somehow it would end this way.'

He pointed the stem of his pipe at Bannerman.

'But please, don't get me wrong. I regret none of it. Only that I have failed. That by my own actions I have put the party I love in peril. As well as the government that has brought light to the darkness of many lives.' He seemed emotionless, almost tranquil. 'Will the child live or die?'

'I don't know.'

He nodded. 'You must think me some kind of a monster. And I suppose history will judge me as such. But you see, Mr Bannerman, what are the lives of a handful of people compared to the well-being of millions?'

For the first time Bannerman felt compelled to speak. 'If you deny the right to life of any one man, simply because he does not fit with your idea of what is good for all, then you deny the rights of all men.' He shook his head. 'And what gives you the right to play God?'

Armsdale shrugged. 'Ah, Mr Bannerman . . . we all have our ideals. And wouldn't we just love to be able to achieve them with a snap of the fingers? But, you know, one has to be realistic. Pragmatic. Sacrifices must always be made. The end has to justify the means.'

'Even at the expense of the very principles you hold dear? Democracy? Human rights? Even if it means murdering a child whose only crime was to see her father shot dead by a man you hired?'

The old man sighed. 'Clearly it is not something we will ever agree on. If I had the time, I believe I could make you understand. But we have no time, and there would be little point now. I have devoted my life to the party, Mr Bannerman. A party which has done more to improve the lives of ordinary men and women in fifty years than monarchs and politicians achieved in the previous five hundred. Do not think it did not pain me to do the things I have done. But I was not prepared to let the work of a lifetime, and this country's only real hope for the future, be destroyed by a man consumed by greed. A man who deceived not only myself and my party, but the many millions of people who saw in him the same qualities we all did. Qualities that could have made him great. Qualities that could have brought so much to so many. Except that behind that bright, shiny façade there was something rotten. A sickness that made a nonsense of all the trust we placed in him.'

He had grown agitated now, and he rose to pace across the room to the window. And there he stood, gazing out into the blackness beyond it.

'How did you find out?' Bannerman asked. 'About Gryffe's involvement in the sale of arms?'

Lord Armsdale chuckled ironically. Bannerman could not see his face. 'He came to me for help. I can still hardly believe his nerve. Neither, I think, will I ever understand his motives. You can live even to my great age, Mr Bannerman, and people will still take you by surprise. He told me he was being blackmailed by a journalist in Brussels. Slater. At first he wouldn't tell me why, but finally I got it out of him. He was desperate. Slater had wrung nearly one hundred thousand pounds out of him over a period of several months, and was pushing for a final pay-off. But Gryffe didn't believe that would be an end to it. He was convinced that Slater was going to blow the whistle on him, regardless.'

The ageing peer turned from the window.

'He degraded himself, Mr Bannerman. Promised to do any-thing if I would help him. Even resign his seat. Clearly he had weighed up the pros and cons of coming to me. He knew it would destroy me to see my party wrecked by him. And he must have calculated that by sacrificing his career in politics he could maintain his association with Jansen, and continue to live in the style to which aspired. He was gambling that I would help him dispose of the threat that Slater posed, rather than risk the party. Or that my own humiliation would be sufficient motivation. He had, after all, been my protégé. Of all those he had taken in, wasn't I the biggest fool of all?'

He put the pipe to his lips but it had gone out.

'So I promised to help him deal with Slater, and then set about destroying Gryffe himself before he could destroy me or my party. I was not prepared to leave anything to chance, Mr Bannerman.'

He crossed to his writing desk and drew a sheaf of papers from a drawer.

'This, if you like,' he held it up, 'is my full confession. I spent many hours composing it last night. I had hoped that perhaps I might not need to use it until after the election. Just ten more days. But, of course, that is not possible.'

He crossed the room and handed it to Bannerman. There were six foolscap pages, closely typed. It was dated and signed.

'The point that I make in it, Mr Bannerman, the point that I would like to stress, is that neither the party nor the government itself were in any way implicated or involved in this affair. The responsibility is mine and mine alone. Perhaps . . . perhaps it will salvage something. The last and only sacrifice I can make now is myself.'

Bannerman flipped through the sheets without looking at the old man. He did not want to feel pity for him. Only contempt, to remember the child lying bleeding on the concourse at Zavantem.

'I don't think that is strictly true,' he said. His voice was cold and unforgiving. 'The cover-up after the killings was just too fast. There had to have been political collusion between the British and Belgian governments. Diplomatic pressures brought to bear. Not to mention the SIS agent who shot at me in Flanders.'

The old man was silent for a very long time. 'What I am going to tell you is for your information only,' he said finally. 'Not for the record.'

'I'll make no promises on that.'

'Then you make it very difficult for me, Mr Bannerman.'

Bannerman shrugged. 'I'll write it as I see it.' He paused. 'Though if you can tell me something that will shine a light on the story then you'd better tell me.'

The former party chairman made his way back to his chair and sank his bony frame into a softness that seemed to envelop him. He relit his pipe and said, 'Gryffe was being investigated by MI5 on government authority. The agency had not fully uncovered all of his activities at the time of his death, but they were on the brink of doing so. I knew nothing about this until afterwards, when the Prime Minister called me to London. It is not unusual for the party leader to ask my advice. We have been good friends for many years and he has often consulted me. Even after my retirement. He told me then, and asked me what he should do.'

He pulled several times on the stem of his pipe, and Bannerman saw the glow of tobacco in its bowl. Smoke rose to hang above him in a pall.

'Of course, the PM had no knowledge of my involvement in the killing of Gryffe and Slater, and for my part I have told him nothing. How could I? He revealed to me that Gryffe was

being investigated, and that they were pulling every diplomatic string available to have the shootings played down. He
also told me they had a man in the field in Belgium who had
discovered Gryffe's involvement in the sale of arms. He was a
man in a state of shock, Mr Bannerman. He saw quite clearly
what all this would mean if it ever got out. Which is why he
was worried about you. About your investigations. It was my
suggestion that they try to scare you off.' He blew a long jet
of smoke into the still air. 'Looking back, I suppose it was bad
advice. It misfired rather badly, didn't it?'

Bannerman remembered the nightmare of that flight in
the dark across snow-covered fields, the chill of approaching
death, the human mess in the crater left by the landmine.

'Yes,' he said. And he folded the statement and slipped it into
an inside pocket. Then he stared without emotion at the old
man. A frail creature destroyed by his own misguided philan-
thropy. And yet, in spite of it all, there was a certain dignity
that clung to him still. Bannerman wished he could feel hatred
for him, but all he could find inside himself was the dull ache
of emptiness. Sad, watery eyes stared back at him.

'I've done what I can,' the old politician said suddenly. 'But I
don't suppose it's enough. You can never undo your mistakes.'
His head dropped and he gazed at his hands resting in his lap.
His pipe had gone out again. 'I think . . .' he said, but could not
finish. When he looked up again Bannerman saw that there
were large, silent tears running down his cheeks. 'Excuse me.'
He rose unsteadily, drawing a handkerchief from a pocket to

wipe away his humiliation and his shame. He rounded his chair and disappeared through a door into an adjoining room.

Bannerman closed his eyes and let his head fall back. He would return to Edinburgh and tomorrow would write a story that would bring down a government. The irony of it lay in its injustice. He thought back on the last ten days. Slater, Tania, Marie-Ange Piard. Gryffe, Jansen, Lapointe. And the old woman. Platt lying dead on a pathologist's table. Du Maurier. Sally. What did he know about any of them? And now old man Armsdale.

A single, loud report startled him and he sat forward in his chair in a sudden moment of fright and confusion. Then he realized what it was. He rose and crossed slowly to the open door through which the old man had left a few minutes earlier. He found himself looking into a small, oak-panelled bureau. Lord Armsdale lay face down on the floor, a pool of blood spreading outwards and soaking into the carpet. Bannerman could see brain tissue spattered across the floor and the wall. The top half of the old man's head was almost blown away and the revolver lay a few inches from his white, clenched hand.

He turned away and wanted to throw up, a hand against the wall to steady himself. No matter how often you saw death you never got used to it.

The door from the hall flew open and Arthur ran in. He stopped as he saw Bannerman at the door to the bureau and then rushed across to look inside. He turned blazing eyes on the journalist, and it was clear from his face that for a moment he thought that Bannerman had done it. Then his shoulders slumped in despair and disappointment, and he accepted the reality. Without a word he turned and hurried from the room.

Bannerman stood a moment longer before going out into the hall. There were footsteps on the stairs and he looked up to see Arthur coming down with a shotgun clutched tightly across his chest. He stopped when he saw that Bannerman had seen him. There was madness in his eyes.

'You killed him.' His voice was taut and brittle. 'Even if you didn't pull the trigger you killed him.' He was fighting for control over some inner demon. 'I loved that old man. I really loved him. I'll kill you for it.' He raised the shotgun.

'Then you would be denying him his sacrifice,' Bannerman said. His voice sounded abnormally calm, in spite of the fear he felt crawling across his skin. 'He made a mistake. And he has taken the only honourable way out. Just as he had men killed to save his party, so he has killed himself in his final sacrifice. His own words.'

The seconds seemed to drag on for ever. The man with the white hair stood tense, the gun still raised.

'You'd better call the police,' Bannerman said. It was now or never. He turned his back slowly and walked towards the door, all the time waiting for the blast of the shotgun. His hand trembled on the cold metal handle.

And then it was over. He was outside, with the cold wind in his face and the door shut behind him. He let out a long breath and stood for a moment watching the trees swaying in the gloom. His feet crunched on the gravel as he walked to the car.

CHAPTER THIRTY-SEVEN

Bannerman stood under a pool of lamplight on Platform Two. Preston train station was almost deserted. One or two shadowy figures stood further along, staring out across the tracks. The sense of loneliness bearing down on him was crushing. Beyond the lights of the nine platforms, red and amber signal lights shone distantly in the darkness to the north, and to the west he saw a far-off twinkling of street-lamps. The world was shut up tight behind closed doors and drawn curtains, except for a few weary travellers and a handful of British Rail night workers.

From the south he heard the sound of the Glasgow train crossing the junction where the lines divided, rumbling past the blackened remains of industrial dereliction. The light from its windows came brightly out of the dark and the train ground to a clattering halt along the length of the platform. Doors opened as Bannerman stepped forward to climb up into the First Class corridor. He found an empty compartment and threw his things into the rack before slumping into a north-facing seat.

The train stood for a few minutes before he heard doors banging and the sound of a whistle piercing the night. Slowly it began pulling away from the platform, gathering speed into the darkness. Bannerman looked across the empty receding platforms. Darkened waiting rooms locked up for the night, shutters pulled down on a news stand. A billboard poster flapped in the rush of air. Tonight's headlines. The top half of the bill was obscured, but he saw the words, *GIRL DIES*, caught in a brief flash of light. The muscles of his chest contracted in a moment of pain before forcing tears to his eyes. Only one thought filled his mind. He had not even phoned to see how she was. She had died alone. And no one cared.

The door of his compartment slid open, but he was barely aware of it. Until the figure standing still in the doorway made him turn his head.

Sally smiled nervously. 'Neil.' She almost whispered his name. 'I saw you on the platform . . .' He stared at her blankly. His mind swam. He wanted to stand up, to take her and hold her. But it was as though he had lost all power in his limbs.

'She's dead,' he heard himself say.

'Who?' Sally frowned.

'Tania. I saw it on a billboard.'

Sally stood for a moment then opened her shoulder bag and pulled out a crumpled copy of the London *Evening Standard*.

'You're wrong,' she said. She held out the paper and Bannerman saw its headline. *SEX ATTACK GIRL DIES*. 'It's some London story,' Sally said. 'Tania survived. I was with du Maurier when they phoned from the hospital. The doctors say she's going to be okay.'

Bannerman felt as though a dam had burst inside him and everything he'd held back for all these years was flowing out. He felt the return of hope and light and love so sweetly. He rose and held Sally's hands and kissed her, and drew her to him.

'I'm so sorry about everything,' she whispered. 'I had to come back. I . . . I had to give us a try.'

He stopped her, pressing a finger to her lips. 'Don't be sorry. It's a bad way to start.'

She laughed and kissed his finger, and he kissed her again and lifted her bag in and slid the door shut. She sat down and looked up at him. 'Did you get your story?'

Bannerman smiled wryly. 'I always get the story.' He walked to the window and saw his own reflection staring back at him. 'It's funny how it seems so unimportant now. Beside the life of a child, beside the chance to love again. After all' – the last of his bitterness seeped out of him – 'it will only bring down a government.'

He pushed his hands into his pockets and felt a small scrap of paper between the fingers of his right hand. A scrap torn from a notebook which had remained undiscovered since a small, loving hand had put it there. He took it out and unfolded it to see three clumsily constructed words scrawled in pencil. LOVE YOU NEIL.